Zorro's Fight For Life

Suddenly they were there — peons and natives, scores of them who had left their huts or come from the fire at the end of the plaza. Denied lethal weapons by law, they carried bludgeons, stones, bits of metal they had picked up around the smithy.

"What is this?" Zorro called to them.

"We will care for this spy, Señor Zorro," a peon called to him. "Ride away, señor, and leave him to us."

"Hold!" Zorro shouted to them as they prepared to rush forward. "Listen to me one moment! As I have said, this man is a spy for the *capitán*. So, he is under that officer's protection. Harm him, and the troopers will seize scores of you, put you in the barracks jail room, beat you, sell you into peonage as a penalty. Those of you with families may never see your wives and children again!"

"But he is a spy!" came a protest.

"You're a plain fool," Pete Jordan complained. "I'm in sympathy with these folks. And I like the kind of work you're doin' to help them. I'll join with you, I said. As for leavin' the *pueblo* because a masked man on a horse tells me to do it — I don't run that easy, Señor Zorro."

Juanita Nuñez rushed toward the nearest group of peons, throwing up her arms.

"You shall not touch the *Americano*," she cried at them. "He attacked a *caballero* in my behalf. Would he have done that if he was a government spy? And you — Zorro!" She whirled toward him, rage in her face. "You are to blame for much of what has happened. Men are beaten because the soldiers think they know you and won't tell your name. My own father is on a pallet in the hut now, half senseless with pain — because of you! Men are in the jail room."

"Kill the spy!" the crowd yelled in still greater fury.

Zorro: The Complete Pulp Adventures
by Johnston McCulley, complete in one series!

The Complete Pulp Adventures, Vol. 6

Johnston McCulley

Featuring

Zorro's Fight For Life

Introduction by
Max Allan Collins

Afterword by
Rich Harvey

Illustrated by
Joseph A. Farren

Rich Harvey,
Editor & Designer

Audrey Parente,
Assistant Editor

Thanks to Max Allan Collins,
for his introduction

Special thanks to
John R. Rose and Pete Poplaski,
for lending their Zorro collections

ISBN-13: 978-1975633189; Retail cover price $19.95

Published by Bold Venture Press
www.boldventurepress.com

Contents

DELL 3

The MA
of ZORR

"The dared

of a rakish hig

who, sim

defied an en

by Johnston McCulley

THE MYSTERY OF McCULLEY'S ZORRO

by Max Allan Collins

I am thrilled to be a small part of the Bold Venture Press six-volume series, *Zorro: The Complete Pulp Adventures*. For this longtime fan of Johnston McCulley's great character — and of McCulley himself — I feel privileged to spend a few moments with you, sharing my enthusiasm for this under-appreciated pulp master.

Noble efforts by other publishers, over the past decade and a half or so — notably the Pulp Adventures "Master Editions" series — have started well but soon sputtered out. Often by the time I learned of a new such publication, its short print run had found the scant available copies spiraling into hundreds of dollars.

My first investment in a *Zorro* book was ten cents — I met the masked swordsman in the Dell *Four-Color Comics* issues starring the character that appeared sporadically starting in 1949 and ending in 1956, replaced a year later by the celebrated Alex Toth take on the Disney version. I have written at some length about those pre-Disney comic books — particularly the four issues drawn so beautifully by Everett Raymond Kinstler — for the Hermes Press volume, *Zorro: The Complete Dell Pre-Code Comics* (2014). I should note that these Bold Venture collections of Zorro make a most effective use of the painted covers of those Four-Color comic books — some of the greatest Zorro images ever created, and perfect for this ambitious and, in my view, overdue and essential reprinting of the original Zorro tales.

Everett Raymond Kinstler illustrated Zorro stories for Dell *Four-Color Comics*.

The first issue I read was Four-Color 538, *The Mask of Zorro*, published in 1954, when I was six years old. Over the next several years I found *The Sword of Zorro* (#497) from 1953, in a second-hand store where you either paid a nickel a comic or traded two for one; then I bought every subsequent Four-Color at Cohn's Newsland, including the Toth issues … and I *never* traded those.

As my earliest enthusiasm in the world of adventure yarns had been *The Three Musketeers*, the sword fighting on display in the *Zorro* comic books was what drew me in — you could practically hear the clang of blades. That and the mystery of a dashing hero wearing a black mask. Of course, Ray Kinstler's magnificent artwork played a huge role, but also fascinating was the Old California setting, and the dual identity of Don Diego Vega and Zorro, which for a youngster watching the *Superman* TV show and reading the *Batman* comic book was fun, familiar territory.

But I think the most compelling thing, for a kid who loved sword fights, was the way Zorro carved a ragged bloody Z into the flesh of the bad guys. *Wow!* Superman and Batman never did *that*!

At some point, fairly early on, I stumbled onto — and was thrilled by — an actual Zorro movie: *The Mark of Zorro* (1940) with Tyrone Power as a perfect foppish Diego and swashbuckling Zorro. It's a great film, one I still return to, and remains my favorite screen incarnation of the character, even including the wonderful Disney version (which *Mark of Zorro* heavily influenced in visuals

Alex Toth illustrated a celebrated run of Zorro comic books, a tie-in with the Walt Disney Productions television series starring Guy Williams.

and approach).

In the 1950s, many local TV stations had after school "kiddie shows" that included cartoons, Three Stooges shorts, and serial chapters you got one-a-day, like vitamins. On one such program, hosted by "Jungle Jay" (who was also "Dr. Igor" on *Acri Creature Feature*) I encountered *Zorro's Fighting Legion* (1939), masterfully directed by William Witney and John English, and one of the great examples of the chapter-play form.

But pre-Disney, Zorro was not a household word among Baby Boomer kids. The character was an enthusiasm of mine that was shared by no one I knew. So when the Disney TV series began in 1957, it seemed a small miracle. It almost felt as though I had wished such a thing into existence! I remember so vividly the night it premiered and that perfect theme song played, instantly searing itself into my kid memory. Most kids of that era, boys particularly, came to know those theme songs by heart, and *Zorro*'s was among the best and most memorable.

With *Walt Disney's Zorro* appearing on TV, Johnston McCulley's source novel, *The Mark of Zorro* (1920, originally *The Curse of Capistrano*) was a cinch for in mass-market paperback publication. That was done by (of course) Dell, with a lovely, evocative cover by Victor Kalin, whose Zorro was reminiscent of both Tyrone Power and Guy Williams. I read the novel again and again,

Thirty-five cents? The cover price did not deter young Max Allan Collins. *The Curse of Capistrano* (Dell 1958), retitled as *The Mark of Zorro.*

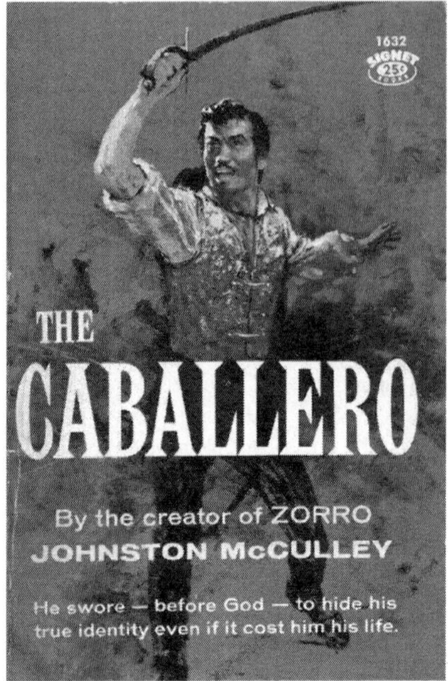

The Caballero (Signet 1959) was among Johnston McCulley's non-Zorro stories repackaged in paperback.

till the covers fell off, then found another copy — and thirty-five cents was hard to come by for a kid in 1958!

All through my teen years and beyond, I never lost my enthusiasm for Zorro, always pleased when one of the film versions showed up "on the tube," though admittedly nothing pre-Disney compared to the 1939 serial or 1940 film. I don't recall how I learned that McCulley had written other Zorro novels and short stories, but I did, and fairly early in the game. So I started looking for them.

I didn't get very far.

With the success of the *Zorro* TV series — and, I presume, the paperback of *The Mark of Zorro* — at least one other McCulley novel hit the stands to take advantage. In 1959, a paperback of a non-Zorro novel, *The Caballero,* was published by Signet Books, who'd done a 1948 edition, presumably a reprint of a hardcover (original publication date unknown). The Old California and swashbuckling action made it a good fit for Zorro fans. Still, it was a substitute....

Meanwhile, none of the author's other Zorro novels hit the reprint racks during a time when the character's visibility was hugely high. This struck me then — and still does — as a mystery. That mystery goes back even farther, because to my knowledge, only an obscure edition of *The Sword of Zorro* (1928) marked any hardcover or paperback reprint of McCulley's Zorro material during years when the character had made frequent screen appearances. The original Douglas Fairbanks silent version of *The Mark of Zorro* had made its masked protagonist a star in the pop-culture firmament. The dearth of the character in print (other than pulp magazines) didn't change with the phenomenal success of the Disney TV *Zorro*, either, which is a real puzzler.

Keep in mind that McCulley was crazily prolific. He was a pulp writer who mined the western form heavily — some consider Zorro a western character, as opposed to a swashbuckling one — and the detective/mystery story as well, with Black Star, the Spider and the Crimson Clown among his contemporary crime series. Many of his westerns, which had appeared in hardcover, were reprinted in paperback by such major publishers as Avon and Signet during the late forties and fifties.

As pulp collectors will tell you — and readers of this series from Bold Venture Press know — throughout those years McCulley also wrote numerous Zorro tales, including novels, sometimes serialized, but (with the exception of *Sword of Zorro*) never published in book form. So a question arises. Why were McCulley's one-shot westerns frequently published in hardcover and then in paperback, when the author's signature and incredibly famous character remained consigned to the pages of pulp magazines?

Two possibilities come to mind. Perhaps McCulley had a lousy agent, or was a poor businessman himself. It seems possible, if unlikely, that the writer might not have realized the impact of his own character and its commercial possibilities. But if that were the case, how did so many films happen? How did the Dell Four-Color comics come to be? And the *Zorro* television series?

Possibly Zorro was such a genre to itself that it resisted niche publishing, not appealing to editors and publishers of westerns, who perhaps considered it a swashbuckling historical series. Likewise, perhaps editors and publishers of historical fiction dismissed the famous character as a western hero. After all, publishers still consign authors to existing boxes.

Still, it's a head-scratcher. Zorro is a character on a level of fame and storytelling interest rivaling the likes of Sherlock Holmes, who filled numerous volumes despite Sir Arthur Conan Doyle's declining interest, and Tarzan, for whom Edgar Rice Burroughs created a shelf of novels. Even the Scarlet Pimpernel (Zorro's precursor) appeared in numerous novel sequels.

For those of us who grew up loving Zorro, not having access to more stories that we *knew* were out there was a great frustration. Some Zorro fans were aware of pulp-magazine collecting and were the lucky few who tracked down many or even all of the elusive Fox's tales.

That's what makes the six volumes of Bold Venture Press's *Zorro: The Complete Pulp Adventures* such an important event, and a genuine gift to lovers of popular fiction. That for decades the talented creator of Zorro — one of the most prolific and skilled pulp writers of his day — was only represented in print by his famous hero's first adventure remains hard to fathom. This is a character who has appeared internationally in some 48 films, 11 TV series, 65 stage plays, 8 video games, and more comic books than I would care to try to count.

Over the years, when I've raised this topic, I have heard on occasion speculation that the absence of McCulley's Zorro fiction in print had to do with the author's lack of skill. He was just another run-of-the-mill pulp writer, I've been told — clearly an opinion shaped by people who haven't read him.

McCulley was a first-rate talent, who could create a sense of time and place with ease, who fashioned vivid characters from stock material, who wrote action well and conveyed mood beautifully. Consider this, from the final Zorro novel, *Zorro's Fight for Life*, reprinted in the pages ahead: "In the early night as the light of the half moon struggled through waves of swirling mist that had drifted in from the sea with a promise of rain to come, Zorro rode."

And when Zorro rides, brother, I am there.

In *Fight for Life*, the reader encounters much that is familiar — Don Diego the apparent effeminate fool, the secretly proud father Don Alejandro, loyal servant Bernardo, the rotund, good-natured but dim Sergeant Garcia, a new evil *commandante* in Capitan Juan Ruelas, put-upon peons, compromised wenches, rich *caballeros*, and of course the greatest masked rider of them all. The basic template is right out of director Rouben Mamoulian's masterpiece, *The Mark of Zorro*, and Walt Disney's lively *Zorro* TV series. That much can't be denied.

But McCulley knows how to enliven things and freshen up his familiar but always fun formula. Two new characters create conflict with our masked hero — cocky *Americano* Pete Jordan, a buckskin-clad traveler who seems tailored for the readers of *West* magazine, where the novel first appeared; and Don Esteban Santana, a cruel *caballero* who is a loutish disgrace to the way of life Diego and his father so highly prize.

McCulley skillfully pits two heroes against each other — Jordan and

Zorro — and one *caballero* against another — Santana and Diego. Soon a plot is put in motion by the crafty *commandante* to ensure Zorro's capture and eventual execution by manipulating both Jordan and Santana.

Did I mention that Zorro was about to ride again?

Saddle up and join him, and tip your sombrero to the folks at Bold Venture Press for publishing six volumes to make a six-year-old Zorro fan's dream come true.

MAX ALLAN COLLINS received the 2017 Grand Master "Edgar" by Mystery Writers of America. He is the author of the Private Eye Writers of America "Shamus"-winning Nathan Heller historical thrillers (*Better Dead*) and the graphic novel *Road to Perdition*, basis for the Academy Award-winning film. His innovative '70s series, Quarry, has been revived by Hard Case Crime (*Quarry's Climax*) and was a Cinemax TV series. He has completed ten posthumous Mickey Spillane novels (*The Will to Kill*) and is the co-author (with his wife Barbara Collins) of the award-winning Trash 'n' Treasures comic cozy mystery series (*Antiques Frame).*

ZORRO´S FIGHT FOR LIFE

Chapter I

Torture at Dawn

IN THE plaza at Reina de Los Angeles, the misty dawn of the autumn day revealed six posts, each about six inches in diameter and eight feet high, set firmly in the ground ten feet apart in a row. Near the top of each post was a short crossbar, from which dangled thongs of heavy leather.

A yawning trooper from the barracks was pacing slowly back and forth in front of the line of posts. Saber at his side and pistol in his belt, he was on vigilant guard, and prepared to keep visitors at a proper distance.

The scene was not an unusual one for the little *pueblo* of Reina de Los Angeles. It simply meant that certain miscreants had been placed under military arrest, found guilty of something, and were to be punished.

As the mist lifted with the approach of the sun, men began appearing and sauntering toward the plaza — workers in the warehouses and shops, stock handlers, peons and natives employed for menial labor, shivering in the stiff morning breeze. Nostrils extended, they sniffed the aroma that came from the kitchen of the tavern nearby.

Men of greater substance appeared next — storekeepers and traders, purchasers of *rancho* produce in wholesale lots, owners of cart caravans, *vaqueros* riding into town for a spree, and travelers along El Camino Real, the king's highway, which linked the missions of Alta California in a long chain.

All passersby glanced at the row of posts, and wondered what men would be begging for mercy and howling with pain within a few minutes. Peons and natives who saw the preparations in the plaza hurried on, dumb of voice and expressionless of face.

They tried to pass unnoticed, for to attract attention might mean disaster for them. A mere whispered protest, the clucking of a tongue in pity, the shake of a head might be construed as a criticism of those in power, and result in the critics being doomed to punishment themselves. Spies were on every side, watching and listening, ready to report, to exaggerate, and even to lie for the slight favors they might obtain.

The people of the *pueblo* knew that this morning's affair in the plaza was at the order of the new *commandante*, *Capitán* Juan Ruelas, who had arrived from Monterey recently to take military command of the district. Ruelas had been at his new post for only a fortnight, but already was known as an extremist in brutality.

IT WAS rumored that Ruelas had been bodyguard for the Viceroy in Mexico, and in that official's behalf had slain two prominent men in duels. With feeling hot against him, he had been sent to Alta California for assignment to duty, and in Monterey the Governor had sent him on to take charge at Reina de Los Angeles.

Now the *pueblo* was thoroughly awake to the new day. Carts rumbled past the plaza with drivers shouting, hoofbeats drummed the earth as riders came and went. The bell of the chapel called the devout to worship.

Groups of men loitered around the plaza and talked in whispers as they glanced at the row of posts and the trooper on guard. Weeping softly, a pretty peon girl emerged from the kitchen door of the tavern and ran toward the chapel, her head shrouded with a ragged shawl.

"There hurries pretty Juanita Nuñez to seek help from the good *Fray* Felipe," a man whispered to his neighbor. "Her father is one of the six to be punished."

From the barracks came a bugle's clarion call and the sound of a drum. The heavy doors were opened, and a procession emerged.

Capitán Juan Ruelas, the new commander of the garrison, marched in the lead. He was a tall, lean man of middle age, with a hawk-like nose, glittering black eyes, a mass of black hair. On his left cheek a scar ran from the corner of his eye to the tip of his chin. His uniform was ornate, heavy with gold braid; and the hilt of his rapier was studded with jewels. Arrogance was in his manner.

Behind him came six ragged, barefooted peons, each marching between two troopers. They shuffled along with heads hanging, their faces without intelligent expression. The way they walked, the manner in which they held their arms and bent their shoulders told that already they had been beaten and tortured cruelly.

In the rear of the procession lumbered Sergeant Manuel Garcia, the burly second-in-command at the barracks, who had been attached to the *pueblo*'s military establishment for several years. He marched between the bugler and the drummer who was beating out the rhythm of the march.

Groups of men left the sides of the plaza and moved slowly toward the row of posts, stopping when the guard motioned to check them. From the tavern came the fat landlord and some of his guests off the highway. From stores and warehouses came other men to witness the sentence being carried out.

At this tense moment, Don Diego Vega reached a corner of the plaza and began strolling toward the chapel, having business there with the old *padre, Fray* Felipe.

Only child and the heir of proud, aristocratic Don Alejandro Vega, Diego was believed by most to be as a thorn in his father's flesh. He did not consort with dashing young *caballeros*, indulge in wild riding, drinking, gambling and fighting, or making love to such wayward señoritas as he encountered. He looked and acted like an indolent fop, almost effeminate. Wildness had no place in his makeup, so he seemed a man set apart from his caste.

Now he walked languidly, with his shoulders stooped. His attire was resplendent, an affair of heavy green silk, bows and buttons, ruffled white shirt and highly-polished boots. Circling his wide-brimmed sombrero was a band studded with semi-precious stones. His scarf was fastened at his throat with a jeweled brooch, and rings flashed on his fingers. A lace-bordered, perfumed handkerchief of silk hung from his left sleeve.

Diego saw the row of posts and the procession stopping before it, saw the men jostling one another to get positions of advantage from which to watch. He changed his course slightly and approached the scene with unhurried steps.

The drummer beat his drum in a signal for silence. Sergeant Garcia bellowed for attention, and *Capitán* Juan Ruelas stepped forward and watched keenly as the six prisoners had their wrists lashed to the crossbars so their arms were stretched to the utmost. Ruelas lifted his hand, and Sergeant Garcia read off the names of the six men, then the sentence passed on them:

> … ten lashes across the naked back, applied with a hearty will, each morning for five days in succession … afterward to be sold into contract peonage to the highest bidder for a term of five years, and to serve at hard labor, the money resulting from the contract to reimburse the government for expenses incurred by arrest, incarceration, trial and punishment.

GROANS came from the condemned men as the sentence was read. A trooper growled at them to remain silent. *Capitán* Ruelas raised his hand again.

"I have adjudged you six men guilty of treason for refusing to aid the authorities in the apprehension of a known criminal!" he shouted so that all around the plaza could hear. "You have refused to divulge knowledge of the identity and hiding place of the notorious masked highwayman known as Señor Zorro —"

"But we know nothing of him ... we cannot tell even to save ourselves ... have mercy on us, Señor *el Capitán!"* The men tied to the posts wailed their pleas.

"Silence! Falsehood will not help you. It is my purpose to run down this masked malefactor and have him hanged! It is the order of His Excellency, the Governor. I shall continue to seize and question men, and have them punished if they do not give me the information I want."

Suddenly afraid at hearing that threat, peons and natives in the watching crowd glanced at one another. Some began to retreat slowly. Through the crowd ran Juanita Nuñez, the peon girl who had been seen hurrying toward the chapel. She tossed her shawl back from her head, darted between two of the troopers, and knelt to clasp her arms around one of the prisoners.

"*Padre — padre,"* she sobbed.

"Cuff that wench away from the prisoner!" *Capitán* Ruelas ordered one of the troopers. "Are we to be interrupted by a woman's caterwauling?"

The trooper seized the girl's thick braid of long black hair and jerked her to her feet. He thrust her roughly away from the post as she shrieked and clawed at him, and shoved her so hard that she sprawled on the ground. As some of the watchers laughed, she struggled to her feet, bent her head, and hurried toward the tavern, sobbing.

A trooper stepped up behind each of the six bound men, and each trooper held a heavy whip. Sergeant Garcia raised his hand and began counting slowly. At each count the whips rose and fell, cut through skin and into quivering flesh. The men at the posts moaned or shrieked with pain.

Some of the watchers turned aside, nauseated, some laughed, others contracted their eyes a little but gave no other sign of disapproval. Diego Vega brushed his scented handkerchief across his nostrils in such a manner that for a moment his view of the punishment was obscured.

And suddenly Diego heard the voice of a strange man behind him growl:

"What kind of a country is this? What kind of people? Beatin' men like that with whips and sellin' 'em into slavery for nothin'! Men like them — they'd have told it quick enough if they'd have known anything about this Señor Zorro. Think they wouldn't have saved themselves a terrible beatin' and bein' sold into slavery for five years?"

Diego saw the stranger clearly as those near him drew away quickly, for men were eager to leave the vicinity of a man who spoke out so boldly against authority. They feared their very presence near him would be taken as an indication that they agreed with his condemning words.

Diego observed that the stranger was tall and lean, not more than thirty. He wore a buckskin suit, and moccasins. His hair was yellow and his eyes were glinting steel-blue. He had at first spoken Spanish, though his accent betrayed he had not been born to the language. Then quickly he had lapsed into English, spoken in the idiom of his section of his native land.

"Be cautious, señor," a trader standing near the stranger dared to advise him in a low voice. "It is dangerous to speak so here, especially for a foreigner. Keep your thoughts to yourself, and so avoid trouble."

But the American refused to be cautioned or suppressed.

"I'M NOT the kind to stand by and keep silent about a thing like this!" he announced in English, seeing that it was understood. "I'm an American — Pete Jordan by name. And I'll speak right out whenever I damned well please about a thing like this. All you men — standin' around quiet, and some grinnin' while other men are bein' beat like dogs!"

Suddenly Diego heard the voice of the buckskin-clad man behind him, "What kind of a country is this?"

"Hush, señor!" the trader warned. "The big sergeant will hear you and report your words to his officer. The officer may have you put under military arrest, and you may find yourself at a whipping post tomorrow. You *Americanos* — well, you're not liked any too well in this country."

"I still say it's an outrage. I've heard tales about the goin's-on in this country. No justice. Worse'n in Taos and Santa Fe, where I've been. Worse'n the Apaches for cruelty. And that man Zorro — he's a brave man to my way of thinkin'. Punishin' scoundrels who mistreat and torture the poor natives and peons. Takin' his life in his hands to do that. Those six men say they don't know who Zorro is or where he hides, and I believe 'em."

"The officer thinks differently, señor."

"And that poor girl — cuffed around 'cause she ran to put her arms about her father!" the American who called himself Pete Jordan ranted on. "And you — callin' yourselves men — just standin' here like I said, and watchin' it and doin' nothin'! Any sensible man could tell those men at the posts don't know anything about Zorro!"

Diego Vega well knew that the American spoke truth. Those men did not know Zorro's identity, for that was known by only three persons besides Zorro himself. One was Diego's father. Another was Bernardo, Diego's mute peon bodyguard. And the third was aged *Fray* Felipe, the Franciscan in charge of the Reina de Los Angeles chapel, and was Diego's confessor.

For Diego Vega, believed by most to be weak, indolent, with water in his veins instead of hot red Spanish blood — because he adopted such a pose to avert suspicion — was himself Señor Zorro! He was the mysterious masked rider of the hills who fought to avenge the wrongs of the poor and oppressed.

And he fought in constant peril. For detection would mean for him an ignoble death by hanging. It would mean the death of his adoring father from a broken heart, and would also mean the confiscation of the Vega estate by the Governor.

Chapter II
Work for Zorro

THE first day's punishment had ended. Three of the six peons had fainted, for with their half-starved bodies they had no resistance to such physical abuse. The other three had slumped against their posts, with blood streaming from their lashed backs, their arms stretched painfully, and were moaning.

A heavy cart was driven up to the posts, and at *Capitán* Ruelas' orders the troopers untied the men and put them on the floor of the cart without any attention being given to their wounds. The cart started toward the barracks.

As others began leaving the plaza, Diego also turned away. His shoulders were stooped, his face a mask against which he brushed his scented handkerchief frequently. Men smiled, the general opinion being that he had not been able to stomach what he had seen.

Diego's intention was to go on to the chapel for his conference with old *Fray* Felipe. Then he saw the outspoken Pete Jordan, stalking toward the tavern like a man enraged. Jordan was talking to himself, but in tones others could hear:

"A damned outrage! ... Those peons were better men than the ones who beat 'em! ... Damned Spanish cruelty! ... The whole race is a band of fiends!"

Diego swerved slightly and brushed against him. "Pardon me, señor, but not all of us," he murmured in English.

"Show me one who is not! You're one of 'em, huh? All duded up to watch other men suffer. You look to me like you're one of these here *hidalgos*, or the son of one."

"I am the son of one, señor," said Diego. "I am a Vega. My father owns a *rancho* not far away. We have many peons and natives working there, and none is mistreated."

"Your family ain't like the others, then," snorted Jordan. "I've heard how things are here. Look at you — a fine dandy! Silks, laces, satin, jewels — on a man! A Spaniard! Bah, you're all alike! You treat peons and natives like dogs. And that trooper — cuffin' that girl around! All alike — all of you!"

"Pardon me, señor, but there goes a Spaniard," Diego said. He pointed to a *padre* attached to the chapel, who was hurrying past on some errand, his hands thrust into the sleeves of his ragged robe. "There is a Franciscan," he went on. "He and his brothers came to this raw land and built missions to educate the natives and teach the Faith. They — "

"To fool the natives and make 'em work for nothin' while the *padres* sat in the shade and ate meat and guzzled wine!" Pete Jordan broke in.

"You are in error, señor," Diego said gently. "The Franciscans are workers. They roll up their sleeves and fasten the bottoms of their robes high and do the hardest work of all, manual labor. They make adobe bricks and erect buildings, dig gardens, set out orchards and vineyards, work from dawn until dark at such toil, in addition to their religious labors. Study the Spaniards more before you pass judgment on the entire race. Every race has its misfits, señor."

"Why don't the good ones take the bad ones in hand?" Pete Jordan asked.

"It is not so easy, señor. It would not be politic for me to explain."

"Afraid to talk out, you mean?"

"Possibly. But we do what we can. We are beset by mean politicians who reap wealth from other men's misery. Undoing the wrong they do cannot be accomplished in a moment, for they are strong and merciless. But they do not represent the whole of the race to which I belong. Keep your eyes and ears open and learn the facts before you judge, señor."

Diego bowed slightly, and turned aside to follow the path toward the chapel. He had spoken daringly, for a purpose. He wanted to judge whether the *Americano* had been sincere in his denunciation of the whipping, or whether he was a clever imported spy who had been told to be outspoken and so draw to him others who felt as he did. Any such sympathizers then could be reported and put under arrest.

DIEGO quickened his stride, for he was late for his appointment with *Fray* Felipe. When they did meet, the *padre* escorted him to a little private room in the rear of the chapel, where they talked in low tones.

In this place of security, Diego's manner changed. His head went up, his eyes flashed angrily. Now his was not the pose of an indolent fop, he was an indignant man.

"The scene in the plaza, *padre* — I cannot endure many more such scenes," he said. "That cruel sentence! The peons had no knowledge of Zorro to reveal, as you know. Because they are suffering in my name, I feel blame."

"No blame is attached to you, my son," assured *Fray* Felipe. "While you remain Zorro at intervals, you are doing a fine work."

"Those men — " began Diego, but the *padre* shook his head.

"I have been unable to help them, my son," he murmured. "*Capitán* Ruelas is a fiend. He denounced me for begging him to show mercy. When I told him I was sure the six men had no knowledge of Zorro, he said, 'There is many a traitor wearing the robe of a fray,' and threatened to give orders that I could not visit and comfort prisoners hereafter."

"Those men can't endure five days of such whipping," said Diego. "Something must be done. Here is a task for Zorro, it seems."

"And so, my son?"

"I do not grow weary of doing Zorro's work, *padre*, but at times it seems so futile. I punish one scoundrel, and two new ones appear in his place."

"I understand. But the constant menace of Zorro may deter some men from unfairness and cruelty."

"I'll think of some plan, *padre*. From here, I'll go to the tavern and find Sergeant Garcia and try to get him to talk. He may reveal some of the new *capitán's* plans to me. Garcia always goes to the tavern for refreshment after inflicting punishment, and wine at my expense will loosen his tongue."

"And I will get in touch with my spy in the barracks," *Fray* Felipe announced.

"What is this? A spy — and in the barracks?"

The old *padre* smiled. "Sometimes Satan must be fought with his own fire, my son. One of the troopers is a devout and compassionate man. He is sick of the service, but must serve his term. I'll go to the barracks presently to see today's victims and salve their wounds, both physical and mental, and my spy will tell me everything he has learned."

"I'll visit you later and talk over what you learn," Diego promised. "Now I'll hurry to the tavern and get at Sergeant Garcia."

AS HE emerged from the chapel, Diego saw peons and natives scampering to hiding places, apparently frightened. Turning to learn the cause of their fear, he saw a rider on a fine horse which bore a silver-trimmed saddle.

The rider was just turning into the plaza from the highway, and traveling toward the tavern.

Diego frowned slightly when he recognized Don Esteban Santana, owner of a fine *rancho* which had been left by his father five years before.

Now Santana was thirty, and during his five years of ownership he had ruined the estate.

Esteban Santana's reputation was most unsavory. He had remained a bachelor, but his affairs with peon and native girls were notorious. He drank and gambled to excess, had a cruel disposition, and made himself obnoxious to those of his own class. He mistreated his *rancho* workers and house servants, rode horses cruelly, quarreled continually with other men, and was always eager for a fight with blades.

There was no love lost between Diego Vega and Esteban Santana, nor did Diego have any respect for the *caballero*. On Santana's part, he resented the fact that the Vega family, Diego included, were respected and admired while he himself was scorned.

He took every opportunity possible to mock Diego's apparent fastidiousness and indolence.

Diego strove to avoid a situation that might lead to some act of Santana's that would result in a challenge. To fight Santana would mean he must fight for his life, for he would be compelled to exert himself and expose his own great skill with a blade. And the realization by others that Diego Vega, a perfumed dandy who loved poetry, was enough of a swordsmen to outdo Esteban Santana no doubt would arouse a certain amount of suspicion that he *could* be Zorro.

IT WAS easy for Diego to guess that Santana had been somewhere drinking and gambling most of the night, for his appearance indicated it. He was slashing with his riding whip at any peon or native who came within reach, jumping his jaded horse at them and laughing when they screeched and fled.

"I'm too late for the amusement!" Santana shouted. "They have whipped the rascals already. Did they howl much? My horse went lame, else I'd have been here to enjoy it. Make way there, scum! Take to your heels when a Santana rides!"

Diego watched as Santana stopped in front of the tavern and aimed a whip lash at the servant who came running to take the horse and lead him to a hitching block.

Santana reeled toward the tavern door and entered, and Diego could hear him shouting for a flagon of wine.

Diego loitered for a moment, and then approached the tavern also. In front of the door, he encountered Sergeant Manuel Garcia. Undoubtedly the big sergeant had observed Diego's approach, and from past experience knew that Diego Vega's purse was easily opened by a hint of thirst.

"Ah, Don Diego, *amigo!*" Sergeant Garcia cried in greeting, blowing out the ends of his enormous mustache. " 'Tis a better day, now that I have had the pleasure of meeting you."

"I understand you have had a very sorry morning so far," Diego said, stopping beside him.

" 'Twas a thing that had to be done, Don Diego. Orders are just that when a good soldier is concerned. Merely a part of the day's toil, let us say."

"The punishment of those six men seemed rather severe to me," observed Diego. "And for them to receive it four days more — "

"Ah, *amigo*, your concern reflects that you have a tender heart. Do not concern yourself unduly. The rascals are as tough as the hide of a mule. Their whines are far louder than their hurts warrant. The new *capitán* was furiously angry because those six peons refused to tell him what they knew of Zorro."

"But suppose they really know nothing at all concerning this Señor Zorro?" Diego questioned.

"But certainly they know much concerning him," Garcia protested. "He is their champion, is he not? He fights their battles, then runs and hides from the troopers. Where does he hide when he is not riding around the hills and attacking people? The man must eat and sleep somewhere. Do you imagine he lives like a hermit in some cave in the hills? And that big black horse he rides — or perhaps a demon in the shape of a horse — must be kept somewhere."

"All that is true," Diego admitted. "But can it concern the peons?"

"It is impossible that no man has knowledge concerning him," insisted the sergeant. "*Capitán* Ruelas has decided to arrest the peons and natives he suspects in groups, and have the truth from them or send them to the whipping posts and peonage."

"How do you like your new superior officer?" Diego asked.

Sergeant Garcia partially closed his left eye — it was almost a deliberate wink — as he said:

"A good soldier, *amigo*, always likes his superior officers, if he is wise. Else, he keeps silent on the subject."

Diego smiled slightly. "Why are we standing here when the sun is climbing into the sky and showering its heat upon us, my friend? Come into the tavern with me, and do me the honor of sharing with me a flagon of wine."

The big sergeant bowed as well as he could, considering his paunch.

"I assure you the honor is all mine, Don Diego. The wine will be swallowed with double the relish since your coin pays for it."

Chapter III

Disgrace to His Family

DIEGO VEGA passed slowly from the bright sunshine to the semi-gloom of the tavern's interior, with the burly sergeant swaggering behind him, The fat landlord bowed low to Diego, led the pair to a small table beneath an open window, and clapped his hands for a servant, who came running.

As they waited for their wine, Diego glanced casually, but quickly around the room. The first person he saw was Pete Jordan, the outspoken American, sitting alone at the end of a table and devouring a hearty meal. Garcia followed his glance with one of his own in the same direction.

"There," he informed Diego in a low voice, "is a rascal. I never saw him before this morning, and know neither his name nor record, but I know he is a rascal. Like all *Americanos*, he has a loud mouth, and is not afraid to open it in talk. He is also a fool."

"How so?" Diego asked.

"He was bellowing around that the poor peons should not have whips laid to their backs. And it was a disgrace, he howled, that a trooper seized that girl and tossed her aside out of the way. Does the idiot want us to kiss our fingers at peon and native girls? That Juanita Nuñez, who works here, is pretty enough, and a lively wench, but she is still a peon."

"I have heard that *Americanos* are always outspoken about certain things," Diego commented.

"The *capitán* has been informed of this man's wild talk," said Garcia. "Any more of it, or another transgression of some sort, and this *Americano* will find himself in the jail room at the barracks. A man from one country should not attempt to run the affairs of another."

"More and more of the *Americanos* are drifting into Alta California," Diego said thoughtfully. "They come across the burning desert country from Taos and Santa Fe, running the risk of losing their scalps to the Apaches. Perhaps thousands of them will come some day and overrun this land."

Sergeant Garcia had intended to make a reply, but said nothing because of an interruption. For at that moment Don Esteban Santana lurched into the main room of the tavern from the patio.

Diego observed that Santana had removed the stains of travel, and supposed he had engaged a room at the tavern for that purpose. Now he swaggered to a table and seated himself on the bench beside it, pounding on the table with his fist.

"Landlord!" he roared. "A Santana waits to be served! When I honor your pigsty with my presence I demand immediate attention."

The fat landlord waddled to the table and bowed repeatedly.

"Your desires shall receive quick attention, Don Esteban."

"I want food — a hot breakfast. I want your best wine. I want your prettiest serving wench to attend me. And along with those things, I want speed."

"As you command, Don Esteban."

The landlord hurried through the door and into the kitchen, evidently gave orders, and was back again filling a flagon of his best wine from a wineskin. He carried the flagon and a tumbler to the table, and bowed again as he placed them in front of Santana.

Santana poured wine and gulped, then looked around the room. His eyes narrowed when he saw Diego Vega at table with the sergeant. He saw the American also, and his lips curled in a sneer.

"Landlord!" he barked.

"*Si,* Don Esteban?"

" 'Tis the law of the land, is it not, that the landlord of a public tavern must serve all who enter?"

"True, Don Esteban — so long as they can pay, and conduct themselves in a proper manner."

"The law works a hardship on you," Santana stated. "You are thus compelled to serve all sorts of men. Men of blood and station, traders, rascals — all sorts. But you should work out a method to segregate the different sorts."

"I do not gather your meaning, Don Esteban," murmured the landlord.

"Confound it, where are your wits this morning? You should have more than one room — say, smaller rooms off the big main room. Put the sheep in the smaller rooms and the goats in this large main room, in a manner of speaking. Then the sheep would not be so much annoyed by the stench of the goats."

HIS gaze flicked over Diego Vega and the big sergeant and rested an instant on the American. Pete Jordan, his head bent as he devoured food, was unaware of Santana's meaningful glance at him.

"I — I gather your meaning, Don Esteban," the landlord said, embarrassed.

"There are some evils, no doubt, that could be avoided readily," Santana continued, eyeing the landlord. "Like when a man of blood and station sees fit to forget his caste and to consort openly with an underling, even to sit at table with him to drink wine. But you could always give such persons a table in the common room."

"Certainly, Don Esteban. Do you desire more wine?"

"When my food arrives. And be kind enough not to interrupt me again, else I may make you sorry for it. I have noticed that troopers from the barracks are your customers. Beware of extending credit to such, señor. But some of them do not need credit, I fancy. They are given free wine by men able to buy."

Santana glanced at Diego and the sergeant as he made the remark, then poured more wine.

"Don Diego, the Santana is trying to pick a quarrel with you, it appears," Garcia whispered. "Perhaps this friendship between us is wrong. I should seek the companionship of men of my own level."

"You will remain at table with me, or I shall consider it an affront," Diego replied.

Diego did have a friendly feeling for the big, uncouth sergeant. The man lived a lusty life and told droll yarns of his military experiences. Besides, Diego Vega reserved the right to choose his own friends.

He knew that Garcia was not in tune with the events, which now were occurring in the town, that he disliked seeing men punished unjustly. When Garcia participated in carrying out that punishment he did so only as a soldier obeying orders — as the sergeant had said himself.

And Diego wanted to keep Garcia's friendship for another reason — Garcia often unconsciously revealed plans of the soldiers to him, and those plans were valuable to Diego, in his rôle of Zorro. He felt no compunction in loosening Garcia's tongue with wine. It was all in a good cause if a soldier disobeyed orders and revealed his superior's plans. Zorro could profit by the revelation.

Diego glanced at Santana again, and found him watching the kitchen door. Santana was hungry and eager for food. And his hunger made him all the more reckless and dangerous.

"If he issues an insult — " Garcia questioned in a whisper.

"I have no quarrel with Esteban Santana," said Diego.

"But he may try to force one upon you, unless there is a distraction of some sort. I dislike to make speech against any man who bears a noble name and came from a splendid family, but there are some who disgrace the names they bear."

"I understand, Garcia. Let us say nothing more about it."

"Two of my troopers are at a table in the corner guzzling wine. If this affair goes far, I'll call to them and manage to prevent serious trouble. The Governor has issued an edict against dueling."

"Behind which no real man can hide if challenged," Diego added.

The kitchen door swung open and a girl emerged bearing a huge tray heaped with steaming food. She was Juanita Nuñez, whose father had been one of the men at the whipping posts. She was a pretty girl, but now her eyes were red from weeping, and her lips trembled.

She balanced the tray on one end of the table and began putting dishes in front of Santana. He leaned back on his bench and watched her. Her hands were trembling, her whole body was shaking as she made a gallant fight to carry on with her work and keep from displaying her grief. A few tears trickled down her cheeks.

"Must you weep into my food, señorita?" Santana asked, his voice sarcastic.

"I beg your humble pardon, Don Esteban," Juanita said, in a choked voice.

"Do you weep because your lover has turned toward another girl, perhaps? With the world so filled with men — "

"I have no lover, señor. The *padre* will tell you that I am an honest girl and go to confession."

"No lover?" Santana shouted, so all in the town could hear. " 'Tis a sad state of affairs for such an attractive girl as you. But 'tis a state that may be remedied, señorita. If 'tis not a lover, why do you weep?"

"Oh, Don Esteban!" she cried helplessly. " 'Tis my father."

"He has been beating you? He guzzles wine too much? He is too lazy to work? Any of those? What ails him?"

SHE put the last dish upon the table, bent, swung up her apron and covered her face as she sobbed.

"My father — he was one of the men — at the whipping post this morning," she managed to say.

"What? Your father is one of the rogues who befriends this terrible Señor Zorro?"

"Never, Don Esteban! He does not know Zorro, and told the truth when he said he did not. But the *capitán* would not believe him. So he was beaten, and will be beaten four mornings more. And he is ill and half starved, and cannot endure it. He will die from it! If he should live, he will go into peonage for five years, be taken away and enslaved, and I'll be left alone!"

"A girl like you need not be alone, señorita," Santana told her, smirking. "I am not without influence. Perhaps I may do something to better your father's condition."

"Oh, if you only would, Don Esteban!"

"If I only would — what? Perhaps you would smile upon me then, eh? Perhaps you would show your gratitude?"

"I'd work for you for my food, señor. I'd work hard from dawn till dark."

"I have several girls who work as house servants out at my *rancho*," he told her. "They manage to get the work done somehow, but none works very hard at it. Certainly not from dawn until dark. Perhaps you would like such a position?"

His meaning was clear to her. She picked up the tray and took a step backward.

"I — I could not go into your house as a servant, Don Esteban. I — I understand what you mean, and I could not."

"Not even to save your father?" he insinuated.

She hesitated only an instant. "Not even for that, señor. My own father would curse me if I did!"

"Come closer!" Santana ordered. "You are trembling like a leaf rustled by the wind. Your maidenly timidity is enchanting." He reached out suddenly and grasped her arm. "A few kisses would dispose of the timidity, señorita. Once you warmed to them — "

"Please let me go, Don Esteban!" she begged. "Your food will be getting cold. And I am needed in the kitchen." She tried to pull away.

"Sit on my lap," he said coaxingly, "I'll give you a coin of gold for two kisses. Where and how could you get a gold coin more easily?"

All in the room were listening, some laughing and some frowning. The fat landlord was clasping and unclasping his hands, for this was his difficulty. To affront Don Esteban Santana would be no light thing to do. Yet the landlord knew Juanita Nuñez for a pious girl, and felt sympathy for her in her plight.

She had worries enough concerning her father, and now this added worry of being annoyed by Santana — it was too much.

"Let me go," she cried again.

But Santana only pulled her toward him forcibly. She dropped the tray and put her hands against his chest to keep him at a distance. Santana laughed mockingly and drew her still closer.

Chapter IV

Tavern Brawl

A BENCH crashed over as a man sprang to his feet and darted between the tables. Pete Jordan, the stranger from the United States, was in action. As all in the room watched, startled, he appeared in a rage at Santana's side.

"Let the girl go, you Spanish scum!" Jordan cried. "Take your drunken girl-pawin' somewhere else!"

There was sudden silence in the big room except for Juanita's wild sobbing as she jerked free. She turned to rush into the kitchen. Santana started to get to his feet, and Pete Jordan thrust him back upon the bench roughly.

"You — " Santana sputtered with rage. "You dare call me scum? You dare say I am drunk?"

"Roarin'." Jordan replied. "A sot if I ever saw one."

He stepped back and allowed Santana to get to his feet. They faced each other for an instant without speaking. Then Santana's hand swept to his belt, and a knife was whipped out of a sheath to flash in a streak of sunshine that poured through a window.

Pete Jordan sidestepped and bent his body. His own knife came from its sheath, and he straightened to his full height as Santana lurched forward and struck.

But Santana's knife did not strike the target and draw blood. Pete Jordan's knife met the other blade and slipped to the guard. The knives locked. Jordan exerted strength and bent Santana's wrist aside and his arm backward, got Santana off-balance. He held him there, bending over him, his face within a foot of Santana's own.

"You poor fool, to draw a knife on me!" Pete Jordan said in a ringing voice. "Got your steel out first and attacked, did you? So I could slit you open now, and it would be self-defense. If you were sober, I'd do it! But I don't slash a drunk man. I just disarm him — like this!"

He exerted strength, and Santana's knife left his hand, to strike a few feet away on the floor of beaten earth and rock flags.

Santana reeled aside, gasping for breath, half choked with his wrath. His voice came in a roar:

"I'll have you whipped like a dog for this! I'll have you hanged. You dare to show violence to a Santana?"

Sergeant Manuel Garcia feared for an instant that the American would end the Santana family then and there. Now he motioned to two troopers at a table in the corner, and they hurried to him.

"Let's stop this," Garcia said, as he got up from the table.

The sergeant waddled forward with the troopers behind him.

"Enough of this señores!" he bellowed. "Calm yourselves. You ruin the digestion of men who feed."

"Sergeant, seize this scoundrel!" Santana yelled at him. "Throw him into the jail room. He tried to assassinate me — all here saw it. He is an accursed *Americano!* For all we know, he might be — Zorro!"

"Everybody saw you pull a knife on me," Pete Jordan said.

"After you assaulted me," snarled Santana.

"I made you quit botherin' a poor girl who is grievin' enough already, that's all."

"You're in league with her, possibly. Of the same sort, you two. Sergeant! Must I, a Santana, be humiliated by such a fellow, and in your presence? Seize him, I say!"

"Be calm, Don Esteban," Garcia begged. "We shall take him to the barracks immediately. And you, Don Esteban, come there yourself to state your charges, as soon as you have finished eating."

"Make the charges yourself," Santana snapped. "You saw and heard."

"But charges made by you, Don Esteban, undoubtedly would carry more weight with the new *commandante*," Garcia informed him.

"That is so. I'll come to the barracks presently. Throw the rascal into your foulest cell. Cuff him a bit as you handle him. Such riffraff should not be allowed in the country"

"I'll be rememberin' that 'riffraff' when we meet again," Pete Jordan told him, as he was led away by the sergeant and the troopers.

SERGEANT Manuel Garcia was experienced in making a report to a superior. He had been making them for years, and always furnished the most minute details. While Pete Jordan was being kept under guard in the corridor, Garcia gave *Capitán* Ruelas a story of the happening, not sparing Don Esteban Santana in the recital.

Ruelas' eyes gleamed when Garcia finished.

"You are a good man, Sergeant," the officer praised. "And, without knowing it, you have brought certain things to the point where my plans may be negotiated in a natural manner and not arouse suspicion. Bring in the *Americano.*"

Ruelas was sitting behind his long table when Pete Jordan was brought into the officer's quarters. The *commandante* sat erect, his palms upon the table in front of him, his face a stern mask.

Jordan stood on the opposite side of the table with a trooper on either side of him. His wrists had been lashed behind his back, but the troopers had offered him no violence. They did not like Esteban Santana, who had publicly classified them as only a little better than ignorant peons, so they would not go out of their straight path to abuse one of Santana's enemies.

"Your name?" Ruelas demanded. "You may speak to me in English. I am a well-educated man."

"Pete Jordan. Citizen of the United States of America."

"So you are an alien visitor. And you did not report your arrival in the *pueblo* according to law." Ruelas' voice was stern and official.

"I was comin' to do that as soon as I had breakfast," Jordan replied. "Last night I made a dry camp a few miles from the *pueblo* and rode on at daylight. Got to town just as you were beatin' those peons in the plaza. Thought I'd eat and then report to you."

"Report then. Give me something besides your name and citizenship. And no lies, or I'll deal with you in a manner you'll not like."

"I started from Santa Fe with two companions," said Jordan. "We had a ruckus with Apaches. The other two boys were killed. I managed to escape by doin' some hard ridin' and hidin' out. Finally got across Apache country and to the friendly Yumas. They ferried me across the river, and I rode on. Wanted to see this country you Spaniards call Alta California."

"You confess, then, that you are an American vagabond?" asked Ruelas.

"Think so? I've got a little letter that might interest you, *Capitán* Ruelas."

Pete Jordan took a soiled, folded piece of coarse paper from a pocket of his buckskin coat, and offered it to the officer. Ruelas broke the seal, unfolded the message and read:

> To All officials of Mexico and Territories Under Rule of the Viceroy:
> The bearer, Pete Jordan, American, has been of great service to me.
> I recommend him to your courtesy and kind attention.

But it was the signature that caused *Capitán* Ruelas to sit suddenly erect and open his eyes wide. He looked up at Jordan.

"This is rather remarkable. This is signed by His Excellency, the Governor of Santa Fe under the Viceroy. He is a particular friend of the Viceroy's. I know this signature well, for I saw it often when I was in the employ of the Viceroy in Mexico. What was the great service you did him, señor?"

"Nothin' much, to my way of thinkin', but he seemed to think it was somethin'," Jordan replied. "I got between him and a man with a knife."

"And what happened, señor?"

"Somehow, my knife jumped out of its sheath and into the rascal's breast. He was out to kill the Governor. Said the Governor had swindled him."

"Ah!" Ruelas leaned back from the table and regarded Jordan through narrowed eyes. "I understand you are handy with a knife, *si*. The sergeant has told me how you disarmed Don Esteban Santana in the tavern. Santana is coming to make a complaint against you. Why did you attack him?"

"He was abusin' a girl, and wouldn't stop when I told him to," Jordan said grimly.

RUELAS smiled, his manner superior. "We do not consider it abuse to attempt to kiss a pretty peon girl. We consider the girl is being honored."

"It's abuse if she doesn't want to be kissed," insisted Pete Jordan. "And I don't see how she'd be honored any by bein' mouthed by a drunken sot."

"Careful, Señor Jordan! The man of whom you speak is Don Esteban Santana, who comes from an old noble family."

"Then the more shame to him for bein' a sot. And that poor girl, *Capitán* — her father was beaten at the whippin' post, and yet she was tryin' to do her work."

"I know, *si!* Señor Jordan, it has been reported to me that you were rather outspoken at the plaza. You said the sentence was unjust, I believe, and made some disparaging remarks about all Spaniards. Later, you defend a peon girl against a *caballero's* advances. Um! Probably by this time, every peon and native in the district thinks you are championing their cause."

"What I said, I'd say again, and what I did I'd do again," Jordan declared stubbornly.

"This letter you have shown me," the *commandante* said, "is all that prevents me having you thrown into the jail room immediately and given ten lashes in the morning ... a great service to the Governor of Santa Fe, who is the Viceroy's friend — um!" He peered keenly at Jordan again.

"Well, *capitán*?" Jordan asked boldly.

Ruelas straightened on the bench. "Sergeant," he ordered Garcia, "leave this man with me. Take your troopers and wait outside until you are called. His wrists are lashed, and I have my pistol handy. Close the door as you leave."

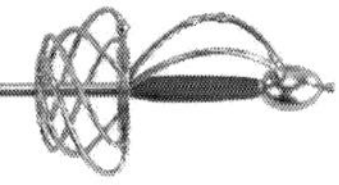

Chapter V
To Play the Spy

GARCIA and the troopers left and closed the door of the *commandant's* private quarters.

Ruelas smiled at Jordan slightly.

"Be seated on that bench," he said, "while I talk to you. I cannot remove your bonds at present, for that might make my troopers suspicious. So you did a service for the Governor of Santa Fe, and he asks all officials and officers to show you kind consideration. Perhaps you would do a great service for me — if there was a handsome reward at the end?"

"It depends on the service, *Capitán,*" said Jordan.

"Quite so." Ruelas bent forward with his elbows on the table and spoke in low tones as Pete Jordan sat down on the other bench and leaned his back against the wall. "The situation in which I find myself is adjusting itself admirably from two different quarters — and you are one of the quarters."

"Maybe I'm dumb, but I don't understand."

"You rant against injustice to peons and natives, and you attack a *caballero* who is affronting a peon girl. All the rascals know of it now, or soon will. They will look upon you as their defender. They will have confidence in you, will talk freely to you after they make your acquaintance. And so you may learn things I want to know, and report them to me."

"Such as?" Pete Jordan questioned.

"You have heard of Zorro? There is a glamour about the rogue. Yet he is nothing but a masked highwayman who attacks and slays men of rank, a fiend upon whose head there is a price."

"Yes, I've heard about his doin's," Jordan admitted.

"I am tired of beating peons and natives to get them to talk and reveal the rogue's identity," Ruelas said, with regret in his tone of voice that was not convincing. "And I was sent to this post to catch Zorro and hang him. I must get results. If I release you with some plausible excuse for not punishing you, you can mingle with the rascals and learn much. They'll trust you because of what you've said and done since arriving this morning. You can give out that you are looking for a *rancho* position or one as caravan boss, or something like that."

"You want me to be a sneakin' spy, that it?" Jordan asked.

"You did a service for the Governor of Santa Fe, and he is no saint from all report. He robs peons and *ricos* alike. I trust you because of this letter you have shown. Serve me in this, and you'll get a heap of gold, also other favors."

"If I don't?"

"Then, señor, you are a boasting *Americano* vagabond, and probably will be sold into peonage and travel with a shipment of such cattle far down into the hot country. A white peon would not live long there, señor — the heat, the humidity, the poor food, the whips of the overseers — " Ruelas waved a hand to hint at other horrors.

"I'm an American, though, *Capitán*, and — "

"A wanderer in this foreign land, no friends at your side. You simply disappear. Your government will never know where you went, even if it is ever learned you have disappeared. And if it was learned and a protest entered, I scarcely think the Viceroy in Mexico, representing the might of Spain, would shiver in his boots at a protest from the uncouth traders, the Yanquis."

"If you ask me, it's in the cards that you folks are goin' to change some of your ideas one of these days," Jordan told him. "This here could be a great land. But it can't be a great and growin' land when a few mistreat the many. Men've got to be equals and neighbors workin' together to make a good and prosperous land. The Americans could do it here, and maybe someday they will."

"Were you a Spaniard, señor, your words would be high treason, punishable by death. It occurs to me that you are trading on this letter from Santa Fe. But do not grow too bold, señor. Let us not quarrel over politics. Will you serve me as I ask? Regardless of citizenship, this Zorro is an outlaw. Your own country would deal harshly with one such. Even if he does avenge mistreated men, as you think, he goes outside the law to do it."

"You want me to make a deal, *Capitán* — is that it?"

"It is. What is your answer?"

"I might be tempted to it on certain conditions."

"What are the conditions, señor?"

"That poor girl, tryin' to work and keep from weepin' over what happened to her father — "

RUELAS smiled at him, as if understanding,.

"Perhaps you are interested in her, Señor Jordan?" he asked. "She is a luscious bit — for a peon. Suppose I release her father and give out I am convinced of his innocence, and perhaps give him a couple of coins for the beating he received this morning."

"That'd be fine. What about the other five?"

"It would be a show of weakness if I released all. Surely you can see that. And the others have no pretty daughters, as far as I know. But I am willing to refrain from having them whipped according to the sentence. I'll give out that I am holding them for further questioning. And later, quietly, one by one, I'll have them released."

"That's good enough. But what's the explanation for you turnin' me loose after me makin' big talk against the whippin', and handlin' this Don Esteban Santana? Maybe this Santana will order you to have me whipped."

Jordan had said the right thing. *Capitán* Ruelas' black eyes flamed.

"Señor Jordan, I happen to be *commandante* in this district. *Order* me to have you whipped, you say? I take orders from nobody less than His Excellency the Governor!"

Pete Jordan got up clumsily, with his wrists lashed behind his back, and paced slowly around the room a moment. Then he stopped in front of the desk.

"I'll make the deal," he said. "I'll want plenty of reward, though, if I get you the information you want."

"You'll get it. I'll give you some money now, so you can live comfortably at the tavern. Travel around the district as if looking for an investment or a position of importance. You have a good horse?"

Pete Jordan grinned. "Well, he ain't much for looks. He looks like a cross 'tween a coyote and a sage rabbit. But he's fast and sure-footed and tough."

"If you need another, let me know, and one will be provided. I'll arrange so we can communicate without actually seeing each other." He pounded on the table and shouted: "Sergeant Garcia! You may come in now."

Sergeant Garcia opened the door and stalked into the room. He saluted his superior officer and waited for orders.

"Take the bonds from this prisoner's wrists, Sergeant," *Capitán* Ruelas commanded. "I am releasing him."

Garcia's eyes widened a little, but he gave no other sign of astonishment. He untied Jordan's wrists and stepped back.

"Don Esteban Santana is waiting, *Capitán*," he said.

"I'll attend to him presently. Give me your close attention, Sergeant. This man, Señor Jordan, is being given his liberty. He will domicile himself at the tavern — and tell the landlord that it is my order he be treated well. Also tell the landlord not to relay that information unless he wishes his property confiscated. Señor Jordan may ride here and there through the district, seeking employment. As long as he obeys the laws, he is not to be bothered by any of the troopers."

"Understood, *Capitán*." Garcia nodded gravely, though he was puzzled.

"If it appears to you that he is overly friendly with such persons as peons and natives," Ruelas went on, "and if he happens to make remarks criticizing our treatment of them, you will ignore his friendships and his talk. Is that clear?"

Garcia's eyes narrowed now instead of bulging, and a hint of a smile flicked one end of his mustache upward.

"It is clear, *Capitán*," he murmured.

"I do not wish to have Señor Jordan and Don Esteban meet each other now. Take Señor Jordan to the rear door, then usher Don Esteban into our presence."

Jordan followed the burly sergeant out of the office and down a long hall to a rear door, which Garcia opened.

"I ask no questions, señor," Garcia said, speaking softly. "What I surmise is my own business. If you ever need help and signal me, I'll respond."

"I don't know what you're talkin' about," Jordan replied. "Your superior officer is lettin' me go free 'cause I didn't understand how things are with you folks hereabouts. I've got to get accustomed to your laws and such."

"I am glad for one thing, señor — that you were not punished for the manner in which you handled the Santana. We troopers do not feel especially friendly toward him."

JORDAN strolled away. Garcia closed the door and hurried to a room in the front of the barracks, where Santana was fuming as he waited.

"*Capitán* Ruelas will receive you now, Don Esteban," the sergeant said.

He conducted Santana along the hall and bowed him into the *Capitán's* quarters, closed the door, and retired. He left Ruelas confronted by an enraged man.

"I have been kept waiting — " Santana began.

"A thing that could not be avoided, señor," Ruelas broke in blandly. "Kindly be seated. I have here some excellent wine from Mexico." As he poured the wine into goblets, he went on, "I have been apprised of what happened in the tavern. I know how you feel about it."

"I want that American scum whipped ten lashes a day for as long as he can endure it and live!" Santana interrupted, his voice trembling with rage. "Then I want him sold into peonage, and I'll see that a friend of mine buys him — one who will not be merciful. I demand that you attend to this at once, Señor *el Capitán*."

Ruelas' eyes flashed. "Did I understand you to say that you *demand*, señor? I am *commandante* here."

"And I am a Santana! Do as I say, else I'll speak to the Governor in Monterey about it. And you, Señor *el Capitán,* will undoubtedly find yourself recalled from this post in disgrace."

"Ah? I happen to know, Don Esteban, that the Governor is much displeased with you at present. He was a familiar of your father in their young days, as you know. I am under orders to show you the error of your ways, also to request you, in the Governor's name, to do him a certain service. And let me say that you will be glad to do it."

"First, let us attend to the affair of the *Americano,*" Santana protested.

"The affair is ended, señor. I have set the man at liberty."

"You — what? Have freed him? Alter he attacked a Santana in public? This is monstrous! Every man of blood will resent it!"

"I doubt that, señor, There are *caballeros* in this vicinity who hold the opinion that you have been disgracing your caste. Let me say, Don Esteban, that perhaps the *Americano* was acting on my orders today when he protested the whipping of the peons — and when, having a chance, he had an altercation with you."

"Your meaning is not clear."

"If I explain, you will keep the matter confidential? Very well, señor. I accept your word of honor as to that. Suppose the *Americano* spoke as he did, attacked you as he did, to endear himself to peons and natives and gain their confidence? I still seek knowledge of Zorro. Understand?"

"Ah! I believe I understand, *Capitán*. But it reflects on me if the rouge goes unpunished for his affront. He carried the thing too far."

"People will soon forget. Avoid, ignore the *Americano*. Now, to your personal business."

Chapter VI

Double Peril

RUELAS refilled the wine tumblers, sipped, looked across the table at the Santana.

"Señor," he said importantly. "I speak for the Governor. You inherited a fine estate, and have managed to ruin it in five years. His Excellency does not deny a young bachelor his wild days, but there should be a limit. The Santana *rancho* is going to waste. There is no management. No great caravans travel up the highway to Monterey carrying the estate's produce. Herds and flocks are not on the increase. Because you are letting the *rancho* run itself."

"Perhaps I have not attended strictly to serious affairs," Santana admitted, a bit uneasily.

"You are heavily in debt," the *Capitán* went on. "You will lose your *rancho* to creditors if something is not done. And that would be a disgrace not only for you but also for all men of noble lineage in the district. Because of the love the Governor bore your father, he will come to your aid."

Santana's eyes brightened, and he bent forward showing keen interest. "Fear of financial disaster has made me act wildly," he said. "It has made me drink to excess, gamble in the false hope of recouping my fortune."

"I know all, Don Esteban," Ruelas interrupted. "And I have the remedy. There is in this vicinity a certain family, both noble and wealthy, against which the Governor holds a special animosity. The head of the family cries aloud that His Excellency is a disgrace to the government, a man unscrupulous in his dealings, a receiver of bribes, a stealer of taxes and all that sort of thing."

"There is more than one like that," Santana said.

"This one has aroused the hatred of His Excellency in particular," assured Ruelas. "The Governor wants him crushed — utterly crushed. But he must have a cogent reason for making a drastic move against him. Aid in this work, and you will be rewarded."

"What could I do to aid?" Santana asked.

"It will be a pleasure for you, too, I believe. How do you stand with the Vegas?"

Santana's eyes flashed. "So! Don Alejandro Vega is the man the Governor hates. I hate him also! I hate his milksop son! Don Alejandro, so noble, so pious. Running around saying I am a disgrace to decent men of my class!"

"Calm yourself, Don Esteban. Tell me — Don Alejandro loves his only son, Diego, does he not?"

"For some strange reason, he does," Santana replied. "Why, I do not understand. Diego Vega has no red blood in his veins. He yawns and gapes, reads poetry and likes lace-bordered handkerchieves. A *caballero* — he? Yet his father loves him."

"It would strike Don Alejandro a heavy blow, would it not, if his only son happened to die an unexpected and violent death?"

"It would crush him," Santana assented positively.

"What are your feelings toward Diego Vega personally, Don Esteban?"

"I hate the little popinjay!" Santana blurted, "He always acts so damned superior. I have tried to taunt him — "

"To combat, perhaps? Taunt him so that in all decency he would have to challenge you? And if he did, and you fought, would you have any great difficulty in being the victor?"

"Over Diego Vega?" Santana tossed back his head and laughed. "It probably would tire his arm to lift a blade! … Ah, you — you mean — "

"Do not try just yet to guess my meaning, but let me suggest a sequence of events," Ruelas said. "Suppose Diego Vega dies violently. Suppose his father tries to have the slayer punished under the edict against dueling. Suppose, being in power here, I declare the slayer had to give combat and so would not be punished."

"Then, Señor *el Capitán* — "

"Then, Don Alejandro appeals over my head to the Governor, and His Excellency upholds my decision. That is all arranged. Don Alejandro would rant and rail, no doubt. Then he could be arrested for treason, and his estates confiscated."

"His estates!" Santana exclaimed. "The wealthiest in these parts! The Governor's share would enrich him."

"And the slayer would not be forgotten when the estate was distributed — so much for the Crown, so much for the Viceroy, the Governor, so much for me for engineering the affair, and so much for the slayer of Diego Vega. A large amount of gold and goods would come in quite handy for you now, would it not, Don Esteban?"

SANTANA'S eyes were glowing, his breath was coming quickly.

"Profit — and revenge," Ruelas said. "Not often does a man acquire both at one stroke."

"The thing would not dare be too evident," Santana reminded. "I am in bad odor already."

"I have a plan for that. I'll call upon all *caballeros* to band together and run down Señor Zorro for the sport of it. You will join the band. It will be expected of you since you are a wild rider and love adventure and fighting. Diego Vega will be approached, also. If he refuses to join the band, it would be easy for you to taunt him with cowardice. No doubt the other *caballeros* would also, in their disgust. Oh, you can arrange the thing, I feel sure."

"I — I could arrange it."

"If he does join, manage to have him killed if there is fighting, or get a broken neck from a horse's stumble. Do I have to plan the little details?"

"Enough, *Capitán* Ruelas. I'll attend to the details."

"I am speaking for the Governor, señor. You will receive a rich reward. And I will receive promotion for handling the affair. It is my hope also to reach Zorro through some plans I have made, catch and hang him, which will mean another promotion and monetary reward. Don Esteban, I am of the opinion that my tour of duty in Reina de Los Angeles will be fortunate for me."

"You have any special suggestions for me, *Capitán?"* asked Santana,

"Stay at the tavern and have your fun. Conduct yourself much as usual, but keep in condition for quick action. Keep away from the Nuñez girl, and let the *Americano* make friends with her, if he can. There is a reason for that which you need not know."

"I understand, *Capitán."*

"Avoid the *Americano*, as I have said before and he will be instructed to avoid you. You two work in different channels, but toward the same end. Perhaps tomorrow I'll make my call for the *caballeros* to band in pursuit of Zorro. Then you will rush forward and be one of the first to volunteer ...."

An hour afterward, old *Fray* Felipe walked slowly along the side of the plaza, receiving the salutations of those he passed, on his way to the Vega *casa* on the outskirts of the *pueblo*. Diego had told him he would visit the chapel later for news, but the *padre* had news that would not await Diego's visit. His excuse for visiting the Vegas was to take the midday meal with them.

Fray Felipe's trooper spy had been at work cleaning the corridor outside the *Capitán's* quarters, and had heard all that had been said inside that private room, and had made his report to the *padre* when *Fray* Felipe had visited the prisoners.

A little later, when *Fray* Felipe, Don Alejandro, and Diego sat in the patio after their repast, the *padre* said:

"Peril comes at you from two sides, Diego. You will once more be in deadly peril as Zorro. Though we think no peon or native knows Zorro's identity, this American, a man I believe to be clever, may get an inkling from something said by one of them, may put one and one together, in a manner of speaking, and do some guessing."

"That is possible," Diego admitted.

"If Ruelas gets the *caballeros* to go after Zorro, they will look upon it as a lark. And they ride like fiends and fight like madmen, as you know. Also, they chased Zorro once and were outwitted, and are eager to even the score."

Diego smiled. "That is to be expected."

"This American, working as he will be to gain the confidence of the peons and natives, may cause many of them to be arrested and tortured — "

"That must be prevented," Diego interrupted with a lift of his hand. "The American must be watched, I held some conversation with him today, and will seek to pursue our acquaintance. And perhaps, while masked, I can warn some of the peons to be on guard against him."

"And a very real danger, my son," pursued the *padre*, "this time to Diego Vega in his own guise rather than as Zorro, you will have to be on guard continually against Esteban Santana. Eager to win the rich emolument offered him, he will hesitate at nothing to gain his end. He is so heavily tarred already that another daub will not hurt him. You stand in the midst of perils, my son. You are fighting for your life."

AFTER *Fray* Felipe's departure, Diego paced around the patio with his hands clasped behind his back and his head lowered, a habit he had while thinking. His adoring father watched from a bench where he sat near the fountain.

Diego finally stopped at the end of the bench and tossed up his head.

"You have decided something, my son?" Don Alejandro asked. "You are a man in a maelstrom of dangers. The troopers will attempt to capture or kill Zorro as a matter of duty. The *caballeros*, if they answer *Capitán* Ruelas' call, will ride after him like fiends, as *Fray* Felipe pointed out. And this *Americano*, Pedro Jordan, will try to form an idea regarding Zorro's identity. He may be dangerous."

"All that is true, Father."

"And as yourself, Diego Vega, you are in peril from Esteban Santana, whose father must be turning over in his grave because of the conduct of his son. Santana hates you, in addition to wanting to carry out the dastardly plot and get gold with which to pay his debts."

"And that also is true. I must avoid riding with the *caballeros*, if possible, and avoid having to challenge Santana or responding to a challenge of his."

"Have you any plans?" asked the father.

"Zorro's horse and costume, as well as his weapons, are hidden at the *rancho*. My idea is this — I'll stroll around the plaza after the siesta hour and show myself. I want to see what the *Americano* is doing, and what Santana is doing. When I return home, we'll go out to the *rancho* in the carriage. From there, I can work as Zorro."

"That would be well, my son," agreed Don Alejandro.

"To my mind, Father, this is something that calls for swift work, for every hour of delay will make my task harder. The task is many-sided. *Capitán* Ruelas must be attended to and revealed as the plotter he is. If other *hidalgos* learn how he has plotted the ruin of the Vegas, they will band together in our defense."

"They will indeed, Diego."

"Esteban Santana himself must be attended to, as also must the determination of the *caballeros* to chase Zorro be broken, by some means. The *Americano* must be exposed, if he is a spy as is indicated, so his talk to peons and natives will have no weight. And above all, Zorro must acquit himself so the peons and natives will know he remains their defender."

"I agree with all you say," said Don Alejandro.

"Then, with your permission, my father — Diego clapped his hands, and a servant hurried into the patio. "I desire to see Bernardo," Diego said.

Chapter VII
Verbal Encounter

BERNARDO, Diego's mute bodyguard, had thought that Zorro would ride the coming night because of the whipping of the peons. He was waiting behind the house for a summons, and within a few minutes after the servant Diego had sent for him arrived, he appeared in the patio.

The eyes of the huge dumb peon were glistening. He bowed low, holding his tattered sombrero in his hands. Diego looked him over. Here was a man in a million unable to speak, but a man loyal to the death, a staunch defender, a man who could and would fight at his master's side.

In that fleeting instant, Diego was remembering how twice Bernardo had saved his life — once when Diego had been sixteen, and a rattlesnake had struck him out in the fields, Bernardo had slashed the wound and drawn the venom from it with his lips when no other help had been near at hand. And again when Diego had fallen from the back of a stumbling horse in the path of a wave of frenzied stampeding cattle, Bernardo had ridden to his rescue on a mule and had pulled him to safety.

Diego voiced no such thoughts now. Instead, he instructed:

"Bernardo, you will have the carriage ready. My father and I will leave for the *rancho* a little later in the day."

Bernardo bowed humbly, and glanced up again. Diego walked over beside him and lowered his voice.

"At the *rancho*," he said, "there will be preparations for you to make. Zorro rides tonight."

Bernardo's eyes glistened again, and he smiled as he bobbed his head, and made the strange guttural sound that Diego knew was meant to indicate pleasure. The mute peon backed to the doorway and disappeared through it.

"Speed — yes, that is what is needed," Diego said, as again he sat on the bench beside his father. "Zorro must strike swiftly and hard, my father. He must hit first one enemy and then another, confuse them all."

A little after the siesta hour, dressed in a change of resplendent attire, Diego

Vega strolled to the corner of the plaza and started toward the tavern. It was the hour for promenade, and fat *señoras* and flirtatious *señoritas* mingled with husbands and fathers as they made the rounds of the plaza, bowed to one another and stopped to chat.

Diego saluted them all, stifling a yawn with his lace-bordered handkerchief at intervals. Knowing what a milksop they thought him, he wished heartily that he could be his real self.

He turned into the semi-gloom of the tavern and went toward the counter. The fat landlord bowed low in his presence.

"In a short time I am going to the *rancho*," Diego said. "I desire a jar of your splendid crystallized honey, for at the *rancho* all has been eaten, and a meal is not complete without it."

"At once, Don Diego."

As the landlord got the honey, Diego glanced around the room. Pete Jordan — a man all would be calling Pedro as soon as they learned his name — was again sitting at a table, eating. Diego accepted the honey when the landlord placed it before him on the counter, and tossed down a coin.

"I believe I'll refresh myself before returning home," he said. "Your best wine, naturally. I'll sit at the table under the window."

As the landlord bowed again, Diego turned toward the table, one he had selected because he had noticed that Juanita Nuñez was attending to it.

The girl came presently with flagon and goblet, and poured when Diego gestured for her to do so. There had been a great change in Juanita since morning, and he remarked it.

"Your eyes sparkle, señorita, and there is a laugh ready on your lips," he told her. "When I was in the tavern earlier today, you were shaken with grief."

"My father has been released from prison, Don Diego," she said eagerly. "And he is not to be beaten again or sold into peonage."

"What miracle resulted in such good fortune for you?"

"It was the *Americano*, the Señor Pedro Jordan. He was not arrested, even after the way he handled Don Esteban Santana."

DIEGO put a coin on the table and shoved it toward her. "That was a miracle, too. Explain it to me."

"I do not understand exactly," she said. "But it seems the *Americano* convinced the *commandante* that he should not be punished for handling Don

Esteban, because in his country any man would do the like to another who mistreated a girl. And I understand he also told the *commandante* that it was ridiculous to think any peon would suffer the lash and peonage rather than reveal all he knew of Zorro if anything was known. So my father was released first of all, and it is said the other five will be, after they have been questioned some more."

"Two rare miracles," Diego told her, a lithe sarcasm in voice and manner. "Does it not seem strange to you, señorita? And the *Americano* — has he presumed to increase his acquaintance with you?"

"Presumed, Don Diego? I feel honored that he gives me the slightest attention. He — he really fought for me, did he not?"

"He did, in a manner of speaking. But did he do it because a sight of you had warmed his heart, or merely because the men of his country always protect women in such a manner?"

"I served him food and drink a moment ago, Don Diego, and he seemed friendly."

"Beware of him, señorita. That friendliness may lead him to seek what Don Esteban sought."

"I — I feel sure, Don Diego," Juanita defended, "that he is a proper sort of man."

"Does it not seem strange to you that he was not punished for how he assaulted Don Esteban?" asked Diego. "The man is a foreigner, an alien *Americano*, and his kind are not liked by our officers. And he assaulted the son of a *hidalgo.*"

"Don Diego, you are trying to make me dislike Señor Pedro Jordan. Why?"

"You are a nice girl, Juanita, and I do not want to find you getting into trouble by trusting the wrong persons," Diego replied.

She refilled his goblet and hurried away. When Diego finished the wine he left the tavern and went out into the sunshine again. He strolled toward the chapel, saluting those of rank who passed. And so he met Esteban Santana, who was making the rounds and also making eyes at every señorita he passed.

"Ha!" Santana exclaimed in mock surprise. "'Tis Don Diego Vega! You will fatigue yourself, señor, tramping around in the hot sun."

"No doubt," Diego replied, brushing his face with his handkerchief. "But I had an errand to do. I could have sent a servant to do the errand, but deemed it polite to show myself in the after-siesta promenade, not having done so for some time. It is expected of one."

"Ah, yes, indeed." Santana was more sarcastic. "I am glad we met, Diego. There is a thing I must speak to you about."

"And what is that, Don Esteban?"

"The new *commandante* is sick of this Zorro rascal running wild. It appears that the troopers are unable to catch him, and no doubt the Governor in Monterey is writing sarcastic epistles about it."

"No doubt." Diego seemed to have little interest in the subject.

"A happy thought has struck the *commandante*," Santana went on. "This Zorro is a notorious law-breaker, a highway man always keeping the peons and natives upset. He is a menace to peace, and must be caught and hanged. Since the troopers have failed, the *commandante* says, why not let the young *caballeros* have some sport?"

"Sport?" Diego asked. "Of what sort?"

"Tomorrow, the *commandante* will issue a request for all *caballeros* to band themselves together and run down this Zorro. What rare sport that will be, Diego! A man hunt. We'll show this rogue that we can outride and outfight him. I only hope that when we corner him I'll be the first to engage him with a blade,"

Diego shrugged slightly.

"Riding and fighting — you think of nothing else," he complained.

"Think of the sport of it, Diego? Doesn't it make the hot blood race through your veins? Think of crossing blades with the rogue! You'll join us, naturally?"

"I dislike tumult, violence, hard riding and fighting," Diego explained. "I enjoy serene composure."

"Certain things are expected of a *caballero,"* Santana reminded him. "Each family of rank must be represented, and you are the only young Vega. Am I to tell the others that Diego Vega will not ride with us? Is your blood water? Do you not relish pounding hoofs, the wind running against your face, the chase, clashing blades?"

"You fatigue me," Diego complained.

Santana glared at him. Persons of rank were approaching, and apparently he thought here was the chance he sought. He would denounce Diego as a coward, and Diego could do nothing except challenge him for it, unless he desired to be stamped a craven by low and high alike.

"So I fatigue you by talking about it," Santana said. "You will not ride with us then?"

"In an hour, I am to start with my father for the *rancho*," Diego explained. "How can I be there with him, and here starting on a wild ride with you at the same time?"

" 'Tis a poor excuse, señor," Santana remarked. "You are trying to avoid helping us run down the malefactor the Governor wishes caught and hanged. Do you not respect the desires of the Governor, you Vegas? Can it be that you are afraid?"

Diego straightened a little, and Santana braced himself for the challenge he felt sure would come. He already saw himself plunging the tip of his blade through Diego Vega's heart. Diego only smiled.

"But you mistake me, Don Esteban," Diego said, brushing his nostrils with his perfumed handkerchief again. "I was only trying to see how I could be in two places at once. Now I have the solution."

"And that?"

"If the band of *caballeros* is formed, get word to me at the *rancho*, and I'll come in and join you."

"Ah!" Santana was disappointed. But there would be plenty of opportunities to pick a quarrel later, if Diego rode with the band. Or he could arrange to have an accident happen to the scion of the Vegas. "I'll see that you have word, Diego."

"Oh, that reminds me, Don Esteban — when I was in the tavern a moment ago to get some crystallized honey, I noticed the *Americano* who affronted you there this morning. How does it occur that he is not imprisoned in the barracks, doomed to be tied to the whipping post in the morning?"

Santana seemed flustered an instant, then recovered. "Oh, the poor lout does not understand us and our manners and customs, Diego. It seems that the Yanquis do not kiss a girl, even one of their lower classes, unless she desires it. Think of a rare custom like that! So I asked *Capitán* Ruelas to release him, after he apologized humbly to me."

Diego bowed slightly. "You have a forgiving nature, Don Esteban," he said. The culminating sarcasm of the scene was in that remark. "And the Nuñez girl's father — I am told he was released by the *commandante*. That seems strange."

"I arranged that also, Diego, on account of the girl. She had been weeping so much, poor thing."

"Pardon me, Don Esteban, for ever misjudging you. I thought you were a man to endure no resistance, a man with a hard heart and only self-interest. And I find you magnanimous. You should exhibit your latent splendid qualities more often, señor."

Santana looked at him sharply. "Do I detect an undercurrent of amusement in your tone, señor?" he demanded,

"I have praised you, and you rebuke me!" Diego protested. "I am, alas, so often misunderstood. Perhaps I do not mingle with persons enough. *Buenos dias, señor!"*

Diego bowed again, brushed his nostrils with the perfumed handkerchief, and turned to saunter along the edge of the plaza, once more bowing to friends and acquaintances.

Santana frowned as he watched Diego lose himself among the passersby. He had a feeling he had been bested in repartee, but was unable to realize exactly how.

CHAPTER VIII

Zorro Rides

IN THE EARLY night as the light of the half moon struggled through waves of swirling mist that had drifted in from the sea with a promise of rain to come, Zorro rode.

His powerful black horse, eager for exercise after much pasture rest, tugged for freedom to run at top speed, but Zorro held him in. He was cutting across the hills by narrow trails he knew well, traveling from *Rancho* Vega to Reina de Los Angeles. The black's hoofs pounded no flinty ground to send news of Zorro's progress abroad, but thudded into soft dirt or turf with little sound.

Zorro rode erect in his saddle, dressed in his black costume, the black mask over his face. His blade was at his side, his pistol in his sash, his long whip coiled and fastened to the pommel of his saddle. In his sash also was a long keen hunting knife that he had learned to use with accuracy and speed.

As he neared the *pueblo*, he redoubled caution, stopping at intervals to watch and listen, always careful not to appear on the skyline and be revealed against the moon-lit sky. The swilling mists obscured him at times, making of him a sort of ghost rider crossing the rolling hills.

Few lights burned in the houses of the town as he approached it. Lights gleamed through the windows of the tavern and the barracks, and a small bonfire had been kindled at one end of the plaza. Around it squatted a few ragged peons and natives, eating scraps of food they had found, while cur dogs waited near them to snatch any small leavings.

Zorro circled the town at a safe distance and drew near a section of small adobe huts where peons and their families lived. At a small distance from the others was the hut where Juanita Nuñez kept house for her father.

Only embers were beneath the cooking pot in front of the hut. Nobody was in sight. Zorro could hear low moans coming from the hut at intervals. Nuñez must be stretched out there on a pile of skins moaning because of the pain caused by his lacerated back. Juanita had not yet retuned front her duties at the tavern, Zorro supposed.

He rode toward a cluster of huts not far away and came upon them from the rear. Around a fire, a dozen men and women were gathered. From the cooking pot over the fire came pleasing aromas. One of the peons had obtained meat somewhere, and he, his family and the neighbors were to have a feast.

They sprang to their feet, alarmed, when Zorro rode around a hut and appeared suddenly before them.

"It — it is Zorro!" a woman cried.

"Be quiet — and be not afraid of me," Zorro said in the deep voice men knew, one entirely unlike the voice of Don Diego Vega.

"We are not afraid, Señor Zorro ... You are our *amigo* ... May you be blessed, Señor Zorro ..."

The mutterings ran on and on until Zorro raised a hand for silence.

"Listen carefully to what I say. I must speak quickly, and get away. Beware of the *Americano* who calls himself Pete Jordan. Today he made a deal with *Capitán* Ruelas at the barracks. He is the *commandante's* spy. For gold, he would betray you. He has worked for the Governor in distant Santa Fe. This knowledge has come to me from a reliable source."

"But he has spoken out against our cruel masters," one peon objected. "And he defended Juanita Nuñez in the tavern, and assaulted a *caballero*."

"That is true," Zorro admitted. "Also, you will notice that he was not punished for attacking Esteban Santana, nor for speaking out against the authorities."

"He had Nuñez released, and — " another began.

"A trick. The *Americano* has done all these things to win your confidence. He thinks that some of you know where Zorro is and where he hides. You do not, but he thinks so. He is to gather evidence for the *capitán*. At any moment he may have you seized and taken to the barracks, and whipped as those men were this morning. Do not be misled by him."

"A spy! He is a spy!"

MORE mutterings went through the group.

"Keep away from him," pursued Zorro. "Do not make friends with him. I tell you the truth. Haven't I fought for you, punished men who have mistreated your kind? I am warning you now, and you will be wise to heed the warning."

"There is a remedy for spies," one man said ominously.

"He is trying to gain the affections of Juanita Nuñez, who is already thankful to him for defending her in the tavern," Zorro continued. "Give her advice, those of you who know her well. Tell her to beware the *Americano's* blandishments. He will only break her heart."

"We shall attend to this *Americano*," one of the boldest said. "He is not one of us, nor a *hidalgo* or *caballero* or of the army. We are not afraid to fight an *Americano* who is a stranger."

"Some of you go quietly to the other hut," instructed Zorro, "and pass my warning along. Tell those to whom you pass it to carry it still further. Warn all to be careful what they say and how they act in the man's presence."

From the near distance came a girl's happy laughter, a rapid fire of talk that could not be understood, and then a man's laughter also.

"Juanita comes home to her hut now," one of the women in the group said quickly.

"And that must be the *Americano* with her," another peon added. "She never has walked home to her hut with a man before. Her father is there now, his back bruised and cut, and she will have to cook his meal. A *padre* came to dress his wounds."

Zorro had backed his horse out of the range of the firelight, and now he wheeled the black and rode slowly back into the deeper shadows. If Pete Jordan was with Juanita, Zorro meant to denounce him in front of the girl.

From the near distance, he saw the fire in front of the Nuñez hut blaze up as fresh fuel was tossed on the embers. In the circle of firelight he saw Juanita attending the pot, then hurrying into the hut for things she needed. Pete Jordan appeared suddenly in the streaks of firelight, puffing at a pipe. He sat down on a rock a short distance from the fire and watched Juanita at her work.

Zorro urged his horse forward cautiously. He did not underestimate the courage or fighting skill of the *Americano*. A man who had traveled the plains from the east to Taos and Santa Fe, who had dared the passage through the Apache country to the land of the Yumas and onto Reina de Los Angeles, would be alert, quick to act in his own defense, a formidable adversary.

As he neared the hut, Zorro got his pistol out of his sash. He had no wish to injure the American now, only to warn the girl against him, denounce him.

Juanita's light-hearted laughter reached him again as he stopped his horse behind the Nuñez hut in the darkness. He overheard some of the talk between her and Jordan as he awaited a proper moment for making an appearance before them. He wanted to move when he could have both in front of him near the fire.

"I'd like to meet this rascal of a Zorro," Pete Jordan was telling the girl. "A man like him — he takes his life in his hands, doin' what he does. If they caught him, they'd string him up without any delay. All the troopers chasin' him around the hills and never catchin' him! And I've heard tell that nobody knows who he is."

"No one seems to know," Juanita replied. "We think maybe he is some man of the army who was mistreated while in service and deserted, and so hates authority."

"That could explain why he can ride and fight as he does," Jordan said. "Somebody must know him, maybe a lot of folks. He has to sleep and eat somewhere, and hide his horse when he's not ridin'."

"No one to whom I ever spoke seems to know," Juanita declared. "They are always guessing. And the punishment he should get always is visited upon others."

"How you mean?"

"Like this morning — my father, for instance. The soldiers are always beating peons and natives to get them to tell what they know of Zorro. He escapes punishment, while others are hurt for his deeds."

"Don't you think he does a lot of good?" asked Jordan. "I've heard he punishes those who mistreat folks and take advantage of 'em."

ZORRO decided the time had come for him to make his appearance. He rode suddenly around to the front of the hut, and light from the fire revealed the black horse, the masked rider in black garb, and the pistol he held.

"Make no outcry!" he warned in low tones, speaking in English.

"You — you — " the girl chocked, alarmed.

"I am Zorro. How is your father, señorita?" He spoke to her, but watched the American and held his pistol ready.

"His wounds have been salved, señor, and he is resting. He will be healed after a time."

"I find you here in the company of a strange alien," Zorro said. "Do you know this man well?"

"I never saw him until today, Señor Zorro, He attacked Don Esteban Santana in my behalf — "

"I have heard of it all. You will do well, señorita, to have nothing to do with this man. He is a spy in the hire of *Capitán* Ruelas. To gain the affection of the peons and gain favor with you, he obtained the release of your father. Do not trust him in anything."

She stepped forward a little and tossed up her head.

"He befriended me, Señor Zorro, in my hour of need. He is the only man except my own father who ever was kind to me."

"I'll handle this!" Pete Jordan said, taking a step forward himself.

Zorro's pistol muzzle covered him instantly.

"Stay where you are, Señor *Americano!* I have no wish to slay you, only to discredit you with the peons and natives and drive you from the land. It would be easy for me to shoot you down now, and ride. I know the deal you made with Ruelas. I know you get a reward if you are instrumental in my capture."

"Hogwash!" Pete Jordan said. "Somebody's been puttin' crazy ideas into your head, Zorro. I like your kind of man. I wanted to meet you, sure! I like a little excitement myself. And I hate to see little folks mistreated by biggies. Give me a chance, and I'll work with you. Together, we might do a lot."

Zorro laughed. "Do you imagine, Señor *Americano*, that you are befuddling me for an instant? Give you a chance to work with me? Zorro works alone. He shares the secret of his identity with none. Give you a chance, señor, and you'd try to trap me for the Governor's troopers!"

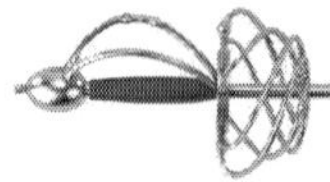

Chapter IX

Authority Is Challenged

SHUFFLING sounds caused by naked or sandaled feet moving on the sandy loose earth came through the night. Shadows flitted where none had been before. Pete Jordan stiffened, and his hand went toward his belt.

"Touch your knife, and I shoot, señor!" Zorro warned.

Suddenly they were there — peons and natives, scores of them who had left their huts or come from the fire at the end of the plaza. Denied lethal weapons by law, they carried bludgeons, stones, bits of metal they had picked up around the smithy.

They voiced no words, but a muttering sound swept through the night. Their sudden appearance, their demeanor was menacing. In the light from the cooking fire, their eyes glittered as they came on, their bodies bent forward, bludgeons held ready.

"What is this?" Zorro called to them.

"We will care for this spy, Señor Zorro," a peon called to him. "Ride away, señor, and leave him to us."

"Hold!" Zorro shouted to them as they prepared to rush forward. "Listen to me one moment! As I have said, this man is a spy for the *capitán*. So, he is under that officer's protection. Harm him, and the troopers will seize scores of you, put you in the barracks jail room, beat you, sell you into peonage as a penalty. Those of you with families may never see your wives and children again!"

"But he is a spy!" came a protest.

"Leave this man to me, señores. I ask it of you. I have a plan wherein I take all the blame — and the troopers have chased me before." He rode closer to the *Americano*. "Señor Jordan, you will leave the *pueblo* before daybreak," he ordered. "And you will not return. If you do not obey, I shall attend to you personally. Is that understood?"

"You're a plain fool," Jordan complained. "I'm in sympathy with these folks. And I like the kind of work you're doin' to help them. I'll join with you, I said."

"I want none of your help!"

"As for leavin' the *pueblo* because a masked man on a horse tells me to do it — that's the very way to make me stay," declared Jordan. "I don't run that easy, Señor Zorro."

"The troopers and their *capitán*, for whom you spy, will not be able to protect you from me, señor," Zorro warned. "I'll manage somehow to get at you."

"Give me a fair chance at you alone, and we'll see who's the best man!" Jordan yelled. "Down out of your saddle, and get your knife from its sheath."

"I have no wish to kill you, Señor Jordan. I want only to have you leave this part of the country."

Juanita Nuñez rushed toward the nearest group of peons, throwing up her arms.

"You shall not touch the *Americano*," she cried at them. "He attacked a *caballero* in my behalf. Would he have done that if he was a government spy?"

"As I explained, señorita, he did that and several other things to get peons and natives to trust him — " Zorro began.

"And you — Zorro!" She whirled toward him, rage in her face. "You are to blame for much of what has happened. Men are beaten because the soldiers think they know you and won't tell your name. My own father is on a pallet in the hut now, half senseless with pain — because of you! Men are in the jail room."

"I have tried to help you — " Zorro began again.

" 'Tis the spy we are after!" a peon shouted.

Others took up the cry:

"The spy! … Kill the spy!"

They disregarded Zorro's shouts for them to stand still. They rushed forward front all sides. Juanita grasped Jordan's arm and drew him backward, thrust him into the hut, which had but the one small door and a single window, and stood in the doorway with her arms stretched from side to side.

"Back!" she screamed at the peons, scarcely heard above the din they made.

"You cannot touch him, unless you kill me first! Back!"

"KILL the spy!" they yelled in still greater fury.

They rushed forward again, those behind crowding those in front. Over the girl's shoulder flashed a knife, and the nearest attacker gave a cry and reeled aside wounded in the arm.

Cries came from those in the rear:

"The troopers! They are coming!"

Hoofs pounded the hard ground of the plaza as some of *Capitán* Ruelas' troopers galloped toward the huts.

"Scatter!" Zorro yelled at the peons and natives. "You'll be beaten if they take you! Run — run!"

They needed no second urging. Scattering to every side, they bent double and ran wildly to get to dark spots from whence they could travel on after a moment's hiding. Some troopers pursued, while others surrounded the hut.

Zorro gave a wild yell of defiance to attract attention, and rode like a fiend, hoping the troopers would chase him and give the peons a chance to escape. Behind him, he heard a chorus of shouts, heard whips cracking against human backs, and the voice of Sergeant Manuel Garcia urging on his men.

Zorro had suspected that *Capitán* Ruelas would not place full confidence in the American, and that he would have a trooper out of uniform watching the man. No doubt that trooper had seen the peons gathering and moving toward the Nuñez hut, probably had seen the masked rider from afar, and had hastened to the barracks to give an alarm.

And now the troopers were thundering through the night, running men down, dismounting to rush into the huts and dislodge all found there — men, women and children — overturning cooking pots and scattering the fires. Men were howling and women screeching, children screamed in fright as everyone in that end of the *pueblo* was awakened.

Zorro knew that at least three of the troopers had tried to pursue him. He circled back to the other end of the *pueblo* and approached carefully. One guard paced back and forth in front of the barracks. A couple of men were in front of the tavern looking toward the scene of tumult.

Zorro touched the spurs to his big black and ran him forward. The guard in front of the barracks turned. From a saddlebag, Zorro took a piece of parchment upon which he had written a note in a scrawled hand and fastened to a bit of metal. He skidded his horse to a stop an instant and hurled this at the guard.

"For your *commandante!*" he called.

He spurred again, and swerved the black just in time. As he had feared, the guard realized that here was Zorro, and lifted his musket and fired. The ball sped past Zorro less than a dozen feet away.

He spurred along the side of the plaza and toward the tavern. The watchers there — the fat landlord and some inebriated man — turned to see what rider was approaching. Again Zorro skidded his horse to a stop and hurled a weighted missive, then wheeled the horse and fled across the plaza and toward the nearest hill.

Leaving the scene of tumult far behind, he rode leisurely to the safety of *Rancho* Vega. In a secluded place there, Bernardo was waiting to take Zorro's horse, costume and weapons.

And Diego Vega, staggering a little from weariness, made his way cautiously to the big sprawling ranch house. Inside it he stopped to tell his father of the night's events, then retired to his couch for rest.

Even as he lay down wearily, a furious *Capitán* Ruelas was shaking with rage as he read for the second time the epistle which had been delivered to him by the guard.

> *Capitán* Juan Ruelas — Your dastardly scheme of the *Americano* spy is known to me. It will be a rare pleasure for me to meet you at a time when you are unable to hide behind a hedge of your troopers' sabers. Either resign your post here, Señor *el Capitán*, and leave, or remain prepared to meet your death.
>
> Zorro

RUELAS cast the parchment on the table before him, gulped wine and strode angrily around his quarters. A few minutes later, Sergeant Garcia entered to report.

" 'Twas a riot of peons and natives among the huts on the hillside, *Capitán*," Garcia said. "Zorro was there, and is now being chased by some of our men, though he got away before our arrival. The *Americano* had taken the Nuñez girl home from the tavern, and the peons and natives were at him, calling him a spy. It appears the secret concerning him is out."

"Read that scrawl!" Ruelas ordered.

Garcia read it. "Zorro! Whence came this?"

"He practically handed it to the guard in front of the barracks while you were gone. No doubt the riot was planned to draw the troopers from their posts here, so he could ride in and toss the thing. A tricky rogue he is — but he may try one trick too many. At daylight, Sergeant, I want twelve men to act as messengers. I'll have requests written. I am calling the young *caballeros* in this district to have some sport in a Zorro hunt."

And at the tavern, at about the same time, the fat landlord and two of his guests were reading a scrawled message on a sheet of parchment spread on the counter:

> The *Americano* known as Señor Pedro Jordan is a spy in the hire of *Capitán* Ruelas. I order him to leave the *pueblo* at once else incur my violent displeasure. Any who show him kindness will incur that displeasure also.
>
> Zorro

Ruelas' trooper scribe worked throughout the night writing copies of the *capitán's* proclamation calling upon *caballeros* to report at the barracks. At dawn, trooper messengers left to carry copies throughout the district.

A troubled landlord called upon Ruelas as he was finishing his breakfast, and asked what he was to do in the light of the message left at the tavern by Zorro the night before.

"Retain the *Americano* as your guest, and we will guard you against Zorro," Ruelas replied. "The *Americano* shows no disposition to leave?"

"On the contrary, *Capitán*, Señor Jordan laughs at the masked man's threat and says a dozen like him could not make him depart."

"Ah! A brave man indeed! Serve him well, landlord, and it will pleasure me."

Only half reassured, the landlord departed.

Ruelas inspected his troop and gave Garcia orders to refrain from bothering him while he caught up on sleep.

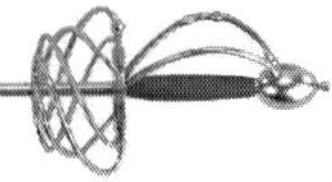

Chapter X

Diego Goes to War

MIDMORNING was approaching when a tired trooper galloped his horse down the lane to the Vega ranchhouse. Don Alejandro happened to be in front of the house instructing a peon in the planting of flower shoots. He accepted the *capitán's* epistle and read it.

"My son, Diego," he said then, "the only young *caballero* of our family, I regret to say, is yet asleep. He had a restless night. I shall inform him of the *capitán's* request as soon as he appears. No doubt he will be glad to ride with the others."

Knowing the reputation of Diego Vega, the trooper opened his eyes wide. Don Alejandro pretended not to notice.

"No doubt you are fatigued," he said pleasantly. "Go to the kitchen and tell them I said to give you hot food and all the wine you desire."

When Diego came from his own room, his father greeted him warmly and showed him the epistle. Diego smiled slightly.

"I have made some plans concerning that, my father," he explained. "Each *caballero* no doubt will have a peon servant to care for an extra mount and carry provisions."

"No doubt."

"The Vega *rancho* will be represented so in a manner worthy of its prestige. I shall ride to the *pueblo* in the carriage."

Don Alejandro's eyes widened. "I'll ride in with you, my son," he said promptly.

"Your company will make the journey far less tedious. I have instructions now for Bernardo."

Diego clapped hands for a house servant, and ordered that Bernardo be called. Within a few minutes the mute peon stood before him.

"Attend me," Diego ordered. "I return to the *pueblo* soon in the carriage, but you will not drive. When nightfall comes, take Zorro's horse, costume and weapons to our usual hiding place a mile from the *pueblo*, and wait there for me. I may come soon or not for quite some time, so take a bag of food and a skin of wine with you. Remain there in hiding and be cautious continually."

Bernardo bowed low, and his eyes glistened as he went from the room. When father and son were alone again, Don Alejandro said:

"My son, Zorro did well last night. Make it your object to see that Diego Vega does as well in whatever situation may confront him. You are dealing with a clever rogue when you deal with Esteban Santana, and with one who hates our family and all we represent. And he is working for high pay, remember."

"I am remembering everything about him, Father."

"If he gets you into a corner where you will have to challenge him to protect your honor," Don Alejandro reminded, "or he can challenge you, you will have to fight with Zorro's skill to save your life. And that would call much unwelcome speculation, as we both well know."

"I am aware of it, Father. Perhaps Diego Vega can be as clever as Señor Zorro when occasion makes it necessary."

"With deadly foes on every side, you are calm, my son."

"A state of serenity is best when important thinking is to be done."

Soon after the noon hour in Reina de Los Angeles, *caballeros* began arriving from the *ranchos*, riding their best horses, carrying pistols, blades and knives. Each brought a peon servant, and most of these led an extra mount.

They reported their arrival at the barracks, left their horses at hitching blocks around the plaza, and trooped into the tavern shouting for wine. Esteban Santana was there before them to make them welcome and try to act as leader. Most of the *caballeros* treated him with distant scorn.

They were like men on a frolic. Hunting down Zorro was considered by them to be good sport. Most of them neither particularly approved nor disapproved of Zorro's actions in befriending mistreated peons and natives or punishing their abusers. It was the excitement of the chase that lured them.

THEY boasted loudly as they drank, decided to draw lots as to which would have the honor of crossing blades with Zorro first if they got him in a corner where he could be made to fight with a blade. They tried to select a leader, but failed because each voted for himself. The election was postponed until later.

They observed the American, Pete Jordan, as he rubbed down his scraggy-looking tough pony at the side of the tavern, and were astounded when Jordan calmly told them in his accented Spanish that he was going to join them in the chase. Santana, warned by Ruelas to avoid Jordan, said nothing. But other *caballeros* frowned at Jordan's announcement.

"Your pardon, señor, but you misunderstand," one of them spoke up. "This man hunt is an affair for a special group of us. I regret that you may not accompany the troop."

Sergeant Garcia, who had been making a list of names, replied to that.

"Your pardon, *caballero*, but *Capitán* Ruelas has issued an order that the señor ride. He is an *Americano* with much experience in tracking. And he has a special interest in pursuing the rogue Zorro, for the rascal aroused a mob of peons against the señor last night." Garcia looked at his list of names. "All seem present except Don Diego Vega."

Santana laughed. "Diego Vega? If Zorro knew he was riding with us, no doubt the masked demon would hide in the hills forever. If Diego Vega pursues the rogue, the rest of us need not exert ourselves."

Some around him laughed also, but others did not. They believed Diego to be a spineless fop, but he was the scion of a noble family, and they did not relish having a man of their own caste held up to scorn.

"Perhaps he will come riding in from the *rancho* yet," one suggested. "It is proper that the Vega *rancho* be represented in this affair."

Another man cried out and pointed. Over the nearest hill, a huge dust cloud was lifting. All turned to look, and grew so quiet that the sound of hoofbeats could be heard.

Into their view over the brow of the hill appeared the Vega carriage drawn by a pair of spirited palominos. They could see Diego and Don Alejandro sitting on the cushions in the carriage seat.

"Dios!" a *caballero* swore. "He comes to a manhunt in a carriage!"

"With his saddled horse hitched on behind," another discovered.

"With jewels on his fingers and a perfumed handkerchief in his hand," commented still another, with heavy sarcasm. " 'Tis the end of Señor Zorro. Never shall he have the pleasure of seeing the rogue hanged. Diego Vega will slit him with a blade if ever they meet."

"Look!" another *caballero* cried.

Over the brow of the hill came a cavalcade of twenty horsemen. Their mounts had been responsible for the cloud of dust that had been observed. They rode four abreast, gay serapes over their shoulders, blades at their sides, pistols in their belts. And they sang the song of the Vegas as they rode.

"*Vaqueros!*" a man yelled. "A band of Vega *vaqueros*? Don Diego seems to think he is leading a host of retainers to war."

Carriage and *vaqueros* stopped at the barracks. Some of the *caballeros*, Santana among them, ran to mount and ride there furiously. *Capitán* Ruelas, his face a picture of amazement, was greeting Don Alejandro.

"*Capitán*, I have brought with me some of our *vaqueros*," Diego was saying. "The hardest riders and best fighters we have on the *rancho*. If Zorro can be brought in, they will do it."

"Your pardon, *señor*, but — but — " Ruelas stammered.

"Why do you hesitate, Señor *el Capitán*?" Diego wanted to know. "Are they not welcome? You desire the capture of Zorro, do you not?"

"But certainly, Don Diego. However, it was understood that a band of *caballeros* was to form the party. And these *vaqueros* — well, for them to be on equal terms, with all respect to them, with *caballeros* … That is to say, some may object."

"Do none of the *caballeros* have peons or *vaqueros* with them?" Diego asked blandly.

"A peon servant or two, possibly. Leading extra mounts, and carrying provisions."

"Ha! But a Vega always travels on such an enterprise with a score of such, Señor *el Capitán*. They will be ready to serve my every need, to furnish me instantly a fresh horse, another weapon, a charged pistol for an empty one. To give me food and drink instantly if I so desire. Each man has his duty. Some are to guard and protect me while I sleep — or if some man should affront me."

ESTEBAN SANTANA'S face was purple with wrath, but he refrained from speech. Thoughts were flashing through his mind like streaks of lightening.

Somehow the secret of the American being a spy had leaked out. Had the secret of his deal with Ruelas to accomplish the death of Diego Vega and the wrecking of the Vegas to his own benefit leaked out also?

The protest he might have started gently was wrecked by the wild yell of one of the laughing *caballeros*.

"Ha! Diego is most thoughtful of us all. He comes to war with a host of fighting men behind him. Let his *vaqueros* ride with us. We'll chase Zorro like a rabbit to its warren. One thing, though, must be remembered — when the rabbit is trapped, the *vaqueros* stand back and let a *caballero* draw blade against him."

Diego brushed his face with his perfumed handkerchief and bowed to them all.

"I'll ride on to our *casa* with my father, señores," he murmured, "and attire myself appropriately for this gay adventure, then return here and rejoin you. Meanwhile my *vaqueros* will water and feed their horses, and refresh themselves with food and wine."

The carriage rolled on toward the Vega house. The *caballeros* laughed and turned away, all except Esteban Santana. He looked after the carriage thoughtfully. He did not join in the laughter.

Chapter XI

Storm Clouds

When Diego and his father had laved away the stains of their journey, they met in the big main room, where food had been set out for them. After they had finished eating and the dishes were cleared away, the table servant disappeared at a gesture of Don Alejandro. Father and son were alone.

"My son, you have astonished the *pueblo* in a new manner," Don Alejandro said. "I think I can understand your idea in fetching the *vaqueros* along. But what are your further plans?"

Diego spoke in a low voice, lest some house servant — and they had been trained to move so quietly that they made little more noise than shadows — should hear and inadvertently mention the overheard words later.

"As the carriage passed the chapel, my father, I noticed *Fray* Felipe standing in the doorway. He gave me the sign of blessing — and another sign."

"Another sign, Diego?"

"One known between us. It meant that he had important news to impart to me. So no doubt he will be coming here soon."

Within a few minutes a summons came at the door, and a soft-footed servant ushered *Fray* Felipe into the room. He sat at table with father and son, sipped wine, and stated the real purpose of his visit after the servant had gone.

"I have had an interview with my barracks spy," the *padre* announced. "He tells me that all day peons and natives have been slipping away from their work and disappearing into the hills. Not only here in the *pueblo*, but from the *ranchos*. Even some of your men, Don Alejandro."

"My *rancho* hands deserting?" Don Alejandro asked in surprise. "Why should they? I treat them extra well."

"They began running away, so my report has it, soon after you and Diego and the *vaqueros* left the *rancho*. Not because of your treatment of them, Don Alejandro. You are always kind and just. But after the mob scene here last night, they fear reprisal. They believe that *Capitán* Ruelas will seize any he fancies and put them to the lash in an effort to learn the identity of Zorro."

"Has the *capitán* made plans of which you know?" Diego asked.

"At nightfall, he will send out all his troopers, since the *caballeros* are here to handle Zorro if he appears. The troopers will scour the countryside, pick up deserting peons and natives, tie them together and bring them to the barracks and toss them into the jail room."

"So if Zorro rides," Don Alejandro observed, "he will indeed face many perils. The troopers are riding the hills. The *caballeros* are waiting only for an alarm in order to pursue."

"That is true," the *padre* said. He smiled then. "But Zorro is warned now."

"Let me think a moment," Diego said. He got up, paced the floor, and finally stopped beside the table. "The troopers will be gone from the barracks, you say. And the *caballeros* will make camp in the plaza and do considerable drinking — "

"*Capitán* Ruelas has invited the *caballeros* to spend the evening in his quarters, and will supply ample food and drink for them, as well as facilities for playing with dice and cards. He would ingratiate himself with them."

"That will leave the Vega *vaqueros*, and the peon servants the others brought to town to carouse in the plaza," Diego said. "And the troopers will be away, except possibly a couple of men on barracks guard."

"What are you planning, my son?" Don Alejandro asked, a trifle sharply. "This is a time for extreme caution, not recklessness."

"The three of us in this room know the task I face," Diego replied. "We know the double plot — against Zorro and against Diego Vega. Zorro has three chief men with whom to deal — this *Capitán* Ruelas, Esteban Santana, and Pete Jordan, the *Americano*. When they are eliminated or discredited, there still will be work for Zorro. I must convince the peons and natives beyond all doubt that he is their firm friend."

"Do any doubt that now?" *Fray* Felipe asked, surprised.

DIEGO sighed heavily, and shook his head.

"I fear so, *padre*. Juanita Nuñez spoke out against Zorro last night. She indicated that Zorro only brought more sorrows instead of good, caused peons to be arrested and whipped for not betraying him. Zorro must show himself stronger than he ever has before."

"And you must rejoin the *caballeros*," his father reminded him.

"Low black clouds are starting to drift in from the sea," *Fray* Felipe said.

"There will be rain. It will be a bad night for those camping in the plaza."

"That might give the delicate Diego Vega an excuse for quitting the plaza and returning to his home," Diego said.

His father had another thought. "Diego, you will have to show yourself at the *capitán's* feast. He will expect the Vegas to be represented, naturally, and that may be a trap."

"What sort of trap?" Diego asked.

"Have you forgotten the plot? Have you forgotten that Santana will be there? Would it be impossible for that rogue to pretend to be deep in his cups and affront you in such a fashion that you would be compelled to resent it and challenge him?"

"I'll have to ward him off, Father. But just now I must change attire and return to the plaza."

Diego changed to rougher riding clothes, and mounted the horse held ready for him in front of the house. He made the horse walk all the way to the plaza, and rode bent forward in his saddle, as atrocious a seat as any man ever had seen. He seemed on the verge of falling off his mount's back.

Dusk was coming on now. The wind had freshened and the black clouds soon would blank out the moon. Mist swirled, and before long rain would commence to fall, a disagreeable drizzle at first, then possibly a deluge. It was the time of year for that.

A huge bonfire had been built in the plaza not far from the row of whipping posts. Horses were tied to those posts now. Many of the mounts had been unsaddled and allowed to roll. The *vaqueros* and peon servants were sitting around the fire, eating and drinking.

Some of the *caballeros* were in the plaza, but the majority were in the tavern out of the rising wind. Diego glanced over the scene swiftly as he approached, and did not see Santana.

The Vega *vaqueros* greeted him with loud shouts, for they were drinking wine and eating food he had provided.

"We are to feast at the *capitán*'s quarters, Diego!" a friend called.

"But I have just feasted at home," Diego explained. "I have eaten enough for two men."

"Then you can spend all your time with goblets of wine."

"Too much wine sours my stomach, *amigo,* and distresses me exceedingly."

"You jest, Diego! What *caballero* ever lived who let wine sour his stomach, unless the wine itself was sour?"

"I may visit the *capitán*'s quarters before the feast is over," Diego told him. "Meanwhile, I'll remain here in the plaza with the *vaqueros*. Someone must be on the watch for this Zorro, not so?"

"What would you do, Diego, if you met him face to face?" his friend asked facetiously. "Ah, I see you have belted on a blade. Would you use it on the rogue?" There was a background tone of laughter in the main's voice.

But somebody else called, and Diego was spared making a reply. One of the *vaqueros* took his reins as he dismounted, and Diego went slowly toward the tavern, shoulders bent and feet almost dragging, as he usually walked.

He entered the tavern and was received in a fitting manner by the landlord and guests. He saw Pete Jordan sitting alone at a little table in a corner, wine jug before him.

Santana was dicing with some of the *caballeros* at a long table in the middle of the room.

AFTER the whipping Diego had spoken to Jordan in the plaza, and in his role of Zorro had spoken to him further the night before. Now as he approached the table where Jordan was sitting, Diego Vega bowed slightly.

"Is this chair reserved, señor?" he asked politely, indicating the one across the table from the American.

"Not at all. Help yourself, Don Diego. I'm a kind of outcast, it seems."

"And how is that, señor?"

"The peons and natives think I'm their enemy, and the fancy gents such as yourself think I'm scum and won't have anything to do with me."

"I have heard that you were attacked last night," Diego commented. "What was the basis of that?"

"This masked Zorro appeared and told them I was a spy in the pay of the *capitán*," said Jordan. "They think I'm out to catch Zorro."

"But are you not, señor? I understand you are to ride with the *caballeros* when there is an alarm and they take up the chase."

"Oh, I'll ride with 'em. I want to see 'em perform. Want to see how they go about tryin' to catch a man in this country."

"Should you catch Zorro, señor, you would be a made man here. A rich reward in gold has been offered. And no doubt the Governor and his officials would look upon you kindly. And, since you are riding with the others who pursue him, the peons and natives will be sure you are a spy anyhow."

"Don Diego," said Pete Jordan, "you seem a bit more decent than the rest of these highborns hereabouts. I've heard that you're not so scatterbrained as others. You're not always hellin' around. Juanita told me that — "

"Juanita?" Diego lifted his eyebrows. "Ah, yes, the girl here in the tavern, whose father was whipped. I trust he is recovering."

"He'll get along all right. Half starved, like the rest of the peons. They don't get much out of life except kicks and cuffs. The sight of it is more'n enough to make a thousand Zorros ride the hills defendin' them."

"I am bewildered," Diego said, and meant it. "One instant you express pity for the lot of the peons, and the next you say you will ride in an effort to catch the man who befriends them. Are you fish or fowl, señor?"

Pete Jordan's eyes narrowed. "That depends upon the man I happen to be talkin' to," he replied. "I'm Pete Jordan, an American citizen, tryin' right now to keep out of trouble in a foreign land."

"I have heard that Zorro tossed a message to the landlord here last night, saying he had ordered you out of the *pueblo*. But here you remain. Do you not fear, señor, that Zorro will visit you?'

"I'm hopin' he'll try it," Jordan declared.

"Ah! You would overcome him, you think?"

"I'd like to have a chance to talk to the rascal alone, without a bunch of others around, that's all."

"Honor me by having wine with me," invited Diego. "I see your glass is empty."

"Thanks, Don Diego, but I've had enough. I want to keep my wits about me. All your *caballero* friends are so soused now that they couldn't shoot straight or sit a saddle well. My horse is ready at a hitchin' block, and I'm goin' to my room and catch some sleep. If there's an alarm that Zorro is in the neighborhood, I'll hit the saddle with the first of them. Thanks just the same. No offense."

"No offense taken, señor."

Pete Jordan got up, bowed slightly, and strode through the door that led into the patio behind the tavern, where there were guest rooms.

Chapter XII
A New Challenge

JUANITA NUÑEZ appeared at Diego's table almost immediately, her eyes sparkling, to ask him what he desired. His favorite wine, he told her.

"You seem happy tonight, señorita," he drawled. "Is it because your father has been released and is at home and recovering?"

"Partly for that, Don Diego, thanks," she told him. "I am glad you talked to Señor Jordan. He is a fine man, Don Diego."

"Are you perhaps falling in love with the *Americano?"* Diego asked.

"He is the first man who ever treated me decently, Don Diego. He is not like the rest. He does not care if I have peon blood."

"I have heard that you defended him last night when the peons attacked him."

"I did — *si!* And would do it again. I know what they say of him, and do not believe it. He is no spy for the *capitán."*

"But the evidence against him, señorita! He is even preparing to ride after Zorro with the others. And Zorro is the peons' friend, I have been told."

"I do not know why Señor Jordan will do it, Don Diego, but I trust him."

"Love is a sickness that always blinds the person it assails," Diego observed. "The whole thing is confusing to me. Kindly hasten with the wine."

She brought it, and Diego sipped a little as he watched those in the thronged room. A *caballero* shouted from the doorway that it was time for them to go to the *capitán's* quarters for the feast, which was being spread in the big barracks room.

Diego finished his wine and got up to go with the others. It might arouse suspicion if he did not.

He went with the others as they trooped across the plaza and on toward the barracks. They went afoot, for most of their horses were unsaddled. They laughed and shouted and swaggered, already tipsy with wine and itching for a fight of any kind. Diego noticed Esteban Santana looking at him repeatedly, with malevolence in his glances.

Capitán Ruelas greeted them at the barracks door, bade them sit on the benches and eat and drink. Troopers kept the goblets filled and the platters heaped with steaming food. Two peons on a dais in a corner played guitars and sang continually.

Diego considered his present situation. He felt like a man completely surrounded with swirling storm clouds. His dual rôle had brought him double danger now. As Zorro, he was beset as usual, but this time from more than one direction. And as Diego Vega he was in peril, also.

As he sipped his wine, he noticed that no sounds came from the stables adjoining the barracks, not the single snort of a horse or a thudding kick in a stall. He already had noticed that Sergeant Garcia was not present to aid his superior in making the guests welcome. And, as the feast got under way and Diego continued to watch carefully, he saw two of the men serving the tables slip out of the room quietly. They did not return.

So *Fray* Felipe's report had been true. The troopers were riding the hills to catch deserting peons and natives and herd them to the barracks. The whipping posts would be in use repeatedly in the morning — perhaps.

And suddenly Diego remembered that about this time Bernardo would be on his way from the *rancho* to the hiding place in a gulch a mile from the *pueblo*, with Zorro's horse and costume and weapons. Bernardo might run afoul of the troopers and be seized!

Capitán Ruelas was announcing:

"If Zorro makes his appearance in the *pueblo*, or is reported in any vicinity, an alarm will be given. The huge anvil at the smithy has been moved out in front of the smithy, and a heavy sledge is beside it. I have stationed a man there to give the alarm."

The *caballeros* whom he was feasting cheered his words.

"Señores," he went on, "your horses have been rested, and with your permission I'll send word to the plaza for your peon servants to saddle them and hold them ready, so no time will be lost in taking up the pursuit."

THEY yelled permission, and Ruelas disappeared for a minute or so to issue his orders. Then he returned to sit at the table and shout for more wine.

Diego had not emptied his goblet. He had been taking only small sips. Ruelas noticed that.

"Don Diego," he said, "you drink sparingly. Is the wine I provide not to your taste?"

"On the contrary, Señor *el Capitán!* It has an excellent bouquet. But it is so potent! Wine makes me sleepy, and I desire to be wide awake if an alarm comes that Zorro is near."

"Ha!" a *caballero* shouted, "Diego has more sense than any of us. He does not forget we are on a serious mission. He would make an excellent soldier. Duty first! Get your enemy, and then empty a wineskin. 'Tis an excellent idea, but one to which I do not heartfully subscribe."

"Perhaps 'tis only a matter of a small and delicate stomach," Esteban Santana roared from down the table. "So wine makes him sleepy! He must swallow a deal if it, for he is more than half asleep always."

There was instant silence in the room. Diego looked up and down the table. He saw the angry flush in Santana's face, saw the black eyes of Ruelas glistening.

"A man may appear to be half asleep when he is meditating on the works of the poets," Diego observed. "Deep thought, I have learned, induces an appearance of semi-somnolence in the thinker. Some men are keenly alert always, but they are men of action only, and generally do not have brains enough to deal with practical thinking."

Some of the *caballeros* laughed riotously. Santana's face purpled with quick wrath.

"Was that remark meant as an insult to me, Don Diego?" he cried.

"I mentioned no names, señor. I was but making a general observation. I was defending myself against the accusation that 'twas wine that makes me appear sleepy."

"I did not like your words, Don Diego Vega! They had a certain ring that was not welcome to my ears."

"I regret it, señor, if your ears have been pained," Diego told him placidly.

One of the *caballeros* sensed trouble coming, and sprang to his feet.

"Let us have no more talk of ears!" he shouted. " 'Tis the ears of Zorro we would carve from his head and nail, to the door of the barracks."

But Esteban Santana got up from the bench upon which he had been sitting, straightened his body and brushed his long black hair back from his face. The *caballeros* glanced swiftly at their host, whose office it was to preserve peace among his guests. But Ruelas appeared to be busy eating, and ignored what was occurring.

Santana stopped within six feet of Diego and stood with his feet apart and his fists jammed against his hips. His nostrils were distended with his deep angry breathing.

"Don Diego Vega," he demanded, "do you presume to judge men? Have you ever spent much time among them? Are you capable of estimating their qualities? Can the qualities of real men be determined by one whose veins pump some mysterious watery fluid instead of good red blood, who reads poetry and brushes his nostrils continually with a perfumed lace-bordered handkerchief of silk?"

"Capitán!" a *caballero* cried. "Put a stop to it! 'Tis wine speaking, not Don Esteban."

Santana whirled toward the speaker. "I shall remember that remark, señor, when I have finished with Diego Vega. I am still waiting for his answer."

Diego's face was white with rage, and he fought to control himself. Here he was in the trap already. He was doing some rapid thinking as he got to his feet slowly, brushed a spot of imaginary dust from the sleeve of his coat, and held his head high.

"As to whether my veins pump a watery fluid instead of blood, Don Esteban," he said, "no man has ever opened one of them to find out."

"Ah? That oversight could be remedied easily, señor."

"Perhaps not easily, Don Esteban."

SANTANA roared with laughter.

"You mean it would take an exceedingly good man to open one? Do the work of poets teach you how to handle a blade? Do the rare perfumes you use fire you to vehement action?"

The *caballeros* were all silent now. Ruelas went on eating, but he glanced down the table without lifting his head. The development of this scene pleased him.

"Different influences act on men in different ways," Diego said. "On me, poetry and perfume exert a softening influence, give me an atmosphere of peace, and I see the world and its people in a kind light."

"Indeed?" Santana sneered. "Something has softened you, as all men know."

"Whereas," Diego continued, knowing that this could be settled decently in only one way, "different things influence you in another manner."

"As, for instance?" Santana prompted.

"Excessive wine drinking, playing at dice and cards in an effort to regain wealth foolishly tossed away, consorting with peon and native women — such things have a tendency to coarsen a man, especially if he be coarse in mind and manners at the start."

"Are you speaking to me, señor?" Santana shouted in interruption.

"Did you not ask me to explain?" Diego inquired,

"Milksop son of an arrogant father!" Santana cried in fury.

He sprang forward and his right arm swept through the air. His right palm cracked against Diego's cheek. Santana took a step backward then, as the *caballeros* sprang to their feet crying out against what had been done.

"For shame, Santana! … Hand your slaps to men used to fighting! … You do not know what you do! … 'Tis the wine in him, Diego!"

Santana stood like a statue, waiting. Diego lifted a hand and brushed it against the cheek where the slap had landed.

"You have called me the milksop son of an arrogant father, señor, and have struck me," he said, his voice trembling with suppressed fury. "For the insult to me, I shall see the color of your own blood. For your insult to my father, I shall kill you!"

"You challenge me?" Santana asked, laughing.

"I do, señor. It is the usual thing under such circumstances, as all *caballeros* know. Did they fail to teach you that? Or did they teach you, but during years of wild dissipation you have forgotten how decent men act?"

"You — "

Santana would have sprung upon him, but two of the *caballeros* caught his arms and held him back.

Capitán Ruelas spoke from the head of the table.

"His Excellency, the Governor, has issued an edict against dueling. My duty compels me to remind you of it. Don Diego Vega, you issued the challenge, so if you fight Santana it must be held that he only protected himself from your assault."

"He assaulted me first, Señor *Capitán*, by striking me after his insults."

"The Governor's act says nothing of such a situation. It mentions only the person who challenges."

"Having given the challenge for just cause, I cannot withdraw it," Diego decided. "But since the challenge followed an assault, I am the aggrieved party, and making certain stipulations."

"It is your right," Santana agreed. "What are the stipulations? Do you ask that we perhaps slap each other with perfumed handkerchiefs? Or see which can read poetry the faster?"

"We fight with blades," Diego said.

The *caballeros* began shouting again.

"Diego, think what you say … You are no swordsman! … Santana has carved men before now!"

"With blades, after the approved manner," Diego repeated coolly. "But by no means at dawn tomorrow."

"You desire a postponement?" Santana asked. "Why not at dawn? 'Tis the usual thing."

"You forget in your hour of heat and wrath, señor, that we have responded to a call from the *commandante* of the district to band together for the capture of a certain so-called outlaw and highwayman. I, for one, am a good citizen, and do not put my own affairs before those of the government. When this Zorro is caught by us, or we disband because we cannot catch him, then I shall be at your service, Don Estaban Santana."

THIS solution had flashed into Diego's mind at the commencement of the quarrel, since Diego Vega could not display decent swordsmanship without arousing suspicion. But Señor Zorro could contrive to meet Santana and fight him on even terms, exert his utmost skill toward a victory.

"Delay will not save you, señor!" Santana shouted at him. "You will do well to spend some hours with your *padre* and prepare yourself for the end. My sword has yearned for an age to have a drink of Vega blood — if there is any in your veins."

Santana turned abruptly, returned to the other end of the table, and reached for his goblet of wine.

"Under the circumstances, Don Diego, I excuse you from further participation in this campaign against the outlaw Zorro," *Capitán* Ruelas announced. "You may return to your father's house. You are not to be disturbed in any way while you await your meeting with Esteban Santana. I regret this affair, Don Diego, but it is now beyond my control."

Diego bowed to him, bowed to the *caballeros*, and brushed his handkerchief across his nostrils lightly as he glanced at Santana and turned to leave the barracks.

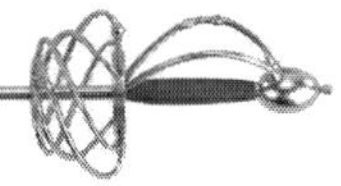

Chapter XIII
Tension Grows

OUTSIDE, Diego Vega found that the mist had turned to a fine drizzle. In the plaza, the *vaqueros* were huddled around the fire with their serapes draped over their shoulders. Loud voices and laughter came from the tavern.

One of the *vaqueros* saw Diego approaching, and called to the others. They all sprang to their feet to be of service.

"My horse," was all Diego said.

They brought it, and one of his friends helped him to mount. He gathered up the reins and rode away from them with the horse at a walk. Once more he was hunched over in the saddle like a man from whom all strength was gone. It had taken Diego serious practice to perfect that ridiculous saddle posture.

A servant took the horse when he reached the *casa*. Diego entered the house, found his father, and began a conversation that was in voices so low no servant could overhear even if he happened to walk close.

"And now, my son?" Don Alejandro asked, after Diego had finished his story of the episode at the barracks.

"I am excused from the *caballero* band, Father. They think I have come home to sweat with fear and perhaps call for the *padre* and prepare myself for death. Do you not understand? The *capitán* gave orders that I am not to be disturbed. So none will know whether Diego Vega grieves in his room — or rides the night as Zorro."

"Ah! Clever, my son!"

"It will be a ticklish business, Father. The troopers are scouring the countryside for peons and natives who have run away from their employment, and I may encounter some of the soldiers. I am even now half afraid for Bernardo. If they catch him with a black horse and Zorro's costume and weapons, it will be a matter difficult to explain."

"Let us hope for the best of fortune, Diego," said Don Alejandro stoically.

"Father," suggested Diego, "perhaps it would be well to send a servant for *Fray* Felipe. If the *capitán* has a spy watching, and he sees the *padre* come here and so reports, *Capitán* Ruelas will be the more certain I am making my peace, to be ready when I face Esteban Santana."

To that his father agreed, and a little later, Diego slipped out of the house unseen. He walked quickly through the drizzle. He had almost a mile to travel to the gulch where Zorro's horse was kept in hiding at times in a little cave with a screen of brush before its mouth.

Diego smiled as he thought of the manner in which he had ridden a spiritless old horse from the *casa* to the plaza and return. It would be quite a different feeling when he was in saddle on the back of his powerful black.

He went on, feeling his way through spots of pitch blackness at times, and frequently stopping to listen. In the distance he could hear hoofs pounding, men yelling, and once the sound of a shot. Sergeant Garcia and his troopers were losing no time in rounding up the peons and natives who had deserted their work.

Again Diego felt fear for Bernardo. The mute peon who had served him with such deep devotion for years — nothing must happen to him!

As he went along the bottom of the gulch and neared the cave where he had a rendezvous he redoubled his caution. He heard nothing to cause him alarm, however. Crouching behind a rock at the side of the gulch, he whistled soft signal.

For a moment there was utter silence. He heard nothing except the rustling of the wind through the brush. Then sounds told him someone was approaching slowly, a cautious step at a time. Diego whistled softly again.

The steps came nearer, shuffling footsteps in the sandy earth. Diego whistled once more. In answer came a guttural sound. Diego called softly, and Bernardo lumbered around some rocks to his side.

Speaking swiftly, in whispers, Diego told the mute the situation. To his question as to whether horse, costume and weapons were safely in the cave, Bernardo made a sound of assent.

"I must ride, Bernardo," Diego said quickly. "The night is dark and misty, but the clouds are breaking in spots, and it may clear to an extent. You must be very cautious. If the troopers catch you here, they may stay here in ambush after you are taken away, to see if someone comes for a rendezvous with you. Understand?"

Bernardo signified that he did.

THE black was saddled and led from the cave. Diego dressed swiftly in the costume of Zorro, putting the garments over his other clothing, belted on his blade, thrust pistol and knife in his belt, and mounted. He gave Bernardo a handclasp and rode slowly up the gulch through the night.

Out of the gulch, he reined in and listened for quite some time. The wind brought sounds from the distance that told him of the troopers' activity. He rode on toward town.

It was a slow journey through the darkness, but Zorro was in no particular hurry. It was a time when haste might bring disaster. An accidental encounter with troopers in the dark, his position betrayed by the striking of a hoof against a rock, by a horse's snort — any one of a hundred things could happen to bring on a conflict he wished to avoid at present.

As he neared town, he swerved to the north, crossed the highway at a distance from the buildings, and circled to come into a shallow arroyo which curved and ran behind the tavern.

He tied his horse to a clump of brush and went afoot through the black night, bending half forward, until he came to the cornet of the sprawling tavern in the rear. A glance at the row of small barred windows high in the adobe wall showed only one light, and toward that one he went.

A shade of sheepskin covered the window except for a small slit at one side, through which the light streamed. Zorro stood erect and peered into the small room. It was one of the cheapest in the tavern, off the patio.

He saw a couch, a small table and a chair. On the table a taper was burning, and beside it was a flagon of wine and a tumbler. On the couch, Pete Jordan was stretched out full length with his hands beneath his head. His eyes were closed, but he tossed to make himself comfortable. Zorro judged he was half asleep.

He retreated to the corner of the building again, and went along the wall until he came to a small gate which opened into the patio around which the guests' rooms were built. Nobody was in the patio, and because of the drizzle Zorro did not think anyone would enter it except perhaps some guest going to his room.

He got through the gate and beneath the nearest arch, went forward on tiptoe, counted the doors, and came to the one he sought. A tiny crack of light showed beneath it,

Flattening himself against the wall in the darkness, Zorro listened for a moment to the din in the big main room of the tavern. He got his pistol out of his sash, held it ready, and stepped to the door. With his left fist, he knocked.

He heard sounds indicating that Pete Jordan was getting off the couch. The bolt of the door was slipped back, and he pressed forward. The American pulled the door open about half way and peered out. He was groggy with sleep, and was groping for the knife in his belt.

Zorro quickly thrust the door wide open, shoved the muzzle of his pistol against Jordan's stomach, and kicked the door shut.

Jordan's eyes were bulging. "You — Zorro!" he muttered.

"Speak to me only in whispers, señor," Zorro ordered. "Sit down on your couch."

He shoved the pistol muzzle again, and Jordan retreated slowly the few feet to the couch and sat down. He was keenly alert now as he looked up at Zorro standing a few feet in front of him with his eyes glittering through slits in the hood mask which enveloped his head.

"Señor Jordan, I ordered you to leave the *pueblo*, and you have not obeyed me," Zorro accused.

"Why should I?" demanded Jordan. Who are you to give me orders? I like it here, for the time bein'."

"You hope to earn gold by acting as spy for *Capitán* Ruelas, señor?"

PETE JORDAN scratched his chin.

"You know, Zorro, you're somethin' of a man," he said. "Comin' right here to the tavern like this, you're takin' mighty big chances."

"I am doing that continually in my work, señor. I warn you again to leave town and not return."

"I ain't feelin' inclined to do that," Jordan informed him. "I'd like to work with you, Zorro, as I said before."

"I work alone. Were I to take an assistant, Señor *Americano*, would I take one who is working for Ruelas, one who is ready to ride with the *caballeros* and *vaqueros* and chase me? Are you of the opinion, señor, that I am not in my right mind?"

"Suppose I tell you, Zorro, that it's all a game with me. I make a deal with the *capitán*. But only because it gives me a chance to get acquainted with the peons, and — "

"And they tried to mob you," Zorro interrupted.

"That's only because they don't understand. Lots of folks, I've found, don't understand when a gent is really tryin' to help them. Always distrustin'."

"Peons and natives of this land," Zorro said sternly, "have learned well the lesson that it is wise for them to distrust everyone expect one another. And sometimes to trust one another even isn't safe."

"I had a letter from the Governor at Santa Fe," Jordan related. "Handed it to the *capitán* to get out of a ruckus myself, and he thought I'd done spyin' work for the Santa Fe official. He offered me gold, and I said I'd take it and work for him. Made certain stipulations."

"Such as?"

"Made him release Nuñez, and that made Juanita happy. And made him agree to go easy on the other men he'd whipped. That was somethin', don't you think so?"

"It was something," Zorro agreed, still more sternly. "Something to give the peons an idea you were working for them. But that was offset by the fact that they learned you're a spy. Stay in the *pueblo* for the time being, if you will, Señor *Americano*. Ride with the *caballeros* when they chase. Catch me if you can. I could exterminate you here and now, but that would not be good sportsmanship. I am holding a pistol pointed at your heart. But if you ride with the *caballeros* and we meet, I warn you to take care of yourself!"

"Thanks for the warnin', Zorro."

"You accept this situation coolly enough," Zorro said, not without a certain hint of admiration. "Did you not fear I might blast life from your body at once, because you did not leave the *pueblo*?"

"Nope. Guessed you wouldn't harm me if I didn't show fight. Got an idea you ain't that kind, Zorro."

"Señor *Americano*, I notice that whenever you speak that word 'Zorro' you raise your voice considerably. Are you perhaps hoping that someone may pass beneath the arches outside the door, overhear you, and give an alarm?"

CHAPTER XIV

Anvil Alarm

EVEN as Zorro spoke he heard a muttering of voices in the patio, heard footfalls. He sprang to the door, glanced once at Pete Jordan and held him under the pistol to keep him from drawing his knife if he felt so inclined, jerked the door open, and darted out. Three men were advancing toward him from the door of the tavern's main room.

They surged forward.

"The girl was right! … There he is! … At him! Remember the reward!"

Zorro whirled toward the little gate, darted through the shadows, got out of the streak of light that came from a single torch burning in the patio. Yelling, the men rushed after him, one brandishing a club, the other two holding knives that gleamed in the torch light.

They were getting too near, and Zorro did not wish them to see in which direction he ran. He raised his pistol and fired over their heads.

Abruptly they stopped, sprang back under the arches in the shadows, flattened themselves against the wall. Zorro darted through the gate and, bent almost double, rushed through the black night toward the shallow arroyo where his horse was waiting.

A sudden clamor shattered the quiet of the night. Someone was pounding the anvil in front of the smithy! The alarm was being given! As he fled on, he was aware from the four words the men who had raced from the tavern had shouted that Juanita Nuñez had told of his presence in Pete Jordan's room. She must have been crossing the patio from the kitchen, heard him talking to Jordan, and hurried to tell the men in the tavern. Then she had rushed to the smithy to tell the trooper on guard there so he would beat the anvil.

Zorro spurred the black up out of the arroyo to the highway and turned away from the *pueblo*, the hoofs of his mount betraying his progress as they pounded the hard ground. In front of the tavern, men were shouting. The doors of the barracks flew open, and *caballeros* lurched out, yelling for their peon servants to saddle their horses. The Vega *vaqueros* already were saddling.

Zorro's mocking laugh was swept back to them on the wind. By the time they could get to saddles, he would be far away, and they would have their night ride for nothing.

He laughed more elatedly because *Capitán* Ruelas had sent his troopers to scour the countryside in the night drizzle, to catch peons and natives and drag them back to the jail room. Soon there would be a tangle of horsemen in the hills around the *pueblo* — troops, *caballeros*, the Vega *vaqueros* — all challenging one another, becoming more and more confused as they chased the masked Zorro. Probably by then he would not be in their vicinity at all.

Zorro raced his black horse through the night over ground he knew well, and after a time turned abruptly to the left from the highway.

The clouds broke and the drizzle stopped. Streaks of moonlight came through. Zorro slackened speed. Anywhere in this section might be troopers searching for the fear-driven peons and natives.

He could still hear the ringing of the anvil, faintly in the distance. Perhaps the sound would recall many of the troopers from their search. Chasing Zorro would be the main object with them. They could run down peons and natives at any time.

Zorro rode with caution, watching the shadows, listening for a shout, the snort of a horse or rattle of a saber. He was circling toward the gulch and the cave where he had left Bernardo. He had to leave his horse, black clothing and weapons, and get back to the Vega house afoot now, and every step was one of possible peril.

Once he saw a moving shadow and stopped his horse behind a ledge of rock. But it was only a trick of a cloud cutting off part of the moon's light for an instant, so he touched with his spurs and rode on.

WHEN he reached the mouth of the gulch he rode slowly along the floor of it, the hoofbeats of the black deadened in the thick sandy soil. At the usual place, he dismounted behind some rocks, recharged the pistol he had fired in the patio of the tavern, then gave the low whistle which was a signal for Bernardo.

He heard nothing except the rustling of the wind through the brush, and whistled again. Again the clouds were swept away and the bright moonlight streamed down, striking the shallow narrow gulch squarely, revealing everything there clearly.

Even a third whistle did not bring Bernardo. Zorro wondered whether the mute had fallen asleep. He began walking forward, leaving the horse ground-hitched behind him, keeping in the shadows of the rocks as much as possible.

Reaching the brush-screened mouth of the cave he whistled again without getting an answer. He put aside the brush that screened the mouth of the cave and slipped inside, groping around, He knew every inch of this place well. It took him only moments to realize that Bernardo was gone!

Fear gripped Zorro. He knew that the faithful peon never would have left the gulch willingly. He slipped outside again, watched and listened, and finally began an inspection of the gulch's sandy floor.

He could see where Bernardo's feet heel tracked for some distance along the gulch. The shifting, sandy, wind-driven earth had not filled the tracks completely, so Bernardo could not have been gone long.

Then Zorro came to an abrupt stop. He saw the tracks of two horses which had come down the side of the gulch. And other tracks told him plainly that Bernardo had been surprised and seized! The mute probably had been caught by the troopers looking for runaway men.

Infuriated, Zorro hurried back to the cave, leading his horse. He removed saddle and bridle and stowed them away, removed his costume and weapons and stowed all of them away behind some rocks, except for his pistol.

It was not Zorro, but Diego Vega who left the little cave and hurried along the gulch, who emerged from it and dodged from shadow to shadow as he started toward his father's house a mile or so away.

Twice he went into quick hiding when he saw men in the distance riding toward town. If identified, there would be considerable wondering why the fastidious Don Diego Vega was walking around on a damp night, especially when he was supposed to be home resting and praying in anticipation of a duel in which he might be killed.

He came finally to the few servants' huts in the rear of the house, and heard nobody around or in them, The main building cast a deep shadow through which Diego passed swiftly. He let himself into the house through a rear window he generally used for that purpose after a ride as Zorro, starting toward the front of the house he stopped abruptly when he heard muffled voices.

Then he made out that it was his father and old *Fray* Felipe who were talking, and hurried into the main room to join them. They got to their feet as he entered.

"My son — ?" Don Alejandro questioned anxiously.

"I was spotted at the tavern — the anvil alarm was sounded — so I had to ride away," Diego told them. "But Bernardo! Bernardo was gone from the cave.

And tracks told me he had been seized."

"Then if the troopers have Bernardo — " Don Alejandro murmured.

He cannot talk, of course, nor write, nor communicate intelligibly except to those of us here who know the meaning of his guttural sounds, and know how to question him so we can get answers."

"That is true," *Fray* Felipe agreed, relieved.

"But will *Capitán* Ruelas not wonder what Bernardo was doing there?" said Diego. "It is known to all that he has been my personal servant for years. Might it not cast suspicion upon me? And if they send him to the whipping post, I could not endure it!"

"I'll go to the barracks and look over the prisoners at daylight," *Fray* Felipe said. "I know the troopers have been bringing in many men. The jail room is crammed with them."

"And *rancho* owners have been corning to town, Diego," his father added. "The *rancho* owners — all of us — and the storekeepers and warehousemen in town, are to call on *Capitán* Ruelas in the morning in a body. We shall demand that he cease seizing men and frightening others away from their work. I have had a message from our *superintendente*, Juan Cassara, and he reports that even some of our workers have become frightened and have fled."

DIEGO drank some wine his father gave him, and sank into a chair.

"We must act with caution, Father," he said. "We know there is a plot against the Vegas. You must appear before Ruelas with the other *rancho* owners to allay suspicion, naturally, but keep in the background. *Capitán* Ruelas would like nothing better than to have you question his authority. Also, if he learns Bernardo's identity, he will question us as to why Bernardo was in the gulch."

"Do you think his captors found the cave?" *Fray* Felipe asked.

"I think not. They could have told a horse had been stabled there, and would have waited for my return. No tracks except Bernardo's were near the mouth of the cave. Even the tracks my horse made when I left for my ride as Zorro had been filled by wind-driven sand."

"Go to your room and get some rest, Diego," his father instructed. "I'll awaken you after a few hours. *Fray* Felipe will go to the barracks after dawn, to learn whether Bernardo is there."

"Sergeant Garcia probably could tell him," Diego said. "The sergeant knows Bernardo well, and no doubt he will be in charge of inspecting the prisoners as they are delivered to the jail room."

Diego hurried to his room, undressed and stretched out on his couch. He was asleep within minutes. It was after dawn when his father awakened him.

Shortly, father and son were eating breakfast in the patio. The sky had cleared, and the sun came up warm.

"*Fray* Felipe has gone to the barracks," Don Alejandro reported. "Juan Cassara is here. He rode in from the rancho a couple of hours ago. He wanted to report to me in person regarding our men deserting. They rushed away in a panic, he says, but some have already returned."

"Where is Cassara now?" asked Diego.

"Having breakfast in the kitchen. I told him to come to the patio as soon as he had finished."

A summons came at the front door, and a servant answered. A moment later, he ushered old *Fray* Felipe into the patio.

Chapter XV

In Brutal hands

FRAY Felipe looked haggard. Evidently he had been walking at top speed, for he was breathing deeply, his mouth slightly open. He sat down on a bench as Don Alejandro motioned for him to do so.

"You have bad news?" Diego asked.

"I have, my son." the *padre* said sadly. "Bernardo was caught by the troopers, and is in the jail room at the barracks. Sergeant Garcia informed me of it."

"Did Garcia release him?" Diego questioned.

"Garcia is a soldier first, my son," the *padre* replied, "regardless of his personal feelings. The *capitán* had given strict orders that all peon and native prisoners be held. They are to be questioned during the day."

"Bernardo must be saved somehow," Diego declared hotly. "He can hear and understand, but cannot speak. Perhaps it the *commandante* knew that — "

The *padre*'s gesture stopped him. "The instant *Capitán* Ruelas learns that Bernardo is a Vega man, he will treat him twice as cruelly. As far as I could ascertain, no man from the Vega *rancho* was taken."

The *rancho superintendente*, came into the patio at that moment from the kitchen, and heard the news.

" 'Tis ill news," Juan Cassara declared. "If someone not of us told the *capitán* that Bernardo is a mute, perhaps he would let him go free. Why not? 'Twould do *Capitán* Ruelas no good to shout questions at Bernardo."

"From what I know of Ruelas, he will put Bernardo at the whipping post just to irk us," Don Alejandro declared worriedly. "I want to go with the *rancho* owners and others to visit Ruelas soon and protest against men being seized. Perhaps I can think of something to do while there."

"You have orders for me, Don Alejandro?" Juan Cassara asked.

"Not at present. Join our *vaqueros* at their camp in the plaza and spend a few hours of relaxation with them. If I have orders for you, I'll find you there later."

Cassara hurried from the house. The others moved around the patio restlessly.

"Something drastic must be done!" Diego's father declared, finally. "This man Ruelas is upsetting everything in our vicinity. No worker should lose a day's toil at this season of the year. There are crops to harvest, olives to be cured, wine to be pressed from grapes, tallow to prepare. Not a *rancho* will have a full cart caravan for market if there is serious interruption."

" 'Tis because of Zorro — because of me," Diego said, in a low voice.

"Think not of that, my son!" Don Alejandro said firmly. "You do good work. This Ruelas must be disposed of somehow. If the *rancho* owners protest to the Governor — "

"The Governor will say that you, Don Alejandro Vega, had influenced the others to do it, and will hold it against you," Diego interrupted. "I'll go to the meeting with you, my father."

"You? But it is supposed that you are at home shaking because you may have to meet Esteban Santana in a duel."

"I'll appear suitably frightened," Diego replied, smiling. "They will think I have gone with you through bravado, trying to make it appear I do not fear the duel."

Fray Felipe left to return to his chapel. And, a short time later, Diego and his father strolled toward the corner of the plaza and then toward the barracks.

The Vega *vaqueros* cheered as they passed, and Diego waved at them. Cassara was with them, and no doubt had told them about Bernardo.

From all directions, *hidalgos* and businessmen of importance were converging upon the barracks. Don Alejandro and Diego joined the group. They waited in front of the building for *Capitán* Ruelas to order them admitted.

Diego glanced around and met the questioning glances of his father's friends. *Caballeros*, showing they had been up through the night and had taken too much wine, came roistering from the tavern to join the group. Diego saw Santana with them, but turned away when Don Esteban glanced his way.

DIEGO watched the guards coming and going, heard the loud laments of the wretches in the big jail room, as they moaned and cried for mercy, half mad with fear. He was looking for Sergeant Garcia, but did not see him.

Then he heard him. The big sergeant strode from the main entrance and bellowed:

"Attention! *Capitán* Juan Ruelas!" The *commandante* appeared, resplendent in a fresh uniform heavy with gold braid. He was wearing his sword, and his hands were adorned with gauntlets with coat-of-arms on the cuffs, made from gold threads.

So Ruelas, it seemed, had no intention of admitting the conclave to his quarters. He would listen to them here, where he could give a quick rejection of their demands and retire to his own rooms.

"I am exceedingly busy this morning, señores," he called in a loud voice. "What is it you wish with me? Please be as brief as possible."

A gray-haired *hidalgo* stepped forward, his face purpled with wrath.

"You are addressing some gentlemen of blood, *Capitán*, and will do well to remember it," he said. "This is not a matter to be thrust aside in a moment. Your arrogance does not become you in the presence of your betters — or before your inferiors, either."

"I have no time to listen to your insults," Ruelas snapped. "If you have no business with me, disperse at once."

Another *hidalgo* stepped forward. "Very well, *Capitán*. We desire to say that your senseless seizure of peons and natives has frightened men so that they run away. We ask that you release our workmen immediately, and let them be assured they need have no fear."

"I am in authority here!" Ruelas shouted angrily. "I have orders from the Governor to do anything and everything in my power to capture the rogue, Zorro. I desire information about him. Some of the peons and natives must be able to give me information about the highwayman's life. I'll get it if I have to shred the naked backs of every peon and native in the district!"

"You exceed your authority, señor!" Don Alejandro shouted.

Ruelas eyed him. "Ah!" he said. " 'Tis Don Alejandro Vega. You are suspected in high places already, señor, of not being any too loyal to the Viceroy and his officials."

"I am loyal enough — but not to upstarts who think they are giants because they have been given a little brief authority."

Diego noticed that Esteban Santana lurched away from his companions and got nearer the barracks door. He heard Santana's sarcastic laugh.

"You are supposed to quail with fear, *Capitán*, when you hear Don Alejandro Vega's voice," he called. "You should get better acquainted concerning the important persons in your district."

"Silence, you shame your class!" Don Alejandro shouted at Santana. "You disgrace the name of gentleman with your drunken orgies!"

Santana shook with rage. "Were you not seventy and silver-haired. I'd put the point of my blade through your heart for that remark!" he cried. "As it is,

I'll make your son your proxy, if his knees are not too weak to carry him to our meeting place."

Diego had taken a step toward his father, but stopped. He had a part to play. But rage seethed through him for the insult to his father, and he promised himself that he would do more than wound Esteban Santana when they met.

The men who had called on the *commandante* surged forward to within a few feet of him. Ruelas dropped his right hand to the pistol in his belt.

"Let us have an end of insult," one of the *hidalgos* said. "*Capitán* Ruelas, we have come about a certain matter. Will you cease seizing our men and beating them? Will you release those you have in the jail room, except perhaps some few you feel you have a reason for questioning?'

"They will he released after being questioned, if I think they know nothing," Ruelas promised.

"But they are not to be beaten and mistreated while you question them. We want them able to return to work."

"I am the one to say what is to be done!"

"Let me call your attention to one thing, *Capitán!* Of the *caballeros* you called to try to capture this Señor Zorro, most are our sons and nephews. If we order them to return home, they will heed parental orders."

"Ah? And have me report to His Excellency that the *hidalgos* in this district refuse to aid in the capture of an outlaw?"

"Report," the *hidalgo* said, "and be damned to you!"

NOW Diego found himself slightly behind the others. And suddenly Sergeant Garcia was beside him, whispering:

"Don Diego! Your mute servant Bernardo, is in the jail room. I'll do what I can, but it may be little. Don Esteban Santana already has informed the *capitán* that the man is your personal servant."

"Poor Bernardo must not be mistreated," Diego said grimly. "He cannot speak."

"I know. I'll do what I can. I must go now." Sergeant Garcia moved away, motioning to one of his troopers to attend to some duty.

"We await your decision, *Capitán!*" a *hidalgo* called.

"I'll commence questioning the prisoners at once — that is all I can say now," Ruelas replied. "*Buenos dias, señores!*"

He turned abruptly and strode through the door to his private quarters.

The angry, disgusted men moved away slowly. Diego walked beside his father. His head was bent and he shuffled along like a man utterly devoid of spirit. *Fray* Felipe encountered them, and they stepped aside to speak with him.

"I have been unable to get to Bernardo and whisper to him," the *padre* reported. "*Capitán* Ruelas has issued orders that no *fray* is to visit the men until he has questioned them. But I'll continue to try to do something." He walked on.

As Diego walked on with his father, he said; "I am going to the tavern, father. I'll pretend that it is because I wish to be seen there so men will not think I am filled with fear arid shivering at home."

"As you please, my son," sighed Don Alejandro. "But return home soon. We must try to think of something that can be done in this situation."

Chapter XVI

In the Midst of Foes

NEARLY everyone had gone to the barracks to listen to what happened, so the tavern was almost empty when Diego reached it.

But Pete Jordan, the American, was sitting at one of the little tables beneath the windows, and Juanita was standing beside the table putting dishes upon it.

The fat landlord bowed to Diego and looked at him as if the scion of the Vegas was a man already dead. Diego nodded to Pete Jordan and sat down at a table near him.

"Don Diego, it would please me much if you sat with me," the American called. "Drinking wine alone is a lonesome business."

Diego thanked him and went to the other table. He ordered a flagon of wine, and Juanita hastened to fetch it.

"It's a sorry business, this grabbin' every man and tossin' him into jail," Jordan said boldly. "Folks wouldn't stand for a thing like that in my country."

Diego had to remember that he was himself now, and not Zorro, and that supposedly he knew nothing of Jordan's deal with Ruelas.

" 'Tis sad," he agreed. "My mute servant, Bernardo, was seized somewhere. Perhaps he was in the hills making his way to our house here in the *pueblo*. I hope he is not being mistreated."

"If he can't talk, they should turn him loose quick enough. You know, Don Diego, things are comin' to a head hereabouts. Everybody seems to be fightin' everybody else. The troopers and *caballeros* are prepared to chase this Zorro. Your *vaqueros* are ready to fight anybody just for the hell of it. The men of importance are mad at the *commandante* because he's been scarin' their workers and drivin' them from their daily jobs. The *padre*s hate the whole tumult. What a country!"

"And where do you stand, señor?" Diego asked, bending across the table. "You are in it, too, are you not?"

"Oh, I haven't done much messin' around yet," said Jordan. "When the alarm was given last night, I hit my saddle with the others, and had the fun of ridin' in the drizzle for a few hours, chasin' shadows. You see, Don Diego, Zorro dropped in to see me and order me out of town again. Came right into the tavern to do it. He's got nerve enough, I'll say that for him! Juanita was on her way across the patio from the kitchen and heard us talkin' in my room."

"You had no opportunity to seize him?" Diego asked.

"Not with him holdin' the muzzle of a pistol in my direction. I've got some sense, if I am what you folks call a Yanqui."

Juanita Nuñez came to the table with another dish for the American. It was easy to see that the girl was infatuated with him.

"You like my *Americano* better, eh, Don Diego?" she asked, dimpling. "He will catch Zorro if he can. And you should want him caught, Don Diego, for he is the cause of all this trouble, of the peons and natives being chased and thrown into the jail, probably to be beaten."

"I have troubles enough of my own," Diego replied.

"Oh, yes!" Jordan put in. "That Esteban Santana. There's a prime polecat if ever there was one! He ever as much as glances at Juanita again I'll cuff him down, and not with my fist open, either. You challenged him, I heard. Good for you!"

"Perhaps it will not be so good for me, señor. He is handy with a blade, and I do not have a reputation along that line."

"I hope you have luck," Jordan said. "He was talkin' in here before he went to the barracks. Goin' to sober up, he said, so he'd be on edge and you couldn't get in a lucky lick at him,"

Diego sipped some wine and glanced around the room. A couple of travelers off the highway had entered and were talking to the landlord. A group of *caballeros* entered, bowed to Diego, and went to a table.

"I must go on," Diego told Jordan. "I hope to meet you again when there is not so much tension, and talk to you of your country as compared to this."

He tossed a coin upon the table, arose, bowed, and went to the door and passed through. Esteban Santana was coming to the tavern alone, and for an instant he and Diego faced each other.

"Preserve yourself until we can have our meeting, señor," Santana said.

Diego looked straight at him. "Don Esteban Santana, for your insult to my father this morning, I shall kill you!" he replied.

"Indeed? Do you expect to pistol me from behind a rock?"

"I shall kill you with a blade, señor. All your skill with the weapon will not save your life. The world will be better off without you."

DIEGO walked on, his whole body trembling. Santana looked after him a moment, laughed and shrugged, then went on into the tavern.

At one end of the plaza where the Vega *vaqueros* were encamped, their horses were staked out and their saddles stacked. They were grouped around a couple of fires, with serapes over their shoulders, still eating and drinking and jesting.

He turned toward the group, and when they saw him coming they sprang to their feet. Diego walked among them. He felt safe here, not only from open insult but also from unkind thoughts. He knew the *vaqueros* liked him. He gave rich prizes for sports at each cattle roundup and at the time of the great slaughter, when cattle were killed with lances for their hides and tallow. The attitude of the workers toward Diego was that of strong men toward a weak lad.

"Do not let my presence disturb you, señores," he told them.

"Don Diego, did you learn anything concerning Bernardo?" Juan Cassara asked.

"He is in the jail room — that much I know. What will happen to him, I do not know — and hate to think."

"No trooper is going to whip Bernardo on his naked back while I'm around!" a *vaquero* cried. "The poor devil — can't talk even if he *had* anything to say about Zorro."

"He has been faithful and loyal to me," Diego said with more meaning than they understood.

"He must have been coming to town when he was grabbed," Cassara declared. "Maybe with a message for Don Alejandro. I hope something can be done to help him. Maybe *Fray* Felipe will put in a good word."

"The *padre* told me only a short time ago that he and the other *padre*s are even denied admittance to the jail room," Diego said.

"What kind of a man is this Ruelas?" another *vaquero* asked, angrily. "Trying to handle his betters as if they were trash!"

"Be cautions in your speech," Diego advised. "The *capitán* may have spies about. And it has become evident that he holds a measure of hostility for the Vegas."

He talked with them a moment or so more, then turned to go home, head bent and feet shuffling as if he did not have the strength to lift them properly as he walked.

Fray Felipe came to the house in the middle of the day. Questioning of the prisoners had started, he reported. Cries for mercy, protestations that they knew nothing, could be heard outside the barracks. Still no *padre* was allowed to enter. All the troopers were being held around the building, were not allowed even to go to the plaza or tavern.

Further reports came during the day, but nothing specific about Bernardo. And just at dusk *Fray* Felipe brought the intelligence that it was reported six men were to be whipped at dawn. The names of the victims had not been given out.

"Not a fourth of the men caught last night have been questioned," the *padre* reported. "Some of them are almost insane with fear, a trooper told me, and some have been badly beaten. *Capitán* Ruelas firmly refuses to let me enter the barracks and give them comfort."

The evening meal was eaten, darkness came. And tonight the sky was clear except for fleecy scudding clouds which were driven in at times from the distant sea. The moonlight would be bright.

"Zorro must ride tonight," Diego told his father, after the *padre* had gone to the chapel.

"I would not deter him, my son," said Don Alejandro. "But the enterprise may be perilous. The cave in the gulch may be watched. And how about your horse?"

"As you know, Father, there is a small spring in a corner of the cave, enough to give a horse water. And Bernardo had put plenty of forage in the cave, so the horse did not go hungry today."

"If he wandered out and away — "

"Let us hope he did not. I might not be able to trace him and get saddle on him."

Don Alejandro lowered his voice. "If Zorro is able to ride tonight, what does he intend to do?"

"Stir up another hornets' nest," his son said promptly, "then watch for an opportunity to punish one or more of the men who should be punished, or to open the doors of the jail room, or to do anything he can to harass those who deserve it."

IT WAS some hours later when Diego got quietly out of the house and around the servants' huts unseen, and started toward the distant gulch. *Fray* Felipe had returned to spend the night. His excuse for being at the Vega house was good, for he was still supposed to be trying to comfort Diego and prepare him for his duel.

As he neared the gulch, Diego kept in the shadows, moved slowly, watched and listened. Nothing indicated the presence of danger. He slipped along the gulch to the screen of brush in front of the cave's entrance, and heard the big black stamping inside.

He crouched and listened a moment more, then entered the cave and spoke quietly. The black gave a quick whinny at the sound of Diego's voice. Diego hurried forward to clutch his mane and pat his glossy neck.

He put on saddle and bridle, then dressed in Zorro's clothing, got his weapons from their hiding place and hooked his long whip around the pommel of the saddle. Mounting, he rode through the brush and stopped the eager horse in the shadows cast by a ledge of rock.

Deeming it safe after a survey, he rode up out of the gulch, kept off the skyline, and turned to swing widely around the *pueblo*. It was in Zorro's mind to create a diversion in the town, cause an alarm, try to draw the troopers and *caballeros* away from the place, and perhaps manage to release the prisoners.

And he did not forget that he was Zorro now, not Diego Vega, and that his own *vaqueros* would pursue him as readily as would any of the others.

The fires in the plaza had been allowed to die to beds of embers. Some of the *vaqueros* were playing cards or dice on serapes spread on the ground, and others had wrapped their serapes around them and were curled on the ground in sound sleep.

The horses of the *caballeros* were picketed, but most of them had not been unsaddled tonight. The *caballeros* themselves were in the tavern, as their wild shouting and singing proclaimed.

Zorro came up back of the barracks carefully and looked over the situation there. Two men were on guard in front, pacing back and forth with muskets over their shoulders. The *capitán's* quarters were dark. Zorro could hear wailing in the jail room. Several horses of troopers were tethered in front of the barracks, saddled and ready for the chase.

Zorro's lips tightened grimly as he girded himself for his night's work.

Chapter XVII
Bite of the Blade

ZORRO wished, first of all, to cause a commotion, do something to attract attention to his presence in the *pueblo*, and inspire a chase that would scatter his pursuers through the hills again.

He rode carefully through the shadows toward the smithy. From the near distance, he could see a weary trooper huddled on the ground beside the big anvil, ready to give an alarm.

With his big black at a walk, Zorro drew nearer and nearer to the smithy and the careless trooper guard. He scanned the scene again. The smithy was at some distance from both the plaza and the tavern, and at a safe distance from the barracks if it came to musket shots.

Zorro was beside the guard almost before the man was aware of his presence. Half-asleep, he stumbled to his feet and saw the masked, black-garbed rider on the black horse.

"You — you — " the trooper mouthed. His musket was leaning against the wall of the smithy, too far away to be reached quickly.

"Do as I say, and you will not be harmed," Zorro told him. "I have nothing against you personally."

"What am I to do?" chattered the guard.

"Pick up the sledge, pound the anvil and give the alarm," Zorro ordered.

"Don't you know that'll bring them all after you? You want to be chased and caught?"

"I've never been caught yet."

"But they're mad to catch you now! The *commandante* has been at them, telling both the troopers and *caballeros* that they are no better than children."

"Do as I have said," Zorro said, "or this pistol I am holding may go off and blow a hole in your head!"

The frightened trooper caught up the sledge and stepped up beside the anvil.

"Keep up the blows," Zorro ordered. "Make the anvil ring loudly. Awaken the whole *pueblo*!"

The anvil rang. Zorro swerved his horse, got the guard's musket, and hurled it far away behind the smithy. He glanced at the plaza.

Vaqueros there were springing to their feet and running toward their horses, looking around wildly as if they expected to see Zorro riding down upon them. *Caballeros* began reeling out of the tavern, shouting, racing for their mounts. Back at the barracks, somebody began yelling.

Zorro swerved the black again, bent low in his saddle, touched with his spurs. The powerful horse broke into a run. His hoofs pounded the hard ground at the edge of the plaza. Zorro guided him toward the other end of the plaza, giving a series of strident mocking yells.

A couple of pistols exploded, but no ball came near him as he rode. Glancing back as he reached the end of the plaza, he saw that some men were in saddles and heading after him. He guided the black into the highway and toward distant San Juan Capistrano. His last backward glance revealed troopers coming from the barracks with their horses at a dead run.

Streaks of bright moonlight revealed him as he rode. Hoofs pounded behind him. Zorro went at top speed for a short distance, then swerved off the highway and up a slight slope where his pursuers could see him clearly against the moonlit sky.

Behind him, he saw the pursuit break up as riders scattered to right and left of his course, as if preparing to encounter him regardless of which direction he turned. He got to rougher country where the sure-footed black began putting distance between him and the pursuit.

Men were shouting in the distance, hoofs were pounding, a few wild useless shots were fired. Zorro's mocking laugh went back to his foes as he rode at top speed.

HE SWERVED again shortly and rode back toward the *pueblo*. But as he topped a sharp slope, he found himself within a short distance of some of the pursuers who had turned that way. They caught sight of him, and with challenging shouts charged after him.

The black was forced to descend into a shallow gulch and travel up the opposite side, and that brought pursuers nearer. Zorro could make out a couple of troopers, and some other riders. And farther ahead three riders were running their mounts in an effort to intercept him.

He drove the black between two ledges of rock. His last glance at these three nearest pursuers showed two of them behind him and one racing ahead. Between the ledges of rock, which ran parallel for some distance, he could not get to either right or left.

He thundered on, gaining ground on the two behind. As he raced around a bend in the rough formation, he saw one rider cutting in ahead of him. The bright moonlight revealed to Zorro the tough little pony that Pete Jordan, the American, had called half coyote and half sage rabbit.

Zorro gathered his reins in his left hand and got his pistol from his sash as he rode madly on. Pete Jordan turned and raced slightly ahead of him. The other two riders were far behind, but coming on between the two ledges of rock.

"Aside, or I pistol you!" Zorro shouted.

Jordan swerved toward him,

"Zorro! Don't worry about me. I'm for you! Bump my pony with your horse — pronto. I'll pretend to fall, and my pony will block the trail. Be quick! One of the men behind is a *caballero* on a speedy horse."

Zorro took the chance that Jordan was not playing a trick.

"Why?" he asked, as he crashed his black against the smaller pony.

"I like what you're doin'. Said I wanted to side you, but you couldn't see it."

Zorro's horse stumbled slightly. Behind thundered the pursuit. Pete Jordan pretended that he had been hurled from his saddle, and sprawled in the trail. He pulled the reins over his pony's head as he fell, and the pony stopped, blocking the narrow trail between the ledges of rock. Zorro raced on into the night.

As he came to a wide open space, he glanced behind. The yells now were being directed toward the American, who seemed to be trying to swerve his pony out of the trail. Zorro used his spurs and did some swift riding again. He disappeared into the darkness in a coulée.

There he stopped the black to give him a breathing spell. The pursuit was scattered now, he knew. Individual riders, and couples, would be watching on every side for a sight of him.

He wondered about Pete Jordan. He had a conviction now that the American had told him the truth. Jordan had pretended to fall in with Ruelas' plans, had decided to ride with the *caballeros* simply because he thought he might be of service to Zorro in an emergency. His resentment of the treatment of the men at the whipping posts had been genuine.

Zorro heard some of the pursuit thunder past in the near distance. Yells came from the east as riders shouted at one another. He decided to ride toward the *pueblo* again, scout around it, see if there was a possibility of releasing the prisoners in the barracks or of getting *Capitán* Juan Ruelas alone and giving him fight.

He rode along the bottom of the coulée slowly for quite a distance, then emerged and started toward the town. No sounds indicated that riders were near. But whatever he did must be done soon, for dawn was not any too far away. He would have to get his horse back into the little cave, and get himself back into the Vega house before dawn.

He approached the barracks from a different direction. When he was only a short distance from the building, a rider suddenly appeared in front of him from behind a stand of brush.

"Look this way, Zorro!" the rider called. "I thought you might return to the barracks. I'll have the rare pleasure of handling you by myself now!"

Don Esteban Santana was before him.

ZORRO pulled up his horse within a short distance of the man.

"Ah!" he said. "It is the Santana. I am holding a pistol, señor."

"So am I, as you can observe. Is it your desire to exchange shots with me?"

Zorro watched him warily as he spoke. "A bullet is no death for a man of blood," he said.

"You claim to be such?"

"My identity is unknown to my enemies. But I assure you, Don Esteban, that my blood is as good as yours, if not better. I at least have not soiled my heritage as have you."

"Beware your words! You are talking yourself into a grave!"

"Is it that you fear to cross blades with me? Can a Santana be a coward as well as a drunken thieving sot?"

"Damnation!" Santana roared. "How do I know you will not pistol me if I get the better of you?"

"You have my word, señor — and it is as good or better than your own. I could have pistoled you at any moment since we met."

"Out of your saddle, rogue!"

Santana sprang out of his own, ground-hitched his horse, braced himself on the ground. Zorro was in front of him almost instantly. Two blades hissed from their scabbards.

The bright moonlight gave light enough, and neither had the advantage. The ground was good here, too. There were no rocks, no rough places to interfere with footwork.

"Would you like to know the man you fight, before you die? Step back and lower your blade a moment, and I'll unmask."

The blades clashed, rang. They parried, felt each other out. Santana gave ground slightly, and Zorro avoided the trap he would have sprung.

"The Governor's reward is as good as in my purse, señor!" Santana called.

"Your purse needs it, depleted as it has been by your wild dissipation."

"For that remark, Zorro, I'll carve you to bits!"

"Less talk and more swordsmanship, Santana."

The blades rang again. Zorro was remembering the insult to his father, the many insults to and mocking of himself as Diego Vega, and Santana's hatred of all Vegas. Zorro's blade became like a live thing, and Santana showed that he felt his first fear. He gave ground again as they circled.

Zorro's blade darted in and found flesh. Santana gave a cry of pain and retreated, trying to ward off another instant attack.

"That touched you!" Zorro called.

" 'Tis but a scratch!" Santana cried. "It only aroused my ire."

"Would you like to know the man you fight, before you die? Step back and lower your blade a moment, and I'll unmask."

Zorro stood still, and Santana retreated a short distance, but not lowering his point. With his left hand, Zorro took the hood mask front his head and tossed it aside.

"Diego Vega!" Santana cried. "You — you are Zorro!"

"So you see, Santana. And now, since you know, this must be your end. The last face you see in this life will be that of a Vega. For your insults to me, and to my father, you are about to die, señor!"

Blade ready, he started forward again. Santana recoiled a step, then gathered courage born of rage. He charged wildly, and the blades clashed, Diego laughed as he fought.

"A swordsman — you?" he taunted. "Say a swift prayer, señor, if you have not forgotten how to pray. You are in need of prayers now. Your deal with *Capitán* Ruelas is known to me. You would kill Diego Vega and so break his father's heart, would you? You would have the Vega estates confiscated and profit thereby? Fight then, señor, and slay me!"

Santana, panting for breath, fighting to retain at least a small measure of strength, gave ground again, until he found his back against a boulder ....

A little after dawn, riders saw Santana's horse without a rider. Investigating, they found Santana. He was stretched on the flat of his back in death, and marked on his forehead with the tip of a blade was the letter "Z."

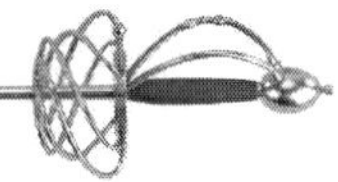

Chapter XVIII

Dawn in the Plaza

CABALLEROS and *vaqueros* had been cleared out of the plaza by troopers, at dawn. They had been compelled to remove their horses to a corral behind the tavern or hitch them to the horse blocks in front of the buildings.

There was sudden activity around the barracks. For word had been passed that four men had been sentenced to the whipping post. Citizens gathered at the early hour. *Caballeros* stood in front of the tavern with goblets of wine in their hands, drinking as they watched.

Into the town came two riders with their horses at a run. They began shouting as soon as they could be heard:

"Esteban Santana! We found him dead! Blade beside him — he'd been run through! A letter Z scratched on his forehead!"

The *caballeros* in front of the tavern stood as though shocked for an instant. Then, with furious yells, they ran to their horses and mounted. Swiftly they followed one of the news-bringers out of the town.

The news spread rapidly. It traveled to the barracks, where *Capitán* Juan Ruelas heard it. The *commandante* became enraged. He threatened to run down Zorro if he had to call on the Governor for reinforcements. He promised dire vengeance on his prisoners unless they betrayed Zorro to him immediately. And he ordered the troopers to proceed with preparations for the morning's persuasion at the whipping posts.

Sergeant Manuel Garcia went about his tasks with a stolid expression in his face. He was a soldier, and did not mind battle, but he was growing sick of beating helpless peons and natives. However, Garcia formed the usual procession from the barracks and the four sentenced men had their arms tied behind their backs and were put in line, two guard troopers to each man. The last prisoner in the line of those sentenced to the posts was Bernardo.

The bugle sounded and the drum was beaten. The procession left the barracks for the plaza. The citizens watched it approach. The Vega *vaqueros* watched it also, and their faces darkened when they saw that Bernardo was one of the men to be punished.

Diego Vega appeared with his father and walked toward the edge of the plaza. *Fray* Felipe had notified them that Bernardo was to be whipped, and Don Alejandro Vega was enraged more than he had ever been in his life.

"If Zorro does not punish this *capitán* — " he whispered to Diego.

"Zorro will do something worse than slay him," Diego promised.

Don Alejandro hurried forward as the procession stopped before the posts, with Diego a step behind him. Don Alejandro confronted the *commandante*.

"That huge peon, known as Bernardo, is my son's personal servant, and has been for years," Don Alejandro told Ruelas, his voice quivering with rage. "He is a mute, cannot speak a word. Are you a fiend, that you send such a man to the post?"

"He was insolent to me," Ruelas replied.

"I protest that he cannot speak!"

"Don Alejandro Vega, you will kindly take your protests elsewhere," the *capitán* interrupted. "I have no wish to hear them. Will it ever dawn upon you that I am the *commandante* of this district, that I act for the Governor?"

"The Governor is by no means a merciful man, but he would never countenance such an act as this," raged Don Alejandro.

"Your words border on treason, Don Alejandro," Ruelas warned.

"I stand by my words! This man Bernardo can be of no harm to you. He is unable to answer questions even did he know the answers."

"He was caught by a trooper running around through the night," the *capitán* said. "He may be in league with Zorro. Whether he is or not, when I asked him a question, he grew insolent."

"How could he be insolent when he cannot talk?"

"He made sounds of disrespect."

"That probably was a guttural sound that meant he did not understand what you wished."

"Enough of this, Don Alejandro. Stand aside, and let us get this business over with."

"Then you will put him at the post? You will whip his naked back?"

"Such is my sentence. Ten lashes. Stand aside, you and your son, else I'll have the troopers handle you."

"You dare speak so to me?" Don Alejandro roared. "Your own punishment is liable to be most severe."

"Are you threatening me, señor?" Ruelas shouted, so all could hear. "Do you deny my authority and that of the Governor? Are you determined to be a traitor?"

RUELAS turned and gestured, and Sergeant Garcia stepped forward and read the names of the four men, and their sentences. Ruelas gestured again and troopers stepped forward to untie the arms of the four condemned peons and to stretch them upward so the wrists could be fastened to the leather thongs.

Don Alejandro stepped forward again, but a trooper barred his path. Another thrust Diego aside roughly. And then it seemed to filter into the mind of Bernardo what this scene meant.

Bernardo had seen men whipped in the plaza. Now suddenly he realized that this morning he would be a victim himself. He had thought that Don Alejandro and Diego would save him. It was in his slow mind that a mistake had been made. But he knew now it was no mistake.

His huge body stiffened, and he became like an enraged beast, he hurled one of the troopers from him and turned as if to escape. Ruelas shouted an order.

It took four troopers to subdue Bernardo and get him to the post. He was half unconscious from the beating he received before they had their way with him. The *vaqueros* were watching closely. Diego heard Bernardo give a guttural cry which he knew was a plea to him for help.

Then Diego saw the *vaqueros* rush to their horses and mount. And they came riding into the plaza yelling defiance. Spectators scattered before them. They pulled up their horses along the row of posts. Juan Cassara, the *superintendente*, was their spokesman.

"Señor *el Capitán,"* he shouted, "the big mute peon is not to be whipped! He is harmless, and has done no wrong. The *vaqueros* will handle any man who puts a whip to his back. Call your troopers back."

"Disperse, or I'll have all your *vaqueros* taken to the barracks and afterward sent to the posts themselves," Ruelas shouted back.

The *vaqueros* began laughing loudly.

"Ask your troopers whether they wish to do battle with the Vega *vaqueros!"* Cassara called. "They are all armed with knives, and some have pistols. They are here now to defend the Vegas and all Vega servants and workmen!"

"Troopers, do your work!" Ruelas ordered thunderously. "The men are lashed to the posts. One trooper to each man. Ten lashes for each, laid on with a will — "

Some of the troopers moved, and the *vaqueros* advanced their horses a few feet. The troopers stood still.

"Obey me!" Ruelas screeched at them. "Sergeant Garcia! See that the men obey orders!"

"Capitán, none of our men will touch the big peon," Garcia replied.

Ruelas drew his pistol. "I order you men to form a line between the mounted *vaqueros* and the row of posts!" he shouted. "I'll shoot the first who hesitates! At once!"

Used to the voice of command, the troopers moved forward and formed the line.

"As for this peon who is causing all this trouble, I'll whip him myself!" Ruelas declared. "I order you *vaqueros* to back your horses! I shall file complaint against any who hesitate to obey, and have the guilty ones sold into peonage! And you, Don Alejandro Vega, I shall charge with treason and have the charge sent to the Governor today by special courier."

The troopers hung back uncertainly. The *vaqueros* gathered their reins and held weapons ready. And toward the plaza came riding at a gallop and *caballeros* who had gone to the spot where Esteban Santana's body had been found.

"Hold a moment!" Ruelas ordered.

He waited until the *caballeros* came up with their lathered horses, listened to their report of Santana's death.

"I call upon you, señores, to drive these *vaqueros* aside!" the *capitán* shouted. "They seek to obstruct justice."

"You are ordering a battle!" somebody in the crowd shouted at him. "Set *caballeros* and *vaqueros* at one another, and you'll have dead and wounded men to explain."

CAPITÁN RUELAS appealed to the *caballeros* again.

"One of your kind has been slain by Zorro. Some of these peons and natives know Zorro's identity. I'll whip them until one man talks and tells what I desire to learn. Will you help hide the outlaw who slays one of your own kind?"

Don Alejandro stepped forward and held up his hands. The *vaqueros* looked toward him.

"This is injustice, señores," Don Alejandro called. "But better injustice to one man than a battle that may cause the death and injury of a score, and the season of bitterness following an affray. I ask you to retire."

"No — no!" the *vaqueros* began shouting.

Don Alejandro raised his hand again in a demand for silence.

"*Capitán* Ruelas," he called, "any trooper who lays the lash on the back of our peon will be a marked man. Sooner or later, some Vega *vaquero* will encounter him alone, and have revenge for the act. I am warning you — and your men. If you order any of them to use the whip after what I have said, it will be a cowardly order."

Ruelas darted forward and seized a whip from one of the troopers.

"I order no man of mine to do what I would hesitate to do myself!" he cried. "And I would not hesitate in carrying out my sentence!"

Chapter XIX
Odds and Ends

VICIOUSLY Ruelas raised the whip. It swished forward, and the lash bit into Bernardo's naked back. The *vaqueros* yelled and started their horses forward again. Ruelas struck twice more and then stood aside.

"There, Don Alejandro Vega, you have seen!" he shouted.

"And remember what I said, *Capitán* — that any who laid a lash on Bernardo's back would be a man marked for severe punishment."

"*Caballeros*, I call upon you to see that the punishment is carried out without further interruption!" Ruelas called. "If you are loyal men, you will obey."

One of the *caballeros* rode forward.

"*Capitán* Ruelas," he said, "we will do our utmost to aid you in capturing the rogue, Zorro. But our fathers and uncles are calling upon us to see that our peons are not mistreated and frightened, and the work at the *ranchos* delayed. It is ridiculous to think any of the poor wretches know anything of Zorro. We ask you to release these four men, and also all those you have in confinement in the barracks prison room."

"You dare refuse?" raged Ruelas. "The arm of the Governor is long."

"The Governor is far away in Monterey, and our fathers and uncles are near at hand," the *caballero* spokesman replied. "We must in this case respect parental authority before yours, Señor *el Capitán.*"

The *caballeros* started riding forward slowly from one side, and the Vega *vaqueros* from the other. The troopers fell back before them.

"You will regret this act!" Ruelas shouted, enraged.

The *caballero* spokesman replied to him: "Señor *el Capitán,* let me give you a word of advice. Your methods as *commandante* are not suitable to this district. You would be wise to ask the Governor to send you to another post. All here will be of sympathy with you, all classes of men, and your efficiency will be impaired."

"You think I will turn my back and run?" Ruelas stormed. "I'll send for reinforcements! I'll sweep this district clean of all who have lifted their hands against authority!"

Some of the *vaqueros* had dismounted. And now they charged forward to the posts and began removing the bonds that held the victims. The troopers were thrust backward, and the *capitán* shouted orders in vain.

Diego hurried forward to Bernardo, who clung to him and whimpered like a child. And *Fray* Felipe suddenly was beside them.

"Let us get him to the house, Don Diego," the *padre* said. "Let us soothe his hurts, my son, both physical and mental."

"This is not the end, *padre*," Diego whispered.

"If I know Zorro, it is not. I do not countenance violence, my son — but I do countenance justice and just punishment."

Diego and *Fray* Felipe led Bernardo away from the line of whipping posts and toward the corner of the plaza. Behind them was a scene of tumult.

The mounted *caballeros* and *vaqueros*, working side by side like equals, now united in a common endeavor, scattered the unmounted troopers, released the three men who had been lashed to the posts along with Bernardo, and then went at a gallop to the barracks.

They seized the jail guard and got his keys, unlocked the prison room and herded the prisoners outside. There, the *rancho* owners had gathered.

"You are free!" one of them shouted. "Get back to your work."

Capitán Ruelas and his troopers, arriving at the barracks, found their prisoners gone. Raging, Ruelas went to his quarters. Sergeant Garcia began giving the usual orders for the day as if nothing unusual had happened.

The *caballeros* had scattered, and the *vaqueros* went back to the plaza, tethered their mounts and repaired to the tavern, where Vega credit had been established. The fat landlord and his servants had a busy morning.

AT THE Vega house, Bernardo had his sore back soothed by *Fray* Felipe, and his sore spirits also.

"Rest in one of the huts, Bernardo," Diego instructed him. "This evening after it is dark, go back to the cave, and take forage for the horse with you. Be sure you are not seen. Have everything ready about the middle of the night, for Zorro has one more ride to make before this affair is at an end."

Fray Felipe hurried away to his chapel, and Diego and his father relaxed in the patio.

"What do you intend doing, Diego?" his father asked. "I proposed Ruelas punishment for the man who put a lash to the back of Bernardo."

"And *Capitán* Ruelas did, so he must receive the punishment."

"Will it be an affair of death, my son?"

"One death is enough. That was a different affair, my father. Esteban Santana sought to kill me, did he not? But this other — it would be murder for me to force Ruelas to combat and slay him."

"Then?"

"So I will try to kill him with ridicule. I'll make him a laughing-stock to such an extent that the Governor will not dare leave him here as *commandante*, since it would reflect on the Governor himself."

"That is an excellent idea, my son."

"People are probably saying now how fortunate Diego Vega is that Zorro killed Santana before he could force the said Diego to fight a duel with him."

Don Alejandro smiled. "No doubt."

"I think I shall go down to the tavern, Father. There are some odds and ends to straighten out."

Don Alejandro opened his eyes some at the statement, but said nothing in reply. Diego left the house and went toward the plaza again, head bent and feet shuffling.

The excitement had died down. Ruelas and his troopers were at the barracks. Most of the *caballeros* had ridden away, and only Juan Cassara and the *vaqueros* remained.

Diego ordered more refreshment for them, and then suggested to Cassara that he lead the men back to the *rancho* and put them to work. After they had ridden away, Diego went to one of the small tables and relaxed on the bench beside it.

Her eyes sparkling, Juanita Nuñez came to his table.

"Some crystallized honey and those little cakes," Diego ordered. "My usual wine, also. This excitement has been almost too much for me."

"It has been terrible, Don Diego!" she agreed.

"Are you still the enemy of Zorro, señorita?"

"No longer, Don Diego. My Pedro has explained to me that he was the friend of Zorro all along, though he does not wish others to know that. And, since Zorro slew Esteban Santana, who mistreated me, I am now Zorro's defender."

"Let the *commandante* hear you have said that, and he will have you in the barracks," Diego warned. "What was that you said a moment ago — *my* Pedro?"

Juanita blushed. "He — the *Americano* — is very dear to my heart."

"Then you are a fortunate girl, providing you are also very dear to his."

"I am certain that is so, Don Diego."

"A rather sudden affair, is it not?"

"Ah, Don Diego, who can tell when love comes and strikes a heart?"

"I'd like to see your *Americano* again, and congratulate him. But what will come of this romance of yours, Juanita? Will Pete Jordan remain in this country?"

"He says he will, if he can find the right work to do," she told him. "And he will care for my father, too, he says."

"He seems like a proper fellow," Diego observed. "Do not forget my cakes and wine."

The girl hurried away. Diego brushed an imaginary fleck of dust from his jacket, extracted his perfumed handkerchief from his left sleeve and brushed it across his nostrils. He heard someone approaching the table, and glanced up to see Sergeant Garcia.

"Join me, *amigo*." Diego invited. "No doubt you are fatigued after the events of the morning."

THE burly sergeant sat down on the bench across from Diego, blew out the ends of his mustache, and nodded.

"Don Diego, I am disgusted," he announced. "So much trouble over nothing! And now because of the way things turned out, my superior officer — I am not in any way criticizing him, understand, but merely stating facts — is making life almost unbearable for every man in the barracks."

"What will be the end of it?" asked Diego.

"That, *amigo*, I do not know. He may send for reinforcements and continue to make trouble. He may be recalled. One thing or the other certainly must happen, for this is a situation that cannot be endured otherwise."

"Perhaps Zorro will punish him for what he has done," suggested Diego.

"Confound that rogue!" Garcia exploded. "He is always stirring up a turbulence. However, he did a good thing in disposing of Esteban Santana. He did you a service, Don Diego, also, in that."

"No doubt," Diego agreed.

"It was cowardly of the scoundrel to get you in a position where you had to challenge him. He knew you would be no match for him in a fight with blades. Ah, well! All that danger is past and gone now."

"It is," Diego agreed. "Now I can go out to the *rancho* again with my father, and prepare for the great slaughter. I shall offer rich prizes again this season for the best riding and horse breaking, and other kindred events."

"I'll hint to the *capitán* that I always go out with four or more troopers to keep order," Garcia said, grinning.

"You will be welcome, Sergeant. What do you think of the *Americano* who is visiting here?"

"An outspoken rogue, but all *Americanos* are that, I have heard. No doubt he is harmless."

"He and Juanita seem to be attached to each other."

"She's a good girl," the sergeant declared.

They talked for a time, and the sergeant left when Diego began nibbling at the little cakes Juanita brought him. And then Pete Jordan appeared at the table. Diego gestured for him to be seated.

"Well, Señor Jordan, you did not get a chance to catch Zorro," Diego suggested.

"Nor do I desire to do so now, Don Diego. After thinkin' everything over, I've decided this Zorro has some good points. Anybody who can stick thorns into the hide of a human bein' like the *commandante* deserves a pat on the back."

"Do you still think all Spaniards are alike, señor?" Diego asked, smiling at him.

"Nope. I figure they're the same as other folks — some bad and some good. That father of yours — I like him. And I sure liked the way them *vaqueros* from your *rancho* handled things. They're my kind of men."

"Did you ever have any experience in *rancho* work?"

"Worked with cattle and horses back home, before I got to travelin' the Santa Fe trail and then comin' on west."

"Juanita was hinting to me that she has fallen in love with you, Señor Jordan," said Diego. "She's a fine girl."

"She's the girl for me," Jordan confessed.

"I was wondering, señor — our *superintendente*, Juan Cassara, who has been with the rancho for a long time, is getting old. He needs a good assistant, a *segundo*. Perhaps you would like to work on the *Rancho* Vega?"

Jordan's eyes glowed. "Wouldn't I, now! I've heard a lot about your *rancho*, and all good. Must be quite a place. Any chance of gettin' the job?"

"I'll see that it is arranged, señor."

"Any chance of — that is, if Juanita and me get the idea of bein' married —"

"The *segundo* would have a little adobe house of three small rooms, señor," Diego explained.

"Well, now, I'm figurin' that Juanita and me will be talkin' to the *padre*. It's been a quick business with us, but we know our own minds."

Diego laughed at him. "Make your plans, señor. We'll even have a wedding feast for you at the *rancho*. My father and I probably will drive out in the morning. You may ride along beside the carriage and see if you like the place."

Chapter XX
Punishment

HEAVY, dark clouds again obscured the moon and the air promised rain. Through the night passed the black horse with the masked rider in the saddle.

Zorro rode with caution, though he knew no troopers were abroad. Reina de Los Angeles was quiet, the people asleep after the excitement. No fire burned in the plaza and it was even quiet around the tavern as Zorro neared the town.

One torch burned on the wall at the entrance to the barracks. One sleepy guard paced back and forth, and at times leaned against the casement, resting.

Zorro dismounted a short distance behind the barracks and tied his horse to a small tree with a knot that could be freed with a single jerk. Afoot and cautiously, he went alongside the barracks building, watching, listening.

Snores came froth the sleeping room of the troopers. Snores came through the opened window of the *capitán's* quarters. Zorro got his pistol out of his sash and held it ready. He also made certain of the readiness of the coil of rope attached to his sash.

At the corner, he peered around and saw the guard standing beside the door, his back turned. Zorro slipped quietly around the corner and approached. The guard heard footsteps when Zorro was within a few feet of him, and turned quickly. He saw the masked man in black, and his eyes opened wide.

"Silence!" Zorro warned in a whisper, weapon menacing. "Turn, and put your hands behind your back."

The trooper did as commanded. Zorro made a few swift movements and lashed the guard's arms behind his back.

"Lie down and stretch out on the ground in the darkness against the wall," Zorro ordered.

Again the trooper obeyed. Zorro lashed his legs with the rope, then made a gag out of a piece of cloth he carried, and silenced the man effectually.

"And keep silent, if you value life," Zorro warned.

He left the guard then and went around to the other side of the building.

There he stood against the wall in the darkness for a time, until he was sure he had not been observed. At last, slipping to the window of the *capitán's* quarters he pushed the casement open a trifle wider.

Zorro crawled through and into the room. *Capitán* Ruelas was asleep, still snoring. Zorro acquainted himself with the placing of the furniture, got his pistol out of his sash again, and stepped to the side of the bed.

He ascertained the position of the sleeper in the darkness, and prodded him gently in the back with the muzzle of the pistol. Ruelas stirred, turned half over, came awake.

"Make no sound, or you die!" Zorro whispered to him.

"Wh-what?"

"This is Zorro. Do exactly as I say, and you will live yet for a time. Disobey, and I'll blast life from your body. It would be a pleasure for me to do so."

"Wh-what do you want?" stammered the *commandante.*

"Sit up on the edge of the bed," ordered Zorro.

He held the pistol muzzle against the *capitán's* body and gripped one of Ruelas' arms with his left hand. Ruelas sat up.

"Walk with me to the window," Zorro ordered now. "If you call for help, you are a dead man!"

"You … wh-what are you going to do with me?" Ruelas demanded.

"We are going to take a little walk."

"My boots — "

"If your feet are cut a little on sharp stones, the wounds will not be so bad as the cuts on the backs of men you had whipped. To the window, and get through it to the ground! Do not forget that I'd relish an excuse to shoot you. There is nothing you can do to avoid this. The door guard is bound and helpless. He cannot come to your aid."

HE COMPELLED Ruelas to get through the window, clad only in a long nightshirt. Zorro dropped out and stood beside him, gripped his arm again and urged him away from the building. They went through the darkness to where Zorro had left his horse.

Another coil of rope came off the pommel of the saddle. Zorro bound the capitan's wrists in front of him, stuffed another piece of cloth into the officer's mouth for a gag and knotted it behind his head, attached the rope to the pommel and mounted.

"One touch of the spurs, and you'd be dragged to death," Zorro warned. "Just keep along beside the horse."

He heard Ruelas grunt as gravel cut the soles of his tender feet. Riding slowly through the black night, he came to the edge of the plaza with his prisoner. No sounds of passersby reached him. The tavern door was closed, and only a dim light was inside.

Zorro urged his horse on. The *capitán* trotted along beside the mount on his bruised feet, grunting and groaning. Zorro stopped at the line of whipping posts in the center of the plaza, and got down from saddle.

"*Capitán* Ruelas," he said, "I am about to give you some of the medicine with which you have dosed others. I am going to make your name a thing of mockery. You will be found in the morning dressed only in a nightshirt that has been cut with a lash across the back. Everyone will know that Zorro took you from your own barracks and brought you to this."

Ruelas groaned some more, but Zorro did not remove the gag. He untied the *capitán's* wrists one at a time, forced each arm upward its full length, lashed it to the crossbar with the leather thongs.

"This will make you ridiculous, Señor *el Capitán*," Zorro said. "Up and down El Camino Real, men will laugh at the mere mention of your name. The Governor, I feel sure, will not endure having an officer ridiculed in such a manner. 'Tis better than shooting you or running you through with a blade."

More grunts and groans came from behind the gag, and Zorro laughed as he got his whip from the pommel of his saddle.

"It would be a rare pleasure to hear you howl, as you have made peons and natives howl," he told the officer. "But I do not wish to attract attention just yet. It is my intention that you be discovered here when people begin to stir at dawn."

He lifted the whip and swished the lash through the air. The first blow cut the skin and stained the nightshirt with blood. Zorro lashed again and again, ten lashes in all. Ruelas slumped against the whipping post.

The whip was coiled and fastened to the pommel again. Zorro got his blade from scabbard, and Ruelas's body flinched and sagged more as the tip of the blade cut between his shoulder-blades.

"That will be enough, I judge," Zorro said. "You do not have the fortitude shown by some of the peons. Take this lesson with you wherever you go next, Señor *el Capitán*."

Zorro returned the blade to its scabbard and mounted the black horse. He rode slowly out of the plaza through the darkness and around some buildings, and soon was away from the *pueblo* and on his way to the cave where Bernardo awaited him.

There he explained to Bernardo what he had done while the peon unsaddled the horse and put the saddle and bridle away with Zorro's costume and weapons.

"Stay at the house until night comes again, then bring the black out to the *rancho* and turn him loose in the pasture," Zorro directed. "Be sure you are not seen. Out there, we will have a season of peace."

Don Diego Vega left the cave and hurried along the narrow gulch, making his way to his father's house ....

AN HOUR after dawn the Vega carriage, driven by a stable hand, rolled away from the house and came along the plaza to stop in front of the tavern. A group of men had gathered there, and all of them were laughing. Pete Jordan was waiting with his pony, to ride beside the carriage as Diego had told him he could.

"Señor Jordan, what is the cause of all this merriment?" Diego asked him.

"That Zorro — he's been up to his tricks again," Jordan explained. "*Capitán* Ruelas was found this mornin' at dawn tied to one of the whippin' posts, wearin' only a nightshirt. His feet were cut by gravel, too. He's been whipped till the blood came. Someone ran to the barracks and told the big sergeant, and he brought a couple of troopers and took the *capitán* away."

"Surprising!" Diego declared.

"He sure didn't look any too much dignified when they took him away, I'd hate to be in his boots. Every man'll grin at him from now on. Oh, that Zorro!"

"But how do you know Zorro did it?"

"Ain't any question about that, I take it. Right between the *capitán's* shoulder-blades a letter Z had been cut, like with the tip of a sword."

Diego smiled slightly as his eyes met those of his father.

"That certainly is amusing, Señor Jordan," he said to the American. "Get into your saddle now, and ride along with the carriage, if you want to visit the *rancho*."

"That I sure want to do, Don Diego. I'd like to work for you folks."

"Then you think now that some Spaniards can be decent?"

"Aw, shucks! I was silly to talk like I did the first time I met you. But that was before I got acquainted with Juanita Nuñez — and that makes a big difference."

The West

Short Stories

Part 4

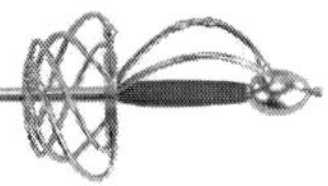

Zorro Shears Some Wolves

Don Diego champions the victims of a cruel and crafty swindler!

WHEN Diego Vega entered the spacious patio of the sprawling rancho house that morning, he could tell after his first glance that something was not as it should have been.

Diego had risen from his couch much earlier than his usual hour. For it was the sheep-shearing season again — a season of hard work and merriment combined, when the regular force of men who worked on the big Vega rancho not far from San Gabriel was augmented by extra workmen engaged for the shearing.

Don Alejandro Vega, Diego's father, always furnished the shearers with an abundance of good food and wine. Prizes were given for the best work. After the labors of the day, huge fires of logs were built near the huts of the workers, and there was music and dancing and not a few fights, the latter generally induced by jealousy over some senorita who had used her eyes too freely and with devastating effect.

The sheep-shearing period was a merry time, and Diego always liked to leave the comfortable Vega house in Reina de Los Angeles and go out to the rancho for the event. Nor was he insensible to the fact that sheep and wool added much to the yearly income of the Vegas.

The shearing had started two days before, and last night there had been much merriment around the blazing fires. Yet Diego appeared in the patio for the early breakfast, yawning and with his eyes still heavy with sleep, which was in itself an astonishing event.

As usual, his father was sitting at the head of the long table which had been placed beneath an arbor. At the table also sat elderly Fray Felipe, the Franciscan *padre* from the chapel in the pueblo, who had given the sheep-shearers his blessing with the usual ceremony. The table was supplied with huge bowls of fruit fresh from the orchard, with large pitchers of warm milk fresh from the cows' udders, hot tortillas, mush, hot meat and other dishes. All that was the usual thing.

BUT Diego felt there was something alien in the scene. Cassara, the trusted overseer of the rancho, was standing beside the table with his hat in his hand and a worried look on his countenance, as if he had just made an unpleasant report. Diego's father also appeared to be worried. And old Fray Felipe was rubbing his chin with a nervous hand, as he always did when some problem was giving him unusual trouble.

"I shall do something regarding the matter immediately, Cassara," Diego heard his white-haired father say. "You did the right thing to bring the affair to my attention immediately. Such injustice must be stopped."

The overseer bowed and left the patio. Diego greeted his father and the old *padre*, and bent his head slightly to receive the *padre's* blessing. When the table servant had served him and returned to the kitchen, Diego looked at his father inquiringly.

"There is trouble of some sort?" he asked.

"It concerns the contract workmen again," Don Alejandro declared. "Each year there is trouble. But this is not the fault of the workmen. However, they are grumbling, which means they will not do their work well."

"What has happened?" Diego asked, as he reached toward the bowl of fruit.

Don Alejandro sighed and gestured, and the *padre* took up the recital.

"It is a new variation of the old game of swindling the peon and native workmen, my son," Fray Felipe explained. "Your father engaged a certain José Arenas, a labor contractor, to furnish men for the shearing."

"But it is always necessary to hire extra men," Diego reminded him. "It is done every season."

"True, my son. This José Arenas arrived with his men and put them to work. They are expert shearers. They were delighted with your father's generosity in food and drink and prize money. Now, all has changed. They have grown sullen, are not careful in their work."

"Dispose of them and get others," Diego suggested.

"I have already contracted with Jose Arenas," his father told him. "Because of the scarcity of work in this vicinity, most of the unattached workers have gone north toward Monterey. We cannot get more help quickly, even if I took a loss on the labor contract."

"But why have the men grown sullen? Why have they stopped working well?" Diego asked.

Fray Felipe bent forward to explain:

"José Arenas and his lieutenant, a man named Quadara, compel the workers to gamble. They cheat the poor dupes and keep the score their own way. When the shearing is done, the men will still be in debt to Arenas, instead of having money in the pockets of their ragged garments."

"So they gamble and are cheated and the score marked up against them," Diego summed up. "Why do the idiots not merely refuse to gamble?"

"Because," the *padre* explained further, "José Arenas has them already in his debt by some means. If they quit him and run away without working out their debts, he can have them seized by the soldiers and returned to him in peonage."

"But why do they not merely refuse to gamble?" Diego persisted.

"Arenas compels them to do so, when they know they will be cheated. If they do not, he will discharge them, and then they will be vagrants out of work, since work now is scarce in this district, and will be seized as vagrants and made by the soldiers to work for nothing except poor food on public buildings and public roads."

"So they are caught in a double trap?"

"Something like that, Diego. If they run away, they will be in trouble. If they do not gamble and Arenas kicks them out, they will be in trouble. So they let the swindler do as he wills, because at least they are where they have good food and drink as they work."

"And Arenas gathers the reward of their toil from my father, charges it off against the debt, and pockets it?" Diego asked.

"That is it," the *padre* admitted. "So the men are doing poor work, and each day the work will be poorer and less."

DON ALEJANDRO added: "And we are short-handed already, Diego, and behind time with the shearing, and the cart caravan waits to take the wool to Monterey for shipment. So many workers have strolled toward the north. Among those who remain, only a few can shear sheep. Something must be done!" He got up from the table and began pacing around the floor.

"There is only one answer to the problem," Diego decided. "José Arenas must be dealt with, and made to repair the error in his mode of life."

"How can he be dealt with, and by whom?" Don Alejandro asked, his eyes glittering a little as he stopped pacing and turned to look at his son.

Diego did not have time to reply to that. There had come a summons at the door. A house servant answered it, and ushered into the patio Sergeant Manuel Garcia, for the moment the commanding officer of the barracks at Reina de Los Angeles.

Garcia was a huge, gruff man, the sort of soldier who carried out orders promptly and without question even if he knew the orders were wrong. In the absence of his *capitán*, who had gone to Monterey to try to explain to his superiors why he had not been able to capture Senor Zorro, the masked rider who fought for the peons and natives against the cruelties of officials and others, Sergeant Garcia felt a weight of responsibility upon his shoulders.

He bowed to Don Alejandro, the *padre* and Diego as he drew off his riding gauntlets.

"Please be kind enough to pardon this intrusion, Don Alejandro," the sergeant begged, bowing again. "I have arrived with four of my troopers — "

"Welcome!" Don Alejandro interrupted. "I always like to have you and a detachment visit us during the sheep-shearing and cattle slaughter. You keep the peace, prevent fights among the men, see that law and order prevail."

"I have come this time on a special mission, Don Alejandro, though it will cast suspicion aside if it is thought I am here with my men to keep peace among the workers as usual."

"A special mission?" Don Alejandro queried.

"I received a communication that Senor Zorro is in the vicinity, and perhaps this will be my opportunity to catch him and earn the Governor's reward."

"Zorro around here?" Don Alejandro cried. "I have heard no such rumor. It may be unfounded."

"A certain José Arenas, labor contractor, sent me word that he had received a scrawl from this Zorro, threatening him with a visit. No doubt he did not wish to trouble you with such matters, Don Alejandro."

"A scrawl sent by Zorro?" Don Alejandro muttered. "Why, that … It is preposterous!"

He glanced swiftly at Fray Felipe, and then at Diego, and then back at the sergeant. Here was something amiss. For Don Alejandro and the *padre* were the only two persons in the world, with the exception of a mute peon servant, who knew that Diego Vega, believed to be a spineless, lazy fop, was also the Senor Zorro who rode the highways and hills with blade, pistol and whip, and punished those who mistreated the downtrodden and helpless.

And they knew that Diego had sent José Arenas no scrawled threat.

"I'll have you and your men shown to quarters and made comfortable, Sergeant," Don Alejandro said, recovering himself and clapping his hands to summon a servant. "Do your duty, whatever it is. And remain with us during the sheep-shearing, if you can, for we are always glad to entertain you."

A servant took Garcia away, and the three at the table were alone again.

"So!" Don Alejandro exclaimed.

"So!" Diego echoed. "Who sent that warning, and for what, and why? Here is some trick! Before the sergeant arrived, I was about to suggest that Zorro should attend to this José Arenas, the swindler of peons."

"And now, with the soldiers here and watching for that very thing — " his father pictured.

Diego smiled. "I am of the opinion that the situation will only intrigue this Zorro and urge him to instant action."

They left the patio, Fray Felipe walking a step behind the others, and went toward the huts, where the men were leaving for the shearing pens. They could see Sergeant Garcia talking to Arenas and Quadara, the assistant, and approached the group.

"What is this?" Don Alejandro inquired curiously.

HE SURVEYED José Arenas — a short, squat, swarthy man dressed rather flamboyantly. Arenas, his appearance told, was cruel, arrogant, avaricious. Now he smirked and bowed to Don Alejandro in a manner almost sickening.

"I had hoped to spare you annoyance, Don Alejandro," he explained, "so said nothing to you, but sent for the troopers. I found a scrawl in my tent, plainly enough tossed there by somebody."

"What did the scrawl say, senor?"

"It said, 'I am coming to pay you a visit. I do not like labor contractors who rob their men.' And it was signed with a letter 'Z,' the mark this Zorro leaves around everywhere."

He handed a bit of soiled parchment to Don Alejandro, who read the scrawl. Diego and the *padre* read it also when he extended it to them.

"What have you been doing, Senor Arenas, to attract the attention of this Zorro?" Don Alejandro asked.

"I really do not know. Some of the men have lost small sums to me gambling with dice and cards. But that happens continually, and is nothing new. I treat the men well — I put them to work here on Rancho Vega, noted for its fine food and drink. This Zorro may have heard some wild, untrue tale about me."

Don Alejandro turned to Garcia. "I leave this matter in your capable hands, Sergeant. I know how eager you are to capture Zorro and earn the big reward."

Garcia eyed Arenas in an unfriendly manner. "I know how some of you labor contractors rob your men with dice and cards," he remarked. "If Don Alejandro ordered you to stop gambling — "

"I cannot do that," Don Alejandro broke in quickly, as Diego touched his elbow. "My own men, the *vaqueros* and others are always playing at dice and cards. They would resent it if I made them quit. And I control only my own property. They could go beyond my acres and gamble to their heart's content."

"And," Diego added, flicking an imaginary spot of dust from a satin coat sleeve, "if the gambling stopped, Zorro would not visit this Senor Arena, and the troopers could not have a chance at catching him."

"Sergeant Garcia, I leave it in your hands, as I remarked before," Don Alejandro said.

They started to turn to go back to the comfortable patio and finish their breakfast. But Diego gave an exclamation of surprise and pointed to a large rock a few feet away. In the sandy dirt beside it was scratched an irregular letter "Z."

"So he really has been here," Diego said. "Were I you, Senor Arenas, I should be trembling."

Arenas was doing just that, and his eyes bulged. He gulped when he tried to speak.

"Sergeant, I — I demand protection," he finally managed to stammer. "It is right I should have it. This — this masked rogue may try to slay me."

"If he does, we'll catch him—either before or after he slays you," Garcia comforted.

Diego turned away with his father and the *padre*, and when they were a short distance from the others began chuckling softly.

"What is so amusing, Diego?" his father asked.

"Senor Arenas is amusing, Father. You know, of course, that I did not write that scrawl. And I noticed that the bit of parchment upon which it was written looked as if it had been torn from the bottom of the labor contract you signed for him, Father. Nobody else hereabouts has any of that parchment."

"And so?" Don Alejandro asked.

"So Senor Arenas wrote that scrawl himself and played his little game."

"But why?"

"So he could send for the troopers. So they would guard him while he went on robbing his men. Perhaps he feared Zorro would hear of his thievery and really visit him, and in this manner hoped to prevent it."

"The rogue!" Don Alejandro muttered.

"I scratched that letter 'Z' in the dirt when none was looking. You saw how he was startled and frightened when he saw it. It proved to me that he had written the scrawl himself. If it had been a genuine message from Zorro, and had frightened him into sending for the soldiers, the scratch in the dirt would not have frightened him so much."

"And now," Don Alejandro pointed out, "he has a sergeant and four troopers protecting him while he swindles his men under their protection. So how can Zorro get at him?"

"I feel quite sure that Zorro will find a way," Diego replied. "And I am of the opinion that he will pay the rascal a visit tonight …. "

WHENEVER Diego went to the rancho from town, he had Bernardo, his mute peon body-servant, take Zorro's black horse, costume and weapons over the hills and to a hiding place in a small secluded canyon.

So he had merely to meet Bernardo, act as if giving the mute orders about something, and whisper:

"Zorro rides tonight. Have everything ready at the usual place and usual time."

Bernardo's eyes were twinkling as he turned away. And Diego entered the rancho house to spend the day resting, yawning, reading the poets, maintaining his pose as a young man of position, practically lifeless.

Dusk came, and the big fires were built back by the huts. The cooking pots were steaming, wineskins were put handy, foremen checked over the results of the day's shearing and sent the record to Don Alejandro, who would award the prizes at the end of the work.

After the evening meal, which he ate in company with his father and the old *padre*, Diego put on a sombrero, muffled his throat with a woolen scarf against the night air, and left the house to stroll down by the fires and watch the merriment.

Off to one side, at the edge of the big orchard, torches burned where serapes were strewn on the ground. Around the serapes some of the peon and native shearers were squatting, gambling with cards and dice. José Arenas was strolling around, watching, and making notes on which men lost. And his assistant, Quadara, was handling the games.

As if amused, Diego stopped near the group and watched the play. Arenas and Quadara greeted him with respect, and Diego noticed that they looked relieved when he turned to go away. He walked on around the fires, listening to the music and singing, watching the dancing, and finally made a cautious observation of the hut and tent occupied by Arenas and Quadara, before the former of which a small fire burned and a cooking pot simmered, a sullen peon in attendance.

Sergeant Garcia and his troopers had their saddled mounts tethered to a line extending between two trees, and the soldiers themselves were dancing and flirting with peon girls from other ranchos who were helping in the Vega kitchens during the shearing. Garcia was drinking wine and boasting of his military deeds to any who would lend him their ears.

Diego returned to the rancho house and went to his own rooms, where he dropped upon a couch to rest. From the distance came sounds of music, shouting, loud laughter, at times angry voices of quarreling men which were stilled promptly.

He knew where the soldiers were quartered, at some distance from where Arenas and Quadara slept. But he guessed that the labor contractor and his assistant would gamble almost throughout the night.

Hours passed, the fires died down, the music and laughter ceased, and the workers finally rested against the labor of the coming day. Diego slipped out of the house and through the patio.

Clouds obscured moon and stars. The big fires were beds of ashes and glowing embers. But over at the edge of the orchard the torches still burned and a few men were squatting around the serapes playing.

Keeping to the deeper shadows, moving cautiously and with scarcely any sound, Diego went toward the picket line where the mounts of Garcia and the troopers were tied. Working quietly as he whispered to the horses, Diego loosened all the saddle girths and bridle buckles. Then he walked on through the night.

"Do not cheat peons and natives again," Zorro waited, "or I shall pay you another visit."

One trooper could be seen by the light of a torch where Arenas and Quadara were gambling with their dupes. Garcia and the others evidently were asleep in the quarters assigned them, no doubt with their boots and weapons within easy reach.

Diego went around the corner of the orchard and came to the secluded spot where Bernardo was waiting. He began getting into his Zorro costume and arming himself. Finally, he mounted the black horse and gathered up the reins.

"Remain here until my return," he instructed Bernardo. "Plans I have in mind may be changed by events, and that delay me. Keep in hiding if anybody else approaches."

Bernardo's guttural sound told Zorro his orders had been understood. He touched lightly with his spurs and rode away through the night.

FROM a position in the orchard, Zorro viewed the gambling layout again. Arenas and Quadara were there gambling with three of the peon victims. The one trooper on guard was leaning against a tree, half asleep.

Arenas got up and strode around the serape upon which the men were casting dice, and stopped for a moment beneath one of the torches. Then he approached Quadara.

"You can finish it," Zorro heard Arenas say. "Be sure to keep the records correctly. I want some cold food and wine, and then some sleep."

"I'll go along with you, senor," the trooper guard told Arenas. "It is my duty to watch over you."

Arenas strolled off into the night with the trooper beside him, headed for the hut which Cassara, the overseer, had assigned him.

Zorro moved his horse a short distance nearer and watched and listened. Quadara was tall and stringy, with badly stooped shoulders. His voice was harsh and his manner domineering. Zorro could see that he had a pistol in his sash.

One of the peons sprang up. "That finishes me," he lamented. "Enough for tonight!"

"Go to your hut and sleep," Quadara told him. "Work well tomorrow, for you are on the way to one of the prizes."

The weary peon staggered away, and Quadara continued play with the two remaining. Zorro heard one make a remark about the suspicious manner in which the dice acted at times, and Quadara sent him sprawling with a blow of his fist.

"Get away from here!" Quadara ordered. "I shall report to Senor Arenas that you said the dice are not fair; and he will deal with you for the remark."

The peon picked himself up out of the dirt and started away. His companion made a final cast of the dice, then followed him. Quadara was alone.

Zorro urged his horse forward, drawing his pistol from his sash. He rode through the soft ground of the orchard and suddenly appeared beneath the torch, where Quadara was folding the serapes upon which the men had been gambling.

Quadara glanced up and saw the masked rider who was dressed entirely in black. His eyes bulged, he squawked his astonishment, then his hand went toward his pistol.

"Do not touch a weapon unless you wish to die instantly," the cold hard voice of Zorro warned.

"You — you are a robber? But I have no money. Senor Arenas has it all."

"I am Zorro, not a robber. I know how you and Arenas have been swindling the peons and natives. Put your hands above your head and walk up close to me. You must be punished."

Zorro transferred his pistol to his left hand and with his right got his long whip off the pommel of his saddle. Quadara was licking nervously at lips suddenly dry from fear. He put up his hands slowly and took a step forward.

"Do not turn and run," Zorro warned. "I can tell that is what is in your mind. A bullet will bring you down if you try it. Come closer!"

Quadara stepped quite close to the big black horse.

"Now, Senor, take your pistol from your sash and hurl it away," Zorro ordered. "And do not try to use it on me, or you are a dead man!"

Quadara obeyed. Then the whip swished through the air and the lash cut into Quadara's back. He screamed from the pain of the blow.

"Yell all you please," Zorro told him, as the lash cut again. "Cry out for help, if you desire."

Quadara tried to turn and run, but the whip curled around him and jerked him back, to fall sprawling. The black horse was urged forward a few feet, and Quadara continued his screams and yells for help as the whip rose and fell upon a writhing target.

"Help! — Zorro is here! … Soldiers! — Help!"

Arenas' assistant shouted at the top of his voice as the cracks of the lash punctuated his words.

There was a sudden commotion, for which Zorro had been wishing and waiting. Men rushed from the huts. Tapers were lit at the fires. Sergeant Garcia and his men tumbled from their cots and emerged into the open, buckling on blades and tucking pistols into belts.

GARCIA began bellowing orders, and the troopers ran to get their horses off the picket line. There was more confusion when they tried to mount. Saddles turned because of the loosened girths. Bridles slipped over horses' heads because of the loosened buckles. Howling troopers ran to catch their excited mounts, and Sergeant Manuel Garcia's bawled instructions rang out above the din.

Zorro continued using the whip, and Quadara kept up his screeching while stretched on the ground with his arms wrapped around his head and his back exposed to the lash. Finally, Zorro stopped the whipping.

"Do not cheat peons and natives again!" Zorro warned. "If you do, I shall learn of it and pay you another visit, and if I do that it will not be a whip I use. You will quit the employ of Arenas at once and leave this part of the country. Do you understand?"

"I'll go—I'll go," Quadara agreed.

Zorro gave a yell of defiance, wheeled his horse, and rode through the patch of light coming from the torch, where the soldiers could see him. Pistols barked and flamed, but no bullet came near him, for the range was too great for accurate pistol shooting.

They could see the masked man as he rode away. And the last thing Zorro heard was Garcia's wild command:

"Into saddles! After the rogue! This time we do not stop until we have him! Pistol him if you must! Catch him unharmed, and I'll hang him without a trial!"

Zorro purposely kept to hard ground so the hoof beats of his horse could be heard. But, aware that the pursuit finally had started, he swung off to one side, pulled the big black down to a walk, and went slowly and carefully through the blackness of the night, circling back toward the huts as Garcia and his troopers rode straight ahead in futile chase.

He neared the huts again. The rushing, frightened horses and excited troopers had scattered the fires. Some of the workers had charged toward the orchard, where Quadara was still howling with fright and pain.

José Arenas was in front of the tent, making wild gestures and shouting incoherent orders to his sheep-shearers, who were trying to keep out of his way. Zorro rode around behind the hut and tent and waited until Arenas was alone.

Lights had appeared in the rancho house, and torches had been set alight in the patio and garden. The scene was one of turmoil, for those newly awakened from deep sleep scarcely knew what they were doing. Female house servants were screaming at nothing, and peons and natives were shouting questions at one another.

José Arenas tuned toward the hut to get something he desired, and stopped with a gurgle of fear. Before him was a huge black horse, and a masked man dressed in black was in the saddle, holding a pistol menacingly.

"Come to me, José Arenas!" Zorro commanded. "At once! Do not cry for help, or it will be the last cry you ever give!"

Voiceless, his flabby body shaking with fear, Arenas waddled forward.

"You — you are Zorro?" he mouthed.

"I am, and you know why I am here. You got my scrawl, did you not?"

"I — I wrote that myself."

"Another fault for which you must pay. It is unnecessary for me to go into details, senor. I know how you swindle men and keep them in your debt and in your clutches and really make slaves of them."

"I — I'll treat them well hereafter, Senor Zorro. I'll give them back their losses!"

"You will do all that — *si!"* Zorro interrupted. "And more. You will treat them as human beings hereafter. You will keep them here and fill your contract with this rancho, then move the men on to other good work. I shall be watching, José Arenas! And the first time you transgress again, you will have a visit from me — perhaps the last you ever will have from any man. Is that understood?"

"It shall all be as you say, Senor Zorro"

"But for what you have done already, you must pay now," Zorro continued. "I have whipped your assistant and ordered him to quit this district. Approach and turn your back!"

ARENAS hesitated. Then Zorro had the whip in his hand again and began using it. The great fear the labor contractor felt could not keep him from shrieking as the blows fell. Men came rushing toward the spot as Zorro continued to use the whip.

And he heard the pounding of a horse's hoofs, and glanced toward the orchard to see Sergeant Garcia riding toward him madly. Something had made the sergeant turn back instead of continuing the chase with his men.

Zorro gave the fat body of Arenas a final cut with the whip and moved his horse aside out of the light as he fastened the whip to his saddle.

Then he charged the black forward directly toward Garcia.

Garcia was holding a pistol ready. In the face of the wild charge, he fired the weapon, tossed the useless pistol aside, and whipped blade from scabbard.

Zorro had no desire to shoot the sergeant out of his saddle. He knew Garcia to be a skilled and loyal soldier doing nothing more than his duty. He thrust his pistol into his own sash and drew his blade.

THE two horses reared as they met, then bumped together. The two blades rang as they clashed.

"Zorro, I have you!" Garcia cried.

But Zorro's blade seemed like a live and powerful thing in his hand. There was a quick thrust, and Garcia lowered his guard. Then a twist of the wrist, and the sergeant's blade was torn from his hand, to sail through the air and clatter to the ground and leave him unarmed.

"Some other time, Sergeant!" Zorro shouted at him. Then he used his spurs.

Through the corner of the orchard he rode, and disappeared into the night. He pulled up in soft ground, reached the rendezvous, handed the reins to the waiting Bernardo, and quickly freed himself of weapons and the Zorro costume.

Then, Don Diego Vega hurried afoot to the corner of the orchard again.

The scene had changed. Two *vaqueros* were riding wildly in pursuit of the troopers. Servants and field workers were scattered all over the place. Diego, his shoulders hunched, his hair mussed as if he had just awakened from a deep sleep, lost himself among the others, and finally came to the vicinity of Garcia.

"You — " the sergeant began. "Why, it is Don Diego! But — what are you doing here?"

"There was so much tumult I could not sleep," Diego Vega replied. "I heard them shouting that the fellow Zorro was here, and came out to see if I could do anything to aid in capturing him."

Sergeant Garcia tossed up his head and laughed. "Don Diego, my friend, you will be more comfortable sitting in front of a fire in an easy chair and reading your poets," he declared. "I fear that capturing Zorro is something out of your line. Why, the fellow disarmed me a moment or two ago—disarmed *me*, Don Diego! 'Twas by an unexpected trick he did it, to be sure, and I shall punish him for it when we meet again. But it shows you what sort of fellow he is."

Diego yawned. "I believe I shall return to the house," he said. "This tumult will give me a severe headache, I am sure. *Buenas noches!"*

"Noches!" Sergeant Garcia replied.

Diego went on like a man half asleep, pretending not to see when the workers and servants he passed knuckled their foreheads to him respectfully. His father would be waiting, he knew, to hear a recital of the night's events.

The Face Behind the Mask

When a beautiful woman baits a killer's trap, the fighting hidalgo, Don Diego Vega, makes a black-cloaked foray into the very jaws of death!

WHEN the messenger arrived from Reina de Los Angeles, he found Don Diego Vega sitting in the patio of the sprawling house on the Vega rancho.

Diego read a volume of poetry lately arrived from Spain. Near him on a bench sat Don Alejandro, his silver-haired father. The house steward brought the messenger to the patio and bowed low before Don Alejandro. "This fellow says he carries an important message to you from the pueblo," the steward reported.

Don Alejandro signed for the steward to retire and for the dusty messenger to approach with the document he held. The messenger bowed humbly and surrendered the document.

"I am to carry a reply," he said, in a low voice.

Don Alejandro stiffened a forefinger to break the seal, glancing at the superscription.

"Diego! This is for you," he said handing it to his son. "What dainty señorita have you so much enamored that she sends you a letter by special messenger? Am I remiss in knowing the close affairs of my own household?"

Don Alejandro smiled as he spoke, knowing well that his son gave little attention to dainty señoritas. Diego smiled also as he replied:

" 'Tis from no señorita, of that I am sure. The writing of my name is too bold and not in a feminine hand, and the message is not scented."

DIEGO opened the message and read it swiftly, lifted his head and was about to speak when he noticed the messenger still waiting.

"Attend me outside the patio wall," Diego directed. The messenger retired swiftly. Diego handed the message to his father and got up to stride back and forth beside the fountain as his father read:

> "Diego, my son:
>
> "Be kind enough to come to me immediately. There is a matter of importance for us to discuss without delay. God be with you!
>
> "Felipe, Fray of the order of St. Francis."

"What do you suppose he wants with you, Diego?" Don Alejandro said.

Diego ceased his pacing and put his hands behind his back. "You will observe, my father, that in the upper corners of the message and in the lower left hand corner, are little scratches made by the pen. Put them together in the order of reading, and what have you?"

Don Alejandro scowled and looked, then lifted his head. "Together, the pen scratches form the letter Z," he said, almost in a whisper.

Diego sat beside him. "Z — for Zorro," he replied, in a whisper also. "Fray Felipe is calling upon me — in the name of Zorro. Something must be sadly amiss." He raised his voice and called the messenger back into the patio. "Who gave you the message to bring to me?"

"Fray Felipe, Don Diego. I am a messenger for the chapel."

"Say to Fray Felipe that I will do as he desires, and he will understand." Diego waved the man away.

"What will you do, Diego?" his father asked.

"We do not know the trouble. There must be no suspicion. So there must be nothing unusual in my actions. I'll return in the carriage, yawning and half asleep as usual, the indolent Diego Vega the people know." He clapped his hands, and the steward came from the house. "Order the carriage. I leave for Reina de Los Angeles in an hour's time," Diego said. "Have Bernardo sent to me in my private room."

He turned to his father again and continued his conversation in low tones: "I have Zorro's black horse and weapons here at the rancho. I'll have Bernardo take them in during the night. It will be dark, with no moon. And a mist is already blowing in from the sea."

Diego left the patio and went to his own private room in a wing of the big adobe ranch house. He walked with shoulders bent as if they carried half the weight of the world, and he yawned.

That was a pose he had maintained in town and at the rancho for some time now. Diego Vega was a weakling, a sort of human spineless jellyfish, people supposed, instead of the fiery young caballero he should be.

But three men knew he also was Señor Zorro, the masked man who rode to avenge the wrongs of the downtrodden and helpless against cruelties visited upon them. The three were his father, Fray Felipe, his confessor, and Bernardo, his mute peon body servant, none of whom would betray him.

Bernardo appeared and received his orders, and nodded and made a guttural sound which meant he understood and would obey. And less than an hour later, propped up on silken cushions in the family carriage, with a silken dust robe across his knees and a scented handkerchief with which to brush his nostrils and keep the dust from them, Diego Vega was being driven along the highway which ran from San Gabriel to the pueblo of Reina de Los Angeles.

HE ARRIVED during the siesta hour. When it was over and the usual late afternoon promenade had started around the little plaza, Diego appeared dressed in resplendent clothing and sauntered toward the chapel, saluting all persons of importance he met.

Aged Fray Felipe had known of his arrival, and was waiting for him. They went to the padre's little private room, where Fray Felipe finished his meal, wiped his lips with a napkin, and eyed Diego.

"You remember the good peon, Gustavo, whose wife died last year after a long and difficult illness?"

"Very well, padre. He has worked for us often around the house and at the rancho. Since his wife died, he lives in his hut alone except for his daughter, Anita, a beautiful girl."

"Too beautiful, I fear," Fray Felipe interrupted. "Perhaps you remember that Gustavo, who loved his wife, acquired the services of a famed physician from Monterey, who happened to be passing through our pueblo on a journey. The physician remained for several days and did the best he could."

"I remember."

"Payment for that physician's services would be something to make a wealthy man shudder. And Gustavo is only a poor peon, a workman who picks up a coin here and there. He promised the physician he would work day and night and send him money whenever he could until the debt was paid, if it took him the remainder of his life."

"An honest fellow," Diego put in.

"Yes. Everybody thought the physician a kind man who would forget the debt, at least never bother Gustavo about it. But it has not worked out that way, my son. Some magistrate in Monterey has put through an order. It was brought here by a certain Capitán Jorge Lozito, himself a magistrate. This Lozito has been sent south by the Governor to see that the laws are stiffened here."

"And — ?" Diego asked.

"The Monterey magistrate ordered Gustavo and his daughter into peonage to work out the debt. Capitán Lozito has transferred Gustavo on a bill of sale for services to the Cabrillo rancho. It means hard toil without pay for perhaps the remainder of his life, for he must work out the amount."

"And his daughter?" Diego questioned.

"She was ordered into peonage also, as being in part responsible for the debt, and her services have been contracted for by Pablo Urista, the wealthy trader. She already has been taken to his house, to act as servant in it."

"Anita, that beautiful and graceful girl?"

"And as good as she is beautiful and graceful, Diego. I am her confessor, and know that. And this Pablo Urista — "

"I know of him," Diego interrupted. "A wealthy, middle-aged bachelor who gambles with dice and cards, consumes vast quantifies of wine and is known for his affairs with women. A girl like that, serving in peonage such a man — " Diego did not go on.

Fray Felipe nodded. "Almost the same as his slave," he said. "How long can she remain unsullied? The very atmosphere of that house is enough to stain her."

"I know of Pablo Urista," Diego said. "Above all else, he loves gold. I'll go to him and buy the peonage-service order from him, release the girl and send her back to her father's hut. I'll bargain for the services of her father, too. If Cabrillo has him, it will not be difficult. The Vegas and Cabrillos are good friends."

"And if you cannot get Urista to release the girl for gold?" Fray Felipe questioned.

"Then, Señor Zorro must take a hand," Diego decided.

"I had that in mind, my son, when I sent for you. To save an honest girl from utter ruin — there is a good fight for Zorro to make."

PABLO URISTA had the largest warehouse and mart in the pueblo. He was a shrewd trader and clever merchant. He handled everything from imported fabrics to raw hides and casks of olive oil, wine and tallow.

Diego sauntered into Urista's establishment, in which at the moment were several fat señoras and their charming daughters purchasing material for gowns. Urista himself, beaming upon everybody, was watching his three salesmen closely. He bowed as low as his paunch would permit when Diego entered.

"Ah, Don Diego!" he greeted.

"I would have private speech, with you, señor," Diego broke in, brushing his nostrils with his scented handkerchief as if to obliterate a stench.

"Allow me to escort you to my office room, Don Diego."

In the office, Diego seated himself and used his silk handkerchief again.

"It has reached my ears, Señor Urista," he said, "that you have obtained a certain young woman in peonage."

"Ah, yes! A splendid girl — beautiful, graceful, with a quick wit about her. I need a girl like that to grace my house and keep it in order, one who can arrange flowers and dress my table when I have guests."

"The girl's father has worked for us in town and at the rancho, and I know the circumstances well," Diego told the trader. "Gustavo is an honest, hard-working man — and his daughter is an honest girl and should be kept so." There was a hint in Diego's speech that Urista could not overlook.

"Don Diego, you wrong me," the trader accused. "I swear to you that no harm will come to the girl while she works for me."

"Thank you, señor. But Gustavo and Anita smart under the taint of peonage. Señor Urista, I desire to buy your peonage contract regarding the girl. Naturally, I expect you to have a small profit for your trouble. And you will not find it amiss, I am sure, if the Vegas express a friendly feeling toward you."

A queer expression came into Urista's face, and he bent forward and spoke seriously: "Now, Don Diego, I really find myself between the devil and the deep sea, as the ancient saying has it. Anyone with a modicum of common sense would know that I'd be gratified and honored to have your family as patrons. And I am not above taking the profit you proffer."

"Then we make the deal? What amount do you require, señor?" Diego asked.

"I — I cannot deal with you, Don Diego."

"What is this?" Diego showed a trace of anger.

"One moment, please. Others than myself are concerned. I must take you into my full confidence, Don Diego, knowing well that a caballero such as yourself, the son of a hidalgo, will not betray that confidence."

"What is your meaning?"

"The whole affair, Don Diego, was fomented in Monterey by high officials."

"An affair of a peon and his daughter? By high officials? What nonsense! Do you dare jest with me, señor?"

"Kindly attend me, Don Diego. Capitán Jorge Lozito, formerly an army officer in Mexico and now a magistrate especially named by the Governor, is here to see the thing through. The physician was ordered to sign a request for payment through peonage, against his will, for he is a merciful man. Capitán Lozito came here with the order and put it through. I was the same as ordered to take the girl. Her father — "

"The Cabrillos will release him to me," Diego interrupted.

"That is well. But the girl … She is the core of the plot. No doubt rumors will be spread that she is receiving indignities in my house. I regret that, for my reputation is not at the best anyhow. But I cannot go against the orders of such a man as Capitán Lozito, else I am ruined. We traders and importers must have the Governor's license or we cannot do business."

"I know that. What is the plot? How does it concern the daughter of a mere peon?" Diego demanded.

"She is bait in a trap, Don Diego — a trap in which they hope to catch Señor Zorro."

GENUINE astonishment was in Diego's voice. "What is this?"

"You know how Zorro is a thorn in the side of the Governor, how eager the soldiers are to catch him and win the rich reward offered. The Governor has sent Capitán Lozito to capture or slay the rogue. Just between ourselves, Don Diego, this Capitán Lozito is one of the finest swordsmen ever to hold an army post, certainly by far the best ever to be in Alta California."

"Indeed?" Diego asked.

"It is expected that Zorro will try to rescue the girl, save her from her predicament. She will be guarded every night. If Zorro seeks to contact her and rescue her, he will stumble into a trap. Sergeant Garcia, our *commandante* here, will be watching with his troopers. And Capitán Lozito will be ready to fight the rascal with a blade and run him through. Just enough to render Zorro helpless, of course, so he can be healed of his wound and afterwards be hanged."

"A pretty plot!" Diego remarked.

"So you see, Don Diego, why I cannot release the girl to you. It would mean my ruin, with officials turned against me. But I give you my word, Don Diego, that she will be protected from all affront and harm while she is in my house."

Diego stood and brushed his nostrils with the scented handkerchief again.

"I understand your predicament, Señor Urista," he said. "I hold you to your word that the señorita will suffer no harm."

"I'll see to it, Don Diego."

Urista ushered him from the warehouse, and Diego strolled homeward thoughtfully.

Diego ate the evening meal alone. He told the house steward that Bernardo might arrive some time during the night, and that he wanted to see him when he did, regardless of the hour. Then, as sunset turned to purple dusk, Diego strolled down to the plaza again, and this time went to the tavern.

The big main room was crowded as usual at this hour. Some men were eating, others drinking, some dicing or playing at cards. The fat innkeeper was shouting and clapping his hands at his native servants. But he bowed and gave his entire attention to Diego when the caballero entered.

Diego refused a goblet of the best wine and ordered a pot of crystallized honey. This gave him opportunity for speech with the innkeeper apart from the others.

"Who is the tall slender stranger dressed so fashionably?" Diego asked.

"He is Capitán Jorge Lozito, Don Diego. A superior magistrate from Monterey on the Governor's business. The sort to toss gold around to draw flatterers to him. I detest the type, but he is good for my business."

"No doubt," Diego replied.

"Do you wish to have him presented to you, Don Diego?" the innkeeper asked.

"Not now. Perhaps we'll meet at some other time."

Diego took his pot of honey and went home. He had seen Capitán Lozito, had observed him well, had noticed that he had the proper build for a good fencer. If Lozito lived up to his reputation, Zorro would have no easy adversary in him should it come to crossing blades in anger.

Pacing around his private apartment in his father's house, Diego considered the affair. The peon girl was but bait in a trap, the trader had said. It was necessary to get her out of the trap.

Were she rescued, she would have to be hidden. If a man or woman subjected to peonage contrived to escape, the penalty was severe when they were caught.

A man might make his way over the hills and join some ship's company and escape to freedom. But a girl could not hide long without discovery.

EVEN an escaped girl could not claim sanctuary at a mission, for the padres obeyed civil law whether they cared to or not. And for anyone, even a Vega, to be caught hiding such would mean a heavy fine at least, and the Governor's displeasure. The Vegas, tending toward kindness and mercy to peons and natives, were frowned upon by the present licentious Governor already. As much as he wished to rescue the girl, Diego did not want to see his father's estates confiscated because of some act of his.

"If I could dispose of this Capitán Lozito, things might be easier," Diego mused. "If Urista could be brought to the point of not wanting to keep the girl — "

He turned abruptly to his cabinet and opened it, and from a secret drawer brought forth sheets of parchment unlike any other in the pueblo. Working rapidly, he made two copies of a warning by lettering with a pen. He held one up to the light of a candelabra and looked at the wording:

> WARNING!
>
> Pablo Urista, the trader, is holding in his house an innocent young girl under the act of peonage. If any deal in trade in any manner with this man they may expect to receive an unpleasant visit from me.
>
> ZORRO.

It was the middle of the night when Diego, dressed in dark clothing, slipped unseen out of the house, went past the quarters of the servants silently, and strolled toward the plaza. Clouds had scudded in from the sea, a slight mist was swirling, and it was dark.

He fastened one of his placards to the barracks building within a few feet of sphere the guard should have been standing but was not. Going on through the darkness, he fastened the second warning to the door of the adobe building where the local magistrate had his offices and courtroom. Then he hurried home, got into robe and sandals, and waited for the coming of Bernardo.

It was almost dawn when Bernardo arrived.

"You accomplished everything?" Diego asked.

Bernardo nodded affirmatively.

"Bueno! Seek your rest. Nothing will be done tonight."

After breakfast the following morning, Diego dressed as carefully as usual and strolled down to the plaza and along one side of it to the chapel. Once more he found himself in Fray Felipe's private room. He explained what he had done, told about the plot.

"Senor Pablo Urista is furious," the padre reported. "A number of persons saw the placards before they were torn down, and now the entire pueblo knows of Zorro's threat. But you object, my son?"

"To make Urista eager to get rid of the girl when the proper moment arrives. Then I'll buy her contract from him and free her."

"But this Capitan Lozito — ?"

"We can tell nothing about that, padre, until the moment for that comes also."

Diego went forth again, and in front of the tavern met Sergeant Manuel Garcia, in charge of the local barracks during the absence of his superior officer, who had gone to Monterey.

Between Diego Vega, the high born and fastidious, and Garcia, the uncouth soldier, was a strange friendship. But that friendship often made it possible for Señor Zorro to know what movements the troopers contemplated.

GARCIA greeted him jovially. "Don Diego! *Amigo!* I had thought you were out at the rancho."

"The wind singing through the trees of the orchard depressed me," Diego explained. "And I had forgotten to take with me a certain book of poetry."

"And you have returned, my friend, to have your delicate nerves upset by a commotion," Garcia informed him. "That pest of a Zorro is acting up again. But this time we'll get him — though the reward may not be mine."

"How comes that?"

"I cannot tell you, Don Diego, because it is an official secret. One thing rejoices me — that Pablo Urista, the rich trader, is being annoyed. No patrons will go near his place today. He is not making any profit, and that is enough to break his heart."

"There always seems to be a tumult of some sort," Diego complained. "If in your official capacity you meet this Zorro, be careful he does not slice off your ears."

Diego walked on and went home, and throughout the day learned news of what was occurring by the simple method of keeping his ears open and listening to the house servants talk.

The peons and natives were nervous and afraid, the reports said; Pablo Urista was raging because he had no trade. Capitan Lozito had gone openly to

Urista's warehouse and had purchased a measure of expensive satin from which to have a coat made, and had declared publicly, "This Zorro, this highwayman and low scoundrel, should be captured and hanged; it will take more than a man like him to keep Jorge Lozito from trading when he desires to trade." But nobody else had followed Lozito's example, and Urista's salesmen were idle.

At the hour for afternoon promenade, Diego appeared as usual. He managed to meet Sergeant Garcia again near the tavern.

"I have heard this Zorro is annoying people again," Diego told the sergeant. "Why do you not catch the fellow and put an end to this turmoil?"

Garcia winked at him. " 'Twill not be long now, *amigo*, until the rogue is in a cell in the barracks, else dead."

"How is this?"

"Certain arrangements have been made for his capture," the burly sergeant revealed. "He is sure to try to release the peon girl. The trap is ready to be sprung."

"But so many traps have failed to catch him?"

"Capitán Jorge Lozito has arranged this one. He is indeed a clever rascal," Garcia declared. "Urista's house, where the girl is held, will be well guarded; I'll have troopers inside it and also in the garden, and they will be well hidden."

"And this terrible Capitán Lozito — where will he be?" Diego asked.

"He will spend the early evening in the main room of the tavern, then retire to his own room off the patio, saying he is fatigued. But after a time he will slip out and go to the vicinity of the Urista house. He hopes to encounter Zorro and have at him with his blade. Confidentially, this Lozito is a wonder with a sword, He expects to wound Zorro but not kill him, and so gain yet a greater reputation."

"The whole affair seems to revolve around this Lozito," Diego observed.

"That is true, Don Diego. Confidentially, I do not like the business. Being a soldier, naturally I desire to see Zorro caught. But the girl — I know her and her father. They are quite decent people. To have such a girl in Urista's house under peonage … it is enough to make a man vomit."

DIEGO strolled on, and passed Urista's warehouse to find the trader standing in the doorway with a sullen look in his face. He bowed to Diego.

"How is it with you today, señor?" Diego asked.

"I am almost undone," Urista wailed. "Have you heard of the placards?"

"I have, señor."

"My business will be ruined. Everyone is afraid of Zorro. I have no trade."

"I heard that Capitán Lozito — "

"Ah, yes! He made a purchase to show his contempt for Zorro, but others failed to follow his example. Come in and make a purchase, Don Diego — anything. You will find the price to your liking. If you demonstrate the courage to trade with me, others will follow your example. Surely you are not afraid of Zorro, a caballero like you."

"I do not fear him," Diego replied, truthfully enough, "nor do I seek to bring trouble upon myself unnecessarily. And, if you will remember, I desired to trade with you a little earlier, and you would not deal."

"Regarding that girl? I wish I could sell her contract to you. I would be willing to take a loss. But that cannot be at the moment."

Diego got away from him and went home for the evening meal. He got word to Bernardo to have Zorro's horse, costume and weapons ready in the usual place at an early hour.

He was careful that night as he got into the costume and buckled on his weapons. He made sure that the pistol was ready for use. He adjusted the scabbard of his blade. He coiled his long whip around the pommel of his saddle with care.

"Await me here," he ordered Bernardo. Then he rode slowly away through the night.

Clouds blocked the light from moon and stars. Swirling mist was in the air again. The night suited Zorro perfectly. He rode cautiously through the blackness toward Pablo Urista's house, which sat in a garden at the edge of the pueblo with no near neighbors.

Faint streaks of light came through some of the windows of the house. The place was quiet. There were no sounds of merriment as often were heard when Urista was entertaining and conducting a gambling and drinking party.

Somewhere in the darkness troopers lurked, Zorro knew. Others undoubtedly were inside the house. But it was not in Zorro's mind to storm the place and carry away the peon's daughter and hide her. She must be released by legal means, so she would not have to live a fugitive, afraid each hour that she might be retaken and punished severely.

In the darkness, sitting in his saddle and bending forward a little, Zorro watched and listened. He saw a flicker of light in the shrubbery — some careless trooper had lit a *cigarillo*.

Zorro knew the ground well here, for he had played around the house as a boy when its former owner had a lad his own age. He gathered his reins, touched with the spurs, and urged his black horse forward.

Purposely, he made a little noise about it. He rode deliberately through a streak of light coming from one of the windows, and guessed some trooper had seen him. Along the back of the patio and not far from it, he urged the horse.

"Zorro! Zorro!" Some trooper shouted the alarm.

ZORRO used the spurs again and rode bent low in his saddle. Firearms exploded behind him, but no bullet came near. A distance from the house, he pulled up his horse and stopped to watch and listen again.

The troopers were shouting, one declaring with vehemence that he had seen the masked rider. Others were yelling that they had heard the hoofbeats of Zorro's horse. Torches flared in the patio and around the house. Zorro heard the raucous voice of Sergeant Garcia giving the order he had hoped would be given — for a trooper to hasten to the tavern and inform Capitan Lozito of Zorro's visit.

Circling away from the house, Zorro rode cautiously through the black night and after a time came to a depression behind the tavern and not far from it, where there were huge rocks and stunted trees and brush. He dismounted, tied his horse in a secluded spot, and went toward the tavern afoot, holding his pistol ready.

The clatter of hoofbeats came from the vicinity of the horse blocks, and light revealed Capitan Lozito riding away furiously in answer to Garcia's message. Zorro walked on to the little gate at the rear of the patio, and got through it.

Lozito, he had learned, occupied the tavern's most sumptuous apartment at the end of the patio. The door was closed, but not locked. Zorro slipped inside the large room, felt his way past articles of furniture and got to a large window which swung outward. He swung the window open and fastened it into place. Dampness rushed into the room, but the wind was blowing in the wrong direction to do so ….

At the Urista house, Capitan Lozito was an angry man as he stormed at Sergeant Garcia and the trooper who had given the alarm.

"You frightened the rascal away, dolts and asses!" he shouted. "Why did you not keep silent? Why not let him work his way about the house trying to find the girl, and in the meantime get word to me? This Zorro will not give up his efforts, possibly. But he will not try again tonight. Continue to guard the place well, however. And tomorrow night we may have better luck. Garcia! Fine that stupid trooper of yours a month's pay for his share in this farce."

Lozito stormed back to the tavern and gave his horse over to a peon stableman. In the main room of the tavern he stopped to buy wine for all. Gulping his own, he went into the patio and walked beneath the arches to the door of his room.

He opened the door to darkness, closed and barred it, and struggled to light the tapers on the candelabra. Then he drew off his gauntlets and tossed his hat upon a couch, and turned.

Before him, standing in front of the open window, was a masked man dressed in black, who held a pistol menacingly.

"Who are you? A robber?" Lozito questioned.

"I am Zorro! Stand steady, señor! This pistol is aimed at your heart."

"Zorro? What do you want here?"

"I issued an order, señor, that nobody was to trade with Pablo Urista, did I not? And you purchased something from the fellow."

"So you have come to murder me?"

"I am not a murderer," Zorro returned. "Though you little deserve it, I will give you a chance for your life. You are an expert at swordplay, I have heard — and you have a blade at your side?"

"And you have a pistol in your hand, Señor Zorro."

"The pistol will be returned to my sash when you have tossed on the couch the one in your belt. Then it will be blade against blade."

LOZITO drew the pistol from his belt and carefully and tossed it upon the couch. He backed to the wall. And suddenly he whipped his blade from its scabbard and charged.

"A foul move, señor!" Zorro cried, as he avoided the other's rush and got his own blade out and ready. "I might have expected it from a man who fights against innocent girls."

Their blades met, clashed, rang. The room was large enough, and both Zorro and Lozito had kicked stools out of their way. The light from the candelabra was as fair to both swordsmen. They circled as they began fighting, each trying out the other.

Zorro caught the feel of his adversary's wrist, and in the first half-minute of the combat knew here was no ordinary antagonist. Lozito would call forth

Zorro caught the feel of his adversary's wrist, and in the first half-minute of the combat knew here was no ordinary antagonist.

all of Zorro's skill and strength.

For Zorro, defeat meant either death on this man's blade, or a bad wound and life thereafter, for a time. Regardless of his real identity and his father's wealth and standing, he would not escape. The Governor would have him hanged as an appeal to the people that he made no distinction in class when a man was guilty of crime, for the Governor was a politician before all else.

And his old father's silvery head would be bowed in grief and shame. His estates would be confiscated, and perhaps Don Alejandro would be subjected to exile if not condemned as an accessory and punished in a more ignominious manner.

Zorro fought with extreme caution. Once, Lozito laughed and began taunting in panted phrases as he fought:

"The great Zorro … a mere novice with a blade … you do not fight some stupid trooper now, señor … soon we shall have a look at the face behind your mask … "

Lozito pressed the fighting. Caught off balance an instant, Zorro felt steel slip in-to his upper left arm. He flinched from the sudden stab of pain. He had been touched — wounded. He could feel the hot blood starting down his arm.

In desperation, he fought madly, driving Lozito back to a corner of the room.

"Help!" Lozito shouted wildly. "Here, to me! I have Zorro here!"

His voice rang through the window and into the night. But it was heard from the patio, by a peon servant bringing Lozito a message. The peon heard the sound of fighting — the ringing of blades, thumping of feet, the harsh breathing of men at the point of exhaustion, and ran to give the alarm.

Pounding feet sounded on the flagstones of the patio. Zorro heard hoarse voices. Somebody pounded upon the doors.

"Break in!" Lozito shouted.

He escaped the corner, but Zorro hemmed him in again. He could feel Lozito's wrist tiring, slowing. And suddenly Zorro took a chance at a dangerous thrust, and won. His blade slipped beneath Lozito's guard, went home to the hilt, and was withdrawn crimson.

Zorro sprang through the window, raced and stumbled into the darkness and got to his horse. There was tumult behind him as the door was smashed down and the wounded man found. Through the night Zorro rode carefully, circling the pueblo, coming finally to where the faithful Bernardo waited for him.

He dismounted and reeled. "I am wounded," Zorro said. "Help me off with my costume and weapons, get me into the house, and hasten to get Fray Felipe, that he may come and dress my wound. Nobody else must know!"

THE FOLLOWING afternoon, Pablo Urista appeared at the Vega house and asked to see Don Diego. He was escorted to a chamber where Diego was in bed, the covers draping his left shoulder and arm.

"I am a little indisposed, señor, and decided not to go out today," Diego apologized. "You have business with me?"

"Zorro fought Lozito last night, and Lozito has a fatal wound, Don Diego.

The local magistrate has agreed to let me sell the peonage contract I have for the girl, Anita, daughter of Gustavo. I give you first chance."

They arranged a price.

"Fetch the girl, and I'll have the gold for you," Diego told him, "Do it at once, for I intend to leave for the ranch in the cool of the evening."

Urista hurried away. Fray Felipe and Bernardo came to the chamber.

"At the rancho, no one will know of my wound until it is healed," Diego explained. "Let them think I have a touch of fever. Padre, I have looked upon danger many times, but last night I looked at death. I will communicate with the Cabrillos and get the release of the girl's father, and the two can return to their hut and continue their normal lives. I'll take the girl to the rancho until I have her father freed."

Then Diego Vega turned his back upon them and went to sleep.

Zorro Starts the New Year

Death stalks Don Diego Vega amidst the gay laughter of a fiesta!

AWAKENED by the sound of voices on the first day of the new year, Diego Vega arose from his couch shortly after dawn. This was a departure from his usual routine, for it was his habit to arise only after the sun had gladdened each new day for several hours.

Wrapping his silken robe around his lithe body, he yawned and crossed the bedchamber to an open barred window and looked out through the patio arches and toward the huts of the peon house servants in the near distance.

Men and women of the huts were up and already going about their duties. The shrill voices of women came from the huge kitchen of the *rancho* house, and appetizing odors of cooking food were in the bracing morning air.

There had been much cooking throughout the day before, and there would be more today. Haunches of meat and fat fowls were to be roasted, *tortillas* baked in heaps, *enchiladas* to be made, little cakes and other dainty pastries to be prepared in large quantities. Skins would be filled with old wines drawn from the great casks in the cellars, and candied fruits, olives — the products of tree and vine — made ready.

This year, it was the turn of those at Rancho Vega to be hosts for a New Year's *fiesta* in the patio for neighboring Dons and members of their families, while musicians played and dancers whirled.

And at the same time, at long tables spread beneath the huge pepper trees at the edge of the orchard, the *vaqueros* and other workmen of the *rancho* would entertain their friends from other estates with a feast also.

Fray Felipe, the aged Franciscan padre from the chapel at Reina de Los Angeles, had arrived at the *rancho* the evening before on his riding mule. He would go around through the crowd, asking that all be blessed during the new year with health, peace and contentment, and material prosperity.

Now, as he stood before the open window, Diego heard his father's stentorian voice giving instructions and realized that Don Alejandro must have arisen long before him. Diego clapped his hands and the door of his bedchamber was pulled open by a peon house servant who had been awaiting the summons.

"Fetch me warm perfumed waters for bathing, immediately," Diego instructed him. "And may this new year be one of blessing and happiness for you."

The servant quickly knuckled his forehead in respectful salute. "And for you also, Don Diego," he replied. "Were all men in high places as kind and considerate as you and your father, the world would be a happier place in which to live."

It was the customary salutation, the usual words to say at the moment, but for once Diego Vega was struck with the real meaning the words conveyed if spoken with thought and sincerity.

Well he knew that there were some men of power and position, of good blood and station, who were not always kind and considerate toward those in lesser circumstances — some who were the social equals of Diego and his father before the world but whose acts shamed others of the caste to which they belonged. Such lowered the prestige of men of good birth and breeding and brought all into a state of disrepute.

Diego had retired the night before considering a certain problem which confronted him in regard to such a man, and had awakened still thinking of it, and the problem was not yet solved in his mind.

He bathed and dressed quickly and hurried to the big main room of the sprawling adobe *rancho* house, where the table was prepared for the morning meal. A smiling servant greeted him. He ate alone, for his father had breakfasted already and Fray Felipe would not eat until after his mass.

BREAKFAST over, Diego strolled through the patio and went in search of his father, finally locating him behind the huts watching a peon stable hand examine the cut leg of a horse.

"Diego, my son!" proud old Don Alejandro greeted, as the peon led the horse away. "A good new year to you! May you live to see many more years start their march into eternity!"

He embraced Diego, then stood back and regarded him fondly, chuckling.

"My son, Diego," he said. "People think he is only a spineless fop, a dreamer and reader of the poets, a *caballero* without spirit. Little do they think that he is also Senor Zorro, who rides and fights like a fiend and makes fools of the troopers who pursue him."

"Let us hope my secret is never discovered," Diego replied, smiling. "I have no itch to swing at the end of a rope and bring disgrace upon you and others of our kind."

Don Alejandro's face clouded. "As one of our kind is doing now. Considering Carlos Fierro — " he hinted.

"I have been thinking of him and his recent actions," Diego said. "The situation is difficult."

"I agree. But something must be done before he disgraces men of breeding. At times I think he has gone insane. He is the last of a fine family; his father was a splendid man. But Carlos Fierro is dragging the family name in filth, disgracing himself and his caste."

"A small amount of such actions can pass without traders, peons and natives thinking any more of it than that a highborn is having some fun," Diego observed. "But if he continues, they will lift their brows and remark that people like us are not the gentlemanly, dignified, respectable people they should be."

"True, Diego. Carlos Fierro drinks and gambles to excess, engages in brawls with men beneath him, and his affairs with peon girls and even native wenches are becoming notorious. Were he only a common fellow, he could be handled quickly — say by Zorro. But, being what he is — "

"Zorro has a problem," Diego said. He always spoke of Zorro as quite another person. "Before now, he has punished rogues for mistreating and swindling the peons and natives and oppressing the poor and helpless. But for him to punish a man with gentle blood in his veins — "

"It would have to be done in a clever manner, Diego," his father said. "Continue to think of the problem and perhaps a solution will occur to you."

Fray Felipe shuffled up to them, the wind whipping his robe around his emaciated form, and gave them his blessing. He, too, knew Diego was Zorro. And he knew about Carlos Fierro.

Scion of a noble family, Carlos Fierro was the last member of it now, and the line would die out unless he married and had children. He held broad acres and had a money chest filled with gold, and his social standing equaled that of any of the aristocratic Dons.

He was now thirty-five, and still unmarried. Tall, strong in body, proud and arrogant, with a streak of cruelty in him — such things could be expected to a certain degree in such a man. But Carlos Fierro was traveling too far and fast along the wrong road.

He did not seem to care anything about the opinions of others regarding himself. He did things that would have disgraced even a man who did not have the responsibility of holding up his caste as a pattern for decent living. And he could not be taken to task for his actions, like an ordinary man.

Fray Felipe had been unable to do anything with him, for he scorned spiritual advice. And for a *caballero* near his own age to remonstrate with him would mean only a duel — and Carlos Fierro already had slain one man and badly wounded two others in duels.

Yet only a man of his own caste could attend to him properly. The soldiers kept hands off because of Fierro's wealth and standing and his friendship for the Governor, who was inclined to be dissolute himself.

Unscrupulous traders, wanderers along the highway, gamblers and their ilk were grinning as they watched a man of gentle blood making a fool of himself like a base-born rogue, descending to their own level.

DON ALEJANDRO spoke now, his eyes piercing as he said:

"I have had word concerning Carlos Fierro. As late as midnight, he was in the notorious house of pleasure recently opened in Reina de Los Angeles, drinking and gambling."

"And no doubt he will come here to the *rancho* today for the fiesta," Diego said.

"We can be sure of that," his father replied. "Carlos Fierro is not so far gone along the road to damnation that he will absent himself from the *fiesta* here and put an affront upon us. I only hope he will do nothing while here to disgrace us and himself."

Fray Felipe spoke bluntly: "It is an affair for Zorro."

"A delicate affair," Diego replied. "Never before has Zorro been called on to punish one of his own class. Carlos Fierro cannot be whipped like a common trickster."

"Why not? He has cheapened himself," the padre said.

"A touch of the lash would bruise his pride," Zorro admitted. "But it would also make him a furious man-killing beast. He would revenge himself on peons and natives. He would resent even a word of rebuke. Scoundrel though he is turning out to be — he is of gentle blood."

"I understand, Diego, how you would dislike to put a lash to the back of one of your own kind," the padre told him. "And, as you say, he would resent rebuke. And that would mean an affair of pistols or blades. If the thing could be done in some way without the spilling of human blood on the first day of the new year — "

"I shall try to think of something," Diego promised.

Loud voices, cheers and the sudden clatter of hoofbeats made the trio turn and look toward the house. Sergeant Manuel Garcia, attached to the *presidio* at Reina de Los Angeles, was arriving with four of his troopers to be guests at the *fiesta* and preserve order among the *vaqueros* and *rancho* workmen.

Diego smiled and started toward the house to make the burly sergeant welcome. Between these men of entirely different stations in life was a strange friendship. Garcia would have defended Diego Vega against a mob at risk of his life. And Diego liked to buy wine for the sergeant at the tavern in Reina de Los Angeles and listen to his humorous boasting.

Garcia had no suspicion that the masked Zorro he often had pursued and never had caught, with whom he even had crossed blades much to his discomfort, was his friend Diego Vega. Like others, the sergeant believed Diego was a lifeless young man whose greatest exertion was reading poetry.

Diego greeted Garcia and the troopers, and the soldiers rode to the stables to put up their mounts and join the feasting. They were acclaimed with wild shouts by the *vaqueros* and *rancho* workmen.

Guests began arriving at the *rancho* at an early hour. *Vaqueros* rode in astride half-wild horses. Workmen came afoot. With young *caballeros* on horseback attending them, carriages arrived from other *ranchos,* and from them descended proud old Dons and their wives and pretty, flirtatious daughters.

Throughout the morning, Diego was busy assisting his father in making the guests welcome. He watched particularly for the carriage of Don Marcos Apodaca, who had a *rancho* a few miles away. Diego knew the twins would be with him — Juan and Inez Apodaca, close friends of Diego from childhood. He and Juan were companions, and between Diego and Inez was a friendship that, in time, might ripen into love and link the two families in strong bond.

Finally the carriage, with Juan riding beside it, rolled down the lane to stop in front of the house. Juan dismounted and slapped Diego on his back.

Don Marcos got down from the carriage and stepped aside to allow Diego to help Inez alight.

Other carriages came, and more riders, and Diego was kept busy greeting his guests. And finally Carlos Fierro arrived, riding a spirited horse.

BY THE time Fierro reached the *rancho* house, the musicians were playing in the patio and people already were feasting in the patio and under the trees at the edge of the orchard.

Diego was in front of the house to greet Carlos Fierro alone, his father having gone to take his position at the head of the first table in the patio to open the feast.

Fierro howled for a peon to care for his horse, and staggered slightly as he dismounted and approached to receive Diego's greeting. The man's face was aflame with liquor and it was rank upon his breath. But his conduct was all that could have been wished otherwise.

Diego went with him into the patio, and Carlos Fierro bowed first to Don Alejandro and then to the others and took his place at the table. As the feasting began anew, the musicians played and a dancer appeared.

She was a peon girl of beauty and grace who danced barefooted on the flagstones of the patio, her colored skirts swirling around her shapely limbs and undulating hips. She smiled as she danced, toyed with a red rose, and finished with a low bow as she stood panting against the patio wall.

The guests applauded, and, coins were tossed toward her. An elderly peon — her father, Pedro — began gathering the coins.

"She is named Bonita," some guest said. "I have seen her dance before. She keeps her father's hut — her mother is dead. Her father works wherever he can."

Bonita smiled and bowed again, and ran beneath an arch to hurry to those feasting beneath the pepper trees and dance for them also. And Diego saw Carlos Fierro get up and start following her.

Others noticed it also, and their glances at one another were eloquent. Fat señoras lifted their eyebrows, the gentlemen at the table narrowed their eyes, and the senoritas allowed their lids to droop as they pretended they had seen nothing.

Fray Felipe excused himself and shuffled through the archway after Fierro. Later, when he could manage to get away after dancing with Inez and a few other girls, Diego walked toward the orchard.

The *vaqueros* and workmen and their friends were laughing and shouting as they brandished wine mugs. Men were playing a lively dance on their guitars. And Carlos Fierro was dancing with Bonita, the peon girl, with an abandon that a *caballero* never should have shown at such a time.

Diego frowned as he walked on, answering the respectful greetings of those who bowed to him. He leaned against the bole of a pepper tree to watch. Sergeant Garcia, waving a wine mug, approached and stopped beside him.

"It ill becomes me to speak of my betters," the burly sergeant whispered, "and the gentleman has friends in high places in Monterey — "

"I understand, Garcia," Diego interrupted. "What is to be done?"

"I would not dare touch him for short of murder, Don Diego, unless a man of gentle blood called upon me to do so."

"And that is to be avoided."

"We can only hope that, before he commits an indiscretion, he will become quiet from the liquor he has taken. He has been swilling wine, but no doubt was well filled with brandy before coming to the *rancho.* "

The musicians had ceased playing and Bonita was bowing. As they watched, Carlos Fierro darted to the girl, seized her in his arms, began whispering in her ear. Fright came into her face and she glanced swiftly at Diego and the sergeant as if asking for their help.

Then Carlos Fierro kissed her before them all. It was not a madcap kiss such as might be given on such an occasion, without any special meaning. He bent her back and seized upon her lips, and his eyes were aflame as he kissed her while she fought to be free of him — kissed her in such a manner that there was sudden silence around the tables and the *vaqueros* and their friends looked at one another questioningly.

The girl broke away from him finally and ran, sobbing as her bare feet carried her around the tables and further away from him. Carlos Fierro was too intoxicated to pursue. He laughed and sank upon a bench and called for wine.

"Watch," Diego told Garcia. "Let me know if he molests the girl. I know of her. She is a decent girl, and her father is at honest workman. Had Fierro been a man of ordinary standing, she would have slapped him."

THE sergeant sauntered away, and Diego turned to go back to the patio, and found Juan Apodaca beside him.

"The swine!" Juan said. "Something must be done concerning him."

"Do not show your resentment when he is looking," Diego warned. "You would be easy meat for his blade!"

They walked back to the patio together. The guests were either sitting at the table or dancing, and old Don Alejandro was beaming upon them, well satisfied so far with his *fiesta*.

Word of what had happened was soon circulated among the patio guests. Servants heaped the tables with more food, and the musicians played, and the gentlemen sipped wine and everybody visited and related gossip.

Diego looked up presently and saw Sergeant Garcia through one of the archways, and got up and hurried to him when the sergeant gestured.

"Don Carlos Fierro is harmless for the moment," the sergeant reported. "I am thankful he did not have to be handled."

"What is he doing, and where is he?" Diego asked.

"Overcome with wine, he staggered to one of the stables and went to sleep on a heap of straw, like — " The sergeant hesitated.

"Like a drunken peon or native," Diego ended, his eyes flaming. "Perhaps he will cause no disturbance."

Garcia saluted and went back to the orchard, and Diego noticed that one of the troopers was on watch near the stables.

The afternoon was waning. The merriment under the trees was growing, and the *vaqueros* and their friends would drink and celebrate the new year until almost dawn, Diego knew.

But some of the others would be leaving for their homes before long, since they had far to ride and drive. Diego was hoping the Apodacas would be among the last to leave, that he would have a little time alone with Inez and Juan while their fathers talked of old days.

Only a few were left in the patio as the night darkened and flaring torches were set alight in the patio and candles in the house. Down at the edge of the orchard the *vaqueros* had built a fire and were dancing around it.

Diego wandered outside the patio and watched for a time, until he saw Bernardo, his giant mute peon bodyservant, and beckoned him. Bernardo was the last of the three human beings who knew that Diego was Zorro — Bernardo the loyal servant who cared for Zorro's black horse, costume and weapons.

"You have been enjoying yourself, Bernardo?" Diego asked.

The mute made a harsh sound in his throat and bobbed his head.

"I will have no need for you this evening." Diego spoke in a voice loud enough to be heard by some in the patio. But in a whisper, he added: "Zorro rides tonight. Have everything ready!"

Bernardo's eyes gleamed. He knuckled his forehead and strolled away and Diego went back into the patio, brushing his nostrils with a scented silk handkerchief, stifling a yawn, pretending to be the lifeless fop people thought him to be.

Inez was talking to some of the women, and Diego and Juan stood inside an arch and made talk about nothing much at all, enjoying each other's company. Again Garcia approached, and Diego excused himself and went to meet him.

"Don Carlos is awake," the sergeant reported. "He is down at the fire. I am afraid, Don Diego, that he intends to steal the dancing girl, Bonita. He was urging her to work in his house, and she refused, and Don Carlos cuffed her father aside when he would have taken the girl away."

"Try to guard her in some manner, Garcia," Diego said, frowning. "Use your own judgment."

Diego rejoined Juan, and they went to a table and sat beside Inez, and the three of them talked as they sipped wine and ate little cakes. And into the patio, after a time, came Carlos Fierro, just as the musicians began playing another dance tune.

FIERRO reeled along the table and stopped beside Inez and bowed.

"Dance with me," he begged.

Her eyes flamed at him. "Not this evening, señor!"

It was an affront to ask her, after carrying on as he had been with a peon dancing girl. Before Diego or Don Alejandro could speak, old Don Marcos Apodaca was on his feet, shaking with rage.

"You forget yourself, Fierro!" Apodaca cried. "My daughter does not dance with a man in your present condition. Nor does she dance with one who hugs and kisses a peon girl against her will."

"So?" Fierro lurched nearer. "You are an old man, Don Marcos, so it is impossible that I demand you fight me for your words. But you have a son — "

Juan sprang forward, a stripling who knew little of handling a blade. His hand cracked against Carlos Fierro's cheek.

Fierro's eyes gleamed in the light of the nearest torch. "At dawn, at the usual place on the San Gabriel road," he said. "Please do not keep me waiting."

"I'll be there before you!" Juan raged. "Try to be sober enough to draw blade from scabbard!"

Fierro took a couple of steps backward and bowed. Inez was weeping softly and the older women were gathering around her. The men crowded forward, old Don Alejandro at their head.

"Señor Fierro, this is a sad occurrence," Don Alejandro told him. "To my mind, you have struck the bottom of the downward path. I ask you to apologize to my guests."

"A Fierro apologizes to no one, señor."

"Then I must ask you to leave my house, señor, and keep away from it hereafter." Don Alejandro's voice rang out like that of a young man. "Perhaps it would be better if you returned to your friends, those who seem to be your own kind — the *vaqueros* and peon workmen at the edge of the orchard."

Fierro's eyes blazed anew. "You are an old man, Don Alejandro Vega, he said, "and so I cannot properly challenge you. But you too have a son to take your battles upon his thin shoulders — though no doubt you are ashamed to call such a weakling your son."

Now it was Diego's hand which cracked against Carlos Fierro's face.

"Ah!" Fierro smiled. "You also, señor, at the usual place on the San Gabriel road at dawn. You and Juan Apodaca can draw straws to decide which of you I shall kill first."

Fierro glared at them all, turned and reeled out of the patio. By the light of the torches at first, and then by the light of a full moon as he passed from the patio, they saw him going toward the stables shouting for his horse.

Those in the patio crowded around Diego and Juan. Neither would have much chance against Fierro, they thought, even if Fierro was staggering because of wine. They were as good as dead, or seriously wounded, already.

"Apodaca, you and your children will remain here for the night," Don Alejandro said. "Perhaps our sons should retire now and get some rest … Juan, I'll have you shown to a chamber. Both of you will want to be alone with your thoughts at such a time. I'll see that neither of you is disturbed."

Don Alejandro had caught a glance from Diego and knew the latter wanted to be free to escape the house unseen. And Diego walked to the table and took a sip of wine, bowed to them all, and turned away languidly.

"You others will kindly continue as if nothing has happened," he heard his father saying. "Let nothing mar our *fiesta.*"

DIEGO left the house unseen through a side door. He slipped quickly past the stables, stopped once in a dark spot to see Carlos Fierro get into his saddle and start toward the scene of merrymaking beneath the pepper trees.

Diego hurried on, and behind an abandoned storehouse some distance away found Bernardo waiting for him with Zorro's horse saddled and ready. Diego slipped on the baggy Zorro costume over his other clothing, put on the mask, buckled on Zorro's blade, put a pistol into his sash, and mounted. Bernardo handed him his long black whip, which Zorro fastened to the pommel of his saddle.

"You will wait here for my return," he instructed Bernardo. "Be prepared to take the horse as usual."

Keeping carefully in the dark shadows, Zorro rode around the end of the orchard farthest from the fire. He stopped in a spot of darkness and looked back. There was a commotion. He heard a girl scream. He heard the hoarse voices of excited men, then a raucous laugh and the pounding of a horse's hoofs against the hard ground.

Caries Fierro, Zorro guessed, had Bonita, the peon dancing girl, on his saddle before him.

Zorro knew in which direction Fierro would ride to come to his own *rancho* far beyond the San Gabriel Mission. And now he touched spurs to his big black horse and cut across a hill and down the opposite slope, and so came into the road again far ahead of where Carlos Fierro was riding.

Fierro was taking his time about it. Hidden behind a ledge of rock, Zorro could hear the man's laughter in the distance and the girl's tearful entreaties to be put upon the ground and left behind.

Hoofbeats came nearer, and he saw Fierro and his prisoner ride slowly through a wide streak of the bright moonlight and come on along the trail.

At the proper moment, Zorro jumped his horse from his hiding place and barred the way.

"Stop there!" he called in a stern voice.

Fierro pulled up abruptly, startled, and the girl screamed again at sight of the masked rider in the moonlight.

"What is this?" Fierro cried. "Who are you?"

"Zorro!"

"You are — What did you say? Zorro? The rogue the troopers are always chasing?"

"The same."

"This is a robbery, I presume? And do you think you will take the jewels I am wearing at my throat without fighting for them?"

"Run away, senorita," Zorro ordered. "Quickly!"

"Let the girl down," Zorro ordered. "You take no girl against her will while I am near, señor!"

"I am Don Carlos Fierro — "

"So I know," Zorro interrupted. "You are a disgrace to your name and lineage. Drunken brawler, stealer of girls — you, a Fierro!"

Carlos Fierro almost hurled the girl to the ground, and she scrambled to her feet and darted to the side of the trail.

"Run away, señorita," Zorro ordered. "Back whence you came, quickly!"

Fierro already was whipping blade from scabbard. And now Zorro wheeled his horse and did the same as Fierro charged. He did not try to use the pistol.

He did not want to slay this man, if such an act could be avoided, and mar the beginning of a new year by shedding blood. But he knew Fierro's reputation as a swordsman and that this would be no easy task.

The girl, screaming, ran on into the shadows and down the road. Fierro charged again, and their blades met and rang. And then they were fighting from horseback as their mounts wheeled and reared.

"To the ground, rogue! I dare you!" Fierro shouted.

He spurred a short distance away and sprang from his saddle when he saw Zorro was doing the same. But it was a foul move, for Fierro had taken a pistol from his saddlebag, and now he aimed and fired and the ball sang past Zorro's head, only a few inches away.

"I could pistol you now, poltroon," Zorro cried at him. "But we'll settle it with blades!"

THEY ran together and met in a patch of bright moonlight where the ground was hard and even beside the trail. Fierro attacked furiously and pressed Zorro back for a distance. And then, having felt out the other's wrist, Zorro stood ground and fought with his best skill.

He felt Fierro's blade pass through the left sleeve of his costume and almost scratch the skin. He tried in vain to make the thrust he wished to make. His wrist was tiring and his breathing was becoming labored.

He had to be victor in this, he was telling himself. He had to triumph over this dissolute bearer of a noble name. For him to fail would mean that Diego Vega would be unmasked as Zorro, that his life would be forfeit if he did not die, that perhaps his father's estates would be seized by the Governor on a charge of treason —

He ceased thinking about it and took the offensive. He knew that Fierro was tiring, too. The life he had led recently, the drinking he had done, the loss of sleep — all had weakened him. Slowly, Zorro drove Fierro before him, meeting every turn Fierro tried to make, keeping him in the bright moonlight where he would be a fair target.

In the distance he heard horses galloping. And down wind came the hoarse voice of Sergeant Garcia.

"Forward! Overtake him! The girl must be saved!"

Zorro guessed the answer to that. Garcia and his troopers had rushed to saddle their mounts after the abduction of the girl, and now were riding down upon the scene. And Zorro had no intention of being taken by the troopers, or of being hanged as the Governor had sworn Zorro would be.

Fierro began shouting, “Here, to me! Zorro is here!”

Zorro heard Sergeant Garcia’s startled answer, and the hoofbeats thundered as the troopers came on. Again Zorro pressed the fighting. He parried a wild thrust and sent his own blade home, trying to wound badly but not to slay. As Carlos Fierro dropped his blade and sagged to the ground, Zorro whirled around and sprinted toward his black horse.

He was in saddle and riding furiously by the time the troopers stopped where Fierro was stretched on the ground, with his mount standing not far away. Zorro could hear Garcia shouting as he rode around behind a ledge of rock, got to soft ground and gave the black the spurs.

The pursuit went in the wrong direction. Riding carefully, Zorro circled and finally got upon Rancho Vega land, and went cautiously to where the loyal Bernardo was waiting.

“Take care of everything,” Zorro ordered.

He tossed Bernardo the reins, got out of his costume and put his weapons aside, and hurried toward the *rancho* house. No one was near the huts, for the merriment continued by the fire at the orchard’s edge, even the house servants being there now.

Don Diego Vega got inside the house and went noiselessly to his own rooms. He undressed swiftly and donned his night clothing, put on his robe and sat beside a window.

Within half an hour, a rider galloped down the lane and stopped at the house. The knocker of the front door sounded. Diego got up and stretched and paced the room. He ran his fingers through his hair to muss it and contrived to get a sleepy expression in his face.

He heard voices sounding through the house and caught the gleam of candles alight when he glanced through the window. And finally came a pounding upon the door of his bedchamber.

“Diego! My son!” he heard his father call.

Diego went across the room again and pulled the door open. Light from the candles struck his face and he yawned. He saw his father and Fray Felipe, with others behind them, including Marcos Apodaca and his son, Juan.

“What has happened, my father?” Diego asked.

“Sergeant Garcia has sent us news. It appears, Diego, that Zorro met Carlos Fierro on the highway and fought with him. And Zorro wounded him badly and escaped. The troopers have taken Fierro on to the mission in a cart, so the padres can attend to his wound."

"Is it serious?" Diego asked.

"So serious that he will no doubt be confined to his bed for some time," Don Alejandro replied. "There will be no duels at the usual place on the San Gabriel road in the morning."

"Perhaps it is for the best," Diego said, yawning again. "Have the ladies retired?"

"All have gone home, my son, except Inez. And she is in her room giving thanks with her dueñña because Juan's life has been spared."

"Then it will be safe for me to come out, dressed as I am, and have a sip of wine," Diego said. "I feel the need of it."

"Brandy should be better, under the circumstances," his father replied, smiling slightly. "Come on out, my son!"

Hangnoose Reward

Don Diego's lash sings a biting tune in the moonlight to bring justice to a tricky scoundrel!

AN HOUR before dawn, a rider clattered into the pueblo of Reina de Los Angeles and brought his jaded riding mule to a stop in front of the barracks. The eyes of the rider, who was a tattered peon, bulged with excitement. As he jumped from the mule's bare back and lurched toward the guard in front of the door, he was panting as if he had been running instead of his mule.

"They've caught him! I must see the *commandante* — no time to be lost," the rider gasped.

Half an hour later, Sergeant Manuel Garcia and four of his troopers left the barracks, riding at top speed, and went south on the road to San Juan Capistrano.

The arrival of the rider and the departure of the soldiers only made a few sleepers turn over on their beds and mumble at being disturbed. Riders were always tearing into the pueblo like madmen, and the troopers were always rushing away to chase some unfortunate who had transgressed the laws.

But, later in the day, all the inhabitants of the pueblo became excited also and gathered in groups around the plaza, and in front of the tavern and warehouses, to discuss what had happened.

Diego Vega, yawning and shuffling, was abroad at the moment having left his father's house to go to the chapel and consider with aged Fray Felipe, his confessor, the state of his soul. He blinked in the bright sunshine, brushed his nostrils with his scented handkerchief, and seemed to be still half asleep —

Zorro drove the frightened man along the corridor

which he was not.

He heard the turmoil in the plaza before he could see what was occurring and learn its cause, for he was walking behind a row of buildings. When he did reach the corner of the plaza, he came to a quick stop to survey the scene.

Peons and natives were running from every direction. Men of business were standing in front of their establishments talking and making excited gestures. Into the plaza from the San Juan Capistrano road, came an unusual cavalcade.

Burly, bombastic Sergeant Garcia rode ahead. Behind him came his four troopers in the form of a square. In their midst was a prisoner, a man with his wrists lashed behind his back and his ankles fastened beneath his mount's belly.

The mount was a powerful black horse. The prisoner was dressed entirely in black, with an empty scabbard at his side — Garcia having taken the blade out of it — and a disarranged sash which revealed plainly enough that a pistol and Perhaps a knife had been yanked from beneath its folds.

Diego Vega moved closer and watched, listening to the voices of the excited men around him. He strolled toward the tavern and finally stopped almost directly in front of it. The fat tavern keeper stood only a few feet away.

"What is it, señor?" Diego asked him. "Why this tumult and shouting? What have the soldiers been up to now?"

"Ah! Don Diego! 'Tis a happy day, no doubt! Zorro has been captured."

"Zorro? You mean the confounded fellow who rides around at night with a black mask over his face and always has the soldiers chasing him?"

"The same, Don Diego. There is a rich reward offered for his capture — and there he is! Does he not look like a vicious rascal? Now men can look at his face and learn his identity. There will be a public hanging of him in a couple of days, as soon as our *magistrado* returns from a trip to Santa Barbara."

"The soldiers have finally caught him?" Diego asked.

LOUDLY the tavern keeper laughed. "Not so, Don Diego! And that is why our good Sergeant Garcia looks so angry, for he will not get the reward. Zorro was caught last night by a certain trader who was camped beside the road a few miles out, one José Mora. We hear that Zorro tried to rob him, and the trader caught him off guard and subdued him. Ah, well, this excitement will be good for my business."

The tavern keeper waddled away to enter his establishment. Diego yawned and strolled on toward the chapel. So Zorro had been captured! The man who righted wrongs for the downtrodden had been taken and would be hanged as a highwayman. Diego quickened his stride and hurried on to his meeting with Fray Felipe. Here was something that called for immediate and thorough investigation.

For Diego Vega himself was Zorro.

As he started to enter the chapel, Fray Felipe emerged.

A trooper was with him and hurried away toward the barracks when the old padre spoke to him.

"Ah, Diego, my son, I am glad to find you here," Fray Felipe said. "It saves me sending a messenger for you. Do you know — ?"

"I have just heard," Diego said in low tones.

Frey Felipe was one of three persons who knew what Diego Vega was Zorro. The second was his father and the third was his mute peon body-servant, Bernardo.

"Come with me," Fray Felipe ordered. As they strode side by side, he whispered: "The man under arrest is a witless fellow known as Big Carlos for his size and strength. You and I, my son, know he is not Zorro. I had thought this was an error made by the soldiers, until a moment ago."

"A moment ago, padre?" Diego echoed.

"The trooper came for me. Sergeant Garcia sent him. It seems this Big Carlos wants to make a full confession, and the sergeant wants me to be present, since our *magistrado* is away on a visit."

"But how can he confess — " Diego began, and stopped.

"Yes, how can he?" the padre questioned. "There is some mystery here, Diego, and that is why I want you with me."

They went to Garcia's office in the barracks.

"Ah, Don Diego, my friend!" the burly sergeant greeted. "I am glad that you, a man of standing, are here with the padre. The fellow is hot to confess, he informs me. Fray Felipe, I want you to listen, and question him if you wish. Don Diego, do me the pleasure of listening also, since you would be an excellent witness if anything goes amiss."

Sergeant Garcia led them through a dank corridor, a trooper unlocked a barred door, and presently they stood before the door of a cell.

"Arise, Big Carlos!" Garcia ordered. "Here is a padre to see you and hear you confess, and a young *caballero* also."

The man in the cell got to his feet and neared the door. He was a massive fellow, and his face betrayed the fact that he might have an amount of animal cunning but was not intellectual in a normal degree.

"Are you the highwayman known as Zorro? Are you the man who has ridden masked through the countryside and — "

"I am Zorro!" Big Carlos interrupted. "You have caught me, but you will never hang me."

"Ha! I'll attend to that," Garcia replied. "So you are Zorro. And you were caught by the trader, José Mora?"

"He caught me, señor. I sought to rob him last night while he was alone in his camp. His two men had gone to the tavern in San Juan Capistrano to have some fun. He caught me off guard and tripped me and made me fall down. It stunned me, señor."

"A blow from a club on the head should not stun a big ox like you," Garcia declared.

"José Mora tied my hands behind my back and threatened me with his pistol, señor. A man came riding by, and Señor Juan told him to fetch the soldiers. That is all. I am Zorro. You have caught me, but you will never hang me."

"The fool says the same thing over and over like a parrot," Garcia complained. "You have heard him, Fray Felipe? Don Diego? You will remember his public confession?"

Diego nodded in assent. "I heard him," Fray Felipe said. "Do me a favor, sergeant. Let me speak to this man alone and see if I can gather more information for you. Sometimes the sight of a uniform makes a wretch frightened and speechless."

"A good idea. Talk to him as long as you desire."

"And allow Don Diego to remain with me. Two witnesses are better than one, and Don Diego being a Vega — "

"Certainly," Garcia broke in. "I thank you, Don Diego, for going to the trouble. I must hurry to the office and greet this José Mora, who caught the fellow. My ears will ring, no doubt, with the tale of his quickness and bravery. I shudder at the thought. And to think a rascal like this trader will get the Governor's reward!" Garcia shuddered and hurried through the door and down the corridor.

Fray Felipe and Diego stepped closer to the barred door of the cell and the padre beckoned for Big Carlos to come nearer.

"My son, you are in sore trouble," the padre said. "Do you realize the possible consequence of your acts?"

"You will never hang me!" Big Carlos repeated.

"But you are a prisoner, and have declared you are Zorro. How do you expect to escape?"

A gleam came into the prisoner's eyes and he laughed softly. "Zorro has many tricks," he said. "Tell me, padre, will the trader, José Mora, get the rich reward?"

"Probably," Fray Felipe replied.

"And when will it be given him?"

"After you have been hanged," Diego put in. "After you have been put in the ground and a lot of papers signed and all that,"

"What is that you say?" Big Carlos gripped the bars and tried to shake them. Before his animal fury, Fray Felipe and Diego retreated a step.

"What ails you?" Diego asked. "What do you care about the reward? Can you not understand, señor, that you are to stretch rope, have the life choked out of you, because you are Zorro? As for the reward, such things take time. Officials have to sign documents, and one must bring the money to this trader. But you'll be dead before all that happens."

"No — no!" Big Carlos yelled.

"Be quiet!" Diego cautioned.

THE guard at the door in the corridor was looking toward them, for he had heard Big Carlos' bellowings. "Do you need help there?" he called.

"Not at all, señor," Diego replied. "Do not concern yourself. We merely said something that enraged this fellow."

A sudden change had come over Big Carlos. He shook his head like a bewildered beast and seemed to be trying to do some concentrated thinking. He looked at the Fray.

"Tell me the truth, padre," he begged. "If they do not hang me, the trader will not get the reward — is that so?"

"It is so. But why — ?" Fray Felipe began.

"But I cannot understand, padre. That makes a great difference in — in everything. Perhaps it is some trick. That is not like I was told."

"Speak softly," Fray Felipe cautioned. "We are your friends, Big Carlos. If you have been tricked, perhaps we can help you. Do not let the guard hear you. How can you have been tricked? For a long time, soldiers have pursued Zorro, and a reward has been offered for his capture. You say you are Zorro. So where does the trick come in?"

"I am not Zorro, really."

"What is this?" Diego asked. He spoke like a conspirator. "Speak softly, as the padre said. This shall be our secret."

"I am not Zorro. How could I be? I do not know how to fight with a blade. I never fired a pistol. I am Big Carlos, a peon. I have been working near San Diego de Alcalá, and have been walking along the highway to get to Santa Barbara, where I have a brother."

"If you are not Zorro, why did you confess to being him?" Fray Felipe questioned.

"José Mora planned it all, padre. He explained how easy it would be. He got me the horse and the black clothes and mask, and the sword and pistol and knife."

"Why should he do that?" Diego asked.

Big Carlos' eyes gleamed again. "Do you not see the clever plot? It was to be pretended that I had tried to rob him and he had caught me and sent for the soldiers. José Mora would claim the reward, and we would divide it."

"How could you divide it when you are in jail? And since he will not get the reward until after you have been hanged, how would you benefit?"

"He was to get the reward, and then I was to escape," Big Carlos explained. "I would be hidden for a few days and then helped to go on to Santa Barbara, or maybe Monterey. And I would have gold. No more hard work. I would have fine clothes and plenty of food."

"How did you expect to escape?"

"I will not tell you. If I do not, José Mora will see that I escape though he does not get the reward."

"I fear very much, Carlos," the padre told him, "that you have been made a dupe. You let Mora make a fool of you. You confessed to being Zorro. Even I and Don Diego would have to testify to that. It is in my mind that the trader will let you go to your death, and then will collect the reward and have it all for himself. Have you known Mora long?"

"Only for a couple of days, padre. I was walking along the road, and he called me to his campfire and gave me food and wine to drink, and told me the plan."

"No doubt," Diego said to the padre, "the trader had been sitting there like a spider in a corner of his web, waiting for the proper victim to come along."

The expression in Big Carlos' face had changed. That face showed fear now.

"If I have been tricked — " he mouthed.

"Tell me quickly — how did you expect to escape?" the padre ordered.

"José Mora explained it to me. The peons and natives love Zorro. José Mora is to stir them up. They will come here to the barracks and drive the soldiers away, and rescue me and take me up into the hills and hide me."

"Now I know you have been tricked," Diego told him. "Listen to me! If the peons and natives love Zorro, José Mora would not dare to stir them up to rescue you. Would they not tear Mora to pieces because he had captured Zorro, the man they love, and handed him over to the soldiers? And the sergeant has just told us that Mora is coming here. Do you understand? Coming here to give more evidence against you, probably, to send you to the rope so he can get the reward!"

Comprehension came to Big Carlos. "Call the sergeant! I'll tell him the truth!" he told Diego and the padre.

"The sergeant would not believe you, for you have already confessed,"

Diego said.

"What can I do? They will hang me — "

"After all you have said, they would not take your word against Mora's now. Nor will peons and natives come to rescue a false Zorro and some of them die in the fighting. I fear you are done for, Big Carlos, unless — "

"Unless what, señor?" Carlos asked.

"Unless the real Zorro learns of your predicament and comes to rescue you himself," Diego Vega replied. He glanced meaningly at Fray Felipe and he spoke ....

WHISPERING swift sentences, Diego and the padre went down the corridor, through the barred and guarded door and toward Sergeant Garcia's office, which in reality was that of his superior officer. But the *commandante* was in Monterey on official business, and Garcia ruled in Reina de Los Angeles during his absence.

They found José Mora with the sergeant. Mora's air was that of a hero. He was short, fat, a little too well dressed for a trader. Jeweled rings were on his fat, dirty fingers and gold rings fastened through the lobes of his ears.

Sergeant Garcia introduced Diego and the padre to Mora, in the sergeant's manner something apologetic for having to do so.

" 'Twas not difficult," Mora was declaring. "The masked fellow threatened me, and I acted alarmed. I pretended to be getting a pouch of money from my cart. He was foolish enough to turn aside — perhaps he thought he heard somebody approaching. A bludgeon happened to be on the cart. I grasped it and whirled and struck him down."

"Yet there is no bump on his head and he does not complain of a headache," Garcia protested.

"Ah, perhaps he has a thick skull. He looks more animal than man," Mora replied. "However, now you have him, and no doubt will hang him. You say he has confessed fully, sergeant?"

"He says he is Zorro," Garcia growled. "Also, he declares that never will we hang him."

Mora chuckled. "I think my sergeant, that we can leave that to you. When will the *magistrado* return?"

"In two days' time. He must pass sentence," Garcia replied, "though in this case it will be only a formality, since the rogue has confessed. Fray Felipe and Don Diego heard him admit that he is Zorro."

Mora fawned on Diego. "I have heard much of your famed family, señor, and am pleased to meet you personally. It is a great honor," he said.

"No doubt," Diego observed. He brushed his nostrils with his scented handkerchief as if to drown a stench.

"I have just moved my camp to within half a mile of the pueblo," Mora continued. "My two men will guard it while I am absent. No doubt I'll spend most of my time in town except the nights. I shall be honored, Don Diego, if you drop in at my camp at any time. I may have some goods that will interest you."

"Our merchants here have excellent stocks," Diego observed.

Mora finally felt the chill in the air. He arose and bowed to Garcia, to the padre, to Diego.

"I must get to the tavern," the trader said. "Free wine will be expected of me, no doubt. Since this locality appears to be a fortunate one for me, perhaps I shall decide to erect a building here and open a trading post."

He backed to the door, bowed again, and went out. Sergeant Garcia closed the door after him and inelegantly spat.

"A rogue!" Garcia decided. "I dislike him, yet he has done a service."

When Fray Felipe and Diego left the barracks, they strolled to the plaza and across it to the chapel. "Have you plans, my son?" the padre asked.

"Padre, you know well that Diego Vega is too lazy to make plans concerning anything. But it is possible that Señor Zorro has plans."

"Ah. I wonder what they can be?"

"If you know nothing, padre, you can truthfully tell anybody concerned that you know nothing."

The padre's eyes twinkled. "That is true saying," he replied.

They parted, and Diego went into the tavern. As he did generally when he visited the place, he asked for a jar of crystallized honey, a thing he liked and which the big Vega rancho did not produce.

The main room of the tavern was filled. José Mora was celebrating his capture of Zorro by buying wine for all and basking in their fawning congratulations. The innkeeper's peon and native servants were rushing around with wineskins and mugs and carrying huge platters of cold food.

"This is good for your business," Diego observed.

"A windfall," the tavern keeper admitted. "I wish somebody would catch a rogue every day."

"I would not be in this Señor Mora's boots, however," Diego observed. His voice was loud enough for peons and naive servants near him to overhear.

"What is your meaning, Don Diego?"

"Zorro, though declared a highwayman, has done much to help peons and natives and avenge their wrongs. They should love him for it."

"No doubt they do," the tavern keeper said.

"This Mora, who looks to me like a consummate rogue — handed Zorro over to the soldiers, and no doubt he will be hanged and this Mora get the reward, blood money."

"That is true."

"If the peons and natives were to gather at the man's camp outside town during the night, they could drive away Mora's two helpers and capture Mora and punish him. It would be an easy thing to do."

"But the soldiers?"

"Ha! They could handle the man before the soldiers learned of it. All they have to do is pass the word and gather quietly and rush the camp. For one, I hope they will do something of the sort. I do not like rogues who dip their hands into blood money. Get me the honey, señor, and say nothing of what I have told you, else I'll be displeased. I do not care to have it seem that I appear in such a sordid business."

"You may be sure I'll keep a silent tongue, Don Diego."

As the tavern keeper got the pot of honey, Diego was thinking that some of the peon and native servants had overheard what he had said, as he had intended them to. The word would spread like wildfire. A leader would appear. There would be a mob at the trader's camp before another dawn. And Zorro would have work to do ....

IT WAS a dark night, which suited Zorro's purpose. At home, Diego had whispered to Bernardo, his mute servant, that Zorro was to ride at a certain time. Bernardo had everything ready including Zorro's black horse, costume and weapons.

Diego slipped noiselessly from the house and went to the hidden rendezvous, and there became Zorro by slipping the black costume over his other clothes, putting on his mask, blade and pistol, and hooking his heavy whip to his saddle.

There was a huge bonfire in the plaza and men were drinking and dancing around it. A couple of troopers watched them. The others were at the barracks resting. Sergeant Garcia was at the tavern getting several portions of free wine himself.

But around the tavern and other buildings and into the plaza there seemed to be a dearth of peons and natives. Those who were there for a time slipped away by twos and threes and disappeared in the darkness.

Zorro rode through the night and watched the road. He heard the whisper of voices at times reaching his ears on the wind. He knew the darkness hid determined men, men who had been cowed by brutality yet had courage enough to act in behalf of one who had risked life to help them.

The camp was beside the road and less than half a mile from the plaza. It consisted of two carts, a small tent, and two spans of oxen. José Mora had a good horse, which he had ridden into town.

Zorro surveyed the camp from a brush-studded hillside not far from it. Mora's two men were sitting beside the campfire, tilting a wineskin at frequent intervals and eating cold food. One sprawled on the ground beside the fire, while the other continued eating and drinking.

" 'Tis in my mind that Señor Mora will give us no part of the reward," one said. "He will spend it all on himself. How he captured this Zorro, I cannot guess. It must have been rare luck. Our employer is not noted for bravery."

The other laughed. "A man's glare can frighten him," he replied.

The conversation was interrupted. From the darkness men rushed — many men. Before the two at the fire realized what was happening to them, before they could reach weapons, they were seized, bound with thongs, gagged with dirty cloths, and rolled off to one side in the darkness.

"We mean you no harm, señors," Zorro heard a peon tell them. "It is your master we want. Be quiet, and no harm will come to you."

Peons and natives melted into the darkness again, and the camp was quiet.

Some time later, far down the road, was a clatter of hoofbeats and a man's raucous song. Filled with wine and intoxicated also by the adulation of those he had furnished with free drink, José Mora was headed for his camp and some hours of sleep.

Zorro urged his horse farther down the hillside until he got unseen and unheard to a place beside the road, from which he would be able to make a quick dash forward.

Mora's song ceased as he neared the camp. The campfire still burned brightly, but neither of his men was in sight Mora stopped his horse and bellowed:

"Juan! Marcos! Where are you, rogues? Come and care for my horse! If you've slipped away and left the camp to go to town, I'll have your hides!"

Mora dismounted with difficulty reeled, started for the fire. The black night spewed men. Brandishing clubs, rods of metal, tools, they rushed upon the trader. Mora gave a squawk of mingled surprise and fear and lurched backward, to bring up against another wall of men.

"What is this?" he squealed. "You rascals — dogs! Keep your hands off me! I'll have the soldiers slay you all!"

They hurled him to the ground as Zorro watched. Their weapons flashed in the light from the fire.

Zorro gave a wild yell and rode his horse forward furiously, and peons and natives scattered before him. Then, when he came to the circle of light the fire cast, and they saw the black horse and masked rider dressed in black, they stopped abruptly, bewildered.

" 'Tis Zorro — Zorro!" they cried.

"Silence!" Zorro shouted at them. "Put that rogue on his feet and hold him. And listen to me!"

Mora had been handled roughly already, but had not been injured much. His clothes were torn, his face was bruised and scratched, and a bludgeon had numbed one of his arms. Above all, he was a terrified man as they stood him in front of Zorro.

" 'Twas not Zorro this man turned over to the soldiers," the masked rider called to them. "It was a poor dolt with whom this trader made a plot. Mora told him he would get the reward, then rescue him and give him half the money. The poor dupe confessed to being Zorro. But Mora intends to let him be hanged and have all the reward himself. This Señor Mora is the sort of man I have been punishing for mistreating such as you."

There was a roll of mutterings, and peons and natives surged forward again.

"Wait!" Zorro ordered. "This affair must be handled as I say. Two of you fleet ones run to the barracks and tell Sergeant Garcia that a big mob is here killing the trader. Be sure you do not mention I am here, or it will ruin everything. All you others will stay here, and yell and make a loud noise until you hear the soldiers coming, then will vanish into the night and save yourselves. Do you understand?"

They shouted at him that they did.

"Wait a moment!" Zorro called. He rode closer to the frightened Mora and took his whip from his saddle. "Señor, I spoke the truth, did I not? That was your little plot?"

"It — it was but a jest on the soldiers," Mora replied, scarcely able to speak.

"All these men know the prisoner at the barracks is not Zorro, for I am Zorro, and I am here. You, José Mora, would let a man be hanged so you could line your pocket with gold. On your knees!"

"Mercy!" Mora begged, dropping to his knees and holding up his arms imploringly. " 'Twas but a jest. I meant to tell the sergeant tomorrow."

"Sergeant Garcia will not think it a jest. It will he a black spot on his record if he has already sent word to his superiors that Zorro has been caught. And you, señor, will be imprisoned for trying to cause the death of an innocent man. That is in your future. But now — "

SINGING through the air, the lash cut across the trader's back. Mora shrieked and tried to wrap his arms around his head. A score of times Zorro lashed him, then ceased. Mora's fine clothes were in ribbons, and blood soaked them.

"Put him on his feet again," Zorro ordered. "Now, do as I told you. Send men for the soldiers. You others howl and make a din until you hear the troopers coming. Put this rascal in his own saddle and tie him there."

They obeyed him swiftly. When Mora was tied in the saddle, Zorro seized the reins of his horse. He disappeared quickly into the darkness, taking his prisoner with him, as the peons and natives began their wild howling, which the wind would carry into the pueblo.

Through the darkness he rode, warning the man behind him to keep silent if he valued his life. Mora did, save for frequent moaning. He had an idea that Zorro was taking him somewhere to inflict torture upon him.

Before they reached the pueblo, Zorro heard and saw troopers riding at top speed past the dying bonfire and into the road. From the distance came the wild howling of the peons and natives. People of the town were gathering in the plaza.

Zorro went far around the plaza, riding where it was dark, and finally stopped in a depression a short distance behind the barracks, where there was no other building.

He dismounted and went on foot, leading the other horse with the trader tied into the saddle.

He tied the horse at a corner of the barracks stables, which he saw were empty, and went on, again threatening Mora with dire things if he made a sound. From a corner of the barracks, Zorro got a view of the situation. Only one trooper was in sight, a man left on guard, and he had his back toward Zorro and was watching the excitement in the plaza.

Zorro was at him before the trooper realized anyone was near. He jammed the muzzle of his pistol into the trooper's back and made him turn. The soldier's lower jaw sagged.

"You — but you are in a cell," the soldier gulped.

"I am Zorro, but never have been in a cell. Inside quickly, if you wish to live!"

He drove the frightened man before him. They went through the corridor, and Zorro compelled the trooper to unlock the cell. Big Carlos came out of it, plainly terrified at sight of the real Zorro.

"You are free. Get into the hills," Zorro told him. "Do not delay. Hurry through the darkness."

He drove Big Carlos before him together with the trooper. When they reached the corner of the building, Big Carlos fled. Zorro forced the trooper to where he had left Mora, made him untie the trader and help him from the saddle. Then they went into the prison room of the barracks again, and José Mora was locked in a cell and left there wailing.

"I wish you no harm, señor," Zorro told the trooper when they were outside the building again. "But harm will come to you if you do not do as I say. Tell Garcia exactly what happened, and you may not be punished by him. He will be glad to have the new prisoner in place of the old. If you let the new prisoner escape, I'll visit you again, and not so pleasantly."

Zorro left him gaping, and rushed around the building into the darkness. As he ran, he could hear the troopers returning.

But he did not hurry to his horse. Instead, he went to a window which opened into the quarters of the *commandante*, got through the window and left it open, and stood to one side of it.

ZORRO did not have long to wait. He heard wild exclamations, and Mora's wails.

In time, boots thumped the stones of the corridor. The door was hurled open. By the faint light from the corridor, Zorro saw Garcia fairly hurl Mora into the room, the trader having his hands tied behind his back.

"We'll get at the bottom of this!" Garcia roared.

As he started to light the candles, a trooper outside closed the door.

The light flared up and Garcia turned. And he saw Zorro standing by the window, menacing with his pistol.

"Be quiet and listen, Garcia!" he ordered. "What, I have to say may please you. I am Zorro. The poor dupe you had in a cell was not. I handled this rogue of a Mora. Look at me! I am not more than two-thirds the size of the dupe you had imprisoned."

"What — what — ?" Garcia gulped.

"This man Mora used Big Carlos as a catspaw. He told Carlos to play Zorro, and that he would get the reward and then see that Carlos was rescued, and split the reward with him. His intention was to let the poor fool be hanged, and then have all the reward himself."

"How do I know this is true?" Garcia demanded.

"A clever sergeant like you can make Mora confess to the truth of it, though it costs him a long prison term. And there is another way. I overheard Fray Felipe and Don Diego Vega talking as they left your barracks. Carlos had told them the story when he learned the reward could not be claimed until after he was hanged. The padre and Don Diego — men whose word you can accept for truth. As for me — you will not capture me tonight, Garcia. Drop your pistol from your sash. Make no wrong move, or I'll shoot to kill!"

Garcia removed his pistol from his belt and dropped it carefully.

"Another score to settle with you, señor," he said. "But if all this is true, at least I thank you for putting a rogue like José Mora into my hands."

Zorro got halfway through the window, still threatening with his pistol.

"Howl your head off now, sergeant," he suggested. "Shoot holes into the black night after I am gone, and have your tired troopers do the same. They have just unsaddled jaded mounts. I'll be far away before they can pursue."

Zorro got the remainder of the say through the window, and ran into the dark night toward the spot where he had left his horse.

Behind him, Garcia bellowed and troopers answered, and a few futile shots were fired into the night. But Zorro rode away wildly, to slow his horse after a time and circle to the spot where Bernardo was waiting, where he could change back into Diego Vega again and get quietly into his father's house and go to bed.

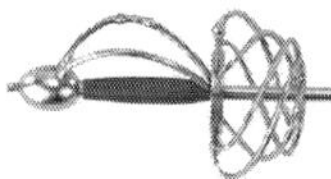

Zorro's Hostile Friends

When evil is done in his name, the masked avenger rides forth on an errand of justice!

WITH a flaming torch to light the way, a barefooted servant preceded Don Alejandro Vega and his son and heir, Diego, as they strolled across the plaza.

There was half a moon, and a rather stiff breeze blew in from the distant sea, a welcome change in the pueblo of Reina de Los Angeles after the heat of the late summer day. From all directions, people were converging on the plaza. For this was the anniversary of the birth of the viceroy, who ruled down in Mexico in the name of Spain's king, and even here in distant Alta California it was an excuse for a social celebration, though there were some who held the private opinion that the world could have struggled along had the viceroy never been born.

At one end of the plaza, a huge bonfire had been built. Seats had been provided for the *hidalgos* and *caballeros* of the vicinity and the women of their families. Indians would give their tribal dances, little knowing they would be honoring the viceroy whose appointed governor was responsible for many of the wrongs and cruelties they endured.

The tavern on the plaza would do a thriving business during the evening and on into the night with men drinking and gaming. And there would be a reception for the pueblo's great and near-great socially at the barracks before the affair ended.

This would be an opportunity for Capitán Carlos Ponseca to strut around and reveal his importance. He was newly sent from Monterey by the governor to take charge of the district and it was understood he had been ordered to win glory, promotion and financial reward for himself by capturing and hanging Señor Zorro, the mysterious masked rider who fought to right the wrongs of peons and natives.

Don Alejandro and Diego strolled along behind their torch bearer until they reached the corner of the plaza, where they encountered many friends. Most of the young dashing *caballeros* had ridden in from the ranchos for the affair, and the dainty señoritas would use their eyes to the extreme during the festivities, each hoping to catch a handsome young husband of station and wealth.

A distance from the fire, peon servants and natives were grouped to watch the program. Two Franciscan padres wandered among them, greeting them kindly. People settled themselves in the seats provided for them, and there was a babble of general conversation.

IT WAS a peaceful community gathering, such as this plaza had seen many times. And into if suddenly came a note of discord. Loud voices were heard — angry, emphatic voices. The beating of horses' hoofs caused a cessation of the vocal din. Into the plaza from the San Gabriel trail came four young *caballeros* on their blooded mounts.

One was supported in his saddle by two of the others. He reeled in the saddle and would have toppled from it had they not held him. The man who rode ahead shouted to clear the way, and stopped his horse in front of the tavern, through the door and windows of which light was streaming, and the others stopped behind him.

"Landlord!" the leading rider shouted in a loud voice. "We have a hurt man with us. Clear a room off your patio! Send for old Fray Felipe, who knows how to mend hurts of bodies as well as of souls. 'Tis Don Pedro Suarez who suffers. Send for the troopers and the new *capitán!*"

Don Alejandro Vega clutched his son's arm, "Did you hear that, Diego? Pedro Suarez has suffered an injury."

"One of my best friends. I must go to him," Diego replied.

For once, Diego Vega, usually yawning and shuffling, betrayed some spirit. He quickened his stride, and his father kept pace with him as they hurried to the tavern.

Some troopers who had been scattered through the crowd to preserve order had hurried there already and were keeping back the curious. Pedro Suarez was being helped down from his saddle. As he neared the spot at his father's side, Diego saw that Pedro's fine jacket and shirt had been cut to ribbons and were stained with blood. His sombrero was gone, and blood matted his hair.

"What is this?" Diego cried. "Pedro, my friend — "

"Help us, Diego," the leader of the group begged. "Let us get him into a room of the tavern. A man has gone for old Fray Felipe. Come help us, you and your august father. Spread word for all the young *caballeros* to come. This is a thing that needs immediate attention from us all."

They got Pedro Suarez into a vacant room, and the fat innkeeper hurried around, clapping his hands for servants, shouting his orders to fetch warm water and towels and cloth bandages, and to stand by to get anything Fray Felipe might need.

Groaning with pain, Pedro Suarez was stretched upon a couch. Diego knelt beside him. Pedro seemed to be only half conscious, only half realizing his surroundings, scarcely knowing those near him.

"We were riding swiftly to get here for the celebration," one of the young *caballeros* was saying. "Pedro's horse stood in the middle of the road, and we pulled up. Pedro was beside the road, his ankles tied and his wrists bound behind him with pieces of a reata."

"Who would do that to him and why?" Diego asked.

He did not get a reply just then. The door was flung open, and Sergeant Manuel Garcia, second in command of the soldiers in Reina de Los Angeles, strode into the room with an air of authority. Behind him shuffled old Fray Felipe, the Franciscan padre beloved by all who knew him, physician alike to bodies and souls.

"Pedro regained consciousness as we were putting him into his saddle," the *caballero* resumed. "He told us a part of it. He was stopped on the trail by the masked highwayman, Señor Zorro."

"What?" those in the room chorused.

"This scoundrel of a Zorro made him dismount, threatening him with a pistol. Pedro was unarmed save for his riding quirt. When he dismounted, Zorro lashed out at him from the saddle with the big whip he uses. He cut him, beat him down, finally smashed him across the head with the butt of the whip and made him unconscious. Then he must have tied him up, for he was that way when we found him."

"But why should Zorro do that?" somebody asked.

"Pedro told us that the scoundrel said, 'You and your kind, proud highborns of wealth, oppress the peons and natives. I'll whip every *caballero* I catch on the trails."

"Pedro Suarez and his father treat their men well, the same as do my father and I," Diego said.

There was a babble of talk as Fray Felipe began stripping off Pedro Suarez' blood-stained clothing and in a quiet voice asked for water and cloths. He had brought ointment with him.

The aged padre glanced up once, at Diego and his father. The faces of the three were inscrutable, but all were thinking the same thing. Zorro had not done this, for Diego Vega was Zorro, and he had been at home all afternoon and this evening. So once more a bogus Señor Zorro rode abroad, and for what purpose it was difficult to guess ….

PEDRO SUAREZ had his wounds dressed and was made comfortable. One of the *caballeros* and a peon servant were left with him if he needed further attention.

Diego and his father went with the other *caballeros* to the barracks to confront the new *commandante*, Capitán Carlos Ponseca. The arrogant capitán had put on his most resplendent uniform for the celebration.

"I regret I was not at the barracks," he told them. "I was having a secret conversation with a man who gave me valuable information about hide thieves. I shall order some of my troopers to patrol the roads, but I have no hope of taking this Zorro. You know better than I how elusive he is, how the soldiers often have pursued him in vain."

"Is it possible you will make no special effort after this outrage?" one of the *caballeros* asked. "Do you not wish to catch and hang the fellow, señor?"

Ponseca's face crimsoned with wrath. "There is a difference now, eh?" he asked. "When Zorro punished unscrupulous traders and cruel rancho superintendents, it was all right with you, eh? But now the fellow has punished one of your own kind, whipped him like a dog. Before this, you viewed the depredations of Zorro with detachment. It was none of your concern, eh? But now you are all for action."

"I do not like your manner and words, *Señor el Capitan!*" thundered Don Alejandro, the eldest present.

"But what else is there to say, Don Alejandro? Have the *hidalgos* and *caballeros* tried to catch this Zorro, if for a lark only, if they have no sense of authority? There are enough young *caballeros* at this celebration tonight to patrol the roads in pairs, to run the fellow down. There is a reward — "

"I scarcely think any of the young gentleman would be interested in the reward Capitán," Don Alejandro broke in witheringly.

"But he told Don Pedro, I understand, that he intended to whip every *caballero* he encountered hereafter. It is skin off your own backs, gentlemen. Give me your aid, and I think we can run down this Zorro. Make it your honorable object. Question your peons and natives — some of them must know Zorro's identity and where he hides."

One of the hot-blooded *caballeros* confronted him.

"We'll do that!" he said. "We'll make our plans and run down the rogue without help from you and your troopers, and bring him to you and let you hang him. We'll do soldiers' work, if necessary, since it seems we have no soldier here in authority able to do it."

"Señor!" Ponseca cried, springing to his feet.

"If you wish to fight about the matter, señor, there are a dozen blades here to accommodate you!"

"Peace!" Don Alejandro cried. "Let us not brawl. I tell you, Capitán Ponseca, that your attitude is wrong. You are on the way to making yourself exceedingly unpopular in this district. My friends and I are not without influence with the governor —"

" 'Twas the governor himself sent me here, and one order was to catch this Zorro," Ponseca interrupted. "I call upon you *caballeros* for your aid."

"You'll not get it!" one of the younger ones shouted at him. "We'll attend to this matter on our own account, not to aid you." He turned to the others. "Let us adjourn to a private room at the tavern, and make our plans."

When they had stormed out of the capitán's quarters, Don Alejandro and Diego got off to one side, away from the others. Fray Felipe came from the shadows and joined them.

"I questioned Pedro after you had left," the padre told them. "He had grown calm and could remember things. One thing he remembered in particular. When the masked man whipped him, his sleeve fell back as he raised the whip. On his right arm, between wrist and elbow, Pedro saw a long scar, such as a wound from the rip of a blade might leave. Pedro saw the scar plainly in the moonlight as the man bent over him, Pedro told me, and is certain of it."

"What is the answer to this riddle?" Don Alejandro asked as they strolled away from the others toward the chapel.

"It appears to me that somebody impersonated Zorro tonight and whipped the first man of blood he encountered. Many *caballeros* were riding to town for the fiesta, and he had only to wait until he met one alone," Diego said.

"And the object, Diego?"

"To infuriate men of blood and make them hunt down Zorro, to have them pester natives and peons with questions, possibly try to beat information out of them. I noticed a few things myself during the past hour."

"Such as — ?" his father urged.

DIEGO continued. "Capitán Ponseca said he was somewhere holding a conversation with an informer. You know how arrogant he is. Would he not make the informer come to his quarters instead of going to him?"

"He may be some man whose usefulness to the capitán would end if people became suspicious," Fray Felipe suggested.

"In that case, would Ponseca have troubled to travel a distance to meet the informer? Would he not have met him somewhere near?"

"That is a good thought, Diego."

"I observed the capitán's horse at the block in front of the barracks as we entered. He was wet from hard traveling and still blowing. Ponseca himself looked fatigued. He was breathing heavily, his hair was mussed and damp with perspiration, and his fine uniform was stained with perspiration under the arms."

"Diego!" his father cried. "You mean — "

"It is my belief that Capitán Ponseca himself did this thing to arouse the *caballeros* against Zorro. He has whipped a man of blood as he would a cur. I have only to see the scar Pedro mentioned, and I shall make it my business to see that!"

"The fiend!" Don Alejandro said. "If that be proved true, he is done in this district."

"If it be proved true, a dozen blades will be at him," Diego observed. "Zorro must vindicate himself. It means Zorro must unmask the capitán if he is guilty. Zorro must face his friends in real life, but who now are his sworn enemies as Zorro. It will be a task"

"A great task," Fray Felipe agreed. "If possible, Diego, let us have no bloodshed. And now — "

"I will hurry to the tavern, where the *caballeros* are meeting. They will expect me, for Pedro is one of my closest friends. And I'll visit Pedro, too, and see how he is getting along."

"I'll go to the plaza," his father decided, "and participate in the celebration. Join me there when you are done, Diego."

Diego found the *caballeros* in a state of wrath bordering on insanity. They had taken charge of a small room, and the inn-keeper's servants had been supplying them with quantities of heady wine.

Diego listened to their plans — for Señor Zorro would want to know them. These then of his own class were inclined to curl theft noses at him. His pose was that of a lazy reader of the poets, and none there could imagine him making a wild ride, fighting furiously with a blade.

"Is there anything you wish me to do?" he asked once, as he stifled a yarn with a scented handkerchief.

"You comfort Pedro as much as possible, Diego," one told him. "He will remain in lodging here at the inn instead of returning to his father's rancho. We'll make this our headquarters until we run down this fiend of a Zorro. And let all of us remember and refrain from slaying him at sight, as we feel like doing. His blood would stain an honorable blade or disgrace an honorable pistol. The thing is to capture him and see him hanged."

Diego shivered slightly as the speech was applauded. He had no desire to be caught and hanged. He must prove to these comrades of his that Zorro had not whipped Pedro Suarez. And he had to use great care during the proving of it.

Plans were made and the meeting broke up. Diego, yawning and looking sleepy, strolled out of the tavern and went toward the group containing his father. The Indians were dancing around the fire, and the crowd was laughing at the antics of a peon clown who hoped to gain a shower of small coins for his efforts.

Outside the tavern, he met Sergeant Garcia.

"What think you of this happening, Don Diego?" Garcia asked. "The *caballeros* will be hotly after this rogue of a Zorro now, will they not?"

"No doubt, Garcia," Diego said, on guard. He and the burly sergeant were on good terms, but he remembered that Garcia was a soldier also. "Had I seen you in the tavern, I'd have bought you wine. Take this coin and purchase some of the best."

"Thanks, Don Diego, my friend," Garcia said, bowing as he took a piece of gold. "What think you of our new capitán?"

"I have not analyzed him," Diego replied. "But his words and actions tonight did not endear him to some."

"It is not for me to criticize a superior officer," Garcia remarked, his voice low in protection. "But I will say this much to you, knowing it will go no farther — I have seen officers I liked better. The trooper's detest him already."

"You know, Garcia, a thought comes to me. It does not seem possible that Zorro would do such a thing. What has he to gain by infuriating men of blood? If he had whipped a *caballero* known to abuse peons and natives, I could understand. But Pedro Suarez is my close friend, and I know him well. He is not guilty of any cruelty to those beneath him in fortune, nor is his father."

NODDING, the sergeant said, "So I know — and the thing therefore puzzles me also."

Diego strolled on to join his father, and presently they left the celebration and went home. Diego sent for Bernardo, his mute peon body servant, one of the three men who knew he was Zorro.

"You have heard men speaking of what happened tonight, and you understand?" Diego asked.

Bernardo nodded.

"You know the barracks well," Diego said. "You know where the new capitán has his quarters. When he sleeps, a window is open, no doubt. Do you think you can get to the window and toss something into the room, and get away without being seen and caught?"

Bernardo bobbed his head with enthusiasm, and his eyes gleamed. He was always eager to have a share in Zorro's plans.

"I will prepare a message on parchment, and weight it with a stone," Diego told him. "Come to me later, and I'll give it you. Toss it through the capitán's window, but not until all are asleep except the guard in front of the barracks. And the guard generally sleeps standing up."

Diego paced around the room composing the message in his mind. After a time he sat at his writing table and penned it carefully, printing the letters in such a manner that it could not be traced back to him He bent toward the candelabra and read what he had scrawled:

> To Capitán Ponseca: — If you would learn what you wish to know concerning the man called Señor Zorro, come at the middle of the night to the bottom of the hill one mile out the San Gabriel road. Come alone arid without fear. I am a *caballero* who must move warily in this affair; I am sure you will understand.

Diego rolled the message around a small stone. "That will fetch the rogue," he muttered.

When Bernardo appeared, Diego gave him the message and instructed him again. And he gave further orders:

"Zorro rides tomorrow night. Have everything ready at the usual place."

In midmorning of the following day, Diego went to the tavern to visit Pedro Suarez. Pedro was sore in body. His face bore bruises from blows he had received from the whip the evening before. But his pride was bruised even more.

Several *caballeros* were in the room. Diego shuffled in and gave them greeting and betrayed a little excitement. He held a small sheet of parchment in one hand.

" 'Tis a message," he announced. "Why it was tossed through my chamber window during the night, I do not know. It seems rather ridiculous."

"What does it say Diego?" one asked.

Diego held it up to the light to read. He had prepared it himself, and had no compunction deluding his friends, since his actions served what he thought was a good end. He read:

> Don Diego Vega: — Inform your *caballero* friends that they can meet Zorro tonight if they follow instructions. Let three and no more be at the Jumble of rocks off the San Gabriel road half a mile out of the pueblo at the middle of the night, and they will be able to seize the rogue who beat Don Pedro.

As Diego ceased reading, they all began speaking at once.

"Three of us?" one cried. "All of us will be there in ambush. We'll meet this Zorro and give him a taste of the whip before we bring him in to be hanged!"

"That would not be playing fair," Diego observed. "It sounds to me as if somebody had planned a trap for Zorro and simply wants to turn him over to you. If more than three go, perhaps the plan will be changed and you will not see Zorro."

"Diego speaks fairly," Pedro Suarez declared. "Why not three go and the others remain on the highway between the spot named and the town?"

"So be it!" another cried. "You wish to be one of the three Diego?"

"I — that is — I am not enured to scenes of violence and excitement," Diego Vega reminded them. "I might make a bad error of some sort."

"Stay you at home then," Pedro said. "When you hear the din when Zorro is brought in a prisoner, hurry to the barracks to see the rogue."

It was two hours after nightfall when Diego slipped unseen from his father's house. Using extreme caution, he got to the place where Bernardo awaited him with Zorro's costume, horse and weapons.

"Wait, Senores!" Zorro called. "Here is the man who whipped Pedro Suarez!"

He got into the costume quickly, buckled on his blade, made sure his pistol was loaded and that his big whip was hooked securely to the pommel of his saddle.

"You will remain here," he told Bernardo. "The waiting will be long, but you may sleep for a time."

HE RODE cautiously back over the hills, keeping off the skyline so his silhouette would not be observed against the background of moonlight. For a time he paralleled the San Gabriel road, then cut toward it and reached it near the spot he had named for his meeting with Capitán Ponseca.

From a patch of black darkness, he watched the highway. He saw a single rider loping along, but could not make out his identity at that distance. A little later he saw three riders in a group and guessed they were the *caballeros*.

The single rider came on along the trail, but the three did not appear in a moonlit patch through which the lone horseman had passed. So Zorro knew the three were the *caballeros*, his friends, and that they had stopped at the place named in the note he had written.

Soon the lone horseman stopped in a patch of bright moonlight, and Zorro saw the light glint from a scabbard and knew Capitán Ponseca was keeping the rendezvous.

He glanced far down the highway toward the town again, and saw six riders coming. But they turned aside about halfway between the town and the place where the three *caballeros* waited. They were more of his *caballero* friends, he decided.

Now he rode cautiously down the road and crossed it where an overhanging ledge cast a deep shadow. He had instructed Capitán Ponseca to await him at the bottom of the hill, and now he went down the slope, but at one side of the trail, keeping his powerful black horse at a walk.

He spotted his man a few feet back from the road. Ponseca seemed to be watching up and down the trail. Zorro urged his horse along a natural hedge until he came to an opening, fearful each instant that either his mount or the capitán's would whinny and betray his presence in the neighborhood.

Now he gathered the reins in his left hand and drew his pistol from his sash. He jumped the black through the opening in the hedge, and as Capitán Ponseca wheeled his mount, Zorro called to him.

"Careful, señor! My pistol is aimed at your heart! Lift your arms high and keep them so until we understand each other."

Ponseca obeyed as he growled a malediction.

"Ride out into the moonlight so I may see you," Ponseca called. "I came alone, as the message requested. If you are a *caballero*, as you wrote, I understand why you must move warily. I'll not betray your identity."

Zorro jumped his horse out into the moonlight and stopped within a few feet of the mounted officer. Ponseca saw the masked man in black costume, the threatening pistol, the eyes glittering through the holes in the mask, and he heard a stern voice order:

"Take your pistol from your sash very carefully, capitán, and drop it on the ground."

"You are — "

"I am Zorro. Quickly!"

Ponseca hesitated a moment, then dropped the pistol.

"Hold your right arm straight up again, *capitán*, and allow your sleeve to drop."

"What nonsense is this?" Ponseca asked.

The capitán raised his arm, the sleeve dropped. Zorro urged his horse nearer, until he could see well in the moonlight. And he saw the scar Pedro Suarez had mentioned. So he was right! Capitán Ponseca had done the whipping.

"Last night, you whipped a *caballero* unmercifully, señor," Zorro said. "You told him you were Zorro, and that you would whip every man of blood you encountered. I am Zorro, and I do not whip men of blood. If I have need of fighting them, I allow them to defend themselves with weapons."

"So you are a *caballero* also?"

"I am, señor. But that tells you nothing of my identity. There are scores of young *caballeros* in the district. And perhaps this is not my district. Perhaps I have come from elsewhere to do my work."

"Why should you, a defender of peons and natives, care if I whipped a *caballero*?" Ponseca asked.

"Had he, a man of blood, been cruel to those unable to protect themselves, I may have whipped him. But Pedro Suarez is little more than a boy, he was unarmed, and had done no cruelty or deception. Why did you whip him?"

"You might have guessed that," Ponseca said. "I thought my act would enrage the *caballeros* and they would help me run down this Zorro."

"Here I am!"

"So you are. And now, Señor Zorro, suppose we draw blades and see what happens. You excel with a blade, I have heard."

"You did not give Pedro Suarez a chance to cross blades with you. You whipped him," Zorro said.

SUDDENLY he thrust his pistol back into his sash and took the heavy whip from the pommel of his saddle. When he saw the move, Ponseca whipped blade from scabbard and urged his horse forward.

But the lash sang. It cut into the capitán's sword arm and made him drop the blade. It drove the officer's frenzied mount back toward a ledge of rock, and he reared and tossed Panseca to the ground.

The lash sang again and wrapped around the waist of the capitán, when he would have run around the end of the ledge, and jerked him back. Zorro drove him back to the rocks, cutting his jacket to ribbons, giving him what he had given Pedro Suarez the night before.

Ponseca ran out into the moonlight, but Zorro cut off his flight with the whip and drove him back yet again. Then the capitán began yelling for help.

Zorro continued his whipping until Ponseca cringed against the ledge of rock whimpering for mercy. Zorro coiled his whip, hooked it to the pommel, and got out his pistol again.

"Mount!" he ordered.

With some difficulty, Ponseca got into his saddle and gathered up his reins. He could not sit erect and gripped the pommel to hold on.

"For this, Señor Zorro, I will track you down if it takes me the remainder of my life!" the capitán threatened.

"It will be your privilege to try," Zorro told him. "Ride close beside me. Make an attempt to attack me or to escape, and I'll pistol you. Try to calm your horse."

They rode through the hedge and along it parallel to the road. Zorro stopped when he was within a short distance of the place where he had told the three *caballeros* to wait. He watched and listened for a time and finally made out where they were waiting.

Ponseca was bent forward across his saddle, moaning. Zorro called softly into the night:

"Come this way, señores! I am the man who wrote the message that brought you here."

He heard hoofbeats, saw shadows coming toward him. When they were within a short distance, Zorro moved his black horse out into a streak of moonlight, catching hold of the bridle of Ponseca's horse and making it move beside his own.

The three *caballeros* caught sight of him, and their hands moved to their weapons.

"Wait, señores!" Zorro called. "Let us be fair in this matter. I am Zorro, but I did not whip Pedro Suarez. Here is the man who did. He has confessed it to me and now will confess to you. He is Capitán Ponseca. He thought it would be clever to whip a *caballero* and to enrage other men of good blood and have them run down Zorro for him."

"What is this?" one of them cried.

"Come closer and listen. Capitán Ponseca, is what I have told them the truth? You whipped Pedro Suarez for the reason I said, did you not? Speak with a straight tongue, or I use the whip again!"

"I — I did it," Ponseca confessed, cringing as he saw Zorro's hand move toward the whip.

"There you have it, señores," Zorro told the *caballeros*. "Take this man and do what you will. And because I have caught him and turned him over to you, allow me to escape from your presence unattacked. I have no fight with you, señores."

"Go your way, Zorro — and thanks," one replied.

Hoofbeats sounded on the highway, and Capitán Ponseca lifted his voice:

"Troopers! Help! I am here! Zorro is here! Seize him!"

So, Zorro thought, Ponseca had troopers in hiding somewhere near the rendezvous. No doubt they were scouting along the road now, trying to find their commander. The thing for Zorro to do was to lead them in chase, so they could not rescue the capitán from the *caballeros*.

He rode furiously out into the highway and stopped in the moonlight. Not far away were Sergeant Garcia and five of his men.

They saw the masked rider in black, too. Garcia shouted, and the troopers gave chase. Zorro sent his black down the highway at furious speed. Behind him pistols barked, and bullets flew close. Wild yells sounded as the troopers pursued.

They were past the spot where the *caballeros* held Ponseca prisoner now, and Zorro put on a little more speed and led them on. The wild shouts of the troopers, the pounding of their horses' hoofs rang among the rocks and echoed along the trail.

Ahead of him, Zorro heard more shouting and realized that the six *caballeros*, who had been waiting for the return of their three comrades, had heard the sounds and were riding to investigate, probably thinking their friends were in trouble.

ZORRO spurred toward them until he reached a dark spot, and there, out of sight of both the troopers and the *caballeros*, he jumped the black off the trail and behind a stand of brush.

The two bodies of riders met almost in front of him. Wild shouts sounded as they recognized each other.

"We are after Zorro," Sergeant Garcia shouted. "Did he pass you? No? Then he turned aside just here. We'll take the left side, señores, and you take the right. After him!"

Zorro spurred his horse on, for the *caballeros* were coming at him as the troopers turned away to the other side of the road. He could not hope to escape without leading a pursuit. If he allowed himself to be caught, no harm would come to him if he unmasked and told what had happened. But he dared not do that and disclose his identity.

If he did, he could not ride as Zorro again. And if some *caballero* in his cups later accidentally revealed Zorro's identity — the governor had a long arm. No doubt he would be hanged, his old father shamed, his estates confiscated —

The *caballeros* caught sight of him and gave pursuit, yelling wildly, driving their mounts to the utmost. But no horse in the district was a match for the black in speed and endurance, Zorro knew.

He crashed through a sea of brush, and they followed. Again pistols barked behind him, and bullets sang uncomfortably near. He urged his black up a sharp slope and came out on a level space where fast going would not be too dangerous.

Now the black rapidly put distance between himself and the furious pursuit. The troopers were far behind, if they had turned back after hearing the *caballeros'* yells. The *caballeros* themselves were being outridden.

Zorro circled carefully and finally reached the spot where Bernardo waited. He dropped out of his saddle, stripped off the costume he wore over his other clothing, tossed his weapons aside.

"Hide everything as usual, Bernardo," he said and dashed away on foot through the night.

He got into the house without being seen and hurried to his own chamber, and there his father came to hear what he had to say. Don Alejandro's eyes gleamed as he listened to the recital.

"Well done, my son!" he praised. "And now for the end of it. Remove your sweat-stained clothing and dress again quickly in something else. There will be excitement soon."

Before long, excited yells came from the plaza. Lights burned in the houses. Men hurried to the plaza to learn what had happened, Diego and his father among them.

The three *caballeros* had reached the tavern with their prisoner, Ponseca. The other *caballeros* were protecting them. Some of the troopers had reached the scene already and seemed about to attempt a rescue of their officer.

Fray Felipe appeared from the chapel and got between the two forces and held his hands high for silence. He gathered the story and repeated it for all to hear. Don Alejandro walked forward with Diego. Other prominent older men of the pueblo joined them.

"What the capitán did was a thing that called for revenge," Fray Felipe was saying. "He whipped an unarmed man who never has harmed a human being. I am Pedro Suarez' confessor, and I know. Now Zorro has punished the capitán in turn. He is held up to public scorn, this officer, and cannot be of service here any longer. So I ask you, señores, to hold your hands and do him no harm. But do you all conduct him to the barracks and see that he writes out his resignation. Send it by courier to the governor at Monterey, and let the courier tell the story of what happened here."

"And see that Capitán Ponseca departs in his carriage with all his baggage soon after sunrise," Don Alejandro added. "His kind are not wanted here."

One of the *caballeros* greeted Diego. "You should have been with us, my friend. How we chased that rogue of a Zorro! We tried to shoot him out of his saddle, but could not. He is as elusive as a ghost."

Diego smiled slightly. He had heard those bullets sing.

"But now that we know the story, we are glad we did not shoot Zorro, the *caballero* continued. "He unmasked the villain, and cleared his own name of the abuse of Pedro Suarez. Yes, I am glad we did not kill him."

"So am I," Diego Vega replied. As he walked on with his father, returning home, he added in a murmur, "It would be a bad thing for a man to be slain by his close friends."

Zorro's Hot Tortillas

The Z in "tortilla" sends Don Diego Vega on a fighting errand!

FRAY FELIPE, the elderly Franciscan padre in charge of the chapel on the plaza at Reina de Los Angeles, had sent that morning for young Don Diego Vega for a consultation relating to the fund for the poor.

The consultation had fatigued Diego considerably, to judge from his manner, which was that of a man yearning for bed and a session of undisturbed sleep. So, as he started home along the side of the plaza, he decided he needed refreshment. He turned through the door of the tavern and into its cool semi-dark depths.

"Ah, Don Diego!" the fat innkeeper shouted in welcome. He came from behind his counter and tried to bend double in a bow despite the ample paunch which did not suit such a courtesy. "My poor pigsty of a tavern is honored by your presence."

"It is, indeed," Diego agreed. He stifled a yawn with a lace-embroidered handkerchief held in fingers which bore jeweled rings. "I have need of refreshment."

"At your service, Don Diego! In addition to a goblet of my very best wine, may I make a suggestion?"

"Make it," Diego permitted, as he sank wearily upon a bench beside a table against the wall, away from the others in the big common room of the inn.

"I have a new cook, Don Diego, who came to me well recommended. His name is Pedro Gomez — "

"There are thousands of persons named Gomez, and at least a quarter of them are also called Pedro," Diego interrupted. "Is there aught else to recommend him?"

"This man — ah, what a cook he is! And he has a specialty which I feel sure will appeal to your taste."

"And that is — ?"

"He takes a tortilla sizzling hot, fresh from the stove, and smears it with a thickness of the crystallized honey you like so well. On top of that he puts a second hot tortilla smeared with a fruit paste of his own making. Atop that comes a third hot tortilla, also covered with a thickness of crystallized honey, and then — "

"Fetch it for me before your stack of tortillas reaches the ceiling," Diego broke in. "And your best wine — which is poor enough stuff, no doubt."

The landlord bowed and hurried out into the patio to proceed to the kitchen to superintend this order personally. Diego yawned and looked around the room.

AT A TABLE near the fireplace lounged a tall, slender man who was a stranger to Diego. His clothes were fine and rings were upon his fingers, and there was something of the sophisticate in his appearance and manner. He wore no blade. He did not look like a prosperous trader; and Diego decided he was a gambler who traveled up and down the highways of Alta California and preyed on the unwary.

The others in the low-ceilinged room were townsmen, travelers off El Camino Real, and a couple of traders loud in their talk regarding the prices of tallow and hides. A single trooper from the local *presidio* sat at a table half intoxicated.

In from the plaza strutted Sergeant Manuel Garcia, second in command at Reina de Los Angeles, an obese and uncouth man whom Diego had cultivated for excellent reason. Garcia blew out the ends of his enormous black mustache and stopped beside the table.

"Don Diego! *Amigo!"* Garcia saluted. " 'Tis a better day since I have seen you."

Diego gestured toward a bench. "Seat yourself, sergeant, and have wine with me," he invited. "I await some special concoction being made by a new cook the landlord tells me he has engaged."

"The rogue's name is Pedro Gomez," the sergeant replied. "I admit that he can cook, but in other matters I would not trust him two feet from his stove.

There is the look of a scoundrel about him."

"I have noticed several strangers around the pueblo recently," Diego said. "There — at that table — "

"He is a gentleman who arrived yesterday. He reported at the *presidio* according to regulations, and his name is Esteban Audelo, so he says. He is from Monterey and is looking for investments for himself and certain associates here in the Southland."

"Investments of what nature?"

"That, *amigo*, is a thing I do not know," the burly sergeant admitted.

The landlord came back to the table and served the wine, and Garcia saluted and drank, while Diego fingered the stem of his goblet. And presently the landlord returned again with a flat silver dish, upon which was the stack of tortillas Diego had ordered, oozing honey and jelly, the whole mess steaming hot.

"Please notify me as to how you relish it," the landlord requested; and waddled away toward his counter.

Diego took a sip of wine and glanced down at the plate. His eyes narrowed slightly, but otherwise he betrayed nothing. Yet before him was a thing rather startling. Baked into the top of the uppermost tortilla, having been scratched in the dough before baking, was a ragged letter "Z."

Sergeant Garcia happened to look 'down and see it at the same time. "What is this?" he asked, his voice hoarse and charged with sudden interest. "The letter Z. Why, that is — "

" 'Tis what people call the mark of Zorro, is it not?"

"It is so," Garcia admitted. "And made on top of a tortilla by the new cook in the kitchen. So! The thing is plain to a man of my broad understanding, *amigo*. Perhaps here is one end of the trail."

"The trail?"

"At the other end of which will be this Zorro's capture! The scoundrel of a new cook — a man I did not like at first sight — is leaving the mark of Zorro on his cookery, is he? And why? To attract the attention of Zorro, no less, and have Zorro communicate with him. A pretty plot! Zorro must be again in the vicinity of Reina de Los Angeles. This Pedro Gomez no doubt is a friend of Zorro's and desires to furnish him with information!"

DIEGO gulped some wine hastily, bending his head forward to hide the sudden gleam in his eyes. He knew quite well that Pedro Gomez, the cook, was not an intimate of Zorro … for Don Diego Vega himself was Zorro, and only three other men knew that — his father, old Fray Felipe, and Bernardo, his mute peon body-servant.

"What are you about to do?" Diego asked the sergeant as the latter finished his goblet of wine quickly.

"I am about to earn the rich reward offered by His Excellency the Governor for Zorro's capture or slaying," Garcia replied. "No doubt it will mean promotion for me, also. Perhaps you will soon see me wearing the epaulets of an ensign, *amigo*, and strutting around the pueblo wearing an officer's blade with gleaming jewels in the hilt — "

"You have not caught Zorro yet," Diego observed.

"I start on that employment immediately, Don Diego. Ha! 'Tis a hot and smoking trail, let us say."

"What do you intend? I dislike turbulence."

"I regret to annoy you, Don Diego, but of turbulence there must be, of necessity, plenty immediately," Sergeant Garcia replied, struggling to his feet. "I'll invade the kitchen and grab this scoundrel by his ears and slam him back against the wall and compel him to confess. I'll shake him as a terrier does a rat! Ha! I'll drag him by his long hair across the stones of the patio floor — "

Diego raised a hand in a languid command for silence. "One moment, Garcia," he begged, his voice low. "Already, persons in the room are watching you. No doubt they think you are quarreling with me. The newcomer you named Esteban Audelo is looking our way. And I have a suggestion to make you."

"I am all attention, Don Diego."

"Let us assume that you rush into the kitchen and accuse this fellow. And then, if he really is an intimate of Zorro, he will know you are on his trail, and will deny everything and afterward be on guard. Would it not be better simply to watch him and see if he contacts any man, and if so whom, and then ascertain whether the person he contacts can be Zorro?"

Sergeant Garcia drew himself up and blew out his mustache. "You, Don Diego, my friend, are an exalted personage," he said. "You do not understand common scoundrels. The best way to handle such is to be abrupt and exert violence. Forgive my absence for a moment — duty calls."

The sergeant hitched up his sword belt, drew out his pistol, and charged like a bull in the fighting ring across the room and through the patio door. The landlord lumbered after him, the others in the room betrayed excitement, and some got up from their benches. But the man called Esteban Audelo retained his seat and watched and listened.

Almost immediately there came from the direction of the kitchen sounds indicating a riot. Sergeant Garcia was bellowing denunciations, the landlord was squealing like a frightened pig, a male voice was raised in lamentations and cries of pain and declarations that its owner had done nothing wrong, and the two peon kitchen maids were screaming.

ADDED to this din were the sounds of furniture being broken, of crockery being crashed against the flagstone floor. Everybody in the big common room of the tavern was on his feet now with the exception of Diego Vega and the man who called himself Esteban Audelo.

The latter continued sipping his wine and watching the door of the patio as if amused. He gestured to a frightened peon servant to refill his wine goblet, and the peon was so nervous he spilled the wine.

"What ails you, fellow?" Diego overheard Esteban Audelo ask. "Are you perhaps concerned in this affair?" And that only frightened the servant more.

The half-intoxicated trooper who had been in the common room had followed Sergeant Garcia into the patio. Now he returned, driving the excited landlord before him and holding the door open wide.

Garcia appeared. His uniform was disordered; his face was a picture of rage mingled with determination. He was pulling along the hapless cook, a tall and rather skinny man whose eyes were bulging and whose face was bruised and splotched with fresh blood. Sergeant Garcia evidently had treated him roughly. Behind them came one of the peon kitchen maids, hanging her head and weeping, plainly enough suffering from terror.

Diego knew the girl. Her father had worked for the Vega rancho until about a year before, when he had been killed by a fall from a horse. Her mother had died long before that, and she had kept house for her father in a miserable hut. Since getting employment at the tavern, she had lived with an old woman, sharing the expenses of food.

"This is an affair for the *magistrado* to settle!" Sergeant Garcia was shouting. "No doubt both of you are rogues. Since you give each other the lie, this not for me to decide. I am a rough soldier, not a solver of riddles!"

He yanked the cook into the middle of the room as those present began pressing back against the walls, and the trooper took the girl by the arm and hustled her toward the outside door.

Esteban Audelo arose from his bench and strode forward as Diego watched. The stranger was smiling slightly as he stopped before Garcia and his prisoner.

"We meet again, Pedro," Audelo said to the cook.

The cook rolled his eyes and tried to kneel. "Save me, Señor Audelo!" he howled. "Tell them I am an honest man. I do not understand the meaning of this — "

Esteban Audelo silenced him with a gesture, and spoke to Garcia: "I knew this man in Monterey. He cooked for a *posada* there. I vouch for his honesty."

"And who vouches for yours, señor?" Garcia barked at him. "You are a stranger here."

"Your *capitán* knows me," Audelo declared. "I have established my identity with him. I have come here as an agent of men of wealth, to see if I can buy a large rancho for them. I have taken a house at the edge of the pueblo — "

"Come along with us to the *magistrado,"* Garcia invited. "The trial will be an open meeting. And you, Don Diego Vega. I hate to trouble you, *amigo*, but if you will kindly come to the trial — ? It will be a great help. You saw the letter Z on the tortilla. Ha! Landlord! Wrap those tortillas carefully and fetch them along. They are evidence." ....

THE *magistrado* was a runt of a man with a bald head and eyes that squinted. He curried favor from those in power, and there was no question concerning his honesty, since all men knew he was dishonest.

As Diego seated himself on a front bench, he looked at the man about to pass judgment, and several thoughts came into his mind. Things were happening in too orderly a fashion. Everything seemed to be going by prearranged plan. The *magistrado* was here in his office already to proceed, when it was notorious that usually he had to be sought when he was needed.

The sergeant told his story quickly, and Diego informed the *magistrado* concerning the marked tortilla, which was exhibited as evidence. The frightened landlord said that he had hired the cook and knew nothing about him except that he was a good cook.

The judge questioned Pedro Gomez.

"I know nothing of it, Excellency," the cook declared. "I got the order to prepare the special tortillas. While I mixed the honey and fruit paste, I had this girl bake the tortillas and keep them hot. For this dish, they are baked fresh, not cold and warmed up."

"Did you not scratch the letter Z on that tortilla?" the *magistrado* demanded.

"No Excellency! I ordered the girl to bake the tortillas. When everything was ready, I put the honey and jelly on them. I did not notice the letter Z — the landlord was in haste for the plate. The girl must have scratched the letter in the dough herself!"

Diego watched the peon girl carefully. It was possible she had found herself in trouble and wished to contact Zorro and get him to aid her, and had taken that crude way of trying it. She was so frightened she scarcely could speak.

"Why did you scratch the letter in the dough?" the *magistrado* yelled at her. "Tell the truth, instantly! Was it a warning to this notorious Zorro? Does he frequent the tavern? Tell me his identity!"

She protested between sobs that she knew nothing ... she did not know Zorro, had not made the letter on the tortilla, was innocent of all wrong-doing.

"You speak falsely," the judge decided. "It is my belief that you know the identity of Zorro and refuse to divulge it. I hold Pedro Gomez, the cook, blameless since he has been vouched for by Señor Esteban Audelo. And I find you guilty of conspiring to defeat the ends of justice. What is your name?"

"Anita Gonzales señor."

"You, Anita Gonzales, I sentence to pay a fine of two gold pieces forthwith."

The girl began screaming. It would take her years to earn that much money, she declared. She was innocent! Could not the *magistrado* be merciful?

"You cannot pay?" the judge asked, knowing well she could not. "Then if anyone cares to pay the amount I shall sentence you in peonage to him until you work out the money at a wage to be settled by the court."

Diego straightened slightly in his seat. The odor of this affair was a thickening stench. The fine was double what it should have been. And this rush to sell the girl into peonage —

"Your honor, I have just engaged a house, and need a maid to work for me," Esteban Audelo was saying. "I'll pay the girl's fine immediately and take her in peonage."

"I thank you, Señor Audelo. The papers will be ready at once," the magistrado said.

More rush, Diego thought. Something was behind all this. He arose and stepped forward and addressed the *magistrado*.

"I do not believe this girl guilty," Diego declared. "Her father worked on our rancho until he was accidentally killed, and she kept the hut for him. Allow me to pay her fine and release her."

The eyes of the *magistrado* gleamed "Ah, Don Diego! You should have spoken sooner," he said. "I have already stated that she goes in peonage to Señor Audelo. Perhaps the señor will release her to you on your payment of the fine."

Audelo shook his head. "I regret that I need a maid badly at my house, and this girl is no doubt a good cook since she has been working in the tavern kitchen."

PEDRO GOMEZ had been released and had hurried away with the landlord. Sergeant Garcia and his trooper went outside. Diego followed them, brushing his nostrils with his scented handkerchief. Soon he saw Esteban Audelo come from the office of the *magistrado* with the weeping girl following him. Diego saw something else that gave him thought — a swift exchange of glances between Audelo and Sergeant Manuel Garcia, and a wink by the former which made the big sergeant grin.

As he strolled homeward thoughtfully, Diego retained his usual pose of a half-awake, spineless fop. He found his august father, Don Alejandro, in the patio, and after a servant had furnished them refreshment and withdrawn, Diego told his father of the entire proceeding.

"What do you think, my father?" he asked, finally.

"Collusion, obviously, between our *magistrado*, a man we know to be a scoundrel, this Esteban Audelo and the local soldiery," Don Alejandro replied. "What is behind it, I have not decided. My son, do you think those marked tortillas were served you purposely?"

"It is hard to tell," Diego replied. "I do not consider that the landlord has anything to do with it."

"And the girl — ?"

"I doubt her guilt in the matter. It would have been a stupid way to attract Zorro's attention, if she is in trouble and wants his help. However, such a girl is not noted for much wisdom."

"Can it be possible that the whole thing was only a means of letting this Esteban Audelo get his hands on the girl? There are men of that sort. Pay a fine, get a girl in peonage, get her into his house — it has been done before."

"It follows," Diego said, "that the *magistrado* would have to be in the deal, and also the cook. If the girl did not scratch that letter in the tortilla dough, the cook must have done so. He looks like a sly rascal."

"If he did, he must be in this Audelo's pay."

"True, my father. And there remain the glances and wink that passed between Audelo and the sergeant. I know Garcia fairly well; he may be a rogue in some things, but I doubt he would help play such a game against a girl."

"Would he if there was a piece of gold in it?"

"I doubt it," Diego replied. "If it was some high officer of the army for whom he engineered the affair, with preferment and promotion as result, I could understand it. The thing now, as I see it, is to rescue Anita Gonzales. I am quite sure she is a good girl."

A servant came into the patio and bowed, and said that Fray Felipe, of the chapel, was calling.

DIEGO and his father stood as the padre was ushered into the patio. They served him wine, and looked at him inquiringly.

"The matter of the girl sold a short time ago in peonage — " the padre hinted.

"We were just discussing it," Don Alejandro told him. "If the girl is in danger, she must be saved. That will be a task for — Zorro."

"I fear for her," Fray Felipe said. "This man Audelo — I know him."

"You know him, padre?" Don Alejandro sat erect and Diego did the same.

"I knew him in Monterey — that is, knew of him," Fray Felipe explained. "He was a *capitán* on the staff of the Viceroy in Mexico, and whenever the Viceroy wished a man of rank removed, this Esteban Audelo picked a quarrel with him, fought a duel — and the man was removed."

"Ah!" Diego said.

"As far as I know, the man is still a *capitán* and in the service of the Governor," the padre added.

"Is he the sort who would arrange to get his clutches on such a girl?" Don Alejandro asked.

"He is. He is known as a dissolute man, a high gambler, a notorious rake," the padre replied.

"Then the thing commences to be plain," Don Alejandro declared. "He wanted the girl in his house, got the *magistrado* to help him for a price, arranged the whole thing — "

"Pardon me, my father, but I understand the man has been in the pueblo for only a very short time," Diego said. "Not long enough to observe the girl often and develop an infatuation for her."

"Um!" Don Alejandro grew thoughtful again.

"However, the girl must be rescued," Diego continued. "As you said, it is a task for Zorro. Merely getting her out of the rogue's house will not be difficult for Zorro. But she must be hidden afterward. And we dare not have her sent to the rancho, for that would show the interest of the Vega family in the affair."

"Leave it to Zorro," Don Alejandro suggested. "I am sure he will find a way." He smiled upon his son.

With nightfall came a mist that swept over the hills from the sea. It swirled around the buildings, dripped from the trees and eaves, made those who went abroad bundle up against its penetrating dampness.

Toward the middle of the night, confusion was added. Into the town from a big rancho came a herd of cattle being driven to the east. The tired, sleepy cattle bawled until the town rang with the sound and milled endlessly around the plaza. Shouting vaqueros drove them back from wandering into the side streets and passages while other vaqueros hurried to the tavern for wine. It was a regulation that no herd could be driven through the town on the highway except during the middle of the night.

Diego Vega got out of his father's house unseen, to hurry through the mist to an abandoned hut at some distance, where his mute servant, Bernardo, waited for him, having been told during the time of the evening meal that Zorro would be abroad that night.

"I do not need the horse tonight, Bernardo," Diego told him. "Only Zorro's clothes and weapons. You will await me here."

He dressed rapidly in the Zorro costume, which he donned over his regular clothes; he buckled on Zorro's sword, examined the pistol and thrust it into his sash, and put the hood and mask over his head. Then he slipped into the depths of the misty night, merging into the darkness, his black costume a part of the night. He carried with him the long heavy whip with which he often had given terrible punishment.

The *magistrado* was a widower who lived alone in a poor house at the edge of the pueblo, hiring a peon woman to come once a week to do the cleaning. He ate at the tavern at a special discount rate granted by the reluctant landlord as a method of protection and favoritism if he ever found himself in trouble with the Law.

ZORRO hurried to this house through the swirling mist. He entered through a rear window which he found open and shortly thereafter appeared before the *magistrado*, who sat at a table scanning documents. The official gave a squawk of fear when he saw the masked man before him, and slumped down in his chair.

"You have guessed my identity, señor?" Zorro asked.

"You — you are Zorro? You have come to rob me?"

"I am Zorro. I have come to punish you, señor, for what you did today. How much gold did you get for releasing that girl in peonage to Esteban Audelo?"

"Audelo? Gold?" the man gulped. "I — I but did my duty in the matter."

The long whip cracked out, and the cringing magistrate howled as the lash bit into his fat body.

"Señor Zorro, let me explain," he begged. "This man came to me and offered me gold to do it — "

"Do what?"

"If they were brought before me — the cook and the girl — I was to listen to their stories, let the cook go and fine the girl heavily and release her in peonage. I thought nothing of it, Señor Zorro, except that this man of wealth and position wanted the girl in his house."

"It was nothing to you that an innocent girl might be ruined by this man with gold in his purse? The Laws mean nothing to you?"

The whip shot out again and bit. The magistrate howled, and began begging for mercy.

"Give me the gold you got!" Zorro ordered. "Every coin! It will go into the poor box at the chapel. Empty your purse, scoundrel!"

Whimpering, the magistrate did as ordered. Zorro stuffed the pouch away in his sash.

"Resign your office tomorrow," Zorro ordered. "Do not forget it, and do not think that any official protection can save you if you do not. Fail to resign and I'll visit you again and carve my sign in your foul heart!"

"I — I'll resign," the *magistrado* agreed.

"What do you know of this affair?"

"Nothing except what I have told you, Señor Zorro. I but did my share as ordered."

The whip lashed out again and again, until the official was cowering on the floor, his arms wrapped around his head, his squawls in competition with the wind that had begun to rage outside.

Zorro darted from the house, coiling his whip. He went swiftly through the fine rain that was commencing to fall, this time to the house which had been engaged by Señor Esteban Audelo.

Zorro knew the house, one of the oldest in the town. It had been repaired for its present tenant. But there was a patio with a crumbled wall, and a garden that was a tangled mass.

In a corner of the dark patio, Zorro crouched to watch and listen. If he was to encounter danger tonight, this would be the place, he knew.

He hooked the coiled whip to a belt over his sash, and got out his pistol, and then went slowly and cautiously along the old patio wall toward a window through which came a shaft of light. That light meant that Esteban Audelo possibly had not retired.

The noise of the milling herd a short distance away covered what slight sounds Zorro made. The smell of cattle was in the damp air. The vaqueros were shouting and singing, and their voices told they had been drinking heavily at the tavern.

Zorro reached the patio door to find it unlocked. He opened it carefully and slipped inside. He was in a hallway dark except for the streak of light that came from the room beyond. He heard voices, and went along the hallway like a shadow and got near the door of the room.

HE PEERED in. Esteban Audelo was sprawled in a big chair at the end of a long table upon which were two candelabra with tapers burning brightly. He held a goblet of wine and was laughing up at the terrified girl who had just poured the drink for him. Anita Gonzales' face was pale and her eyes wide with fear.

"Do not be alarmed, my pretty one," Audelo was saying to her. "I mean you no harm. Were I inclined to a love adventure, there are certain dainty señoritas I know. A peon girl, regardless of how pretty she may be, is not to my liking."

He gulped the wine, and motioned for her to fill the goblet again, which she did nervously.

"You, my pretty, are but bait for a trap," Esteban Audelo continued. "After the trap is sprung, you will be released from your peonage, and I'll have returned to me the gold I paid as your fine. So cease being frightened."

"I am — what did you say, señor?" she asked.

"Bait for a trap. 'Tis this fellow Zorro I want. And how easier to get in touch with him than by what was done today? He rushes around in a mask protecting peons and natives, does he not?"

"You would — would meet him, señor?" Anita asked.

"That is my desire. You know him?"

"But no, señor! Nobody knows his identity. I have heard the peons and natives talking of it. He is what you call a big mystery."

"He'll be a dead mystery when I'm done with him," Audelo boasted. "I'll tell you a secret, my pretty — I was sent here to finish off this Señor Zorro the soldiers seem unable to catch. A great swordsman, is he? Ha! We shall see as to that. I am not without skill with a blade; my pigeon. If he walks into the trap, you will have the rare delight of watching me play with the rogue for a time and then run him through. He does not know he will be facing a man who worked for the Viceroy and settled His Excellency's enemies."

"You would — kill him?" the girl asked.

"Certainly. And strip the mask off his face and see his features. And then return to Monterey and spend the gold the affair will bring me. If only the rogue comes!"

Holding his pistol ready, Zorro strode into the room. "I am here, Señor Audelo," he said.

Audelo bent forward, his palms flat upon the table, his feet braced beneath him. Anita gave a cry of fear and cringed against the wall. Her arrest and doom to peonage, her fear of her employer, and now the sudden appearance of this masked man with a pistol — the culmination unnerved her.

Zorro was watching Audelo carefully. "Well, señor?" he said. "I am here, as you can see."

"And as I desire it, señor," Audelo returned. "Do you intend to pistol me? Let me tell you that you have walked into a trap."

"I'll walk out of it, señor, when I have dealt with you."

"Señor Zorro, you'll never leave this room alive. If you shoot me down, others will be at your throat. Sergeant Garcia and his troopers are stationed at every door. They were in hiding, awaiting you, and no doubt witnessed your entrance to the house. You found the door unlocked, did you not?" Audelo laughed.

ZORRO swerved around the table so no door would be at his back. He did not doubt that Audelo spoke truth. He was in a trap, had walked into it blindly. But he had been in traps before.

"Señor Zorro, I have heard overmuch of your skill with the blade," Audelo was saying. "I believe you are badly overrated. If you do not care to pistol me,

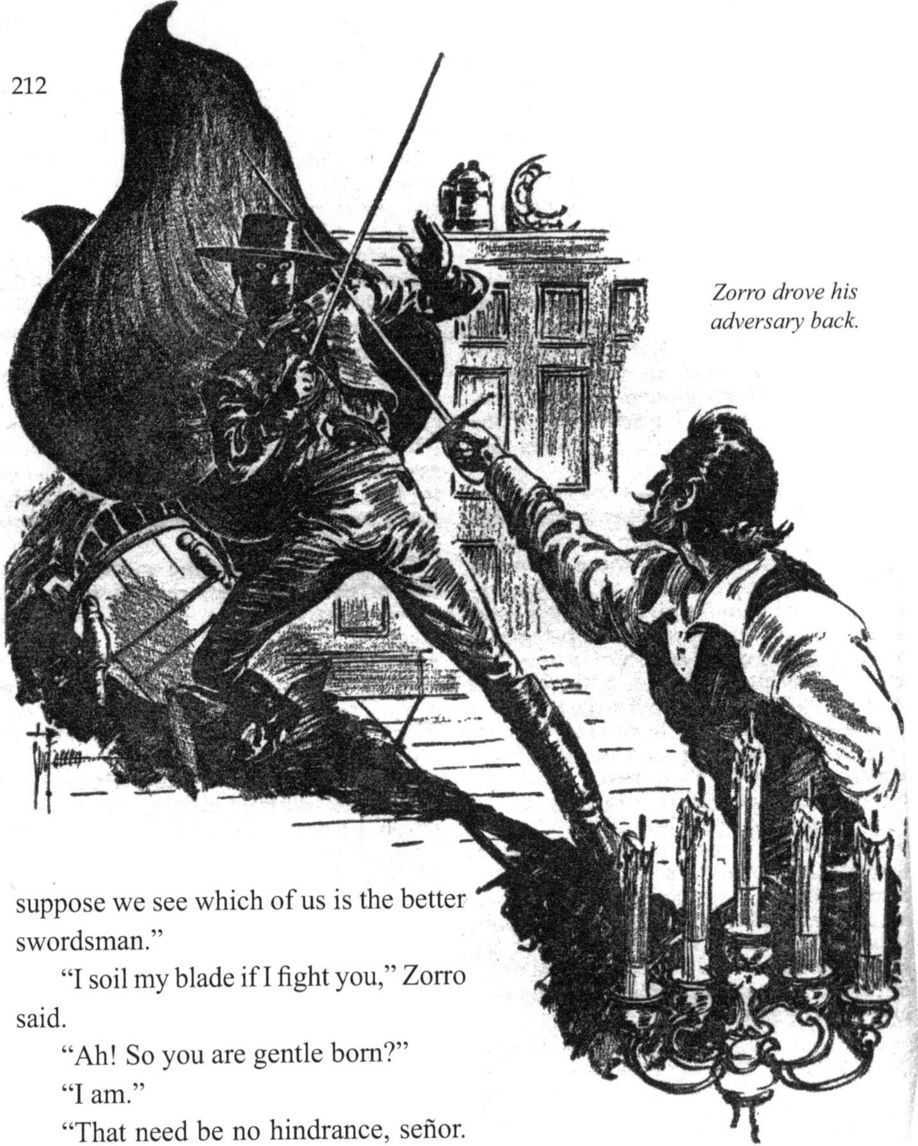

Zorro drove his adversary back.

suppose we see which of us is the better swordsman."

"I soil my blade if I fight you," Zorro said.

"Ah! So you are gentle born?"

"I am."

"That need be no hindrance, señor. So am I," Audelo declared.

"You foul your blood, then!"

"Señor!" Audelo raged, getting out of his chair, but keeping his palms flattened on the table. "I am a *capitán* in the service of the Viceroy, and also in the service of His Excellency the Governor of Alta California. Do I qualify?"

"Draw your blade, señor. On guard!" Zorro replied. "And kindly be honorable enough, in this instance, to fight me without aid from any troopers who may be near."

Audelo's eyes blazed. "I will fight you fairly," he declared, "and as I fight I will be remembering that remark."

"Let the girl go home," Zorro requested, "since she has served her purpose here. She will only be in our way."

Without glancing at Anita, Audelo spoke, "Get you gone. Tell the troopers I have released you."

Zorro heard her gasp, then the swish of skirts as she hurried from the room. Audelo stepped away from the table, back toward the wall, and his hand went to the hilt of his blade. Zorro heard steps in the hallway, saw a face at a door, and knew that Audelo had spoken the truth — troopers were all around him.

"Into the trap you came, like a foolish rabbit," Audelo chuckled, as he prepared for fight. "The cook was put in the tavern at my order, and he marked all the hot tortillas. I thought word of it would get to Zorro, and that after the girl was blamed and bound in peonage to me Zorro would try a rescue. Well, señor, here you are!"

AUDELO whipped out his blade, Zorro lunged forward, and they were at it.

Knowing this man's reputation for ability with a blade, Zorro moved with extreme caution. The first few seconds were enough to reveal to him that here was a rare swordsman, that perhaps this time he was fighting for his life. Audelo's eyes were mere gleaming slits, and his lips were set in a firm straight line. The expression of a killer was in his face.

The blades rang, the room was heavy with their breathing as they fought. From the near distance came the bawling of the cattle around the plaza, and the wild cries of the vaqueros. The tapers in the two candelabra on the long table cast a good light.

Audelo attacked, and Zorro retreated around the table and to the wall, but there stood and engaged furiously. And then Audelo attacked again, with great fury, but only to be beaten back.

Zorro became the aggressor in turn, drove his adversary aside and backward, Audelo turning aside every trick he tried.

"So you have met your master at last?" Audelo cried.

Zorro felt the tip of the other's blade rip his sleeve. A slight fear came to him. And he remembered that he must be the victor here, else be slain and his identity revealed. And that would bring double sorrow to his father, for old Don Alejandro would grieve at the passing of his son and heir, and also because he would be exposed as a man with a price upon his head. No doubt the Governor would even confiscate the Vega estate.

Those thoughts gave him added courage, and he renewed the combat with vigor. He felt Audelo giving way before him, and his caution was renewed. But in a moment he knew this was no trick, that the man before him was tiring, was not so certain of victory as he had been.

Zorro urged the fighting again. And when he felt that he was to have the victory he considered other things. Victory over this man would not be enough, if Garcia and his troopers were standing ready to seize him. He must win, and then escape.

He gave ground, let Audelo come after him, and finally got close to the long table again, with an open window behind him. And again he pressed the fighting, suddenly and unexpectedly, and Audelo was caught off guard. Zorro's blade darted out, he lunged, and the *capitán* of the Viceroy dropped his sword and started to fall forward, blood gushing from the wound in his breast.

Zorro sprang backward. His blade swept in a wide arc and sent a candelabra crashing to the floor from the table, the tapers being extinguished. Another sweep of the blade, the second candelabra crashed, and the room was in darkness. And, even as Sergeant Garcia's voice bellowed a warning, Zorro was through the window and in the tangled garden.

He heard men crashing toward him, and turned and ran, blade still in hand. Through the swirls of mist and fine falling rain he charged the short distance down the side street to the corner of the plaza.

Cattle were milling there as the half-intoxicated vaqueros tried to herd them on their journey again. And Zorro was among them, his blade now in sheath, his black figure bending and dodging and darting. The pursuing troopers could not get at him, could not get around the cattle in time.

Zorro was out of the herd at the mouth of another dark passageway. Through the darkness he sped, the wind drowning all sound of his progress.

And finally he came to where faithful Bernardo was waiting to take the clothes and weapons of Zorro.

A few minutes later Don Diego slipped quietly into his father's house, to find Don Alejandro sitting at a table.

"Everything is well," Diego said. "All I need now is a cup of hot wine, and then some sleep."

Vallejo brought out his pistol and fired

An *Ambush* for *Zorro*

Wily soldiers stage a little drama to snare Don Diego Vega!

FOR three days a torrential storm which had driven in from the sea had been drenching the coastline of Alta California from Santa Barbara to San Diego de Alcala.

Trees bent before the force of the storm. Some were stricken to earth by the angry blasts. Rills turned to rivers, hillsides were drenched, highways became tracks of slick mud. Stock on the open range at the ranchos stood with heads lowered and hides flinching beneath the steady pelting of cold rain.

In the pueblo of Reina de Los Angeles, the plaza had become a quagmire. The buildings were stained with dampness, the adobe walls spotted. Vegetation sagged with its weight of sodden foliage.

But dawn of the fourth day revealed a cloudless sky. By the time the sun was an hour above the horizon buildings, trees and shrubs were steaming. Faint streaks of drying earth appeared on the roads, and people knew the storm was at an end.

They came forth to attend to business they had neglected during the storm, to make social visits, and to chat about other storms which had visited the land. And finally Don Diego Vega emerged from his father's house, his raiment resplendent as usual. He strode carefully around the pools of water to get to the plaza and go to the chapel.

There he visited for a time with aged Fray Felipe, the tender-hearted Franciscan who attended to all religious matters for the Vega family. When their talk ended, the padre went with Diego to the door and stood there with him. He had christened Diego and watched him grow to manhood, and being Diego's confessor knew things about him which other men did not know.

AS THEY talked, there was a sudden commotion at the corner of the plaza. In from the south along the muddy highway rolled four lumbering ox-drawn carts piled high with goods. Some trader's outfit, Diego supposed, that had been caught on the highway by the storm. The oxen and the high solid wooden wheels of the carts were plastered with mud. The men who goaded the oxen were wet and muddy also.

Ahead of this small caravan rode the trader on a good horse. He was yelling, and his long whip cracked, not at the patient laboring oxen, but at the backs of four men who staggered along a few feet ahead of him.

Diego and the padre saw at a glance that the four men were peons or natives dressed in rags, their feet bare. Even the continual application of the whip did not make them flinch and shiver more than the damp cold that had penetrated to their bones. They plodded along like dumb cattle, their heads bent, their countenances indicative of a state of utter hopelessness.

"What beast in human form is this?" Diego muttered, as he watched the infuriated face of the trader.

The carts were coming slowly along the side of the plaza, past the tavern. The man on the horse was berating the four he kept on the move by flogging, his shouts ringing around the plaza.

"Kick the mud, dogs! ... I'll strip the hide from your dirty backs! ... I'll soon have you in the cell room at the barracks!"

Men were emerging, from the tavern and other buildings to see what was causing the commotion. The caravan came on toward the chapel, the leader shouting and the whiplash cracking.

In front of the chapel was a water cask with gourd dippers kept there by the padres for public use. The four unfortunates saw it, and with strange cries broke away from the lash to hurry toward it. Before the mounted man, who had glanced back at the carts, could reach them, they had grasped the gourd dippers and were running water into them from the spigot.

The rider turned and saw, gave a roar of rage, and spurred forward with whip uplifted.

The four men now were drinking like animals who had been thirsting for a long time, spilling the water over their chins and down their breasts in their nervousness. The lash sang and struck the back of one. As he reeled aside with a cry of pain, old Fray Felipe stalked forward angrily, his hand uplifted.

"Stop, señor!" the padre cried in a voice whose strength belied his years. "Are you an inhuman monster?"

"Ha, a padre!" the rider said, bending forward in his saddle with his wrists crossed upon the pommel. "A padre. One of the sort who pets vermin like these and makes them unsatisfied with their lot. Attend to your chapel, padre, and I'll handle those misbegotten Sons — "

"Stop, señor!" Diego spoke this time. "You cannot address a fray in this manner."

"Can I not? And who are you, my fine señor, that tells me I cannot? A popinjay from your appearance, a pretty boy the señoritas like to chuck under the chin."

Diego straightened and his eyes flashed a little. But Sergeant Manuel Garcia, second in command at the presidio in Reina de Los Angeles, had come up behind Diego and the padre. The uncouth sergeant was Diego's friend.

"This gentleman you have addressed so is Don Diego Vega, señor!" Garcia thundered at the trader. "Use more respect when you speak to him!"

"Vega? Ha, I have heard of the Vegas," the man on the horse replied.

"They pet and pamper their peons and natives. They over feed them and make life for them a bed of roses. Thereby they upset the balance of everything. Such acts make the scum get large ideas as to their importance."

THE four men had finished drinking and were huddled together trembling. Fray Felipe pointed to them.

"Look at these men! They seem to be famished, and were suffering from thirst — "

"They had some gruel at dawn yesterday," the rider cut in. "Thirsty? Pools of muddy water are along the highway; the earth is saturated with it. But then, of course, being in somewhat of a hurry, I did not give them time to stop and drink." He bent forward again and leered at the padre.

"Who are these men?" Sergeant Garcia asked.

"Two are peons and two natives, bound to me by the laws of peonage."

"And why do you treat them in this manner?"

"Because, señor, one of my carts started slipping over a cliff in the slick mud day before yesterday. These four men did not jump when I shouted to them to get at the cart; get the oxen free and save everything — "

"The cart would have crushed us all — it was falling already," one of the unfortunates wailed.

The rider raised his whip, but Sergeant Garcia motioned for him not to strike, and strode forward.

"Your name?" he demanded of the trader.

"I am known as José Vallejo."

"Vallejo is an honored name in Alta California, señor, and you will do well not to disgrace it — especially since I feel certain the name is not really your own."

Garcia had been appraising the rider carefully, and the latter grinned down at him. It seemed to Diego and Fray Felipe that the sergeant's manner changed slightly, and that he became a little respectful.

"Señor Vallejo, as you term yourself, it will be a fortunate thing for you if Zorro does not learn of your brutality to these men," Garcia said.

"Zorro? Ha! The masked man who rides a black horse and gallops around being chased by troopers who always fail to catch him!" Vallejo scoffed. "Sometimes I have thought you fail purposely."

Garcia's eyes glittered. "Such talk about the soldiery may get you into difficulties," he declared. "Where go you from here?"

"I intend to put these cattle in the prison room at the barracks for safekeeping, then take the carts to a camping spot a mile out the San Gabriel road," José Vallejo declared. "There I shall leave my oxen goaders on guard and return to the tavern for food and refreshment and mayhap some fun with dice and cards.

After a day, of rest, I shall take my caravan on toward Monterey!"

"Very pretty, señor. But first of all you will go to the barracks and report to the *commandante* and get his approval of your fine plans."

"Rather than bother traders continually with reports and such, you soldiers would do better to catch this Zorro," Vallejo said.

"If Zorro learns of your cruelty to these men, he may ignore the soldiers and punish you, señor. You will learn you cannot mistreat even peons and natives in such a manner with impunity," Garcia said. "I'll lead the way to the barracks, and do you give your arm a rest from wielding that whip."

Garcia strode off. The four unfortunates followed him, and José Vallejo rode behind them, cracking his long whip at intervals. Then came the carts, passing slowly, the oxen pulling with heads lowered, plopping great hoofs down into the deep mud.

Diego and Fray Felipe were left alone, standing side by side. Others who had been watching and listening went back into the buildings.

"Did you give this Señor José Vallejo particular attention?" Diego asked.

"Not particularly. What have you observed, Diego?"

"Notice how he rides. Is his seat in the saddle that of an ordinary trader? Or is it the seat of a military officer who cannot disguise the fact even out of uniform?"

FRAY FELIPE'S eyes gleamed an instant. "Ah!"

"And observe those carts, padre. The third one in line, in particular. There is not the slightest breeze at the moment, eh? Those carts seem to be packed with bales of hides on the way to market, do they not?"

"So it would seem, Diego."

"Then why should the bales in the third cart move slightly, especially at the end? With no wind, what would lift the corner of the covering a few inches?"

"What is your conjecture, my son?"

"That we have been watching a drama, padre. The trader is an army officer, perhaps on the personal staff of His Excellency the Governor. And the third cart has men in hiding, possibly soldiers, beneath that upper layer of hides."

"And the purpose?"

"Is plain, padre. The fellow mistreats men who are unable to resist. That is a thing for which Zorro punishes men. There was mention of Zorro during the talk. The drama occurred where men could see and hear. Anybody who is friendly to Zorro's work would speak about it to others. And if Zorro hears of it, he may seek to punish this pseudo trader."

"Ah!" Fray Felipe said, his eyes twinkling again. "You think this is a trap to catch or slay Zorro?"

"I do, padre. Nor is that all. I saw a signal of a sort pass between José Vallejo and Sergeant Garcia, and after that the big sergeant treated Vallejo with more civility, though keeping up a pretense of censure. Possibly our *commandante* here, and Garcia, his second in command, know of a plot and were waiting Vallejo's coming."

"If Zorro should make a move, then, he might find himself in difficulties," Fray Felipe hinted. "Soldiers with guns would pop out of that cart, and the trader would become an officer most proficient with a blade. And our local troopers might be on the scene also."

"Quite true," Diego replied. "And if Zorro does not attack and punish the trader after his mistreatment of those unfortunates, those who now look to Zorro for help will lose faith in him."

"And what does Zorro intend to do?" the padre asked, looking straight at him.

"Zorro will take thought on it," Diego Vega said, smiling slightly.

Fray Felipe's reply was a whisper:

"May good fortune attend you, Zorro, my son … "

At home, Diego related the entire episode to his father, proud, dignified Don Alejandro Vega. The latter strode back and forth across the broad main room of the house, his head bent in thought.

"I believe you are right, Diego," he said, finally. "It is an attempt to ambush Zorro. Were it not for one thing, my son, I'd advise that you ignore the entire matter. But, as you say, unless you punish this José Vallejo for his brutality, those for whom you fight, those you seek to help, will lose faith in you. The instant a champion of the downtrodden shows he is vulnerable, the downtrodden shrug their shoulders and look for help elsewhere."

"I have decided Zorro rides tonight," Diego said.

"You will have to use great care, my son. Zorro has dodged pitfalls and evaded traps so far, and for that reason alone he must increase his vigilance."

Diego called a house servant and ordered that Bernardo, his mute peon bodyservant, be sent to him. And when Bernardo joined him in his own rooms, Diego spoke in a low voice that could not have been heard even by anyone passing in the hall.

"You have heard concerning the trader, José Vallejo?" Diego asked.

Bernardo nodded assent and made a guttural sound which indicated his anger.

"Zorro rides tonight. Have the horse and weapons in the usual place at the usual time."

Bernardo's eyes gleamed. He bobbed his head and hurried from the room.

LATE that afternoon, Diego wandered around the house and grounds with a volume of poetry in his hand. But though he pretended to be considering the work of the poet, he was only listening to words and phrases dropped by the peons and native house servants as they lounged in their adobe huts in the rear, or went about their tasks in the patio and the house itself.

He learned that the four unfortunates had been put into the prison room of the barracks for safe-keeping. The cart caravan had made camp at the camping grounds on the San Gabriel road, and José Vallejo, leaving his oxen handlers on guard, had returned to the pueblo and was seeking relaxation.

That night there was a bright moon. Slipping out of the house, Diego went through the shadows to the abandoned storehouse a short distance away, where Bernardo was waiting. He had Zorro's black horse, costume and weapons.

Diego put the costume on over his other clothing, donned the black mask and hood, belted on his sword and stuck two pistols into his sash. To the pommel of his saddle he hooked the coiled long whip whose stinging lash had punished many cruel men. Diego Vega disappeared, and in his stead was Zorro. The pose of fop disappeared, and now a stern avenger mounted the black horse.

Since toddling babyhood, Diego had gone back and forth between Reina de Los Angeles and the vast Vega rancho in the vicinity of San Gabriel mission. He knew the country well even at night.

He rode carefully through the shadows, away from town and away from the highway. Finally he turned toward where the highway curved between two hills. Screened by thick brush on a hillside, he looked down upon the camping ground.

A small fire was burning, and the oxen handlers were squatting around it, eating and drinking from a wineskin. The night breeze carried their voices to Zorro, but he understood only a snatch of talk now and then:

"… Señor Vallejo will do the handsome thing by us if he succeeds in this … 'tis outrageous to doff our uniforms and be oxen goaders … we are more fortunate than our comrades in the cart ... but they were out of the pelting rain at least."

So those men supposed to be oxen goaders were soldiers also, Zorro realized. Four of them, and possibly half a dozen more armed troopers in the cart beneath the covering of skins. And, for all Zorro knew, perhaps Sergeant Garcia and some of the troopers from Reina de Los Angeles were in ambush in the vicinity also.

Zorro got a pistol from his sash, aimed carefully and fired. The bullet zipped into the embers of the fire and sent them flying into the faces of the men squatting around it. The ominous crack of the weapon sang in their ears as it was echoed among the rocks. None had seen the flash of the pistol.

They sprang up in alarm and ran toward the carts, shouting at one another, their words betraying the presence of the hidden men. Zorro moved his black horse along the screen of brush and down nearer the highway. From this new position he fired again, after reloading his weapon. The second pistol remained in his sash untouched.

This time, the bullet thudded into the side of one of the carts. And this time one of the men had seen the pistol's flash. He yelled and pointed. Zorro gave a wild yell that rang among the rocks with multiplied sound, and at a curve where the light of the moon was cut off he rode across the highway and upon higher ground on the opposite side.

From a new point of vantage, he looked down upon the camp. He could hear the men jabbering. Those hidden in the cart had not been decoyed out of it by his shots. The oxen goaders grew quiet. They kept to the shadows cast by the carts. They were watching, listening.

ZORRO aimed his pistol and fired again, and yelled as he fired. The bullet struck a rock beside the road and screamed its song of ricochet. And now from the cart came men carrying muskets, six of them, and they darted to cover in the darkness and opened fire at the hillside.

Zorro rode behind rocks and sought cover and listened to the fusillade. He could understand the feelings of the men down in the camp. An unknown was shooting at them, a bullet might fly at them from any direction. They faced a mysterious enemy they could not even see.

He changed position and fired again. Once more his bullet struck a rock and glanced into the brush with a nasty whine. And again the muskets spoke until they were emptied of their charges, and the slugs from them whistled harmlessly among the rocks and clumps of brush on the hillside.

The wind was sweeping the sounds of firing along the curving highway, driving the echoes of gunfire toward the town. Then one of the men rushed across the highway to where a riding mule had been tethered for the night, and a moment later was bending low over the mule's neck and racing along the sloppy road toward Reina de Los Angles. He was carrying news of the mysterious attack to Señor José Vallejo, Zorro guessed.

Along the hillside, Zorro started riding cautiously toward the town. Before he had gone far, he heard hoofs pounding the road below him. The moonlight revealed seven mounted men. It glinted from the sabers at their sides. He heard the voice of Sergeant Manuel Garcia raised in stentorian orders. The troopers raced toward the cart camp. So, then, it was a plot in which the local soldiers were playing a part.

The troopers passed him and rushed on. Zorro rode down the hillside and stopped in a dark place at the side of the highway. The wind blew sounds from the town to his ears. Before long, he heard the pounding of a horse's hoofs. This time, a lone rider was approaching.

The rider came into view, his mount laboring in the deep slippery mud. The moonlight revealed him to Zorro as the man who called himself José Vallejo. He loped on toward where Zorro was in hiding.

Suddenly Zorro jumped his big black horse out of the shadows and swung him beside Vallejo's on the latter's right hand. The moonlight clearly revealed the masked man, dressed in black, and the pistol held ready in Zorro's hand.

"Rein in, señor!" Zorro commanded.

"What is this?"

"I am Zorro, señor. Your little trap was not at all clever. Your men at the camp are afraid of shots from the dark. The troopers of Sergeant Garcia have ridden there, and no doubt are searching the shadows for me in a waste of time and effort. And here you are alone with me — beater of defenseless men!"

"And you, the brave Zorro, with a pistol in your hand!" Vallejo replied. "I appear at your mercy. So the trap failed? Know, then, I am no trader."

"Your seat in the saddle tells me you are an army officer."

"True. And you, I have often heard, are a wizard with the blade. Dare you fight me with that weapon, fairly?"

"I always fight fairly, señor," Zorro said, sternly. "But do you? Let us dismount here where the moonlight is bright enough for our purpose. I'll return my pistol to my sash when you have drawn blade."

VALLEJO growled an imprecation and almost threw himself out of the saddle. He led his horse aside, whipped out his blade, and stood ready.

"This is to be the end of you, Zorro," he boasted. "I have something of a reputation as a swordsman. No country lout like yourself can best me. I'll run you through, strip off your mask to see your face, and collect the Governor's reward as well as the promotion he has promised me!"

Zorro got down out of his saddle. He took the coiled whip from the pommel and attached it to his sword belt on the left side. He sidestepped to avoid a small rock, and whipped blade from scabbard.

Vallejo took the offensive. Zorro felt him out for a moment, and knew the other was good with a blade, but not so good as men Zorro had vanquished in the past. The footing was bad, and both were careful on that account. It was not a place for speedy footwork.

At any moment, Zorro knew, Garcia and his troopers might come riding back, for the wind was carrying the sound of the ringing blades down the highway toward them. And the man who had gone for Vallejo on the riding mule might return, see what was happening, and hurry back to the town for help, in which case Zorro might find himself between two fires.

A quick end of this must be made, but Zorro had no wish to end it by sending the point of his blade into his adversary's heart. He stood, then pressed the fighting, and as Vallejo retired before his onslaught, Zorro's blade darted in. There was a ringing of metal and Vallejo's sword was torn from his hand to arch through the air, catching and reflecting the light of the moon, and crash against some rocks at the side of the highway.

Vallejo reeled aside. His hand went to his belt and he brought out his pistol. It was discharged, and the ball brushed against Zorro's left sleeve. Vallejo hurled the pistol, but Zorro bent and allowed it to go over his shoulder. As he did so he got his sword back into its scabbard, and suddenly the whip was in his hand.

Vallejo's wild cries for help were ringing down the wind. He hurled himself forward for a hand-to-hand clash now that Zorro was not holding a sword. But Zorro made no effort to draw a pistol and shoot him down.

The lash met Vallejo as he charged. It wrapped around his body, bit and drew blood. It jerked him off his feet and sent him on his hands and knees in the mud. And then it fell upon him in a rain of blows, cutting his garments, lashing his body.

"The whip for being a craven and trying to pistol me!" Zorro said. "The whip because you used it unmercifully on defenseless men! I could have run you through or shot you down, but the whip is best for a man such as you."

He continued lashing as he talked. He beat José Vallejo down into the mud, broke his spirit, brought him to the stage of pitiful whimpering. Zorro stepped back.

"Get up!" he ordered. "Quickly, if you want to live! Get into your saddle!"

He jerked Vallejo to his feet. He tossed Vallejo's blade and pistol aside. He drove him lurching toward his horse and forced him into the saddle. Still holding the whip ready, Zorro started mounting his own horse.

Sounds came to him from the highway near the cart camp. He could hear Sergeant Garcia shouting to his men. Then came the noise of horses pounding through the mud with what speed they could.

Zorro rode his black beside Vallejo's mount. Vallejo was clinging to his saddle, bent forward.

"Ride! With speed!" Zorro ordered.

HE urged his black into a lope, then a slow gallop, and kept Vallejo's mount beside him. Sounds of Garcia and his troopers came nearer. But now Zorro was beyond the slippery hill, and got more speed out of his own mount and Vallejo's.

Around a curve, they went on at still greater speed. And toward them Zorro saw coming the man on the riding mule, who had ridden to town to warn Vallejo. He pulled the mule to one side out of the highway as the riders bore down upon him. Too late he realized they were Vallejo and a masked man.

Zorro lashed with his whip again. Vallejo's horse got part of the blow, and sprang forward with added speed. But Zorro sent the black after him, and reached out to grasp Vallejo's reins.

They came to the plaza, and some peons scattered out of their path. In front of the tavern, Zorro pulled both mounts to a stop. The tavern door opened, and a streak of light shot out to mingle with the bright moonlight.

Zorro toppled Vallejo from his saddle. As the soldier yelled for help, Zorro cut him with the whip again. Men rushed from the tavern to see the punishment.

Garcia and his troopers were almost to the plaza now. Zorro whipped out a pistol and sent one shot over their heads. As they scattered to right and left, he spurred the black and dashed across the corner of the plaza, turning toward the mouth of the highway leading to San Juan Capistrano.

Pistols exploded behind him and bullets flew, but none came dangerously near. He bent low and rode furiously. A glance behind showed him that Garcia and his troopers were coming on, except one man who had stopped beside Vallejo.

Out the road a short distance, where there was a curve with high banks on either side, Zorro left the highway, rode behind a fringe of brush, and doubled back as Garcia and his men raced along the highway below him.

He got down into a depression and followed it, carefully, circling to an old cattle trail. This he followed back toward the town. He swung wide as he approached, to come in from another direction. And in time he came to where Bernardo waited for him.

"Zorro has ridden well," he said to the mute, as he stripped off the black costume and tossed it aside with his weapons. "Take good care of the horse. Get the mud off him speedily!"

Through the shadows, Diego Vega raced toward his father's house. He passed the huts of the servants unseen, went through the patio, got inside and went to his own room.

Within a few minutes, he had discarded the clothes he had been wearing, put on others, and wrapped a thick dressing gown around his body. He went into the hallway and to the big main room of the house, shuffling in his loose sandals. His father, Don Alejandro, was waiting. "All is well, my son?" Don Alejandro asked.

"All is well, my father. José Vallejo has been punished. No doubt the servants will be gossiping about it in the morning," Diego said. He reached for the goblet of wine Don Alejandro had been quick to pour, sipped, smiled slightly. "I believe I'll read poetry for a time, and then seek out my couch."

Zorro Gives Evidence

While the court sits in judgment, Don Diego Vega pleads his case with a flashing blade!

DURING the hour of promenade that afternoon, Don Diego Vega, dressed in his resplendent best, sauntered along the shady side of the plaza in Reina de Los Angeles and went in languid fashion toward the sprawling tavern.

As he strolled, he stifled his yawns with a scented lace handkerchief, shuffled a trifle, and sagged, forward as if the heavy weight of the entire world rested upon his shoulders. He acknowledged the salutations of friends he passed with feeble gestures, which was strictly in character.

For those of the pueblo long had taken Diego Vega to be a young caballero without fire and spirit, a sort of spineless fop, and they pitied his illustrious proud father, Don Alejandro Vega, because he had an only son and heir who read the poets instead of cutting the wild antics of others of his kind.

This side of his character, however, was a pose, a means to an end, as the old saying has it. Three persons — his father; old Fray Felipe, the Franciscan who was his confessor; and Bernardo, his mute peon bodyservant — knew another side of his character and guarded the secret from the world.

Diego may have seemed to be more than half asleep as he took his afternoon stroll, yet he was keenly alert to all that happened around him, his eyes and ears continually busy. He observed the usual persons — proud hidalgos and strutting young caballeros; fat señoras and their dainty señoritas crowding into the warehouse where the trader had opened bolts of fancy cloth just received for sale; barefooted peons and ragged natives going about their tasks, half-starved and mistreated unfortunates in a land of plenty.

Diego turned his head aside briefly as a horseman rode past and sent a cloud of fine dust in his direction. He put his scented handkerchief to his nostrils and mouth to keep out the dust. When he lifted his head again and glanced toward the tavern, he beheld that something was amiss.

Sergeant Manuel Garcia, second in command at the presidio of Reina de Los Angeles, was striding toward the tavern, cutting across the corner of the plaza in his haste. It was no new sight in the pueblo to see Sergeant Garcia striding toward the tavern, for there he spent his hours of recreation, bellowing and showing off his importance and gulping all the free wine that came his way.

BUT, just now, Garcia had four armed troopers marching two by two behind him, with measured military stride. And the burly, obese, uncouth sergeant had upon his red moonlike face the expression of a man going about serious official business. Diego also noticed that from the corner of the plaza came *Capitán* Pedro Chavez the new *commandante*, who had arrived at the post from Monterey less than a month before. *Capitán* Chavez was riding his charger, and two mounted orderlies were behind him.

Diego gradually quickened his pace. The manner of all the soldiers was purposeful, and Diego wondered whether some foul malefactor was about to be seized and taken into custody. If so, he must be a malefactor of importance, for *Capitán* Chavez would merely have sent his sergeant else and not put in a personal appearance.

Diego contrived to reach the door of the tavern slightly in advance of the sergeant and his men, and he stood back to watch. Sergeant Garcia bellowed orders, and two of his troopers ran around to the rear of the tavern building as if to prevent an escape by somebody inside. The other two troopers entered the tavern, and Garcia turned to see whether the capitan was coming along with his orderlies.

"You appear to be busy, Garcia," Diego observed.

The sergeant whirled to face him, and blew out the ends of his enormous mustache.

"Ah, Don Diego, *amigo!*" he greeted. "'Tis my ill fortune to meet you under these circumstances. Were I not in charge of a certain piece of work, I would have time to sit at table with you and enjoy a mug of wine — with which you are always kind enough to furnish me."

Diego smiled slightly. "Perhaps we can attend to the wine after your work is over," he hinted. "What troubles you of the soldiery now?"

" 'Tis for our new *capitán* to say, Don Diego. His will be the pleasure of being present at the capture — if we make it — and his glory while others do the work. It is against orders for me to mention upon what task we are engaged. But remain in the near vicinity, Don Diego, and you may be surprised."

Diego nodded and went through the doorway and into the tavern, where he sat on a bench beside a table beneath the open window. Juan Oviedo, the fat tavern-keeper, approached him and bowed as low as he could, considering the size of his paunch. Diego ordered wine, and the servile Oviedo hurried to get it himself instead of assigning the task to a native servant.

Diego glanced swiftly around the room. He saw a dozen men — some townsmen and others travelers off the highway — sitting at tables and eating, drinking, or playing with cards or dice. The troopers who had entered had taken up stations. Diego saw one beside the fireplace from where he could command the front door, and the second at a door which opened into the patio. As Oviedo server the; wine, Sergeant Garcia strode into the place, and behind him stalked the arrogant *Capitán* Chavez and his pair of orderlies. The Tavern-keeper bent low again and rubbed his hands together as he gestured for the *capitán* to be seated. Oviedo knew from sad experience that it were best to act the humble man of no consequence before an officer of the troopers.

But the *capitán* was not there, it appeared, to partake of the tavern's hospitality and afterward leave forgetting to pay. He held his head high, and his manner was domineering as he beckoned Oviedo to approach.

"*Señor el Capitán?*" the tavern-keeper questioned.

"Where is your nephew, fellow?" Chavez demanded to know.

"I believe he is in his room off the patio, resting," the tavern-keeper replied.

Capitán Chavez whirled to Garcia. "Fetch the rascal to me," he ordered. "And have one of the men guard this Oviedo."

The tavern-keeper was terrified instantly. "What has been my crime, *Señor el Capitán?*" he wailed. "I am an honest man. I work hard!"

"Be silent!" Chavez ordered.

DIEGO sipped his wine and watched and listened. He had known Juan Oviedo from boyhood, and liked the usually jovial tavern man. And he knew that Oviedo was extra careful not to transgress any of the laws, even the new ones which were published almost every time a courier arrived from Monterey. Oviedo reported suspicious characters to the presidio, and ejected card sharps and men who cheated at dice.

Diego heard a minor tumult in the patio, a man's voice lifted loudly in protests and then through the doorway came Sergeant Garcia and his two troopers holding the arms of a rather handsome young man Diego knew to be Benito Oviedo, the tavern keeper's nephew. Sergeant Garcia held a pistol, a sword wrapped in black cloth, and a dagger.

The prisoner was brought to a stop before the *capitán* and held securely.

"You are Benito Oviedo, nephew of the tavern keeper?" *Capitán* Chavez asked.

"Such is my name, *Señor el Capitán,*" the prisoner admitted.

"From where did you come to Reina de Los Angeles, and when — and why?" the officer demanded.

"I came from Monterey about ten days ago, *Señor el Capitán*. I came to visit my uncle and see whether I could find employment here."

"I have heard you fancy yourself a handsome rascal at whom all females roll their eyes," the *capitán* charged.

Benito Oviedo bowed. "We handsome men know how it is," he replied.

"Do not show insolence, or I'll have you whipped in the plaza! What is your means of livelihood?"

"I have worked at different things, *Señor el Capitán*. I have had luck with cards — honest luck. I am at good *vaquero*, good enough to be the *superintendente* of some *rancho*."

"You perhaps have many faults; but modesty is not one of them," Chavez observed. "Attend me! Is it not true that you have a rather fine black horse pastured secretly about a mile from the pueblo?"

Benito tossed up his head. "So that is it! I have such a horse — *si*. But there is nothing wrong about it, *capitán!* I found the horse wandering loose along the highway, and he followed me. I judged him to be an animal of value. So I thought I would keep him safely until the owner happened along, and claim a reward for finding the animal and caring for him."

"A pretty tale!" Chavez scoffed. "If you kept the horse hidden, how did you expect the owner to see him and reward you?"

BENITO answered instantly, though with pale face. "I expected the owner of such a fine animal to go about bewailing his loss and offering the reward. If

I had exhibited the horse here at the tavern, perhaps a score of men would have tried to say they had found him."

"Is it not true that you have ridden the horse recently — and at night?"

"That is true — *si,"* Benito admitted. "Such a spirited animal needs exercise if he be kept in condition, and I did not care to exhibit him by daylight, as I have explained."

"I see the sergeant has found a sword among your belongings. Explain that."

"It is an old blade given me a year or more ago by a man who owed me money and could not pay. I hoped to sell it sometime for the value of the debt."

"Can you use a blade?"

"I can, *capitán.* The same man taught me; he once had been a soldier in Mexico."

"I know you can use a blade, for the other evening you fenced with two of my troopers in the plaza and disarmed them both with ease," Chavez said. "What about this pistol my men found?"

"I have had it for years. It is good to have a pistol if one is caught on the highway at night. There are many thieves and cutthroats."

"And the black cloth in which your blade was found wrapped — what of that?" the *capitán* persisted.

"A piece of old cape I have had for a long time, *capitán.* I wrapped the blade to protect it from rust."

"You were observed at an early hour this morning cleaning your pistol and polishing the blade at the rear of the tavern."

"That is true," Benito confessed. "I keep them clean."

"And the trooper who observed you noticed something rather strange." *Capitán* Chavez' manner suddenly became more stern. "You stood like a fencer on guard, facing the adobe wall. You darted in and out like a man fighting, practicing with your blade against your dancing shadow on the wall. And you made lightning-like lunges and made scratches on the wall with the point of your blade. You scratched — the letter Z!"

Diego straightened a little on his bench and sipped more wine as a chorus of gasps came from those in the room.

Benito Oviedo looked sheepish. "I — I was trying to see how it could be done," he replied. "I have heard so much of Señor Zorro, the masked man who rides the hills and carves the initial Z on his foes and leaves it here and there as his mark."

"That is all you have to say, señor," Chavez demanded.

"I have answered your questions *Señor el Capitán*."

"And now listen to me. At night you ride a black horse you keep mysteriously hidden, as does Zorro. You are an excellent swordsman, as is Zorro. That rogue wears a black mask and hood to hide his features, and from this black cloth you say once was part of a cape a section has been cut, as we all can see — enough cloth to make such a mask and hood. Your comings and goings are mysterious. You have gold with which to gamble. And these night rides — what of them?"

"There is a certain peon girl two miles out of the pueblo who is filled with fire and likes gold. Need we say more?"

"You need say nothing more, señor, but I have a last word," *Capitán* Chavez announced. "All you have told me is lies. I order you under arrest for murder, highway robbery, and treason. You will be taken straightway to the barracks and placed in the prison room. You will be tried before the *magistrado* in the assembly room of the barracks tonight an hour after the evening meal. And no doubt, rogue, tomorrow at sunrise you will be hanged. You are Zorro!"

Diego Vega clutched his wine mug, and for an instant his body tensed, as exclamations of surprise rang around the room. The evidence was damning, but all this was a mistake, as Diego well knew. For he, Diego Vega, was Zorro ...

THE fat tavern keeper waddled forward, horror in the expression of his face.

"No, no *Señor el Capitán*!" Juan Oviedo cried. "My nephew is a young rogue, perhaps, and a loafer and a wastrel, but he is not a masked highwayman!"

"It is natural for you to defend him, since he is of your own blood," the *capitán* observed. "And perhaps there is another reason for your defense of him — you may have guilty knowledge of his deeds and be an accessory to them."

"No, no! I am an honest man."

Chavez raised a hand in a demand for silence. "We shall see at the trial," he said. "Meanwhile, this tavern must be run for the accommodation of those who hunger and thirst and desire lodging. Continue with your labors, Oviedo. But I shall leave Sergeant Garcia and one trooper here to guard you. As for your nephew — troopers, take him away!"

The second trooper who had come with Garcia and the two orderlies lashed

Benito's arms behind his back and thrust him out of the tavern. The trooper prodded him along, and the orderlies and *Capitán* Chavez mounted and followed. They went toward the barracks.

In the tavern, the first trooper remained lounging near the doorway watching Juan Oviedo. Sergeant Garcia strode to the table where Diego was sitting, and sprawled on a bench across from Diego.

"There you have it, Don Diego, *amigo*," the sergeant said. "At last the rogue of a Zorro is where he belongs. In the morning we'll stretch his neck. And our *commandante* will no doubt claim all the reward for the rascal's capture, curse it!"

The townsmen were hurrying out of the main room of the tavern, for with Juan Oviedo under suspicion and his nephew arrested, they did not wish to remain, for fear they might be accused of too much friendship for the suspected men. There remained only three travelers who were eating at a table in a corner.

"Landlord!" Garcia shouted. "Wine here!"

Juan Oviedo served them with hands that trembled. A terrible fear was in his face.

"My nephew is not guilty of being Señor Zorro," the tavern keeper declared. "It is all a terrible mistake."

"How about the evidence?" Garcia asked.

"I know how the affair appears, but he is innocent," Oviedo persisted. "Everything he said was the truth."

"Perhaps he has you fooled," the sergeant suggested. "He has the look of a clever rogue."

"He is a rogue of a sort, as are so many of our young men," Oviedo admitted. "But that does not make him a masked highwayman. He is my brother's son — "

"Let him explain, then," Garcia interrupted, "and prove his innocence. The trial tonight will be public, and he will have a chance to talk."

A crowd of peons and natives was gathering in the plaza, news of the affair having spread. Garcia emptied his wine mug and waddled to the door and went out to see if there was any disorder. Juan Oviedo bent across the table and spoke to Diego in whispers:

"Help me, Don Diego! They must not hang my brother's son and so disgrace my own name. I have worked hard here to make a success of my tavern."

Diego stopped him with a gesture. "Let your nephew, Benito, tell every move he has made the last several months, where he has been and with whom. If he was not in this part of the country when Zorro committed some of his depredations, then it follows he could not be Zorro. Let him explain where he was and what he has been doing."

"But he cannot do that, Don Diego. I throw myself upon your mercy and tell you something in confidence. If he told the truth about where he has been for several months and what doing, he would doom himself."

"How is this?"

"He is not Zorro. He never robbed and slew men or did any of the things Zorro has been accused of doing. Yet, were he to tell the truth, they would hang him."

"For what?'

THE innkeeper licked his pallid lips before answering.

"Benito is a smuggler. He worked with a crowd around Monterey, and then down near San Diego de Alcalá. And recently His Excellency the Governor issued an edict that all men proved to be smugglers should be hanged. That, of course, is because smuggling lessens the revenues, a share of which the Governor puts into his own pocket. Benito is a rascal and rogue, but only a smuggler — not a murderer or thief. He could tell the truth and prove it, and escape doom as Zorro, but bring it upon himself from another quarter."

Diego rubbed his chin thoughtfully, then sipped his wine. "Smuggling is a serious offense, but in my mind not serious enough to hang a man for," he said. "If the real Zorro learns of this affair, he may appear and prove Benito's innocence. If he should, get your nephew from this vicinity and tell him to stay away — and to change his mode of life."

Sergeant Garcia came back into the tavern, and Juan Oviedo hastened to refill his wine mug. But Diego waved more wine aside, and sighed and stood.

"I must go home," he said. "All this excitement — it is too much for me. I shall have a terrible headache, I know, and I had intended to read poetry and meditate this evening."

He shuffled out of the tavern and went along the side the plaza toward his father's house. Don Alejandro was sitting in the patio, and Diego told him all that had occurred.

"This Benito is a rogue and deserves punishment for 'his transgressions, but not hanging for being Zorro," Don Alejandro declared. "What will you do, my son?"

"Diego Vega will do nothing, my father," Diego smiled. "But Señor Zorro may attend that trial tonight. You must attend, my father. Every man in the pueblo will be there. You may tell any who inquire for me that you think I have gone to my couch to nurse a headache."

Heavy fog came over the hills from the distant sea before nightfall. The fog did not keep men of the pueblo from going to the barracks in time for the trial before the *magistrado*. Men of all ranks hurried there after the late evening meal, those of high birth and station to have reserved benches, the assembly room of the barracks to be filled by others. Then the doors would be closed to keep still others outside, while they waited for the verdict.

Diego took advantage of the fog when he slipped out of the house to be shrouded in its swirling clouds as he got through the patio and made his way past the huts of the house servants without being observed. Through the mist he hurried to the spot where he knew Bernardo, his faithful mute peon body servant would be waiting with Zorro's black horse, costume and weapons.

Working swiftly, Diego drew on the costume over his other clothes, donned the black mask and hood, buckled on his blade and thrust a loaded pistol into his sash, and hooked his long black whip over his saddlehorn.

"Attend me, Bernardo!" he whispered. "Get to the spot I told you, behind the barracks. Be ready to take the horse. Be sure you are not seen."

Bernardo slipped away through the foggy night, and Zorro gathered his reins and touched the horse gently with his spurs. The big black traveled at a walk away from the buildings and along a hillside, and finally approached the barracks from the rear.

Zorro was doubly cautious as he rode. Yet he could tell that the assembly room had been filled and the doors closed and locked. A crowd of men who could tot get in were huddled in front of the barracks trying to keep out of the wet. And There they were handled by all the troopers except those on duty in the room of trial.

Zorro dismounted in a small depression behind the barracks, and Bernardo slipped up to him through the night.

"Mount the black and wait here," Zorro instructed. "If I give the signal, ride. That will be only if 1 think I do not have time to mount and ride myself. If you ride in my place to decoy them, make the big circle I have explained to you, and put up the horse as usual. I'll care for my costume and weapons."

Bernardo got into the saddle and gathered the reins, and Zorro went noiselessly through the darkness to the rear of the barracks building.

A REAR window was open for a short distance to let fresh air into the stuffed room. A rear door, Zorro found quickly, was unlocked. He listened at the window.

Capitán Chavez was presenting his evidence to the court. Zorro could hear the audience mutter as each damning bit was introduced. He heard Benito Oviedo's wild denial. He heard gruff Sergeant Garcia warn those in the room to cease from making demonstration.

Zorro listened at the window until Chavez finished giving testimony. Juan Oviedo was then grilled by the *magistrado*. The tavern keeper, badly frightened, protested his innocence and that of his nephew.

But there remained the fact that Benito could not explain where he had been at the time Zorro had committed some of his depredations — dared not do so without condemning himself as a smuggler. Zorro knew the time was approaching when he would have to appear on the scene if Benito was to escape the rope of death. He got to the door and opened it slowly and carefully, and stepped inside. He was in a dark hallway at the other end of which was another door opening into the assembly room back of the *magistrado*'s bench.

Zorro listened at the door a moment. *Capitán* Chavez was engaged now in a recital of the things Zorro had done, and indulging in a furious denunciation of Benito Oviedo. He was also hinting that Juan Oviedo, the uncle who operated the tavern, must have known of his nephew's activities, and that possibly Juan was not the sort of person to operate the tavern. From time to time, Benito shouted an angry denial, and Sergeant Garcia shouted in turn for him to keep silent.

Zorro could hear that a downpour of rain had started. It slashed against the adobe walls of the barracks and roared on the tile roof. He knew all the men of the town were either in the locked courtroom or huddled in front outside. He had little fear of an attack from behind as he carefully opened the door beside which he stood, opened it a tiny crack at a time and peered into the room.

The attention of all in the room was centered upon *Capitàn* Chavez as he addressed the *magistrado*. The officer was pleading that he had made a case, and asking that Benito Oviedo be adjudged guilty and sentenced to die at sunrise on a scaffold to be erected in the plaza, where the general public could witness the execution.

Zorro adjusted his mask, tugged to settle his black gloves better on his fingers, and took his pistol from his sash. He opened the door wider. He had to take only two swift steps and jump upon the low rostrum where the *magistrado*

"I am Zorro!" cried the masked man in ringing tones

sat in a pompous attempt at dignity.

Capitán Chavez was concluding his address.

"Without doubt, this man is the notorious Zorro. You have noticed that he cannot account for his whereabouts and actions at certain specified times when Zorro was active in his nefarious pursuits. Benito Oviedo is Zorro, and should pay the extreme penalty for his acts."

Zorro took the two swift steps, and instantly was on the rostrum at the *magistrado's* side.

"Look this way *señores*!" Zorro's voice rang out in stern command. Certainly it was not the voice of the languid Diego Vega.

Every man in the room looked at him, at the pistol he held menacingly, with its muzzle resting against the head of the terrified *magistrado*.

"Do not make a move, señores, or I'll put a pistol ball through the head of your judge. The man you have been trying is not Zorro. I am Zorro! My presence here now at my own peril is proof enough you are making a mistake. It is almost an insult to me and my work, señores, that you think Zorro could be what this man is — a lazy rascal, and vain boaster. Are you content?"

No voice answered his immediately. The troopers in the room were armed with sabers and pistols, but awaited orders. Sergeant Garcia was like a man turned to stone as he waited for his superior to speak. *Capitán* Chavez was glaring at Zorro and saying nothing. But finally he yelled:

"It is a poor trick! This man is not Zorro. He is a friend of this Benito Oviedo trying a subterfuge upon us!"

"Hold!" Zorro shouted. "I'll prove I am Zorro. And make no hostile move while I do it, else your *magistrado* dies."

HE PRODDED the judge with the muzzle of his pistol, and the judge gave a squawk of fear. All before Zorro were motionless.

"If you are Zorro, prove it," Chavez finally said.

"Sergeant Garcia," Zorro called, "you crossed blades with Zorro once — remember? I disarmed you after giving you a slight wound in the shoulder. At that time I made a remark about you which was heard by no other man. I said, 'You are too fat and short of wind to be a good swordsman.' Do you remember?"

"Why, that — that is true," Garcia admitted.

"You — Carlos Ruiz! I whipped you once for abusing your peons. No man was near enough to hear what was said at the moment. You said to me, 'Do not kill me, Senor Zorro. My wife is about to have another baby.' Is that true?"

"It — it's true — none but Zorro could know it," the man confessed.

"Are you satisfied, *capitán?*" Zorro asked.

"Satisfied only that you are a rogue and liar. You are no more Zorro than I. I say you are a friend of this Benito Oviedo, and that he is Zorro, and that he could have told you of the things regarding which you have just spoken. Your trick does not work here, señor."

"Then we come to the last extremity, *capitán,*" Zorro said. "Zorro has the name of being an excellent swordsman. Would you cross blades with me in fair combat?"

"At once?" Chavez yelled. "Nothing could please me better. But you fight with a pistol in your hand."

"I transfer my pistol to my left hand, to make sure of fair play, and hold blade in my right," Zorro said "'Twill take but a moment for the matter to be decided. But if any man here makes a false move as we fight, I'll shoot you down like a dog, *Capitán* Chavez!"

Chavez had barged forward, tugging at the hilt of his blade, and men crowded backward away from the rostrum to give a space for fighting. It was fairly silent for a moment then, save for the noise the downpour of rain made as the wind slapped it against the walls of the building.

Zorro sprang down to face the *capitán*, whipping out his blade and transferring his pistol to his left hand. He stood in front of the door by which he had entered and made sure nobody got behind him.

Chavez approached, the blades touched. The watchers saw some swift footwork, heard the blades ring, and then *Capitán* Chavez gave a cry of rage and pain, and dropped his blade and reeled against the rostrum, throwing a hand to his face and bringing it away stained with blood.

On the *Capitán's* forehead, for all there to see, were three shallow cuts made with one darting thrust by the tip of Zorro's blade, and the cuts formed the letter Z.

"I leave my mark on your forehead, *Señor el Capitán!"* Zorro cried. "Is that proof enough for all here? This fellow you have been trying is innocent at being Zorro, so release him. I regret *señor*, that you cannot claim the reward for his capture."

A roar came from the throats of those in the room, and they began surging forward. Zorro noticed that the front door was unlocked and jerked open, and knew he could not linger now. He laughed mockingly and darted to the door through which he had entered, dashed through it and slammed it shut behind him. And an instant later he was outside in the driving rain, running from the building.

He heard men coming around the building at him from both sides, heard the raucous voice of Sergeant Garcia giving commands. So he laughed loudly again, and the wind carried the mocking laughter through the stormy night. And, because that was the signal, Bernardo kicked at the big black's flanks and the horse rushed away toward the San Gabriel trail.

"Mount and after him!" Garcia bellowed. "The rogue escapes! Run him down!"

The horses were in their stables, and it would take some time to saddle them and start the futile pursuit. The sounds of the black horse's hoofbeats grew faint and died away. And Zorro went slowly and carefully up the hillside through the storm and in time got to his father's house, to strip off his Zorro costume and weapons and hide them in Bernardo's hut, and then get to his own rooms unseen.

He stripped off his wet garments, put on a dressing robe and sandals, and went to the big main room of the house. And there his father, Don Alejandro, joined him after a time.

"Well done, my son," Don Alejandro said, his eyes glistening with pride. "The *magistrado* released Benito Oviedo, but ordered him out of the pueblo as a vagrant. And *Capitán* Chavez is bathing his slashed brow, and no doubt thinking how to ask for a transfer to some other post. He will not want to remain here, for the sly grins of other men are obnoxious to a sensitive person."

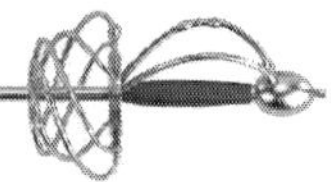

Rancho Marauders

Murder baits a trap for the masked avenger — to test his wit and his skill with a flashing blade!

FROM almost every point of the compass came the buzzards, carrion birds gathering for a feast. They wheeled gracefully in the deep blue of the California sky, spiraled lazily downward, and suddenly dropped from view beyond the distant range of hills.

It was soon after dawn when they were noticed first. At Rancho Vega, the *vaqueros* saddling their horses for the day's work, prior to eating breakfast, saw the birds and shuddered. Juan Cassara, the veteran *superintendente* of the great rancho, saw them and wondered what tragedy the presence of so many of the birds presaged.

Dull peons, natives imbued with superstition, even persons of education and intelligence, were inclined to shiver when they saw buzzards. Some foul instinct seemed to direct them to gather at a certain spot. And men shuddered when a number of the birds gathered, for that could mean but one thing — death.

Don Alejandro Vega, the silver-haired master of the *rancho*, awake and out of the sprawling house at dawn, saw the wheeling buzzards from one of the patio arches. He watched them for a short time, then shouted for his *superintendente*.

"Cassara," he ordered, when the man stood before him with sombrero in hand, "take four or five *vaqueros* and ride over the hills and learn what the presence of so many buzzards means. Only a dead horse or cow, perhaps — but learn what it is."

CASSARA bowed and hurried away, calling to some of the *vaqueros*. It was almost two hours before they returned, for it was quite a distance to the range of hills and over its crest. And they returned with lathered mounts on the run, so Don Alejandro knew something more than a dead horse or cow was concerned. He awaited the report at the end of the patio, and Diego, his son, came from the house and joined him.

"What is happening, my father?"

"A huge flock of buzzards went beyond the hills, my son. I sent Cassara and some of the men to learn the cause. They are just returning."

The vaqueros turned toward the corral for fresh mounts, but Juan Cassara rode on to dismount a short distance from Don Alejandro and Diego and approach afoot, his manner that of an excited man.

"What did you find, Cassara?" Don Alejandro asked.

"We found a score of slaughtered cattle, killed for their hides, their stripped carcasses left behind, Don Alejandro. There were many hoofprints of shod horses, and ruts made by heavy carts, and tracks of both boots and bare feet. The ruts run to the San Gabriel highway, where the carts could have turned in either direction and lost themselves among passing vehicles."

"So we have hide thieves and marauders again," Don Alejandro said. "I thought we had cleaned the district of them. A few wild peons led by some scoundrel, I suppose. What of the herd guard?"

"He was José Gomez, the old man, formerly one of the best vaqueros on the rancho," Cassara replied. "We found his body, Don Alejandro. The thieves had stabbed him to death."

"*Dios!*" Don Alejandro exclaimed. "So they have added foul murder to their theft! Have the body brought in after the investigation, and I'll send for a padre to conduct a service. Anything else, Cassara?"

"A significant fact, Don Alejandro, that may point the way to the thieves and the murderer. In several places near the scene of slaughter, scratched on the ground, evidently with a stick, we found the letter Z. That establishes the identity of the leader, the man responsible for José Gomez' death, does it not? 'Twas Zorro, the masked night rider. May the soldiers catch him, and may I see him hanged!"

Don Alejandro and his son, Diego, exchanged swift glances. For Diego Vega, regarded by most as only a fashionable fop who read poetry, was in reality Zorro, who rode to avenge wrongs against the poor and oppressed. And Diego certainly had led no band of hide thieves to slaughter the cattle of his own father and cause the death of a faithful old rancho worker.

Don Alejandro gestured for Cassara to return to his duties, and went back into the patio with Diego.

"What now, my son?" he asked.

"There are several possibilities, my father. Some master rogue may be trying to put the blame for his deeds on Zorro. Or it may be a trick to discredit Zorro in the eyes of the peons and natives whose battle he has been fighting, and who love him."

"If it is the latter, Diego?"

"If the peons and natives believe that Zorro has recruited a band of thieves, and has caused the death of an old peon, they will turn against Zorro, never trust him again, never listen to him or help him — and his good work will end."

"And so?"

"So it is Zorro's task to learn the truth and clear his name of this deed."

"That is true, my son. I must write a report of the affair and have a *vaquero* ride with it in all haste to the barracks at Reina de Los Angeles. Soldiers must be sent to make the legal investigation."

Sounds of hoof beats reached them, and they went to one of the patio arches to peer through and see who approached. Along the road and toward the *rancho* house came five troopers.

"They are Sergeant Manuel Garcia and some of his men, from the barracks at Reina de Los Angeles," Diego said. "I can identify the burly sergeant even at this distance. What brings them here so early in the morning? They must have started from the barracks before daylight."

"I am glad they rode this way," Don Alejandro replied. "'Twill save me the task of sending a man with a message."

The riders turned their jaded horses into the driveway and loped toward the house. Don Alejandro and Diego went to the front verandah to greet them. The-horses were covered with sweat and dust, and the riders looked fatigued from hard travel.

SERGEANT GARCIA dismounted and advanced alone, while his four troopers bent wearily in their saddles. He saluted Don Alejandro and Diego respectfully.

"I understand you have some trouble here, Don Alejandro," the sergeant said.

"How did you learn of it so quickly and manage to get here so soon?" Don

Alejandro asked. "We did not know it ourselves until a very short time ago."

"As to that, the explanation is simple," Sergeant Garcia replied. "In the middle of the night, two peons came to the barracks and told a wild tale. They had been seized in the hills, they said, and compelled to join a band of hide thieves led by this notorious Señor Zorro. The herd guard, they reported, was seized and stabbed to death. They watched for an opportunity and escaped from the others and brought the report of the deed to us."

"Remarkable," Diego observed.

"Evidently a brace of honest fellows, Don Diego," Garcia said. "They are being detained at the barracks for their own safety, for they fear some of the band of thieves may slay them for making the report. They seem to be fellows with more than the usual intelligence of their kind."

"What will happen to them, Sergeant?" Diego asked.

"They will be given some slight reward, and protected. At the barracks at present is the inspection officer, *Capitán* Marcos Marino, making his regular rounds. He says he may take the two with him to Monterey, being ready to travel north with his escort in a couple of days."

"To Monterey? For what?" Don Alejandro asked.

"So that His Excellency the Governor may question them. The two claim they have been traveling toward San Diego de Alcalá, and may have picked up information regarding Zorro from peons and natives they have met along the way. His Excellency is determined to do everything possible to capture Zorro and hang him."

"Take your men to the huts and have breakfast," Don Alejandro said. "Cassara will furnish you with fresh mounts and lead you to the scene. I'll have the herd guard's body brought in and will send for a padre."

Sergeant Garcia thanked him and rejoined his men. They rode around to the rear, the sergeant shouting for Cassara.

"What do you think now, Diego?" Don Alejandro asked.

"Several thoughts have come to me, my father. Would two peons, caught in such a plight, hurry to tell their tale to the soldiery after their escape from the band of thieves? Is it not true that peons and natives generally keep as far as possible from the troopers? Not even hope of a small reward would get them to go to the barracks with the tale. They would simply follow the highway to some ether vicinity."

"Excellent reasoning," Don Alejandro praised.

"I'd like to see those peons, my father. All this trouble and turmoil, the murder of old José Gomez, the slaughter of our cattle — it upsets me. I shall take the carriage and drive to our house in Reina de Los Angeles, where the atmosphere is more that of peace."

"Perhaps that would be well, my son," Don Alejandro replied, smiling slightly.

"And what would be more natural, my father, than that I carry to the barracks your written report of the affair? And would I not desire to have speech with this *Capitán* Marcos Marino and thank him for his interest? And would not I, as a representative of the Vegas, see the two peons and perhaps give them a coin each as reward for doing what they are credited with doing?"

"You seem to think of everything, my son. And, having done these things — ?"

"I would retire to our house and remain in seclusion, resting — or so it would seem to everyone. My further actions would depend on what I had learned. It would not surprise me much if Señor Zorro rode tonight — and not to lead hide thieves!" This time, it was Diego who smiled.

"You will have Bernardo, your mute peon servant, drive the carriage?"

"He is my favorite coachman, my father."

"Very well, Diego. I'll have a house servant order the carriage made ready."

THE Vega carriage, drawn by a splendid team of black colts and with Bernardo, Diego's huge mute peon bodyservant, acting as coachman, pulled up in front of the barracks at Reina de Los Angeles.

Diego Vega, dressed in resplendent attire which contributed to the general belief that he was a fop, yawned, brushed his nostrils with a scented handkerchief, and descended from the carriage languidly, like a man compelled to perform an onerous duty. The trooper on guard at the barracks entrance saluted him.

Passing came old Fray Felipe, the Franciscan in charge of the chapel at Reins de Los Angeles. He was Diego's confessor, and one of the three who knew Diego was Zorro. Diego bent his head, and the padre gave the sign of blessing.

"I am glad to see you, my son," Fray Felipe said. Then, lowering his voice, he added: "I have heard what has happened. See me as soon as possible."

The padre walked on, and Diego sent word that he wished speech with *Capitán* Marcos Marino. He was escorted to the officer's quarters, and there he found the *capitán* and a burly man much over-dressed, who was introduced to him as Carlos Garza, a trader.

Capitán Marino was a stranger to the district, and Diego never had met him before. But the officer knew the wealth, social standing and power of the Vega family.

"I am distressed, Don Diego, that such a thing happened on your father's *rancho*," the officer said, bowing. "You may be sure we will do everything possible to apprehend this scoundrel of a Zorro and see that he pays the penalty for his crimes."

"I have here a written report from my father, *Señor el Capitán*, regarding the affair," Diego said, offering the document. "Sergeant Garcia and his four troopers reached the rancho before my departure, and the sergeant asked me to tell you he has started an investigation."

"This Zorro, pretending to aid the poor and oppressed — I always have declared he is a rogue winning the confidence of peons and natives so he can recruit a band of thieves," *Capitán* Manno said. "He is a menace and must be exterminated."

"Are you certain, *Señor el Capitán*, that Zorro is responsible for this?"

"I am firm in that belief, Don Diego. The two peons who came here willingly and reported the affair said he was the leader."

"The man responsible must be punished," Diego said. "The herd guard was José Gomez, an old *vaquero* with our *rancho* since before my birth. My father desires everything done to punish the man responsible for his slaying. I do not pretend to understand the business of the soldiery, *capitán*, but — is anything special being done in this affair?"

Capitán Marino smiled slightly. "You may safely leave that to us," he replied. "Señor Garza, here, is also putting pressure on us. He has caravans of carts carrying valuable merchandise traveling the highway, and does not wish to have Zorro and a horde of his rascals rob them."

Diego had been observing Garza closely, and his estimate of the man was none too high, Also there seemed to be a spirit of comradeship between the trader and the arrogant officer did not ring true. It was well known that traders were held in scorn by high officers of His Excellency's army.

"It is my wish," Diego told *Capitán* Marino, "to see the two peons who reported the outrage to you. My father has instructed me to reward them slightly."

"I'll conduct you to the cell room," Marino offered. He turned to the trader.

"Señor Garza, you will await my return."

DIEGO thanked the two peons, and through the bars handed each a piece of gold. He watched them closely, listened to them as they voiced servile thanks, and with difficulty repressed a smile. Then he left the barracks, the *capitán* escorting him to the door, and drove in the carriage to the chapel to see old Fray Felipe.

"A frightened peon came to me this morning for confession, my son," the padre told Diego. "And outside the confessional he related things concerning this affair. He was solicited to be a member of the band that committed the outrage."

"Did he know anything of importance, padre?" Diego asked.

"It is a plot of some sort. The two peons who reported at the barracks — "

"Are not peons," Diego said, smiling, "They overact the part. Their speech and movements betray them. Their hands are not hard, scratched, calloused. Their feet were bare, but have not been so long, for they are white through the film of dirt, and the men stepped as if walking in bare feet hurt them — "

"I suspected as much," Fray Felipe said. "Do you realize, my son, that this places a murder charge against Zorro? And it was an old peon he is supposed to have slain, so the peons and natives will turn against Zorro — "

Diego nodded. "I have considered all that, padre. Zorro must make a move at once. What think you of this Inspection officer, *Capitán* Marino?"

"He is a trickster if I ever saw one, Diego. And I know he is high in the Governor's confidence."

"The trader, Carlos Garza — ?"

"I never saw him before, or heard of him. He, too, is acting a part."

"My thought," Diego admitted. "And he has the bearing of an old military man."

"I have heard," the padre continued, "that in the cool of the evening *Capitán* Marino is to start north with the two peons, to take them to Monterey. He will be attended by two troopers, and *Señor* Garza has given out he will ride along, so as to have protection."

Diego strode around a moment, and made decision. "Zorro also will ride tonight, padre," he said.

THERE was half a moon, and scudding clouds obscured it at times. Dressed in black with the black hood over his head, Zorro rode his black horse carefully away from Reina de Los Angeles and parallel to the San Gabriel trail. And beside him came Bernardo on a big riding mule.

"Listen carefully, Bernardo, and do exactly as I say," Zorro told him. "We must not be seen together, for that would endanger you and possibly expose my identity. If we are met, separate from me instantly, and you will simply be returning to the rancho on your mule after driving me to Reina de Los Angeles."

Bernardo made a guttural sound that meant he understood.

"If occasion arises, we will execute the trick I explained to you. Otherwise, you will return when I tell you, and await me in the usual place to take my horse, costume and weapons."

They made what speed they could with safety until they neared the mission at San Gabriel. Then Zorro left Bernardo hidden in a ravine and went forward alone. He left his black horse a short distance from the mission buildings and went on afoot. Below an open window, he stopped. Looking into a bare adobe room, he saw one of the padres mending a harness, and called him in whispers.

"Zorro!" the padre exclaimed when he glanced out and saw the masked man in a streak of moonlight.

"Listen carefully, padre," Zorro said. "You have heard what happened at the Rancho Vega, no doubt. I swear to you by the saints I led no thieves nor knew anything of the affair.

"I believe you, señor," the padre said.

"I hope to expose the man responsible for José Gomez' murder and for the hide thefts. But when I expose him, there must be somebody near who can speak afterward, a reputable witness. Get another padre — the elderly Fray Celestino will do admirably — and a couple of important men if you can, and go quickly and with secrecy to the little canyon where the highway is narrow, and wait there in hiding."

"It shall be done, my son."

Through the night, Zorro returned to where he had left Bernardo. They rode a short distance, and Zorro left Bernardo in hiding again, and rode on alone a distance farther to the little canyon. There, high up among the rocks, he dismounted and watched the trail that came from Reina de Los Angeles.

WITHIN the hour, the two padres arrived on their mules, and two other men were with them. Zorro mounted and found them down beside the trail.

Zorro's pistol menaced them.

"You do not know me, *señores*," he said. "But I assure you that I had no part in what happened at Rancho Vega. This is a trick to turn the peons and natives against me, to get me accused of murder. I know you all, though you do not know me. I ask you merely to watch and listen, so you may give testimony later. And I ask you not to try to learn my identity.

"You — " he bowed to the two men the padres had brought along, both hidalgo rancho owners who had happened to be at the mission guest house — "are justice-loving men I know well. You show kindness to those of low station, and I know you will see justice done. I want my name cleared of this foul deed, but I cannot appear as myself. For the reward is still out against me, and if I am caught I will be hanged."

He rode away from them and resumed his former position up among the rocks.

After a time he saw riders approaching from Reina de Los Angeles. As they neared him, Zorro saw them clearly in a streak of moonlight. *Capitán* Marino. Carlos Garza and the two men who had been playing peon were laughing and chatting as they rode.

This narrow canyon, a spot where the road was low and sheltered from the wind, was a favorite place for riders on the way to San Gabriel, and Zorro was hoping that these riders would stop here to ease their mounts. And so they did.

Almost directly below him, the *capitán* gave the signal for the stop.

"A swallow of wine would not go amiss," Zorro heard him say. The breeze carried the words along the little canyon, and Zorro knew the padres and the *hidalgos* with them could hear.

"'Tis a pretty trick," Garza was saying, "and let us hope Zorro will enter the trap. We should have some results from our hard work last night."

"You have the profit of the hides," Marino replied, with a laugh.

"I gave them to the rascals who helped me," Garza said. "It was my idea that the affair would draw Zorro out of hiding. With a murder charge against him, he will do something to prove his innocence. The old peon had outlived his usefulness anyhow. And he had to be kept quiet."

"All classes of men will rise against Zorro now," *Capitán* Marino declared. "The peons because now they'll think he is a thief and murdered one of their own kind. And the *rancho* owners because he has raided one of their herds — they will have their *vaqueros* scouring the hills. And sooner or later they'll learn something concerning Zorro and run him down for us. The idea was mine, and the Governor praised me for it."

"And what do I get?" Garza asked.

"Promotion to a captaincy," Marino replied. "You will look better back in uniform, for you certainly are a clown as a trader. And these two youngsters who played peon — they'll get promotion and reward."

"Pass that wineskin again," Garza said.

Zorro worked his black horse slowly down to the trail. Suddenly he charged to within a short distance of them and stopped in a streak of moonlight. His pistol menaced them.

"Your hands in the air, *señores*!" he ordered.

"Zorro!" Garza squawked.

"I am Zorro — *si,"* the masked rider confessed. "I have been much interested in your conversation, *señores*. So you would make men think I am a murderer and thief, would you? And you, Garza, with an old man's blood on your hands — "

One of the pseudo-peons made a quick move, and Zorro's pistol barked. The man reeled aside and dropped the weapon he had drawn.

"At him!" *Capitán* Marino shouted. "He has fired his pistol — "

"And have another loaded one," Zorro added, drawing it from his sash.

He hurled his empty weapon full in the face of the second pseudo-peon, and the man screamed and put his hands to his eyes. The big black horse sprang forward at a touch from Zorro's rowels, and knocked Garza aside. Zorro wheeled to ride back, in time to see Garza bringing up a pistol.

Zorro's second weapon spoke as Garza's flamed. Garza's ball passed within inches of Zorro's head. But Zorro's struck Garza in the shoulder and hurled him to the ground.

MOONLIGHT flashed from the blade *Capitán* Marino had drawn. The officer slashed at the black horse and missed.

And then Zone had vaulted from his saddle and his own blade was out, and the two swords met and rang.

"Now, rogue, I'll stretch you to earth and rip off that mask!" Marino yelled madly.

"Others have tried that, *señor*," Zorro taunted as he fought.

He heard hoofbeats, and through the moonlight came the two padres and the pair of *hidalgos* that they had brought along.

"You heard, *señores?*" Zorro yelled at them.

"We heard, Zorro," one of the *hidalgos* replied. "We'll handle this affair from now on."

Capitán Marino disengaged and retreated to a place where footing was better. Then he came forward again, and Zorro met his charge. And as he met it a peculiar call came ringing down the canyon.

It was the signal from Bernardo that danger was near. The mute's eerie cry was like the scream of a wild animal. Bernardo could not speak, but he could give that terrifying cry.

Capitán Marina was a good man with a blade, Zorro found. He could not disengage and dash to his horse and ride for safety. For the *capitán* was pressing him. And into the end of the canyon, seen clearly in the moonlight, came Sergeant Manuel Garcia and his four troopers.

"Garcia!" Marino yelled. "To me! Zorro is here!"

The troopers spurred forward.

Zorro launched a wild attack, and his blade went home. He darted past Marino as the latter dropped his weapon and clutched at his side. Then Zorro was in saddle and driving the big black up the slope of the canyon wall.

GARCIA and his men came charging. Zorro descended to the canyon floor again as they passed, reached the trail and rode madly. The troopers turned to pursue.

Around a bend, he gave a cry of his own, and Bernardo appeared in the trail on his mule. Zorro swerved his black aside into the darkness. Bernardo bent low on the mule's back and rode on in Zorro's stead. Garcia and his men dashed past Zorro and pursued Bernardo. Zorro knew they would not catch Bernardo's swift riding mule, and that Bernardo would circle through the hills and get safely to the *rancho*.

He knew also that the *hidalgos* and padres would take the men he had wounded to the mission, and that the truth would spread. So he rode cautiously back toward Reina de Los Angeles, unsaddled his horse and put him into the hiding place, divested himself of Zorro's weapons and costumes and left them near the horse for Bernardo to find when he returned safely along about daylight.

And not long afterward Diego Vega had entered his father's house unobserved, and in the seclusion of his room was bathing the perspiration from his body and preparing for sleep.

The next day, in mid-morning, he strolled to the plaza and to the chapel, where Fray Felipe met him.

"Well done, my son," the padre said, smiling. "The truth is out. Hidalgos and peons both know Zorro had nothing to do with the murder and theft at *Rancho* Vega. Charges will be filed against *Capitán* Marino, you may be sure, and Garza will be punished for the killing of old Jose."

Zorro's Stolen Steed

Pursuing troopers catch Don Diego's black horse — and with it bait a trap for the rider of the night!

THE head servant of the Vega casa in Reina de Los Angeles appeared in the patio, where Don Alejandro Vega and his son Diego, were sitting beside the gurgling fountain, half asleep after a heavy midday meal.

The head servant was a peon whose hair had grown gray in the house service of the Vegas. He was unusually well trained, hence Don Alejandro and Diego knew something was amiss, else the servant never would have intruded the patio at such an hour.

"Well?" Don Alejandro asked. His tone was that of a grandee prepared to admonish severely if this intrusion proved to be unworthy of a breach of house rules.

"Your pardon for disturbing you, Don Alejandro, and yours, young master. But Don Diego's mute bodyservant, Bernardo, is at the kitchen door, and we make out from his actions and his guttural rumblings that something ill has happened, and that he desires to see Don Diego immediately. He nodded his head vigorously when I asked him if that were so. He appears to be in a state of great excitement, so I was bold enough to come here at once."

Diego was upon his feet. He glanced quickly at his father and received a nod of permission.

"Let us have Bernardo here immediately," Diego ordered.

The servant disappeared, and in a short time returned with Bernardo at his heels. The gigantic mute peon bent and knuckled his forehead in respect to

Diego and his father. At Diego's gesture, the house servant left the patio.

ONE glance at Bernardo was enough to reveal that he was greatly excited over something that had occurred. He made strange guttural sounds, and lines of agony were in his face — the agony of a man unable to talk, yet with important information to impart as speedily as possible.

"You are ill? … someone has been hurt? … there has been a fire among the buildings? … something is wrong in the pueblo?" Diego asked the questions in turn.

To each, Bernardo shook his head negatively. His agony seemed to increase, as did his guttural rumblings.

"Calm yourself!" Diego ordered. "Let me try to get at it. Has the matter something to do with — " Diego did not finish the sentence, but dipped a finger into the water of the fountain, and on the flagstone quickly wrote the letter Z.

Frenzied guttural sounds came from Bernardo's throat, and he bobbed his head up and down in excitement.

"Something to do with Zorro," Diego said in a low tone to his father.

Bernardo, Don Alejandro, and Fray Felipe, the aged Franciscan padre at the pueblo chapel, were the only persons who knew that Don Diego Vega, considered a spineless fop, was also Zorro, the wild masked rider of the hills who punished the oppressors of peons and natives.

"What could it be?" Don Alejandro asked. "Something surely has happened. I never saw Bernardo so excited before. What a cruel thing it is to be born without the power of speech!"

Bernardo showered gutturals at them again, then sprang forward and knelt beside the fountain, where there was a space of bare dirt between two of the flagstones. With a forefinger, he began drawing something in the dirt. Diego bent over him to watch.

"He is trying to draw something — looks like a horse," Diego said to his father.

Bernardo rumbled again and bobbed his head.

"It is a horse?' Diego asked.

Bernardo nodded that it was. And then, as Diego watched, the mute bent forward again, and with his forefinger drew a ragged letter Z on the animal's hip.

"You mean Zorro's horse?" Diego asked.

Bernardo nodded that he did. Then with a wide gesture, he wiped out the sketch and the letter, and gestured on toward the fountain.

"Listen carefully, Bernardo," Diego commanded. "The horse of Zorro, is it sick? … dead? … has it been hurt?"

Bernardo shook his head to those questions, and seemed to be trying to explain with sweeping gestures.

"Is the horse gone?" Diego asked.

Bernardo nodded assent.

"Did he break out of the little corral?"

Bernardo indicated the horse had not. He knelt and drew in the dirt with his finger again — a circle meaning the corral. He put a horse in the corral. He walked his two fingers forward like a man walking, make tracks around the gate of the corral, and drew a line to show the gate had been pulled open.

"Somebody stole the horse?' Diego asked.

Bernardo's excitement showed Diego had guessed correctly.

"Did the soldiers find him? No? Thieves — ?"

The mute nodded furiously again.

"Could you tell how many?'

Bernardo held up three fingers, then another. Three thieves, and possibly four, that meant.

"Zorro's costume and weapons, are they safe in the hiding place?"

Bernardo nodded that they were.

"Thanks, Bernardo," Diego said. "Do not go near the corral again. Stay around the huts here at the house. Get something to eat, and rest."

BERNARDO stumbled away through an arch of the patio, and Diego sat beside his father. They spoke in low tones, lest some softly walking house servant overhear them.

"There has been a band of horse thieves working through the *rancho* country recently, my son," Don Alejandro said. "It is possible they stumbled upon the little hidden corral and took the big black. They may not know he belongs to Zorro."

"I branded the letter Z on his hip two years ago in a moment of silly bravado," Diego muttered. "My splendid black horse, so well trained! How many adventures I have had upon his back! How many times his strength and intelligence have saved me — "

"Cease moaning and concentrate on what to do," his father interrupted.

"The corral, of course, must never be used again," Diego said. "If the thieves get away with the horse, I shall have to train another, and Zorro's work will end until the new horse is trained. But I'll never find another like the one stolen."

"Troopers have been watching for the thieves," Don Alejandro reminded him. "Only fine saddle mounts have been stolen, and it is thought they are being taken on the Sonora trail into Mexico and sold there to unscrupulous buyers. If the soldiers catch the thieves — "

"If they do — what?" Diego asked. "Other owners of stolen stock can claim their animals. But can I go forward and say the big black is mine — can I claim the horse bearing Zorro's brand?"

"Here is an enigma worthy of the genius of Zorro," his father suggested.

"And can I trail the thieves and attack them as Zorro and regain my black horse? What horse will I ride while I do that? Have I another I have trained so well? Would Zorro dare risk himself in a tight corner on a strange horse?"

"The horse probably was taken during the night," Don Alejandro said. "We can do nothing but await developments."

"I wish I had left the horse out at our rancho," Diego mourned. "But I thought I might have need of him close to me."

They were silent suddenly, listening. From the distant plaza came sounds of a din. Men were shouting, and boots were pounding the hard earth as men ran. Don Alejandro and Diego moved toward the door to enter the house, and in the doorway met the head servant again, and saw he was excited.

"What is the tumult, Estéban?" Don Alejandro asked him.

"The soldiers have caught horse thieves, Don Alejandro! The report is they were taken on the Sonora trail. Two thieves were shot and killed in the fighting, and two taken prisoner. Twelve horses were recovered, and the soldiers have them now at the plaza. It is said the thieves have confessed but will be tortured and questioned further at the barracks during tonight, and hanged in the plaza in the morning."

Diego went with his father to the plaza, where half the men of the pueblo had congregated. Diego appeared his usual indolent, foppish self. He stooped as he shuffled along beside his father, and brushed his nostrils with a scented lace handkerchief. His manner said that all this tumult annoyed him.

"Is there danger of the horse, if he is among the stolen animals, recognizing you, my son?" Don Alejandro asked.

"No danger of that. I always dressed in Zorro's black costume, with my mask, before going to where Bernardo had the horse saddled and waiting. And I always used the voice of Zorro, and not my own, while with the horse. But he would recognize Bernardo quickly, for Bernardo always saddled him and got him ready, and petted him."

They came to the edge of the crowd, and peons and natives stepped aside to let them pass. They caught sight of the big black horse with the other stolen animals which had been recovered by the troopers. The big black stood with head upflung, a proud animal who seemed to look with scorn upon the chattering men around him.

DIEGO saw Sergeant Manual Garcia, of the barracks, who was in command of the detachment of troopers that had caught the thieves. And the burly sergeant saw Diego in turn.

"Ah, Don Diego, *amigo*, a greeting to you!" the big sergeant roared in welcome. "Look what we have here! We have not caught this rogue of a Zorro yet, but we have his black horse. Look, what a monster he is! Strength and stamina and intelligence in that animal! Small wonder our poor army horses could never catch him."

"What will you do with the stolen stock, sergeant?" Diego asked.

"The horses have their ears notched, and may be reclaimed by their owners. But that big black — nobody will put in an ownership claim for him, eh?" The sergeant roared his laughter. "A little dangerous for the rogue to come forward and ask for his horse. So he will be condemned by the *magistrado*, Pedro Casillas, as unclaimed stolen property, and sold."

"Ah? I would not mind buying him and sending him out to the Vega rancho," Diego hinted. "He is indeed a splendid animal."

"Ha! Don Diego, amigo, do not waste your gold. The Vega rancho is overrun with fine horse stock now. And there is perhaps a curse of some sort on this mount of a rascal of a highwayman who will yet be caught and hanged. He would bring you bad luck. And there is another thing — " Sergeant Garcia lowered his voice.

"And that — ?" Diego questioned.

"Pedro Casillas, the rascal of a *magistrado*, who is by no means averse to lining his pockets with tainted gold, is already arguing about the sale of the horse to Carlos Avalos, the rich trader, who stands over there dressed in fine raiment and with jeweled rings on his fingers and struts around to ape his betters."

Diego brushed his nostrils with the scented handkerchief at mention of the trader's name. "What does Avalos want with the horse?" Diego asked.

"Ah! He has a certain scheme, in which I am to play a part. Step aside with me, Don Diego, where there are not so many open ears."

They walked aside with Don Alejandro.

" 'Tis like this," Garcia told them in a low voice. "Carlos Avalos buys the animal and takes him to where his trader's caravan is encamped a mile out of the pueblo on the San Juan Capistrano trail. Then he awaits the moment Zorro will make an effort to regain his horse, if the rogue has that much courage. And Zorro will come into a trap — for I will have troopers watching for his arrival. This time we'll have the rogue! And — naturally — the reward for his capture will be split by me with *Señor* Carlos Avalos, with the rascal of a *magistrado*, Pedro Casillas, coming in for a small share."

" 'Tis a pretty plot," Diego admitted, his eyes twinkling.

A trooper called the sergeant, and he hurried away. The deal for the horse had been consummated. Avalos, the trader, seized the rope looped around the big black's neck.

"You are now mine, you black demon!" Avalos shouted, so that all could hear, "You have a new master. Behave yourself, or you'll know what a lash really means. Come with me."

Avalos jerked on the rope unusually hard, and the noose halter tightened around the big black's neck. The horse gave a choked scream and reared. Avalos was yanked off his feet. The black struck at him with a forefoot and knocked the trader flying into the dust. He would have gone ahead with punishment, but men seized the rope and kept him back.

Don Alejandro had seen Diego tense, and warned him swiftly in low tones.

"Careful, my son! You can have vengeance for mistreatment of the horse later?"

IT was well that his father had spoken so. For Diego saw Avalos struggle to his feet and yank a whip from the hands of a man standing near.

"Hold that black demon!" he yelled. "Hold him well. I'll teach him — !"

He sprang forward and cut with the whip. The lash slashed the black's neck. Then the horse indeed became a demon. He jerked off their feet the men who held the rope, struck with his feet, tried to bite. The crowd scattered and ran. But one of the men took a quick turn around a post with the rope and they circled the black around the post until the rope was wound and the horse was snubbed.

Zorro gave his wild cry a third time.

"Keep him so until some of my men come to take him to my camp," Avalos panted. "I'll punish the demon there! A highwayman's horse, is he? If this Zorro doesn't like the way I treat his mount, let him come and tell me about it!"

Diego touched his father on the arm. "Let us get away from this spot and return home, before I betray myself," he whispered. "Zorro has a score to settle with *Señor* Carlos Avalos, and with Pedro Casillas, the *magistrado*, for selling the horse to such a beast!"

Back at the house, Diego went among the huts in the rear and located Bernardo and took him aside.

"Listen carefully, Bernardo," he instructed. "After fall of night, you will get the costume and weapons of Zorro and take them cautiously to the little ravine a half mile out the San Juan Capistrano trail."

Bernardo nodded that he understood the order.

"Wait there in hiding until I come and help me dress and put on the weapons. Do not forget to bring my whip."

For the remainder of the day, Diego wandered around the house, sat in the patio, read poetry, ate fruit, and conducted himself in the usual manner, so the house servants would not grow suspicious of his actions.

He shared the evening meal with his father, and while one of the servants served meat and poured wine, he remarked so the man would hear:

"I have a headache coming on, I fear, my father. With your permission I'll retire early and rest."

"You have a plan, my son?" Don Alejandro asked, when the servant had left the room.

"A bold one, my father. Perhaps it would be best if you knew nothing of it in advance."

"Use great care Diego. It may be a dangerous trap. Nothing ill must happen to you."

"I know that," Diego said, nodding. And he did know what it would mean if it was learned that Don Diego Vega was Zorro. The angry Governor would have him hanged despite his noble blood. His father, no doubt, would be exiled to Mexico or Spain, and the Vega estates would be confiscated and the money gobbled up by the Governor and his henchmen. And his father would die of disgrace and shame that his only son and heir had been executed publicly, like a common thief of the highway.

Diego contacted Bernardo again when he came to Diego's rooms after the meal, to see if there were special orders, as the mute did every evening.

"You will take the black's saddle and bridle and gear with you to the spot I mentioned," Diego ordered. "I'll explain the remainder of my plan when we meet in the ravine."

There was a half moon that night, with clouds scudding in from the sea and half obscuring it at times. Diego got out of the house without being observed, and walked cautiously to the distant ravine. It was almost midnight when he reached it.

Bernardo was waiting. Diego dressed swiftly, and became the masked Zorro. He buckled on his blade, thrust knife and pistol into his belt, and coiled the long whip to carry in his left hand.

"You will wait here until I return," he instructed. "If I get the horse, I'll ride him bareback, and do you be ready to help me bridle and saddle him here."

Again he strode away through the night, but now as Zorro, the masked righter of wrongs, the avenger.

He knew the terrain well and kept in depressions and dark areas as he approached the spot beside the highway where he knew Carlos Avalos' caravan was encamped. He had learned that Avalos had five peons in his crew, but did not fear them. They would not have weapons, since it was against the law for peons to go armed. And they would bolt at the first sign of violence.

BUT Zorro did not know how many of Garcia's troopers might be at the trader's camp, nor where they would be hidden. So he used extreme caution as he neared the camp, stopping frequently to listen and watch for moving shadows when the moon was not hidden by clouds.

He came finally to the crest of a high bank overlooking the camp, and went prone on the earth to make reconnaissance. A small campfire was burning in the center of the camp. A tent was pitched near the fire. The carts were parked in a row at the side of the highway. Two men were squatted beside the fire — peons half asleep with their heads bent on arms that crossed their knees, serapes draped around their shoulders.

And Zorro saw the horse. The big black was tied to a heavy post, and around him had been constructed a tiny corral of logs and brush. The horse stood proudly, head uplifted, watching, listening.

No sounds told Zorro where troopers might be hiding. Perhaps, he hoped, since the hour was so late, Avalos and Sergeant Garcia had decided Zorro would not make the attempt to recover his horse tonight.

Zorro got to his feet in a dark spot beside a huge rock. He watched and listened for a time longer. Then he made his way cautiously down to the level of the highway and crouched in a spot of darkness there. He cupped his hands to his mouth, and gave a long, piercing peculiar cry.

From his position, he could still see the horse. The animal reared up and hurled himself against the makeshift corral at the end of the rope which held him to the post. He squealed when Zorro gave the cry again.

The horse's squeal served a good purpose. Carlos Avalos, half dressed, rushed from his tent, a pistol held ready. The two men at the fire sprang up and darted to the side of the row of carts. And Zorro saw a trooper emerge from a shadow and hurry toward the fire.

Zorro gave his wild cry a third time. The horse became a raging demon. He reared and tugged, squealing at every move. He snapped the heavy rope and charged against the corral and crashed through it and was free. He stood proudly in the middle of the highway as Avalos and the trooper started toward him.

Zorro gave the cry again. The horse charged along the highway toward the sound of his voice. At the proper moment, Zorro ran out into the moonlight and called again. The black swerved and ran to him, squealing, and stopped. Zorro swung upon his back and grasped the horse's flowing mane and kicked with his heels.

Troopers appeared suddenly in the trail. Firearms were discharged and bullets flew near Zorro as he bent low over the black's neck and rode like a madman. The troopers were shouting and running for their horses, which had been hidden behind the rocks.

Zorro heard Sergeant Garcia bellowing orders. A mounted trooper appeared in the trail before him, and Zorro whipped out his blade and charged. The trooper fired a pistol, but the shot went wild as the man's horse swerved. Zorro slashed with his blade as he passed, wounding the man, and rode on.

Before the pounding hoofs of the pursuit could be heard, Zorro was around a curve in the highway, and left it to ride carefully up a bank and down into a depression. He got back to where Bernardo was waiting, sprang off the black's back, and helped the mute put bridle and saddle on the horse.

"Go to the end of the orchard in the pueblo," Zorro told the mute. "Wait there for me."

He did not return to the trader's camp, but rode to town and to the house of Pedro Casillas, the *magistrado*, who was a widower and lived alone except for an old peon male servant. Zorro put the black at a low stone fence and cleared it. He crashed through the garden and stopped at the front door, to bend from the saddle and pound on the door with the butt of his pistol.

"Casillas! Hasten!" he called in a voice not his own.

AS LIGHT gleamed through a window, Zorro heard a bolt being withdrawn, and the door was opened to reveal Casillas in a heavy nightshirt and a tasseled sleeping cap holding a taper aloft and blinking sleep-heavy eyes.

"Out here, *señor*, or I pistol you!" Zorro told him. "At once!"

Before he realized what he was doing, Casillas obeyed the rough command. Zorro swerved the black into the streak of light from the taper. The *magistrado* gulped and his eyes bulged.

"I am Zorro! Cheap thief that you are, you will put every peso you got from the sale of my horse to Avalos in the poor box at the chapel immediately. If you do not, I shall visit you again when you least expect it, and send a pistol ball into your obese carcass!"

"I — I — it shall be done, *señor*," Casillas gulped.

"Do not forget it, if you wish to live. Come forward another step."

"I but did as the law requires — " Casillas whimpered.

"Do not lie to me!"

Zorro had thrust the pistol back into his sash and grabbed the coiled whip on his saddle. And now the lash sang through the air to cut into the *magistrado's* fat. He dropped the taper and howled, his wild cries ringing through the night, and turned to run back into the house. But the whip encircled him and jerked him back, and then the lash cut and stung, and the louder Casillas yelled and cried for both mercy and help, the more Zorro was pleased.

For he had heard riders down by the barracks, and presumed some of the troopers had returned from their wild futile chase, and knew the cries would attract them. He gave Casillas a last cut with the whip, and rode.

He circled the town, where lights were appearing and men were shouting at one another. Parallel to the highway, he rode with caution back toward the trader's camp. He saw two troopers pass with mounts at a run, going toward the town.

Past the camp, he turned the black down into the highway and stopped to reconnoiter. He could see Avalos at the fire, which had been built up with fresh fuel. Two of his peons were near the trader. Nobody else was in sight.

Zorro loped the black forward slowly, watching the shadows, pistol held ready. Finally he passed through a wide streak where a high bank cut off the light of the moon and jumped his horse toward the fire.

Carlos Avalos whirled around to see vengeance rushing down upon him. The frightened trader fired the pistol he held, and the ball went wild. His peons yelled and began running down the highway toward the town.

Since the trader had fired his pistol, Zorro tucked his own into his sash and got his whip again. The lash caught Avalos as he was darting into his tent, and jerked him back and sent him sprawling. Zorro's whip sang and cut, and Avalos made a wild outcry as he tried to shield his head with his arms.

"Scoundrel!" Zorro barked at him, "Mistreater of horses! Did you hope to hold my horse in your miserable corral? Leave this vicinity at dawn, señor, with your caravan, and do not let me find you near Reina de Los Angeles again, ever."

He lashed until Avalos' cries became only whimpers. And then he coiled his whip and attached it to the pommel of his saddle again, and tightened the reins, then and rode.

And he rode into fresh trouble.

In the trail ahead, revealed clearly by the moonlight, Sergeant Manuel Garcia sat his horse and waited, bending forward in his saddle, pistol held ready.

"Yield yourself, Señor Zorro!" the burly sergeant shouted. "Yield, or I fire! Stop your horse, toss aside your weapons — "

Zorro spurred and charged, bending low in his saddle.

Sergeant Garcia fired, and the ball from the pistol burned across Zorro's left sleeve. Garcia tossed his pistol aside and drew his blade.

"I thought you'd return here, rogue, when you deemed it safe!" Garcia yelled. "Heard my troopers returning to the pueblo, did you? Thought the trader was alone? Come at me, scoundrel! I'll earn the Governor's reward alone!"

Sometime long before, Zorro had crossed blades with the burly sergeant and had wounded him slightly. But perhaps Garcia had practiced swordsmanship since then. Zorro did not wish to injure Garcia unless it was unavoidable. Diego Vega posed as the sergeant's friend, and the sergeant let drop words that put Zorro often on guard.

But now he charged, his own blade flashing through the moonlight, and put the big black straight at the sergeant's mount, which also was a large powerful animal. The black staggered the other horse, and Garcia's cut and thrust both missed. Zorro did not cut with his blade.

He gave a quick thrust as the mounts bumped again, and the point of his weapon went through the sergeant's right shoulder and made him quickly drop his blade.

"Bad fortune for you, sergeant!" Zorro yelled. "Until the next time — adios!"

One trooper came thundering toward them. As Zorro spurred away again, he fired his pistol at the trooper to deter pursuit, and saw the soldier turn aside to help the sergeant.

Away from the highway, Zorro rode with extreme care, coming finally to where Bernardo was waiting. He sprang out of the saddle and began removing the costume of Zorro.

"Ride the horse to the *rancho* and hide him in the usual place, Bernardo," Don Diego Vega instructed. "Hide the costume and weapons also. Use great care."

As Bernardo began gathering up costume and weapons to make them into a bundle for carrying, Diego strode away through the streaks of moonlight. Some time later he slipped into the house, to find his father waiting.

"It is well, my son?" Don Alejandro asked.

"Pedro Casillas has been punished and ordered to put his stained money into the poor box. The trader has been whipped. The big sergeant has a wound in his shoulder. And the horse of Zorro has been recovered, and is now on his way to the rancho, where he will be safe. All is well, my father — " Don Diego Vega replied.

Zorro Curbs a Riot

The black robed avenger strikes again in the cause of justice!

ON his way that afternoon to visit Fray Felipe at the little chapel on the plaza in Reina de Los Angeles, Don Diego Vega came to the door of the tavern from one direction as Sergeant Manuel Garcia approached from the opposite.

It is possible the burly sergeant had noticed Diego sauntering that way and had planned deliberately to meet him at the tavern door. For there never was a time when Garcia would not empty a mug of wine at another man's expense.

"Ha! Don Diego, amigo!" Sergeant Garcia thundered, lifting a hand in salute. " 'Tis a better day now that I behold your countenance. Were I in funds — present lack of which is due to the rascal of a paymaster who has a little senorita hidden away in a hut near the mission of Santa Barbara, and hence is always slow making his routine journey south of that post — were I in ample funds, I say, I would stand you a goblet of the landlord's best, my dear friend, in celebration of this rare meeting."

Diego laughed a little. "Let not that bother you, Garcia," he replied. "I have a coin with me and feel the urge to spend it in your company."

So, a moment later, they sat at table in a corner of the common room of the tavern, beneath an open window through which came a wisp of breeze. A bowing and scraping fat landlord put wine before them — Diego's was the best goblet in the house and Garcia's in an earthen mug — and backed away with Diego's coin grasped firmly in his fat fingers.

"You appear slightly fatigued, Sergeant," Diego suggested. "Or perhaps

Salas snatched up his pistol from the table.

you are perturbed by some recent happening. The life of a sergeant of troopers, I surmise, is not always a happy one."

" 'Tis the life of a dog!" Garcia complained. "Bad enough when the usual routine is followed from day to day, but when there are additional cares! — Why did I not have sense and become a sailor?"

"Had you done so, no doubt you would be a pirate by now," Diego declared. "With a cutlass strapped around your fat middle, a brace of pistols in your belt and possibly a patch over one eye. What troubles you, Garcia? Is it the new *capitán?*"

GARCIA muttered a string of words which revealed in a profane manner just what he thought of his new superior, who had come to take charge of the presidio at Reina de Los Angeles less than a fortnight before.

"*Capitán* Carlos Salas!" he said, in a low mutter that only Diego could hear — for, after all, a sergeant cannot go around denouncing a superior officer with impunity. "For no reason, as far as I can see, he orders that the stockade be repaired."

"I saw troopers working at it, and wondered," Diego admitted.

"It has not been used for years, not since the latest native uprising, when it was constructed so that the rascals could be herded in it, corralled in a manner of speaking, until their hanging time came. Now comes the order to drive new posts, to fill in the gaps with fresh earth, to erect corner boxes where armed sentries may take up their positions. And, why? The cells of the jail room are empty save for a couple of peons who have disturbed the peace. Why finish a work that could care for a hundred or more culprits, were that necessary? There is no reason in it. 'Tis only that this new officer desires to reveal authority by making troopers work like dogs when there is no need of such labor."

"There may be a reason of which you know nothing," Diego suggested. "Perhaps the new *capitán* does not desire to take you entirely into his confidence. He, too, may have mysterious orders from a superior, and instructions to keep the reason secret."

"That is possible, though I doubt it," Garcia replied. "And there is another regulation to irk the men. Starting tomorrow, all troopers must remain in barracks after the sunset meal, with arms at hand, until the following morning. They cannot visit the tavern, gather around the fire in the plaza, or slip through the shadows and keep tryst with a dusky damsel. What think you of that?"

"Perhaps it is punishment for some fault, or a measure of discipline," Diego hinted. "They may have been growing lax. Or, it may be that the *capitán* has intelligence that suggests serious trouble is coming, and wants the men where they can be put into action quickly."

"Trouble? Who would cause trouble here to such an extent that I could not quell it myself with a man or two?"

"It generally is the unknown that causes peril to descend upon us," Diego told him.

It was before the hour when the frequenters of the tavern gathered, but now in from the plaza came a man. He was short, swarthy, squat, overdressed, with flashing gems on his fingers and in his scarf. His boots were fine, and his sombrero had a wide leather band studded with semiprecious stones.

Diego noticed that the landlord bowed to him as to a good customer, but not with the deference he used toward Diego and others of his social standing.

The newcomer glanced around the room, and then stalked past other tables and benches and came to where Diego and the sergeant were sitting,

"Your pardon, señores, but this is the table at which I usually sit," he declaimed, pompously. "I appreciate the slight breeze that comes through the window. Will you kindly betake yourselves to another table and allow me to sit here?"

Diego looked up at him in amazement Sergeant Garcia almost choked on his wine. The landlord began lumbering across the room.

"We are comfortable as we are, señor," Diego said, his voice with an edge on it. He brushed a handkerchief across his nostrils as if to stifle a stench. "There are plenty of empty tables, it appears."

"But this is the table I desire. Know you that I am Carlos Pedroza?"

"Both the name and any importance that may be attached to it are unknown to me, señor," Diego remarked. "I am Diego Vega."

"Ah! And some importance attaches to that name, surely," Pedroza replied, with a tinge of sarcasm. "The son of the Vegas. I have heard you prefer the works of the poets to a blade. But there is no danger of course in reading poetry."

Diego's eyes glittered as they searched those of the other man. "The belief of the ignorant," Diego observed. "Poetry can and often does incite the reader to valiant deeds."

"Bah! The words of a woman. My table. If you please!"

"But I do not please, Señor Pedroza. This is a public tavern. The landlord placed me here with my friend, the Sergeant. So, here we remain."

"Unless I desire to remove you with force!" Pedroza said.

THE landlord finally arrived, his hands uplifted in horror.

"Señores!" he begged. "You do not understand. This is Don Diego Vega, Señor Pedroza, son and heir of a hidalgo who is not without great power in the district. Do yourself a kindness by revealing your courtesy to him!" He turned to Diego. "Don Diego, this Señor Pedroza is a wealthy trader resting in the pueblo for a time. He has come south, I understand, to procure laborers."

"A trader and a labor procurer!" Diego observed. "It was my thought a stench was in the air."

Pedroza whirled upon the landlord. "Decide at once, señor! Does this popinjay remain at the table, or do you order him away from it and give it to me?"

"Don Diego remains," the landlord replied, immediately. "You are here today and gone tomorrow, and Don Diego is here always. It would he bad business to decide against him."

"And you will find it is bad business to decide against me," the trader said. "*Capitán* Salas is my personal friend. I shall speak to him of this matter, and you may find hereafter that the soldiers continually observe that you are breaking regulations."

Diego laughed a little. "If *Capitán* Salas in that manner affronts a gentleman of blood, he may find representations made to the Governor in Monterey, asking for the officer's removal and demotion. If you will remove yourself to some corner for a few minutes, while I conclude my conversation with the good sergeant, you may have the table, for even now I am late for an appointment at the chapel."

Pedroza's face blackened. He retreated a step as Diego and the sergeant watched him. Diego gestured for the landlord to furnish more wine, and brushed his handkerchief across his nostrils again. The trader darted to the table again, and said, "When the tempest comes, the storm may wreck the house of Vega!" And then he turned and hurried out into the plaza.

Diego lifted his eyebrows slightly in question as he looked at the sergeant.

"He came a few days ago," Garcia reported. "He has visited our new *capitán* every day, and they eat and drink together. That is all I know."

As he left the tavern and continued to the chapel, Diego was busy thinking. It was unusual for even a rich trader to speak so to a man of blood and display arrogance to him. He was sure this Carlos Pedroza was not intoxicated. From what, then, did his sudden burst of courage come, if not from wine or rum?

The sudden activity repairing the old stockade, the arrogance of this trader, his friendship with the commandante of the barracks — such things might mean something of importance.

Fray Felipe, the aged Franciscan who operated the chapel and was Diego's confessor, met him at the door.

"I am glad you came when I sent word to you, my son," he told Diego. "There is something afoot, and I would confide it to you. I have had several inklings from natives and peons, and have put them together and built a supposition."

"And what is that, padre?"

"A few days ago, four men came to town — in the wake of the new officer.

They were dressed as peons, and were barefooted else in tattered sandals. But their talk was too good for peons and they did not have the usual lack-luster eyes of such, and their feet and hands were not tough enough with calluses."

"Then?" Diego questioned.

"They were watched by some friends of mine who are genuine peons. And this new officer — I have had word of him from brethren in Monterey and Santa Barbara. He is a familiar of the licentious Governor, and wherever he is sent cruelty to the poor occurs."

"Ah!" Diego said. "You think these four men are working with him?"

"I am sure of it. They have approached peons and natives in our vicinity, and their words have been relayed to me. This is something that must have immediate attention, Diego, my son — say front such a man as Zorro!"

"So?' Diego stepped nearer the padre.

FRAY FELIPE was one of the three human beings who knew that Don Diego Vega, who posed as a lethargic popinjay, was in reality Zorro, the wild masked rider of highways and hills, who righted the wrongs of lesser men.

"These strange men, my son, are inciting the peons and natives to a local uprising. They plan to meet on some certain night and raid the big warehouse of Señor Vallejo, our local merchant. They are told that to each man is to go a cooking pot, a new serape, a bolt of dress goods for his women, a measure of excellent wine and a small cask of olives — and whatever else the man desires and may seize."

'What else?" Diego urged.

"My friends have been reporting it all to me. Why should the strange men work up the local peons and natives to this rash act? What would they profit! I have discovered they are known to this Carlos Pedroza, the trader, for he holds conferences with them stealthily. The trader is a familiar of the new *capitán,* and the officer, a man of the Governor's, is familiar with our *magistrado*, a scoundrel who also is the Governor's man."

"But — the plot?" Diego persisted, "Pardon me, padre, but get to the meat of it. Time may be precious."

"It is my supposition based on what I have leaned: suppose this raid is carried out, suppose the soldiers seize a number at the peons and natives; suppose they are brought before the *magistrado!* The *magistrado* finds them guilty, and what follows?"

"It could be a hanging matter," Diego observed.

"Perhaps for a couple by way of example. And the majority would be assessed large fines they cannot pay — and sold into peonage."

"Ha!" Diego interrupted. "And I have it that Señor Caries Pedroza is a labor procurer as well as a trader, and that he is friendly with the *capitán*. The big stockade is being repaired. It may contain a large number of men. And Sergeant Garcia informed me a few minutes ago that the troopers are being held in barracks each evening and night, though there seems no necessity for it."

"So you see it, Diego, my son? The poor peons and natives will be duped into the raid on the warehouse, the four men who incite them will not be caught by the soldiers. Of if caught will be allowed to get away! The peons and natives will be sold into peonage for a pittance to Carlos Pedroza — and the trader will sell them perhaps in Sonora. The financial returns will be split between trader, officer and Governor!" Fray Felipe choked with indignation.

"You spoke correctly, padre, when you said this is an affair in which Zorro should interest himself," Diego said. "Let me know anything you ascertain."

"I have it that the four so-called peons are to have a meeting tomorrow night it the canyon east of the pueblo, when they will talk to peons and natives and seek to inflame them."

"An uninvited guest will be at the meeting," Diego declared. "I have had words already with the trader in the tavern. I understand now what he meant when he hissed at me that when the tempest comes it may wreck the house of Vega. He will turn the mob on our house as well as upon the warehouse, he means."

"Look there, my son! The four men who pose as peons are standing now at the corner of the plaza. Notice that each wears a red band on his tattered sombrero."

Diego observed them well. As they strode on in front of the buildings, he noticed that their manner was not that of homeless peons. He touched Fray Felipe or the arm.

"No doubt, padre, Senor Zorro will be present tomorrow evening at the meeting in the canyon," he said ....

THE night was dark and wet, for a heavy mist had blown in from the distant sea. On his black horse, Zorro rode cautiously by a circuitous route to the rim of the canyon. Before he reached it, he saw the reflection from a fire in the swirling mist.

He knew this country well, and stopped the horse at the top of a narrow pathway which wound down among the rocks to the canyon's floor. Flame were leaping from the fire below, and men were gathered around it — almost a hundred of them, ragged peons and natives always searching for a ray of hope.

Zorro urged his black horse down the path, going slowly and carefully and making no noise the sound of the wind did not drown. The wind also carried words to Zorro's ears, and he saw one of the four bogus peons standing atop a rock and addressing the mob.

"This is the night to strike … mist and darkness … troopers will be snug in their barracks, get what is your due, men … we will break in the doors of the warehouse. Be sure you carry no weapons, for there is a law against our kind holding them … "

Zorro listened to a lot more of the same, and finally picked up their plans:

"We will leave here at the middle of the night, and do our work before the dawn. At that hour troopers sleep soundest, and also men of the town … make for the hills or your homes after it is over ... hide your loot ... let this night's work be a warning to those who oppress you."

In his black costume, with his face masked, with a blade at his side and pistols in his sash, and his long whip coiled on the pommel of his saddle, Zorro rode on down the path until he was on the canyon's floor.

Between him and the fire and the men surrounding it was a level stretch of sandy land free from boulders or clumps of dry brush. Zorro touched his black steed with his spurs.

The big horse thundered toward the fire, and even in the soft earth the pounding of his hoofs was heard. Those around the fire sprang to their feet in and some began darting to spots of darkness behind the rocks.

But a man recognized the rider from costume and horse and began shouting, and others took up the shout:

" 'Tis Zorro, our friend! Zorro has come to help us! Now we cannot fail!" Zorro, as he rode on, was watching the four bogus peons. They gathered together near the fire. Zorro stopped his horse a short distance from the leaping flames and held high his hand in a gesture for silence.

He got, instead, a chorus of yells:

"Help us, Zorro! Lead us! We cannot fail if you do!"

At his second gesture, they grew quiet, stood respectfully at a short distance, listened.

"Bring the four strangers nearer to me." Zorro ordered.

Men grasped their arms and urged them closer the black horse. Zorro bent forward in his saddle. His eyes gleamed through the slits in his mask as he looked them over.

"Am I your friend?" Zorro yelled at the mob.

"Si!" They all they cried.

"Then listen to me while I talk." He spoke rapidly, exposing the plot, and heard their cries of rage. He jumped the horse forward to stop them when they would have torn the four bogus peons to pieces.

"If you value my friendship, obey me now," Zorro thundered at them. "If you do as I say, I'll punish those who have tried to do this thing."

They were suddenly quiet, waiting for his orders,

"Gag the four men with pieces of their shirts," he said. "Fasten their arms behind their backs. Take them back to the town, going carefully and silently, and tie them securely to the posts at the and of the plaza, where horses are tethered at times."

They shouted that they understood and would obey. "At the corner of the plaza," Zorro continued, "is a heap of hay gathered for the use of the troopers. When you have tied the men securely, set fire to the hay, and toss upon the heap any trash you can find, so the blaze will be large. Shriek and yell as the flames begin to leap. And then pay careful attention to this — scatter quickly and hurry to your homes and so dodge the soldiers. And leave the rest to me."

HE bade them extinguish the fire, which they did by throwing sandy earth upon it. Then they bound and gagged the four peons and urged them toward the mouth of the canyon, Zorro leading on his black horse.

Through the black misty night they went to the edge of the pueblo, and there Zorro halted them and repeated his orders, and rode away as the mob started on again.

He went in a wide circle around the buildings and finally approached the rear of the barracks. In a depression there, he dismounted and ground-hitched the trained black and went forward afoot.

Lights burned in the barracks, but there was no noise. Lights also gleamed in the quarter of the *capitán*, and Zorro could hear talk and laughter and the tinkling of glasses. He drew near a window and crouched beneath it.

One side of the wooden shutter was fastened back, and Zorro could hear, and by lifting his head cautiously could peer into the room. *Capitán* Salas was sprawled in a huge chair at the end of the table. Pedroza, the trader, was on a bench at the table's side. And the local *magistrado*, an evil old man known to be the unscrupulous tool of the Governor, sat on still another bench. All had wine before them, and in the center of the table was a silver platter heaped with little spiced cakes.

"This night will be profitable for the three of us, and also for the Governor," *Capitán* Salas was telling the other two. "The last report I had from our men was that they expected fully a hundred peons and natives to be with the mob. The troopers should round up almost all of them. And of course we can seize any others we wish, and charge That they were with the rioters."

"A good and profitable business," Pedroza agreed. "We'll put them in the stockade under heavy guard, and the blacksmith of the pueblo can iron them together. They'll step along on the way to Sonora, I promise."

"I am ready to do my part," the *magistrado* declared. "I shall even deliver a stern speech against their treason." He laughed, and lifted his wine mug again.

Zorro crouched again beneath the window and looked down the slope toward the plaza. He saw a tiny light, another, the first flame leap up. He watched as the flames ate into the dry hay under the top layer of mist-drenched strands, as trash caught. Then there came a sudden chorus of wild yells.

Zorro heard *Capitán* Salas rush to the window above him, open it wide and thrust out his head. The head disappeared at once, and Zorro heard the officer's frantic words:

"The fools have started it earlier than we planned. Stay as you are until I give the alarm."

Zorro risked lifting his head again. Salas had rushed to the hall door, and was shouting for the guard:

"Sergeant Garcia, at once!" he thundered. "Tell the troopers to prepare and arm. There is a riot."

In a moment, Garcia came to the door and saluted.

"Take every man except the door guard!" *Capitán* Salas ordered. "Peons and natives are rioting. Round them up and put them into the stockade under guard. Grab every one of them! Ride!"

Garcia hurried away, bellowing commands. Zorro crouched close to the wall a distance from the window, and watched and listened. He could hear the troopers getting dressed, grabbing weapons, running to the stables. And after a short time there was a shouted command from Garcia, and they all rode forth, down the slope, toward the scene of the disturbance.

Zorro was hoping the peons and natives would scatter and hide in time. The soldiers would spend considerable time searching for them, Zorro knew, and would find the bound and gagged men tied to the hitch posts. He should have time in which to do his own work.

He went swiftly to the corner of the barracks building and saw the one trooper standing guard there. The man was looking toward the plaza, at his charging comrades and the fire. Zorro was at him before he knew it, had thrust the muzzle of a pistol against his spine.

"Silence, if you would live!" Zorro said.

The trooper turned and saw the masked man, He backed into the building at Zorro's command, stretched on his face on the floor of the sleeping room and had his arms tied behind his back and his legs lashed together. Then he was gagged and tied to a bunk.

ZORRO hastened into the corridor again. Handling a frightened trooper was one thing, but what he intended doing now was quite another. *Capitán* Salas had the reputation of being a brave man and something of an expert with the blade.

Zorro still held the pistol. His whip was looped into his belt on his left side beneath his second pistol. And the scabbard which held his deadly blade was in such a position that a swift draw of the weapon was possible.

He stopped at the door of the officer's quarters and listened.

"Listen to the rascals yell!" Salas was saying. "Garcia and his men are rounding them up. We'll have the stockade filled with them."

Zorro threw open the door sad stepped into the room. "Look this way, señores!" he cried at them.

They whirled, scattered, half crouched, their eyes bulging as they saw the masked man before them. The *magistrado* gave a squawk of fear and cringed against the wall. *Capitán* Salas let his hand drop to the hilt of his blade.

"Zorro — 'tis Zorro!" the *magistrado* said.

"You are correct, señor," Zorro replied. "And you three are precious scoundrels to build the plot you did against helpless natives and peons. As you will learn when the sergeant and his men return, not many will be caught. Nor will you seize any of those innocent, or you will hear from me."

"Indeed, Señor Zorro?" Salas said, laughing a little. "Do you forget that you are an outlaw with a price on your head — and that I am an officer of the soldiery?"

"A disgrace to the service!" Zorro told him.

Pedroza, Zorro noticed from the corner of his eye, had flattened back against the wall, and his right hand was groping toward his sash. But as he whipped out the pistol he wore there, Zorro fired the one he held, and Pedroza dropped his weapon and reeled back with a broken right forearm to nurse.

"So!" Capitan Salas cried. "Your pistol is empty, Señor Zorro, but you have a blade at your side. I shall honor you by crossing swords with you. We'll soon see the face behind that mask.

Zorro had a second pistol in his sash, but made no attempt to bring it forth. He exulted in the ring of blades, in the feel of another man's wrist strength. So he whipped out his own weapon from scabbard and darted to a corner of the room where there was no furniture.

Salas came at him, and they engaged. Pedroza had sunk to the floor against the wall, and was moaning with pain, and the *magistrado* cringed in a corner and was a menace to no one.

Zorro swung aside after parrying, for light from the candelabra on the table was in his eyes. Through the window he caught sight of the leaping flames down in the plaza. He heard the shouts of the troopers and the pounding of their horses' hoofs as they searched for fugitives.

Salas made a desperate attack, his rage at being confronted in his own quarters by Zorro overcoming his caution. Zorro's blade point ripped satin and touched skin, but the *capitán* retreated and came at him again.

Zorro heard someone shouting not far from the barracks, and knew he should end this and be gone. He attacked with sudden fury. The point of his blade darted out, and *Capitán* Salas recoiled with a cry of rage and pain as he felt the pain on his forehead.

"You now wear the sign of Zorro on your brow, señor!" he heard the masked man say.

Salas retreated to the table as if to come at his antagonist in a new charge. But, instead, he dropped his blade to clatter on the flag stones of the floor, and clutched at a pistol resting on the table beside a candelabrum.

Zorro sprang forward, and his blade slashed through the air again, catching and reflecting the candlelight. Blood spurted from a wound on Salas' right arm, more from another wound in his shoulder, and the *capitán* staggered back against the wall and collapsed there.

Zorro whirled toward the corner where the *magistrado* crouched. He scabbarded his blade and suddenly held the whip taken front his belt. The *magistrado* screeched like a man under torture as the lash cut into his hide.

"A lesson to you all!" Zorro said, as he coiled the whip swiftly and attached it to his belt

HE retreated to the hall door, tuned to dart through it. And be came face to face with Sergeant Garcia.

"So 'tis you, fiend of Hades," the burly sergeant roared.

Garcia sprang backward and tugged at his scabbard to get his saber. Zorro had no wish to harm Garcia who was useful to him as a mine of information, wine often loosening the sergeant's tongue. So he sprang backward, slammed the door shut and shot the bar into place, and dashed across the room to the window.

He got a leg over the sill, glanced out, dropped to the ground. Garcia was bellowing in the barracks. Someone was shouting answers at him from the front. Before Zorro could get free of the streak of light that came through the window, a trooper appeared at the corner of the building, saw him and fired a pistol.

The bullet sang past Zorro's head. He did not fire his last shot in reply, but plunged into the darkness and ran. Garcia had returned to the barracks with one man for escort, to make a report to his officer, Zorro supposed.

He reached his horse and got into the saddle. He heard Garcia bellowing, saw the trooper mount and start riding furiously toward the plaza to warn the others that Zorro was abroad. Then, Zorro rode.

He was lost in the darkness instantly. His horse's hoofs made no sound of pounding in the soft mist-drenched earth. Behind him, he left sounds of shouting and hard riding as Garcia tried to get men into action for pursuit.

He circled the town and approached the place where his horse was kept hidden. In a short time, Zorro had disappeared, and Don Diego Vega made his way carefully into his father's house, hurried to his rooms, reappeared in dressing robe and muffler, with his hair tousled, to find his father and some of the servants in the big main room off the patio.

"What is the tumult, my father?" he asked.

"'Tis only a small disturbance of some sort at the plaza," Don Alejandro Vega replied, his eyes twinkling as he looked at his son. "Return to your couch and get your rest, Diego. Such things always give you a headache."

"My father, let us go out to the rancho for a time," Diego begged. "It is so calm and peaceful there. Here in the pueblo there is always trouble and turmoil. How can man commune with the poets?"

Three Strange Peons

Zorro rides through the night to face three flashing blades of a trio bent on his capture!

RECLINING on the soft cushions of the family carriage, Don Diego Vega was more than half asleep as the vehicle rolled and lurched along the rutted road. Bernardo, his mute peon body-servant, acted as coachman and handled the reins in an expert manner.

It was a warm day in summer, the hills and valleys of Alta California bathed in a friendly sun. Diego was traveling from Reina de Los Angeles to the Vega rancho near Mission San Gabriel, where his father was busy with affairs.

Bernardo had just turned the carriage off the main highway and into a winding road which led to the rancho buildings. The horses trotted around a curve in the road, and Bernardo made a guttural sound, his only mode of speech. Diego was alert instantly, sitting erect. From long association, he had learned to distinguish what the different tones of Bernardo's gutturals meant; and the sound he had just heard indicated astonishment and warning mingled.

Bernardo glanced at Diego and nodded ahead and to the right. A short distance back from the road was a tumble-down abandoned adobe shed, generally inhabited only by scurrying small lizards and the black ants upon which they fed.

Now, three men were in front of the hut, squatting around a cooking fire; they wore ragged pantaloons, tattered sandals and sombreros filled with holes. A glance revealed that much to Diego, and a second, as the carriage rolled on toward them, told him they were not Vega rancho workers.

"Stop the carriage when you reach the spot," Diego told Bernardo.

As the mute slackened the horses' speed, Diego reached beneath a cushion and drew forth a pistol he always carried on these trips, for highwaymen prowled the trails at times. He examined the weapon, and held it from view as the carriage stopped.

Those at the fire got slowly to their feet, took off their tattered hats and knuckled their foreheads in a show of respect.

"What men are you?" Diego demanded.

One stepped forward. "We are travelers on our way to San Diego de Alcalá, where we expect to find work."

"Why did you stop here?"

"What hidalgo asks?" the spokesman for the trio asked.

"Are you daring insolence? Take care I am Diego Vega, and you are on my father's rancho. Wandering strange peons are not welcome here. There has been too much thieving."

The spokesman bowed. "We meant no insolence, Don Diego. We thought you might be someone without a right question. We saw this empty hut from the highway, and decided to come here and eat and rest."

"What are you cooking in the pot?"

"Mutton and frijoles, highborn. The pot is our own, and we have used only dry brush for fuel. We got the food from a padre at San Gabriel this morning. He will vouch for it, no doubt."

"You are merely homeless wanderers going to, San Diego de Alcalá to seek work?"

"That is all. We mean no harm. We are honest men."

"Approach," Diego ordered, still keeping his right hand and the pistol from their view.

THE three shuffled forward, their manner that of men with a burden of hopelessness upon their shoulders. Diego looked them over carefully.

"You have been lying to me. You are not peons," he accused. "Your clothes are tattered — *si*. Mud plasters your feet and legs. But strip and wash, and I doubt not we'll find your skins are not coarse and toughened from exposure, nor your hands from hard toil."

"I assure the highborn — "

"Silence! A real peon would not argue with a hidalgo. Nor would he dare take charge of a hut on private property without permission. And he would have better sense than to start a cooking fire at the edge of a sea of dry brush at this time of year, when it is easy to start a conflagration. Your abject manner is assumed; you do not hunch your shoulders properly and did not knuckle your forehead correctly. And you forgot one important thing — you did not dull the gleam in your eyes."

Diego exhibited his pistol. "Tell me the truth, now, or I'll hold you here with my firearm while the coachman drives to the house and sends vaqueros to me. They'll knock you about, bind your limbs, take you to San Gabriel and call soldiers."

The leader of the three laughed. "You have penetrated our disguise, Don Diego. But it would expose you to ridicule if you sent for soldiers. We carry official passes."

"Explain that to me."

The man glanced toward Bernardo. "For your ears only."

Diego yawned and got out of the carriage and looked up at the mute. "Bernardo, drive forward a hundred paces and stop, so I may have private speech with these men," he ordered.

Bernardo did as commanded, but turned his head to watch.

"And now?" Diego asked the trio.

"Don Diego," the spokesman said, "we are cornets in the service of the Governor. We are of good blood, and were newly commissioned in Mexico three months ago, and sent to Monterey for service with the Governor of Alta California. We are here on a special mission."

"You have credentials?" Diego asked.

"Each of us carries a pass signed by His Excellency, ordering military and civil officials to give us any aid we ask."

"Let me see one of the passes," Diego ordered.

The spokesman got one from the depths of his ragged clothing and extended it. Diego took it in his left hand, and did not look at it until the man had stepped back. Then he read the pass swiftly. He knew the Governor's signature, having seen it often on documents.

"Are all the passes like this?" he asked.

"They are identical, Don Diego."

"No name is mentioned, only 'bearer'. Perhaps you men slew the owners of the passes and stole them to use yourselves."

"You yourself judged we are not peons."

"But you may be educated rascals without official standing, hoping to use the passes for your own benefit."

"Since you are a hidalgo without doubt, and are Don Diego Vega, of a family we know for its loyalty, perhaps I may explain our object in being here."

"Do so," Diego suggested.

"We are participating in a plot for the capture of a great rogue who is a thorn in the flesh of all officialdom. All efforts to catch him have failed. We three are young, adventurous, and have known moments of peril in Mexico which have demonstrated — if you'll pardon my seeming boast — our courage. Also, we are unknown in these parts."

"And so?"

"So, His Excellency decided to send us to make a capture through cleverness. All we need is to be placed in the near vicinity of the rogue, and we'll handle him! Dead or alive, but preferably the latter, the Governor said, that the rogue may be hanged publicly. For us, success means promotion and a reward of gold."

"Who is this great rogue you would catch and win fame and fortune?" Diego asked.

"He is the one known as Señor Zorro. Is that interesting?"

"Indeed, I find it so," Diego admitted.

AND indeed he did — since Diego Vega himself was Zorro.

"I am remembered of certain facts," Diego said. "This Zorro had crossed blades with many good swordsmen and left his mark on them as he escaped unscathed. He has been chased by the troopers of His Excellency until they have worn paths over the hills, and never has been caught. He appears to be a clever rascal. When so many good men have failed, how do you hope to cope with him successfully?"

"Ah! We are all good at fence. Has this Zorro ever fought three good men at once?"

" 'Tis scarcely a fair game, that," Diego observed.

"With an equal, no. But Zorro is a masked highwayman with a price on his head, a traitor to the Governor because he stirs up the natives and peons. Dead or alive, His Excellency told us. The means of accomplishing our success, he left to us."

"I cannot see how you can succeed," Diego declared. "Why do you come as peons, for instance?"

"That is a part of our plot, Don Diego. We will mingle with the peons and natives in the vicinity of Reina de Los Angeles, and keep our ears open. Without doubt, many of them know Zorro's identity, and how and where he hides and when he is to move."

"The peons and natives are superstitious regarding this Zorro. Because he has not been caught, and because he seems to fight always to aid the poor and oppressed, they believe he is under a sort of divine protection. They would be cautious in speaking of him."

"We'll win their confidence, and they will talk," the spokesman boasted. "We'll contrive to meet this Zorro and handle him!"

"Confidence in one's self is an excellent thing — but overconfidence is as grease on the downward path to ruin," Diego remarked. "However, if you would mingle with local peons, there is a small canyon a mile beyond the pueblo, on the San Juan Capistrano road, where peons and natives are allowed to gather, build fires and cook, and eat and sleep if they have no homes and are wanderers."

"We thank you for the information, Don Diego," the spokesman said.

"Before you depart, kindly be sure the fire is extinguished," Diego warned.

He yawned, brushed his nostrils with a scented handkerchief, and turned to stroll toward the carriage.

"So that is the sort of popinjay they breed in this Alta California!" the spokesman whispered to his two companions. "I could have taken away his pistol and jammed it down his throat!"

Diego Vega would have smiled had he heard the remark. But the three would not have smiled had they heard what he said to Bernardo as he got back into the carriage:

"It is fortunate that my big black horse is hidden in the canyon here at the rancho, Bernardo. Zorro rides tonight. You will have everything ready an hour before moonrise."

BUT the sky was not entirely clear that night. In from the distant sea came scudding clouds that at times obscured the face of the bright moon, causing alternate brightness, and shadow. And through the shadows rode Zorro on his powerful black horse, wearing his black costume, his face obscured by the usual black mask. At his side was his blade; in his sash were pistol and poniard.

Zorro rode leisurely across the hills by trails he knew well, keeping off the highway and swinging to the left to pass Reina de Los Angeles by a safe margin and travel on to the canyon of which he had told the three young cornets.

He had no wish to slay the three, for as yet they had done nothing to confound him. He understood their youth, their adventurous spirits and their rash daring. And he knew such men are dangerous, not taking precautions older men in years and experience would take, but dashing in and liable to make a lucky thrust at any time.

However, their work must be stopped, and if Zorro met and defeated them, and placed his mark upon them, their efforts would come to an end. He realized that at any time he could cease his hazardous pursuits and remain simply Diego Vega, the young *caballero* noted for lassitude and reading poetry. But as long as he remained Zorro he checked, at least in part, the oppression of helpless peons and natives by their cruel and unscrupulous enemies.

Having passed opposite the pueblo, Zorro bore to the right again until he was riding slowly in the protection of a high ridge of rocky land parallel to the highway. He used extreme caution as he neared the small, narrow canyon. He could see the reflection of the fires the peons had kindled there.

It was a place for gathering, such as homeless wanderers established in later years. They built their fires, cooked what scraps of food they could obtain by begging, rested in the fire's warmth if there was drizzle or wind to chill the air.

From the side of the brush-covered canyon, he looked down upon the scene. Not more than a score of men were huddling around the fire tonight. On the breeze were carried to Zorro's nostrils odors of cooking food.

He rode cautiously down the slope through the brush to the sandy floor of the canyon, keeping in the dark spots as much as possible. Behind a heap of rocks half shrouded with dry brush, he dismounted and ground-hitched his horse. Carefully, he went toward the fire. From a spot not far from it, he crouched behind a rock to watch and listen. The breeze coming toward him up the canyon carried talk to his ears.

The three young cornets were there, and from what Zorro saw and heard, he knew they had been made welcome and had gained an audience because they had brought food with them for the common pot. Zorro knew nothing would open the hearts and loosen the tongues of hungry men better than a gift of food.

THE one who had acted as spokesman in the afternoon was talking to the others.

"We have heard a lot concerning this Señor Zorro," he was saying. "You men are fortunate to have such a friend. In the north, our kind meet with no mercy. We work like dogs, yet we almost starve. I would like to see this Señor Zorro, for it would be a great honor to see such a man."

"He comes and goes," one of the local peons said.

"You should do all you can to aid him — help him hide, see that he gets food."

"We do not know who Zorro is," another local peon replied. "He comes and goes, as my friend has told you. The troopers chase him, and always lose him in the hills."

"Somebody must know him. A man cannot live hidden and entirely alone. Is it that he fears to trust you men?"

"We do not think that it is," the local man replied. "It is that he wishes to keep his identity a secret from all. It has been said he is a man who suffered much in the past, and so is trying to help others. And some declare he is a *caballero* — "

"But that is nonsense!" the spokesman interrupted. "Why would a *caballero* fight and run risks to help such men as you? More likely he would put a lash across your backs for the fun of it."

Zorro was watching carefully from his hiding place. He had seen the local men glancing at one another peculiarly. And now the one who had been talking to the spokesman got upon his feet as if to toss more fuel upon the fire, but instead seized a stick of wood and turned back suddenly.

"You talk too much of Zorro and little of anything else," he told the spokesman. "You three men — we do not know you. You may be spies. Perhaps you are not even of our station. Just now you made a mistake in your talk. You said 'such men as you,' instead of 'such men as us,' and 'a lash across your backs,' as if our backs were not like your own."

"Nonsense! You are too suspicious," the spokesman said, hastily, getting to his feet also, and his two companions doing the same. "All we know of Zorro is what we have heard."

"You sought to learn whether any of us know Zorro and where he hides," the local peon accused. "Your questions were too searching. We would fight or die for Zorro — understand? We would kill any man who threatened his safety."

"Why all this rage, *amigo*?"

"Do not call me friend until you are accepted as such."

"I do not like your manner," the spokesman said. "We bring meat for the pot, and this is our reward. Perhaps you are eager to fight with me.

"Ha! Peons do not fight with one another except seldom, but combine to fight their enemies. If we thought you were spies, we would seize you now and beat you until your senses left your body. We do not like you. The meat you brought is cooking in the pot. Dump it out and carry it with you, and leave at once. We are hungry, and the meat smells good, but we will starve before we eat meat furnished by traitors."

"Let us seize the three and hold them until we learn more of them!" another local man cried.

ZORRO saw the spokesman spring aside, and his companions with him. From beneath their ragged clothing, they drew weapons. A pistol appeared in the hands of the spokesman, and the other two brandished blades which flashed in the light of the fire. Zorro guessed the blades had been next their skins, the hilts under left armpits and the scabbards running down inside their ragged pantaloons. They had only to grasp the hilt, throw a leg back and whip the blades from their scabbards.

"So! You carry weapons, and it is a great offense for men such as us to have them," the local man yelled. "You are spies, as I thought. You would have us tell you of Zorro, so you can tell the soldiers."

"And you, or some of the others, do know about Zorro," the spokesman of the cornets declared. "The troopers will torture your knowledge out of you. Stand — all of you! I'll shoot down the first who moves!"

Zorro darted away from the rocks and got into his saddle quickly. He knew the peons were in peril. If they tried to fight, some would be wounded or slain; if they were taken captive, they would be taken to the barracks, and the soldiers would beat them.

And they could tell nothing of Zorro, for none knew his identity or place of residence. They would declare they knew nothing, and the troopers would not believe, and would torture.

Zorro urged the black quickly through the brush and to the edge of the canyon's floor. As he did so, as he went out into the open with the moonlight striking him, he saw the spokesman of the comets jump aside again, and heard him give a yell:

"Troopers! Sergeant Garcia! To us! Capture these rogues!"

Zorro jumped the black forward, yelling as he did so, calling for the peons

The men drew their weapons as Zorro approached

to dart into the brush and rocks and escape. For the spokesman's call told Zorro that troopers were in hiding on the sides of the canyon. Zorro's yells disconcerted the cornets for a moment and they heard the thunder of his horse's hoofs as he dashed forward.

" 'Tis Zorro!" a peon yelled.

The peons already were running wildly away from the fire, bent half double, trying to make their escape. In the brush, they would be like rabbits, and it would be difficult for the troopers to capture them.

The cornet's spokesman discharged his pistol, and Zorro, as he continued riding madly, saw one of the escaping peons reel aside and then plunge on into the brush, and knew he had been wounded.

Men shouted and the brush cracked as troopers rode wildly down the slopes to the canyon's floor. The three cornets were still beside the fire, and now the one who had fired the pistol and had no time to reload, got a blade from beneath his ragged clothing also, and stood beside his companions.

Zorro saw that all the peons were in the brush now, where rocks and shadows obscured them. And he knew the troopers had seen his wild ride in the moonlight, and they would leave off chasing the peons in an effort to capture him. He could hear the hoarse voice of Sergeant Garcia, his old enemy, giving orders: "Catch me this Zorro! There is a reward!"

Zorro charged on toward the fire. But suddenly he turned the big black and rode madly into shadows as fleecy clouds obscured the moon for an instant. So many hoof beats were sounding among the rocks that the troopers could not distinguish where he rode.

Finding the end of a narrow trail he knew, Zorro urged the black up it. He swerved the mount aside behind a ledge to give him rest, and listened.

Garcia's troopers were charging through the semidarkness in every direction. The sergeant was shouting for them to ride to the canyon's upper end, thinking Zorro had gone there. Zorro looked down into the canyon and saw the three comets standing near the fire.

They had come to the canyon without mounts, naturally. And the troopers had not paused to leave horses for them, not with thoughts in their minds of the reward they would get if Zorro be caught. They had natural resentment at three young officers coming to the district and taking the reward after the local troopers had chased Zorro for so long without success.

In the distance, Zorro heard a trooper yelling: "There he rides!"

The pounding of a trooper's horse had been mistaken for Zorro's passage. Garcia yelled an order, and all the troopers pursued toward the upper end of the canyon. It would be some time before they realized their mistake.

Zorro urged the black down the winding narrow trail and to the canyon's floor again. Then he used his spurs, and the black's hoofs spurned the sandy ground as he dashed forward. Bending low in his saddle, Zorro grasped the reins and bore down upon the fire.

" 'Tis the masked rogue coming at us!" one of the cornets yelled.

The three scattered, holding their blades ready. Zorro swerved the black and stopped him at the correct instant.

"So, rogues, you wish to see Zorro, eh?" he yelled at them. "Here he is!

How do you like the sight?"

He had his blade out now and held ready. And suddenly the cornets saw a pistol held in his left hand, too.

"One at a time, señores!" Zorro told them. "Who would cross blades with me first?"

The spokesman of the trio darted forward, and Zorro bent from the saddle to engage him, and the blades clashed and steel rang. A swift parry, a lunge, Zorro's blade darting like the tongue of a snake in the light of the fire — and his adversary dropped his blade.

"My face — my face!" he screeched.

"Only some scratches on your forehead forming the letter Z," Zorro called. "You will bear my mark always, señor."

He wheeled the black just in time. The third young cornet had whipped out a pistol, and now he fired and the ball brushed Zorro's left sleeve. The big black sprang forward at touch of spur, and Zorro's blade flashed.

"Through the shoulder for you, señor, since you tried to pistol me!" he cried. "Go back from whence you came, young gentlemen. Tell the Governor to send better material for me to work on."

Wild yells were rolling down the canyon, and the thudding of hoofs came nearer. Sergeant Garcia was leading his men back. Zorro sent a mocking laugh ringing among the rocks of the canyon, and bent low in the saddle and rode.

Pistols exploded far behind him. A few balls whistled near. Then, Zorro was out of the canyon and riding the short distance to the broad highway. He turned into it and ran the black toward the pueblo. But when he was a distance away he turned off the highway and sought the hill trails again, to make a circuitous trip around the pueblo and go on through the hills to the Vega rancho, where Bernardo would be waiting to take Zorro's horse and costume and weapons, and Zorro could become Don Diego Vega again.

Zorro Nabs a Cutthroat

The black-clad avenger battles to clear his name of a false murder charge!

DIEGO VEGA arose early that morning with the idea of going to the chapel on the plaza and making confession to the aged padre, Fray Felipe, stationed for the time being at Reina de Los Angeles.

He breakfasted on fruit, a bowl of warm milk and honey cakes, then strolled out into the fresh morning air, observed that the sky was destitute of clouds and that the day would be uncomfortably warm later on, and directed his steps toward the chapel.

At the corner of the plaza, Diego became aware of a scene of excitement and a tumult near the tavern. He heard the stentorian voice of Sergeant Manual Garcia of the local barracks, and saw a small crowd collecting. He also saw a man's body stretched on the ground, the town physician bending over it.

Diego quickened his stride, but not too much, for it was his pose to appear indolent, a being in whom lethargy resided, a man who seemed almost insensible to the stirring emotions that seemed to dominate the lives of others about him.

As Diego neared the group, he saw other men running toward the scene; and the peon girls who worked in the kitchen of the tavern were shouting with strident voices.

Some peons and natives noticed Diego's approach and stepped out of his path with a show of respect and much knuckling of foreheads. For Diego was the only son and heir of Don Alejandro Vega, who had the best house in town,

Zorro's horse thundered forward.

a great rancho near Mission San Gabriel, and a chest filled with gold and precious stones, according to common report.

As Diego drew closer, he saw Fray Felipe beside the prostrate man, and it was evident the padre had been attending to the rites of the church. Sergeant Garcia glanced around and saw Diego and hurried to him.

Between the burly and uncouth sergeant and Diego, the fashionable scion of a noted family, was a strange friendship, for they were as unlike as possible for two men to be. Diego bought the sergeant wine at the tavern and listened to his boasting; the sergeant enjoyed the free wine and Diego enjoyed the bragging, so it was a fair exchange.

"Don Diego, my friend, approach no nearer," Sergeant Garcia warned. " 'Tis no sight for a man with a delicate stomach. And brush your scented silken handkerchief across your nostrils, *amigo*, lest your sense of smell be offended by the odor of blood."

"There has been some act of violence?" Diego asked, using his handkerchief as the sergeant had suggested.

"There is what remains of Pedro Aguilar, the rich trader," the sergeant explained. "His body was found beside the San Gabriel trail a couple of miles out of town by Juan Cadena, the leather worker, who brought the information to the barracks. We sent out a cart to fetch in the body."

"He is dead? An accident?" Diego asked.

"He has been dead for hours. He was murdered. His pouch wherein he carried gold and the leather belt in which he kept valuable jewels to sell are both missing, and his pockets have been turned inside out. Murdered and robbed, plainly enough."

A man thrust his way forward, removed his battered sombrero and bowed to Diego. He said, "Don Diego, I am Juan Cadena, the leather worker. I found the dead man behind some brush at the side of the road, and hurried to the barracks to report the affair. I was coming to town to deliver some work."

"A gruesome experience," Diego commented. "Let me look."

He stepped forward, and as some of the others stepped back had a good view of the body. Pedro Aguilar's flamboyant attire was disarranged and stained with blood and dirt. His fingers had been stripped of the expensive rings he usually wore. The trader's throat had been cut from ear to ear. And on his forehead, as if scratched there with the point of a knife, was the letter Z.

" 'Tis the mark of the murderer," Sergeant Garcia declared. "Señor Zorro again! Now the rogue has come out under his true colors. A hero aiding, the poor and oppressed, is he? A man who hides behind a mask and punishes those who knock peons and natives about, eh? The rascal who boasts the soldiers cannot catch him. Now he reveals himself for what he really is — murderer and thief! And he leaves his mark for all men to see, in a manner of boasting."

DIEGO VEGA was startled though he did not reveal that fact by facial expression. For he, himself, was the unknown Señor Zorro, the masked avenger of those who suffered wrongs and could not help themselves. And he was quite certain that he had not slain Pedro Aguilar, the trader.

Juan Cadena spoke again. "How long is this terrible Señor Zorro to ride the hills uncaught? There is a reward for his capture or death, but the soldiers are unable to accomplish either."

Garcia's face purpled. "Let us hear no more criticism of my troopers," he warned. "Why not capture him yourself and earn the reward, if the task is so light?"

"I meant no offense," the leather worker replied quickly, retreating a step because of Garcia's belligerent attitude.

Diego inspected Cadena. He lived alone in a hut near the road about half way to San Gabriel. He was an excellent leather tooler, and gave out that he had learned the trade while a prisoner of the Moors, having been captured and enslaved by them while a sailor. Cadena was middle-aged, short, squat, greasy, foul in dress. He earned a few coins by his work, bought materials and food and cheap wine, and seemed content.

Fray Felipe stepped up to Diego. "Good morning, my son," the aged padre said. "Here we have a terrible example of man's inhumanity toward his own kind."

"Violence and thievery — it is dreadful," Diego admitted. "I was on my way to the chapel, padre."

"I'll walk there with you, my son. I have done all can here. I understand the deceased had many bad qualities — but it is not for us to judge. No doubt he had many enemies, and one may have waylaid him."

" 'Twas Zorro waylaid him!" Garcia thundered. "He even left his mark on the man's brow. A common murderer and thief — this masked rogue who says he aids the poor and distressed! Now we shall redouble our efforts to catch him."

Diego caught Fray Felipe's glance and started to turn away. Fray Felipe, his confessor, knew he was Zorro. And no others knew except Diego's father, and his mute peon body servant, Bernardo. He did not fear any of the three ever would betray him.

But there came an interruption that stirred the interest of the group anew. Down the San Gabriel trail and toward the plaza came a rider with his horse on the run. He saw the group near the tavern and spurred that way. They identified him as the *superintendente* of a rancho near the San Gabriel mission. His eyes were twin globes of excitement as he sprang from the saddle of his lathered horse and lurched toward Sergeant Garcia.

"Carlos Lopez, your courier — is he expected?" the rider asked.

"Expected and longed for, since he brings the pay for the detachment here," Garcia replied.

"I started to town with two of my men, to order supplies," the rancho man explained. "We saw the courier's horse standing beside the highway; we recognized him from the coat of arms on the saddle blanket. So we investigated — "

"Get to the meat of it!" Garcia growled.

"Sergeant! We found him — Carlos Lopez, your courier and paymaster. Found him with his throat cut from ear to ear, and his money pouch gone — "

"What?" Garcia roared. "Lopez dead — pay money gone — "

"It must have happened during the night," the rancho man continued. "What causes a paymaster to ride at night?"

"Because he was delayed in the vicinity of Santa Barbara by a torrential storm," Garcia replied. "No doubt he came riding on so we would have our pay today. What did you observe at the scene of crime?"

"Lopez evidently had dismounted, for his horse's reins were grounded. In the tall grass were indications of a struggle — blood everywhere. The courier's uniform had been half torn off him, the pockets turned inside out, his pouch gone, and papers if he carried any. And on the dead man's forehead had been scratched the letter Z."

"Zorro again!" Garcia cried. He beckoned one of his troopers. "To the barracks! Tell the troop to saddle! So this Zorro slays and robs an official courier and paymaster, does he? 'Twill be his last atrocity. For this we shall run him down, catch and hang him; if it takes the entire army of His Excellency to accomplish that end!"

As they walked toward the chapel Fray Felipe said to Diego, "Several years ago, a highwayman roamed along the trails and killed and robbed men in such a fashion."

"But he did not cut a letter Z on his victims' brows," Diego said.

"That is true. The criminal who is at work now no doubt does so to throw suspicion on Zorro, to discredit him with the very people he helps."

"It must be shown that Zorro is not doing these things," Diego said. "And the only way to prove that is to catch the real criminal and reveal he is not Zorro."

"The real criminal may be one of a hundred men such as roam along our highways, my son. He must decoy his victims in some manner, perhaps by pretending to be hurt or in trouble, and then strike them when they draw near."

"That could be the method, padre. A sudden grapple, a keen knife drawn across the throat, a quick scratch on the brow, and then a robbing of the slain man's body. Perhaps it is wrong to have suspicions — "

"Not in such a case, my son, should they lead to the guilty man."

"Then — I have no fancy for Juan Cadezia, the leather carver. He has a shifty eye. Have you ever seen the tools a leather worker uses, padre?"

"I believe not, my son."

"One is a blade so thin and narrow and keen that it could almost take off a man's head with a single slash. And there is another with a little curved end, and duller, with which they turn back little bits of leather — such as could make a scratched Z on a brow without cutting too deeply."

"And so, my son?"

"Zorro will ride tonight, padre. He will patrol the highway in a certain vicinity, and watch. I have it in mind to drive out to our rancho. I'm sick of the town, and shall go home now and prepare for the journey."

"May good fortune attend you, my son," the padre said.

AN hour later, resting comfortably on the deep cushions in the seat of the Vega carriage and pretending to be more than half asleep, Diego left the town and began the journey along the dusty highway. Bernardo, his mute body servant, acted as coachman.

Diego had told Bernardo what he knew and what he intended to do, and with guttural rumblings Bernardo had indicated that he understood. Zorro's black horse, costume and weapons were at the rancho, and from there Zorro could start on his night's work.

Sergeant Garcia and his troopers had galloped out of town long before Diego's departure; and when the carriage was only a short distance along the highway it met the troopers returning. Bernardo stopped the horses at Diego's command, and the sergeant reined in beside the carriage.

" 'Twas a dastardly crime, Don Diego!" Garcia reported. Poor Carlos Lopez, who never did a man an injury! A faithful courier of His Excellency the Governor, and a paymaster who never stole a coin. 'Twas as reported — his throat cut from ear to ear, and the Z marked on his brow."

"You have suspicions?" Diego asked.

"As to the method of the crime, perhaps. As to the real identity of the criminal, no. It is my belief that the victims were stopped in some manner that would not make them expect violence, possibly by a man pretending to be hurt or ill and asking aid. The guilty man? In this case, he is Zorro. But who knows Zorro's real person?"

"Could it not be some rogue trying to throw the guilt on this Zorro by making the mark?"

"Why should he, Don Diego? Zorro is wanted already for a hanging matter. Could we chase him faster than we do now, regardless of how much we are infuriated because a comrade was slain and our pay stolen?"

"You have plans?" Diego asked.

"I have. If the killer tries his work tonight, 'twill be the end of him. We'll capture or kill, as proves necessary, tear off his mask, learn at last the true identity of this Zorro who has been as a thorn in the hide for so long."

GARCIA lifted a hand in salute, shouted an order, and went on with his troopers. Diego supposed that the body of the slain courier had been taken to the mission at San Gabriel, since that was the nearest proper place.

The carriage rolled on. Going around curve in the highway, the horses almost ran down Juan Cadena, the leather worker, as he plodded homeward from the town. His hut was only a short distance back from the road and a little ahead.

Diego ordered Bernardo to stop the carriage again. "Señor Cadena," he asked, "are you not afraid to be alone in your hut with a murderer prowling around the countryside?"

Cadena squinted, spat in the deep dusty and laughed. "Why should such a man bother one like me, Don Diego? I have neither gold nor jewels for him to steal. I would not be worth the killing. Cold frijoles and mutton left in the bottom of my cooking pot — that is all he could hope to get from me."

"Have you any idea as to the guilty man?"

" 'Tis the masked demon known as Zorro, surely. It is my idea that he is preparing to leave this part of the country, possibly fearing the troopers may catch him finally. So he is killing and robbing to get gold for a journey somewhere."

"Why should he leave his mark on the victims?"

"To show mockery toward the troopers who have not been able to catch him."

Diego eyed him an instant, then glanced away and yawned. Juan Cadena had stated a good reason for this season of brutal crime — a man was gathering funds with which to travel. Perhaps his words reflected a thought in the leather worker's own mind, Diego mused.

Diego pointed ahead. "Is that not your hut over there?"

"It is my poor abode, Don Diego."

" 'Tis a sty a decent pig would disdain," Diego commented. "You should apply yourself more to the work you do and get you a place in town." He sank back upon the cushions and brushed his perfumed handkerchief across his nostrils in a gesture full of meaning. "Drive on, Bernardo!"

As the carriage started again and passed the plodding Juan Cadena, Diego's keen eyes were busy. He saw where the brush was thick and high behind Cadena's hut, where rocks studded the hillside. A horseman could ride down close to the hut behind that screen of brush and rocks without being seen even on a bright moonlit night.

Zorro was the horseman who did it some hours later after night had come. The full moon swam the sky, but fleecy scudding clouds obscured it momentarily at times. Zorro rode with extreme caution, his big black horse held down to a walk, and he stopped now and then in a dark spot to listen and watch.

He crossed the highway in a place where it was narrow and blacked with the shadows of rocks and ascended the slope on the opposite side. Finally he found himself on the ridge above Juan Cadena's mud hut.

The brush was dry, and gave forth sounds of his progress when Zorro urged his horse through it. So he dismounted at the side of some rocks, ground-hitched his horse and went on afoot.

He had feared a dog, but no dog yelped an alarm. Zorro went carefully, step by step, his right hand gripping the butt of the pistol he carried in his sash. He was careful that the scabbard of the blade he wore did not strike against a rock or crash into the brush and give warning of where he passed.

When he came to the rear of the poor hut, he found a small window devoid of glass and curtained with a sheet of some thick cloth. The curtain was askew, and standing at the side of the window Zorro could see most of the hut's interior.

A single small taper was burning. Zorro saw that the front door, made of slabs of undressed wood, was barred securely upon the inside. Juan Cadena was crouching against the wall and beside an old box of some sort.

ZORRO blinked and accustomed his vision to the faint light of the interior. He drew in his breath sharply when he finally got a clear view of what Juan Cadena was doing. The leather worker had a sheet of leather on the box, with some of his tools beside it. But his hands were busy with something else.

He had rings which flashed in the bright light, and was pouring them from one of his hands to the other repeatedly, and in his face was an expression of gloating, of avarice, of lust for wealth.

He put the rings down upon the sheet of leather, reached into a small aperture in the hut's wall, and brought forth what Zorro immediately recognized as the courier's portfolio and money pouch.

An instant later Cadena was pouring coins back and forth from hand to hand, muttering. And finally Zorro could make out words:

"… take a fortune with me … go to Mexico and live like a king … they'll search for Zorro, never for poor Juan Cadena, the leather worker … not quite enough yet … must have more … may meet a traveler on the trail tonight … go closer to the mission, that's it … may find some gay young caballero riding home with his skin full of wine … rings on his fingers and his pouch filled with gold … "

Here was all the evidence any man would need to establish Juan Cadena's guilt. But Zorro, the man wanted himself, and for whose capture or death a reward was offered, could not ride to the barracks and tell what he had seen. He had to get his information to the officials in some other way.

And that was a necessity, if Cadena's guilt was to be established to the satisfaction of all men and Zorro's name be cleared of the infamy of murder.

He watched as Cadena put his loot back into the aperture and fitted a rock neatly into the hole, as he brushed aside some dirt that had fallen to the floor and straightened his sheet of leather. Then Zorro saw Cadena stand up and straighten, bend forward and thrust one of his keen knives into his belt, and another of his leather-working tools.

He was still muttering: "… mark the letter Z on his brow so they'll blame Zorro for it … pretend to be hurt and call for help … grab him and slash his throat … "

Cadena extinguished the taper and unbarred the door as Zorro watched and listened. He lurched out into the moonlight, still muttering, and Zorro watched from the corner of the hut and saw him turn down the highway toward San Gabriel.

As swiftly as he could without causing too much noise, Zorro went back up the hillside through the brush and rocks and got to his horse. In the saddle, he rode parallel to the highway, and where there was a clear space watched until he saw Juan Cadena trudging along through the streaks of moonlight and shadow at the road's edge.

Paralleling the highway, but keeping on the hillside and in the protection of the brush so he would be unseen, Zorro kept opposite the half-mad Juan Cadena. Once a carriage came along the road headed toward Reina de Los Angeles, and Zorro saw Cadena go into hiding in the brush and let it pass. A coachman and a servant were in the driver's seat, and a rider following and it was something Cadena could not handle.

Zorro reached a place where he had to descend to the highway himself for a time to get across a rough formation of land where it would be dangerous to ride his horse in the semidarkness there. He reined in beside some rocks and looked ahead. Cadena was still keeping to the edge of the road, stumbling along with his body bent half forward.

No doubt the leather worker had reached a spot he thought would be ideal for what he intended doing, for Zorro saw him crouch against a rock and half sprawl on the ground in a place where the moonlight did not strike and reveal him. And there Cadena waited like a beast of prey on watch.

Zorro rode slightly nearer and backed his mount into the deep shadows and kept him there. No travelers were in sight on the highway in either direction. But Zorro knew one might appear at any moment, riding out to some rancho from Reina de Los Angeles or hurrying toward the town to spend the night.

THE slight wind had died down. The scudding clouds had disappeared and the bright light of the full moon was not obscured now even at intervals. Zorro urged his horse a little nearer the leather worker, careful not to crash through the brush and give an alarm of his presence.

Then, from the direction of San Gabriel came the distant sound of hoofbeats.

Zorro saw a shadow move against the rocks and knew Cadena had heard it also and was preparing to operate if the rider was one he fancied might have loot worth the taking. Zorro gathered his reins, felt of the hilt of his blade, adjusted his long whip on the pommel of his saddle so he could get it free and uncoiled with a jerk, and pelt of the pistol in his sash.

He would have to let Cadena go far enough to show his murderous intention, Zorro knew, and yet reveal himself in time to save the rider's life if the leather worker attacked. He had to be prepared to shout at the proper instant, to jump his horse out into the highway and charge forward.

Around a distant bend in the road loped a rider, plainly seen in the bright moonlight. Zorro watched as Cadena moved around the rocks and got to the edge of the road. As the rider loped on toward them, Zorro urged his horse still nearer and bent forward in his saddle.

The rider seemed to be a man heavy in body, and he rode bent forward as if fatigued. His sombrero was pulled down low over his forehead, and a muffler was over mouth and nostrils almost up to his eyes to keep out the trail dust. As the rider came nearer, Zorro saw Juan Cadena lurch out into the highway, staggering, reeling, clutching at his throat, pretending to stumble and be on the verge of collapsing on the ground. Zorro heard his wild lament:

"Señor — help me! … I am choking! An illness has seized upon me — "

Zorro saw the rider draw rein and look at Cadena, who now was upon his knees and pretending to be unable to stand.

"Señor … aid me!" the leather worker called.

Zorro used knees, reins and spurs and jumped his big black horse out into the moon-drenched highway.

"Do not dismount, Señor!" he shouted wildly at the rider. "It is a trick! The rogue is a foul murderer!"

Zorro's horse thundered forward even as he yelled the warning. He saw Cadena lurch to his feet and straighten his body, saw the moonlight glint on the blade of the knife he held. He saw the rider draw up his horse and swerve the animal aside slightly.

Then Zorro was upon Cadena who was like a wild man now that he found himself in an unexpected trap. He knew the masked rider dressed in black to be Zorro, whose mark he had put upon the brows of his victims.

ZORRO swerved his horse just in time to avoid the murderous slash Cadena made with his keen knife. He swerved the black again before Cadena could recover his balance, slashed at the man's head with the heavy pistol he held, and the leather worker went dawn.

"Dismount now, señor, and help me bind this rogue," Zorro called, watching Cadena and not glancing toward the rider.

He got no answer and turned quickly to see what had become of the rider. The latter's muffler had fallen off his face now, and in the bright moonlight, Zorro saw the round, ruddy face of Sergeant Manual Garcia.

Garcia held a pistol that covered him. Garcia was bent forward in his saddle and ready to charge.

"So 'tis Zorro," the sergeant said. "Drop your pistol, señor, or I fire! You are under arrest."

"Garcia!" Zorro cried in surprise.

"The same, Señor Highwayman. I removed my uniform and dressed in this manner to ride along the highway, hoping the murderer would try to attack and rob me."

"A good plan," Zorro replied. "There he is, Garcia, Juan Cadena. I became interested when I heard I was being accused of his crimes because the letter Z was scratched on the foreheads of the victims. In the wall of his hut, you will find his loot, even the courier's portfolio and the money he was carrying. No doubt you can get the truth out of him."

"No doubt," Garcia said, not relaxing his guard an instant.

"I am Zorro, but I do not murder and rob, so kindly remember that in the future. There is your man, Sergeant — rope him and take him to the barracks and deal with him. And for this service, allow me to ride away now unmolested."

"Ha! That is a horse of a different gait," Garcia declared. "You are a thorn in the hide of the Governor, Señor. Both profit and promotion await the man who takes you. And I have you now! Too long have you mocked at the soldiery. Drop your pistol and submit yourself to me, Señor Zorro — for the reward says 'either dead or alive.' Much as I'd love to watch you being hanged, I'll not hesitate to shoot."

Zorro had not expected to make a deal with the stubborn sergeant, who was an honest soldier, as he knew. He had been talking, hoping the sergeant would relax and could be caught off guard. And now Zorro dug with his spurs and used his reins and made the black charge forward and swerve aside at the same time.

Garcia fired, and the bail from the pistol brushed Zorro's sleeve; the black had swerved just enough to cause the miss, but it had been a near thing. Zorro's horse crashed against that of Cardena, and Zorro slashed with the pistol, but missed Garcia's head.

"Your murderer will get away!" Zorro shouted at him.

But Garcia was too wise to be caught by that subterfuge; he did not even turn his head to glance at Juan Cadena.

"We can pick the rogue up any time. 'Tis Zorro I want now," Garcia yelled.

He had swung his mount aside, and now he jerked blade from scabbard and charged against Zorro despite the pistol the latter held. Zorro thrust the pistol into his sash unfired and whipped out his own blade.

ONCE, a long time before, he had crossed blades with Garcia and did not fear the sergeant's swordsmanship. Nor did be desire to shoot the sergeant or wound him with a blade save enough to stop him and put him out of the fighting. Zorro and Manuel Garcia were foes, but Don Diego Vega and Garcia were friends of a sort.

The horses came together, the blades clashed and rang. Zorro warded off the first blow and crowded nearer. The blades met again, Zorro's darting like the tongue of a snake in the moonlight.

Garcia gave a cry as his sword was torn from his hand to describe an arc through the air and crash to the rocks at the side of the highway. He reeled his horse backward.

"You are disarmed, Señor," Zorro called to him. "Your pistol is empty and your blade is gone. I could have slain you, Señor — give me credit for not doing it. Now I'll ride, and possibly we'll meet another day."

"You have not escaped me yet, Zorro," Garcia yelled, enraged. "My troopers are posted in hiding up and down the highway — it is a part of the trap we laid." He fumbled in his sat, brought out a whistle and blew several sharp blasts.

Zorro wheeled his big black and rode toward Reina de Los Angeles. As he started he heard the thunder of hoofs behind him, and he guessed some of the troopers had heard Garcia's shot and the clash of blades and had started to investigate.

As the black carried him around a curve in the road, Zorro saw the troopers charging toward him through the moonlight, and far behind them another pair emerging from behind a mass of rocks at the highway's edge.

He knew every foot of this country. And caught between the two forces, with Garcia bellowing, commands in the near distance, he put the black at a steep bank on the side of the road. The black went up it like a mountain goat. Pistols barked down in the road, and several balls flew perilously near Zorro, but none found the target.

Zorro's ringing mocking laugh sounded in the night. He used his spurs and sent the black flying along a narrow cattle trail. Pursuit came, but sounds of it soon dwindled in the distance.

And when he had gone far enough toward Reina de Los Angeles to lead the pursuit astray, he tuned to the left and made a wide circle over the hills and reached Rancho Vega. There, in a secluded spot, the faithful Bernardo was waiting to take Zorro's horse, weapons and costume.

Zorro stripped off the enveloping costume as he whispered news of the happening to the delighted Bernardo, and then hurried through the shadows and past the huts of the field hands to the sprawling ranchhouse.

An hour later he was stretching on his cot in night attire, Diego Vega again, prepared to take some hours of good sleep and arise and stroll around like the spineless fop many men believed him to be.

Zorro Gathers Taxes

The black-clad avenger faces flashing swords to right the wrongs of greed!

THAT midmorning the beating of a drum sounded at the barracks in Reina de Los Angeles. Down the slope came burly Sergeant Manuel Garcia, and behind him was the drummer, and on either side of the drummer a trooper carrying his musket. The sergeant carried a roll of heavy paper, and the group marched at the beat of the drum toward the proclamation board fastened to a post at the corner of the plaza.

The scene meant to the residents of the pueblo basking in the warmth of the sun that some sort of edict was about to be fastened to the proclamation board, and that it would be well for every resident to learn the statements thereon and comply with them promptly.

The group stopped, the sergeant fastened the paper to the proclamation board, the drummer ruffled his drum.

"Get to the tavern, take a table, save a place for me, and order mugs of good wine," Garcia ordered the three men. "The tax-gatherer pays, and our *commandante*, Capitán José Villa, gives us permission. I'll tarry another moment here."

The men hurried toward the tavern, and Garcia turned to read again the information on the paper. From every direction, drawn to the board as scraps of metal to a magnet, came men in different stations of life.

A tradesman looked over the sergeant's shoulder and read, shrugged and turned away, for the proclamation did not concern him. A cart driver did the same. A passing caballero deigned to peruse the paper, laughed a little and went on to a rendezvous. Only ignorant peons and natives remained standing near the post, those who held battered hats holding them in their hands respectfully. They could not read.

"Señor Sergeant, be kind enough to tell us what the words mean," one bold man requested.

"You would grieve to learn it," Garcia declared. "Why should I have the guilt of turning your pleasant day into one of pain?"

"Does it concern our kind, kind sergeant?" another asked.

"On this paper," Garcia informed them all, "is a long list of names compiled by the local *magistrado* and one of the Governor's men. If your name is on the list, you are concerned. Otherwise, not. Can it be that there is a man so ignorant that he cannot read his own name?"

"Some of us merely make the mark," a man said.

GARCIA chuckled. "And half the time you do not know upon what you make it, so afterward are surprised to find yourselves in rare difficulties. Ignorance is a terrible thing. Here comes Fray Felipe, the good padre of the chapel. He will read it to you — and pat your ignorant heads as you moan and wail."

Sergeant Garcia blew out the ends of his enormous mustache and turned to strut toward the tavern. He had no wish to remain and listen to the fiery denunciations of the padre after he had read the proclamation.

Fray Felipe lifted his hand in blessing as the men around the post bowed their bared heads for him. The elderly, emaciated padre squinted his eyes and read, and shook his head sadly while an expression of pity came into his face.

"A grievous thing," he muttered. "Another abuse of power. Another act of oppression against those powerless to rebel."

"Is it something bad, padre?" a man urged.

"First there is a long list of names of men in this part of the country," Fray Felipe replied. "Those are the ones concerned with this edict. Now I shall read you what is required of the men whose names are here."

"It will be something bad," a man near the padre muttered, making a decision based on events that often had occurred before.

"It is a declaration," the padre continued, "that taxes are due from the men who bear these names, together with added fines for hiding indebtedness. These taxes must he paid within three days' time at the barracks, counting this day as one, or the man who does not or cannot pay will be seized and inducted into the Governor's army, and be sent to Sonora, in Mexico, where the army is at present fighting the fierce natives."

The peons and natives began moaning and rocking their bodies from side to side.

Coming across the plaza on his way to the chapel to pay his devotions, Don Diego Vega both heard and saw them, and turned that way.

Diego, dressed resplendently as always, continually brushing a scented silk handkerchief across his nostrils as if common dust and the odors of common men affronted his sense of smell, nevertheless was not the popinjay most believed him to be.

It was but a necessary pose, a protection for the man who lead a dual life, who was an indolent dude one hour, and the next a wild masked night rider, Señor Zorro, who with blade and pistol and whip avenged the wrongs of the oppressed. The son of a hidalgo, scion of a family of noble blood and famed name, risking loss of life to defend those incapable of their own defense.

When Diego reached the spot, the peons and natives bowed and knuckled their foreheads. Fray Felipe turned quickly.

"Ah, Don Diego, my son!" he greeted. "Here we have a new edict that will cause much misery!"

Diego stepped forward another pace and read swiftly, exchanged glances with the padre, and asked, "Why do not the fellows pay the tax?"

A CHORUS of strident voices assailed his ears: "We do not have the money, kind Don Diego! … We were taxed only a short time ago! … Our wives and children will starve if we are taken to be soldiers, and we may be killed far south in Sonora …."

Diego lifted a hand. "Your din fatigues me," he declared. "I regret to see you inconvenienced. But there is nothing I can do about it at the moment. The paper is signed by Juan Castro, the *magistrado*, and by Carlos Mendez, the tax gatherer and army recruit agent for the Excellency, the Governor. That makes it both legal and official. You must comply"

"We can run away to the hills — " a man suggested.

"And if you do the troopers will run you down. They will not stop until they have you all. They will watch the roads, seize your relatives as hostages, see that you do not take ship. And when you are taken you will be sold into lifelong peonage and possibly be sent far away south to the Hot Country, there to work until you die. As many of you as can, pay the fines."

"We do not even know how much is owing," one said.

Fray Felipe replied to that: "I'll send one of the young padres to stand here by the board and read the names and tell each man his amount." He turned to Diego. "You were coming to the chapel to see me, my son? We can walk there now together."

They went to the chapel, where Fray Felipe led Diego to a private spot where their conversation would not be overheard.

"Another case of foul oppression," the padre said. "I have had word of this man, Carlos Mendez, from the north. He has done his terrible work north of Monterey and now has come to our beloved Southland."

"And his scheme?" Diego questioned.

"Our present Governor, appointed not for ability but because he is a familiar of the Viceroy in Mexico, loves money, and cares not by which means he gets it. Carlos Mendez carries the Governor's authority. He collects false taxes from peons and natives, even forcing them to sell the few poor sheep and goats they have, takes the ragged clothes off their backs, has been known to compel some to sell their pretty daughters to raise the tax. He gets a percentage, then the Governor falsifies reports and takes his percentage, and the remainder goes to the Viceroy with the reports."

"The usual beastly scheme," Diego commented.

"But there is another angle, my son. Carlos Mendez really recruits for the Viceroy's army, and gets a bonus for every man. So you may be sure he will either get tax money or the man he says owes it."

"It means death for them in either case," Diego observed.

"We of the missions have been working quietly, and have some evidence in this matter that might cause the Viceroy to recall the Governor and punish him, and certainly would be the undoing of this tax gatherer."

Diego frowned, "Evidence, padre?"

"That Carlos Mendez does not send in to the Governor all he collects, nor the Governor to the Viceroy. In this case, Mendez will take out perhaps a third, and split that amount with Capitán José Villa, our *commandante* here. There will also be an amount handed to Juan Castro, our *magistrado*, who will in return take any step Mendez suggests. Three rogues preying on the bodies, lives and souls of men unable to fight back. And also preying on the Governor and the Viceroy — "

"You have such evidence, padre?" Diego showed sudden increased interest.

"What we need is the first list of taxes collected, opposite the names of the victims. From that, another list is made, after the deductions I have mentioned. If we had both lists, and sent them to the Viceroy through our channels — " The padre hesitated, for he knew a suggestion was enough.

"If I were this man Zorro everyone is speaking about," Diego said, smiling slightly and half winking his left eye, "I would do certain things to wreck and ruin these worthless cheats."

"Such as?"

"If I were Zorro, I would let the tax gatherer and his associates gather all they can today and tomorrow. And tomorrow night, while the money is being counted, I would try to get it back, and in some manner return it to the victims."

"That is all?" the padre asked.

"I would try to get the list, so the money could be returned fairly. I would try to get proof to be sent to the Viceroy that would show how he, too, is being swindled. And, by the way of justice, I would endeavor to punish the three rogues who think nothing of bringing pain to men's bodies and worry to their minds as long as they profit by the act."

"A good determination — and one dangerous to carry out," Fray Felipe commented. "Capitán Villa, I have heard, is an expert swordsman and also handy with a pistol. A rogue like the tax gatherer is sure to go around armed. Juan Castro, the *magistrado*, is an old woman and not to be feared in the line of violence. But there will be soldiers within call — "

"Pardon me, padre, but I doubt that," Diego interrupted. "It is my idea that the three rogues will handle the money in some place where soldiers will not be near. Even the barracks would be risky for them. If you were a betting man, padre, I would offer you a wager that the three will meet at the house of Juan Castro, giving the impression the *magistrado* is trying to ingratiate himself with powerful men by furnishing them with an evening's entertainment."

"Ah, Diego, if you could— Pardon me! If Zorro could do what you suggest, it might result in much good. Our rascal of a Governor would be recalled, the tax gatherer punished by the Viceroy, and for his share in the business Capitán José Villa have rank stripped from him. Then we might have a better and more humane *commandante* sent to this post."

LEST a too-long visit arouse suspicion, Diego left a few minutes later. He found excitement in the plaza. Peons and natives were talking in groups. Several of Sergeant Garcia's troopers were strolling around fully armed and with their ears open.

The rascal of a tax gatherer, Diego had noted, had not put on his list the name of any peon or native who worked for the rancho owners, for he did not wish to antagonize the hidalgos. The list was of men indulging in free enterprise, raising a few sheep and goats, or sowing grain in a small field, or peddling, as many peons and natives did, wares from place to place.

During the day, Diego, wandering here and there on pretense of examining merchandise in the stores or visiting friends, observed harried men going to the barracks to give over the few coins they owned. Others were trying frantically to sell sheep, goats, skins, little jars of wine and olives and tubs of tallow to raise the amounts put opposite their names on the proclamation which had been read to them.

The following day it was much the same, only more men were hurrying to the tax gatherer. A few, more frantic than the others, had said farewell to their wives and children and had taken to the hills to be fugitives.

Capitán José Villa, it appeared, was putting Sergeant Garcia and his troopers at the command of Carlos Mendez. They continually checked the list of names and marked those who had not yet appeared, and they jailed several men they knew could not pay, to be held as recruits for the army.

That day, Diego returned home at dusk, shortly before it was time for the evening meal to be served to him and his father, dignified Don Alejandro. The latter, with Fray Felipe and Bernardo, Diego's mute peon bodyservant, were the only three who knew Diego was Zorro.

"You have made plans, my son?" Don Alejandro asked, as they sat at table and the servant had retired to the kitchen.

"A few. Others must be made on the spur of the moment."

"You will ride the black horse as usual?"

"I met Bernardo as I arrived home, and instructed him to have everything ready."

"Good fortune ride with you, my son. Every time Zorro rides, I worry and pray until he returns safely. You are the only one left of our family to follow me when I am laid to rest. Moreover, if you were caught you would be hanged, and our estates confiscated, and if that occurred I would die within a short time."

"Why so morbid this evening, Father? Do you have a premonition that things may go wrong?"

"Not that exactly, but I fear it each time I know Zorro is riding. The least mistake, the least suspicion — do not forget the large reward the Governor has offered for Zorro's capture."

A fresh breeze had come in from the sea, and after nightfall a cold mist enveloped the pueblo. It drove indoors many who otherwise would have been abroad and made people keep near their fires. The cold dampness seemed to permeate everything and all persons.

THERE was light and merriment and noise in the common room of the tavern, however. Sergeant Garcia and several of his troopers were there, sitting on the benches around a couple of tables and indulging in rounds of wine, at the expense of the tax gatherer.

Through the night, Zorro rode cautiously on his black horse. In his black costume, with the black mask and hood shrouding his features, he merged into the blackness of the night. His blade was at his side, a pair of loaded pistols were in his sash, and his long black whip, with which he could give terrible punishment, was fastened in a coil to the pommel of his saddle.

He neared the low, long and squat house inhabited by Juan Castro, the *magistrado*, a widower who lived with a single peon man-servant who attended to all his wants. Dismounting and going forward afoot, it took Zorro only a few minutes to learn that a part of his plan had been ruined. The house was dark except one kitchen window. No sounds told of a gathering of the three rogues. Peering cautiously through the window, Zorro saw the elderly peon servant devouring meat and drinking wine at a table, which he certainly would not have been doing had Juan Castro been at home.

Mounting again, Zorro rode to the barracks, left his horse in a secluded spot a distance from the building, and made his way to the side of it where the *commandante* had his quarters. All the rooms there were dark. No sound of roistering soldiers came from the common room of the troopers. A guard paced before the main door, shoulders hunched against the drizzle. Zorro got near enough to overhear him speak to a comrade:

"A fine thing, to leave the two of us on duty on a night like this."

"The tax gatherer left us a jug of wine, amigo."

"True. But Garcia and the others are making merry at the tavern. The *capitán* is gone. The cells are filled, with peons and natives destined for the army, who bother us with their continual wailing."

"I'll relieve you in a moment, amigo, and you can come in out of the wet and guzzle wine until time to relieve me."

Zorro made a circuit of the barracks afoot, keeping out of the few streaks of light, checking on what he had heard. He came finally to a front corner of the building and peered around it. The guard who had been there had gone inside. His comrade was before the door now, standing with shoulders hunched and his musket leaning against the wall; he was looking down the slope toward the tavern on the plaza, from whence came sounds of roistering.

ZORRO was upon him before the guard realized the presence of another in his vicinity. Zorro's eyes gleamed through the slits in his mask as he levelled a pistol at the guard's heart.

"Not a sound! Stand still and obey everything I say, or you die!" Zorro ordered in a whisper.

"You — you are the man they call Zorro!"

"True. I would have some speech with your commander. Where is he?"

"He is not at the barracks, Señor Zorro," the terrified guard stammered in low tones. "I overheard something about a card game in a room of the tavern. The *capitán*, the gatherer of taxes, and the *magistrado*, I believe. No doubt the tax gatherer will fill his purse with the others' coins, though our *capitán*, according to report, is clever with cards and dice."

"Where are the sergeant and the others?"

"They are at the tavern also, the tax gatherer having stood treat. He left a jug of wine for my comrade and myself. It is our poor lot to be chosen as guards."

"Inside with you!" Zorro ordered. "And make no sound."

He drove the trooper before him, a terrified new recruit Zorro did not have to fear much. They went along a long corridor and came to the soldiers' common room, where the other guard was drinking from a wine cup.

The man was caught with his musket a distance from him and no pistol in his belt. He half strangled on a gulp of wine in his surprise at sight of Zorro and the other guard holding his hands high.

"Get your keys!" Zorro ordered him. "Be quick, for tonight I am in a mood for shooting. Lead us to the cells. Open them, and release the men being held."

They paced into another corridor, where men gripped iron bars and peered between them.

"Zorro! … 'Tis Zorro come to aid us!" the cries began.

He whirled, to see burly Sergeant Garcia lurching toward him as he tugged to get his own blade free.

"Silence!" Zorro ordered them. "I am compelling your release. Take to the hills, and remain there until you learn it is safe to return. Be cautious in your traveling."

He backed away as the guard unlocked and opened the doors, and kept at a safe distance as the prisoners surged toward him.

"Go quietly," Zorro ordered. "The night is black and misty. Use caution, and you will earn freedom."

They rushed past him and out into the night, and Zorro drove the two guards to the entrance, and gestured for them to enter the dark corridor leading to the *capitán's* quarters.

"Remain there without sound for quite a time," he told them. "If you emerge to give an alarm, you may meet a bullet out of the dark."

He hurried to the entrance again, darted out and around the building, ran to his black horse and mounted.

He circled cautiously and came up behind the tavern in a deep gulch drenching rain had washed through the decades. The reins dropped over the black's head, and Zorro got out of the saddle and up to the lip of the gulch to watch and listen. Bent half double, he went through the darkness, stumbling over a stone now and then, until he reached the corner of the tavern building in the rear.

A DIN came from the common room in front. He went to the gate of the rear patio and glanced in. Nobody was in sight. A flaring torch burned on either side of the patio, and the shadows were deep beneath the covered arches under which people walked to get to the doors of the tavern's rooms for guests.

Zorro had half expected to see a trooper on guard, but none was there. He backed to the corner of the building and went along the wall, stopping at each window to listen. At one window, a tiny streak of light came through where the two drapes had not been drawn together entirely. Zorro stooped and peered inside.

There were the three men he wanted. They sat on stools around a table. Goblets were before them, half filled with wine. A jug stood near. A large tray heaped with fruit and slabs of bread and cold meat was on another smaller table near them.

They had tossed off their headgear. Capitán José Villa had removed his sword belt and put the weapon upon the cot. Juan Castro was unarmed. Carlos Mendez, the tax gatherer and enslaver of men for gain, had a pistol in his sash.

Castro, the *magistrado*, was writing furiously. He tossed aside his pen and straightened.

"It is done," he announced. "I have prepared the duplicate fine lists, and corrected my own papers to conform with the new list."

"We have cut a third off the total, and there may be more to come tomorrow," Mendez, the tax gatherer, gloated. "The figures will not be questioned."

"And here in this bag we have the third, ready to divide amongst us," Capitán Villa added, laughing a little. "And in this larger bag, the two-thirds which you, Señor Mendez, have to account for to the Governor."

"Everything is in order," Mendez agreed. "Let us split our own proceeds. We'll make three piles of it."

"Let us first rest and do some drinking and eating after counting all the money and making out the papers," the *capitán* suggested.

The other two agreed, and the *magistrado* reached for the jug of wine and began pouring into the goblets. Mendez got the tray of food and put it upon the table.

Though the best guest room in the tavern, the apartment was only about fifteen feet by twelve. The tables, stools and cot completed the furnishings. The single door opened into the patio, and there was but the one window.

Zorro got away from the window and went to the patio gate. A moment later, he was through the gate and in the darkness beneath the arches, moving to the door of the room where the three rogues were sitting.

Zorro got out his two pistols, glanced around the patio again, tapped on the door with the muzzle of one of the pistols, and spoke in a muffled, excited voice: "Capitán Villa! … Capitán Villa!"

There was sudden quiet inside the room. "Who do you suppose — ?" Zorro heard the *magistrado* say.

"Probably a trooper with an urgent message," Villa's voice replied. "I'll have him skinned alive if the message is not of importance."

"Capitán Villa — please!" Zorro implored outside the door. "The prisoners have been released. Zorro has been to the barracks!"

That brought instant action from those inside. "Zorro!" Capitán Villa echoed. Boots thumped the floor.

ZORRO heard the other two getting to their feet. The door was pulled open. Zorro, pistols held ready, hurled himself against Capitán Villa's body and toppled him back against the table, and was inside instantly with the door kicked shut behind him. "Stand steady, señores!" the masked man ordered.

"Wh — what — " Villa was gulping.

" 'Tis the masked rogue!" the terrified Castro cried. "He attacked me once — "

"The highwayman, eh?" Carlos Mendez roared.

Zorro moved his pistols. "Quiet, all of you — or I fire!" he ordered. "I have released the prisoners —! I know your damnable plot. So you profit on men's misery! Stand back against the wall by the window! At once!"

He advanced a step. They obeyed. They held their hands high above their heads at Zorro's further command.

"For this, Señor Zorro, I'll run you down and see you hanged if it takes me years!" Capitán Villa declared.

"Others have tried it, señor, and so far have failed. Do not make a move, any of you! Thanks for gathering all this tax money for me. You have separated your stolen share from the rest, as I know. I want the money, and those two papers, the true list of money collected, and the false one made after the theft. They are to go to the Governor by special messenger in quick time."

"You — you would — " the *commandante* began.

"I would expose you three to the Governor. Being a thief himself, he probably expects honesty from his associate thieves. No doubt to clear himself, he will deal harshly with you three."

Zorro stepped to the end of the table, thrust one pistol back into his sash as he watched the men before him, drew the two bags of money toward him, and glanced once to see they were tied with thongs. He picked up the papers and thrust them into his sash.

"Now, señores — " he began.

Carlos Mendez, the tax gatherer, made the move. Better even than the other two did he guess what the Governor would do when apprized of their duplicity. Mendez crouched, his hand flashed to the pistol in his sash. His shot and Zorro's came at the same instant. The slug from Mendez' pistol almost touched Zorro's left ear. Zorro's pistol ball crashed into the tax gatherer's breast, and he slipped to the floor.

Juan Castro, the cowardly *magistrado*, was on his knees in the corner, whimpering like a frightened child.

Capitán Villa had stepped aside nearer the cot, but still held his hands high.

Zorro watched him as he grasped the two bags of money in his left hand.

"Poor coins of small value, stolen from men to whom even the smallest coin is of the most importance," Zorro said. "All three of you deserve death."

"No — no, Señor Zorro!" the *magistrado* cried.

"Silence, or you'll get it instantly!" Zorro thrust his discharged pistol into his sash and continued watching Villa as he fumbled for the second loaded weapon. Then, the *commandante* made his move.

Villa's hand swept down and he grasped his sword belt. An instant later, as Zorro retreated to the door, still tugging at the pistol in his sash, Villa had swept blade from scabbard and was lunging forward.

Zorro's back thumped against the door. Villa was shouting wildly for help as he charged. Zorro's pistol came free, and he fired, and through the surging cloud of smoke saw Villa reel aside. Zorro got the door open, backed to the patio. "Stand right there, Zorro!" a stentorian voice ordered him.

He whirled, to see burly Sergeant Garcia lurching toward him as he tugged to get his own blade free.

And, at the same instant, Capitán Villa, with a bullet in his upper left arm but his right arm undamaged, came into sight with blade held ready.

"Let me have him, sergeant!" Villa demanded. "Arouse your men and help take this rogue after I've wounded him. You will share in the reward."

Zorro backed to a defensive position where light from the torch would aid him and bother his opponent. Garcia began bellowing for help, but did not leave the scene.

Blades clashed, as Zorro and Villa felt each other out an instant. The eager *commandante* sought to slay the masked man and recover the money and exposing papers; he wanted no live Zorro a prisoner and able to talk.

Villa's onslaught, incautious but vicious, drove Zorro backward a few steps. Sergeant Garcia came on to back up his superior as he continued shouting.

Zorro advanced swiftly, and Villa stood. Blades rang and clashed, then Zorro saw his chance. He got through guard and lunged, and his blade went through Villa's body and the hilt crashed against the *comandate's* chest.

As men came pouring into the patio from the common room, Villa gasped and slumped to the flagstones of the patio floor. Zorro's blade, coming free, was up instantly to meet Sergeant Garcia's wild charge.

Garcia's method of swordsmanship was vicious rather than clever. Zorro warded off the furious onslaught, and ran his already-red blade through the sergeant's right shoulder. Then he turned and ran through the darkness beneath the arches to the patio gate.

As he darted through, he crashed against a trooper who had circled the building. Zorro crashed the hilt of his blade into the man's face and ran on.

Guns cracked behind him as a couple of the troopers who had been in the common room opened up with their pistols. But the darkness, the swirling mist spoiled their aim. They came charging through the dark, shouting.

Zorro slipped over the lip of the gully and got to his horse. He got the sacks of money into his saddlebag, and mounted quickly and gathered the reins.

Cautiously, he started his horse. The shouting men in pursuit were drawing nearer. Zorro swung his big black up out of the gulch on the opposite side. His voice rang through the night in mockery: "*Señores, a Dios*!"

Then he used his spurs and rode ....

The following morning, Don Diego Vega went toward the little chapel, shuffling along as if unduly fatigued. Beneath his arm he carried a bundle. It appeared to be a bundle of old clothes he was taking to Fray Felipe to be given to the poor. It was just that — but in the bundle two bags of money were hidden.

"I'll take charge of it, my son," the little old padre said. "I'll take the papers also, and see them forwarded. In some manner, the money will be returned to those who paid the unjust tax. You have done well, my son."

"Your thanks is reward enough, padre," Don Diego said.

"Capitán Villa may survive, and the tax gatherer also, to be dealt with by the Governor. Let us hope that in time someone will deal with the Governor also. As far as the *magistrado* is concerned, he will shake himself to death with fear, probably. Yes, my son, you have done well."

"So much talk fatigues me," Diego complained, brushing his scented handkerchief across his nostrils. "These are such turbulent times."

He glared at the trader through the slits in the black mask

Zorro Rides the Trail

The trader used an ox goad, not on oxen — but on men! Here, indeed, was a chore for the masked rider who left his dread mark behind — The Mark of Zorro!

AT DUSK that day, Don Diego Vega, dressed in splendid holiday clothing, left his father's house in the little village of Reina de los Angeles. A few feet behind him followed his mute bodyservant, Bernardo, walking with a graceful, panther-like stride, his eyes and ears searching for sights and sounds which might signal danger for Diego.

This had been a fiesta day. The afternoon before, Diego had ridden in from the Vega ranch, near San Gabriel, to represent the family at the celebration. An attack of rheumatism had kept his father from making the journey.

He had gone to the religious service at dawn in the little chapel on the plaza. He had watched peons and natives, traders and travelers up and down El Camino Real, the king's highway, gathering for the fun. Then he had returned to the house to spend some hours resting and dozing.

Now, at dusk, he was starting out to make a duty call on an old friend of his father's. He never made it.

A short distance from the house, a barefooted peon came hurrying toward them. Both Diego and Bernardo knew the man well. He helped around the chapel for food given him by old Fray Felipe, the Franciscan in charge. The peon stopped, took off his battered sombrero and knuckled his forehead to Diego in a respectful gesture.

"Well?" Diego asked, stopping and brushing a scented silk handkerchief across his nostrils.

"A message from Fray Felipe, Don Diego. He asked me to hurry." He handed Diego a scrawled note, and turned away.

"One moment!" Diego said. He took a coin from his purse and tossed it to the peon. The man bobbed his head, grinned and muttered his thanks, then disappeared.

By the light of the full moon, Diego had no trouble reading what Fray Felipe had written:

> *Come to me at once, if you, can, my son. There is a thing you should know. The matter is urgent.*

Diego drew in his breath sharply. Fray Felipe would not have written such a note and sent it by messenger unless forced to do so by an emergency. He put the note in his sash and changed his course toward the plaza. The visit to his father's friend was forgotten.

Having his plans changed abruptly was nothing new to Diego Vega. Considering the dual life he led, it could not have been otherwise.

DIEGO VEGA, scion of a wealthy and noble family, without set hours for business or work, could plan a day according to his own wishes. But his other self — Señor Zorro, the masked man who rode his black horse at night and punished those who mistreated helpless peons and natives — might be found in the middle of a whirlpool of a time when he had planned to be peacefully engaged elsewhere.

From the plaza came the din of voices, shouts and laughter, strains of music and singing. Fires were burning, food was cooking, free wine had been set out by merchants and traders. The dancing around the fires would continue until the celebrants were exhausted.

Without attracting attention, Diego went along the side of the plaza and toward the chapel. Loud laughter came from the tavern across the square, and Diego heard a man screaming. A fight had started there. Diego supposed. That was the usual thing toward the end of a fiesta day.

Fray Felipe was waiting for him in the chapel doorway. He greeted Diego with a smile. Diego told Bernardo to wait for him, and followed the old padre to a little room he called his private quarters.

"Your messenger caught me just in time, Padre," Diego said. "I was starting for Don Juan Cassara's house to give him my father's greeting."

"I'm glad you came so promptly, my son," Fray Felipe said. He motioned Diego to a stool beside a small square table, and seated himself on another stool.

"You wanted to see me, Padre?" Diego asked.

"Yes. Today I have been made aware of a species of cruelty I didn't know existed, and of a species of animal in human form, which I shall not elevate by calling a man. I have given what medical aid I could to seven men since noon-time, and possibly twice that many more did not come to me to receive it."

"Tell me, Padre," Diego said.

"Yesterday a rich trader came here from a town to the south. His name is Pedro Tavera, and he has a caravan of eight ox carts encamped a mile from the village. He has a crew of five peons."

"And so?" Diego said.

"He has decided to remain here for the fiesta. He is arrogant, ruthless and unscrupulous in business. He is short and thick in body, drunk with material success — a peon raised by wealth to the point of making him intolerant of his own kind."

"And the cruelty — ?" Diego said.

"Many men like this Pedro Tavera carry a whip with a short lash, as you know. Sometimes they punish natives with it. This man strikes any peon or native unfortunate to come within his reach. And he does not use a whip, my son — but an ox goad."

"An ox goad?" Diego's face showed his surprise.

"Yes. A common ox goad—a short, heavy stick of wood with a sharp spike set in the end of it. He drives the spike into the thighs and hips of those he attacks."

"And they are — ?"

"Peons and natives. They don't dare strike back, because they know they'd be punished with more cruelty. Two of the wounds I treated today are such as to almost cause permanent lameness."

"Did he punish these men for serious faults?"

"For amusement, my son. He laughs and says he knows how to make the scum jump. He's over at the tavern now, drunk, boasting of big business deals. He struts around, buying wine for the house, trying to impress everyone with his importance."

Diego nodded, and got up from his stool. "I know the kind. You say his camp is a mile south of here?"

"Yes."

"And his five men?"

"He gave them some money and let then come to the fiesta. He got Captain Salcido, the commanding officer here, to furnish him with two troopers to guard the caravan."

Diego's eyes gleamed. "I hadn't intended to visit the tavern this evening," he said, "but I've changed my mind. It seems to me that this calls for the attention of a man we both know — a man who leaves his mark behind."

"Who leaves the letter Z behind," Fray Felipe whispered. "Being your father confessor, I know your secret my son. I don't suggest extreme violence, and cannot approve of it. Least of all do I think you should take a human life for any cause. Punish where punishment is deserved and not given by the authorities, but always remember to punish with justice and not with malice."

"Give me your blessing, Padre," Diego

Fray Felipe gave it. "May you be well guarded in your work tonight, my son."

ALTHOUGH Diego dropped into the tavern at intervals, his entry on a fiesta night, when the place was filled with drunken men, was astounding. Generally his visits were to cultivate the friendship between himself and burly Sergeant Juan Garcia, of the troopers. As Diego, he enjoyed the sergeant's quaint sayings; as Zorro, he obtained information as to what moves the troopers were making to capture and hang the man with a price on his head.

When he entered the place now, the fat landlord saw him and hurried toward him. "Welcome, Don Diego," he said. "I am delighted to have you here again. But the company tonight may not be to your liking."

"Indeed, señor?" Diego raised his brows slightly.

"Mostly drunken rascals, Don Diego. Very quarrelsome, No young caballeros of your quality are present."

"A place to sit, and a glass of your best wine," Diego said.

The landlord bowed. He led Diego through the crowd along the wall, seated him at a small table, and clapped his hands to summon a servant.

"If anyone troubles you. Don Diego, Captain Salcido is present," the landlord whispered. "And Sergeant Garcia is there in the corner."

"Ah Ask the good sergeant to come to my table," Diego said. "And bring a glass of wine for him."

Garcia plowed a path through the crowd and sat opposite Diego.

"A great pleasure to see you again, amigo," Garcia said. "This is a rough night. The scum of Alta California seems to be here — not meaning you, amigo. It's no place for a fine gentleman such as yourself. Any of these men would slit your throat for that jeweled brooch you wear, or carve you to ribbons for one of your rings."

"I'm leaving soon, Garcia."

"And I'll have a trooper see you safely home."

A howl of pain and a burst of drunken laughter came from across the room. A barefooted peon screeched as he tried to get through the crowd and out of the tavern.

"He's at it again," Garcia said to Diego. "That man roaring with laughter is Pedro Tavera, a rich trader. He carries an ox goad and jabs men with it."

"Then why don't you put him under arrest and confine him in the barracks?" Diego asked.

"Ah! Notice, please, that Captain Salcido, my superior officer, sits at the table yonder and laughs. Is that your answer, amigo? This Tavera is wealthy, and probably has friends in high places. Some of our official rogues in Monterey may not be above profiting from goods smuggled in by a trader."

"I understand," Diego said.

"It's things like this that cause us to be pestered by that rascal of a Señor Zorro. He may learn of the incident, if he is in the locality. Zorro! Blast him for a ghost of a man! My troopers and I have run the legs off our horses trying to catch him."

Diego was watching Pedro Tavera as the trader stood in a cleared space in the center of the big room. He was brandishing his ox goad and looking around for someone to jab with it. The tavern servants were doing their best to avoid him.

"More wine for everyone!" Tavera shouted at the landlord. "This is fiesta day. My purse is open. Drink to the long life and success of Pedro Tavera."

When one of the tavern servants came to his own table, Diego waved him aside. Pedro Tavera noticed it. His eyes glinted. He gripped his ox goad and swaggered across the room. He stopped by Diego's table.

"I am Pedro Tavera," he said. "I ordered free wine for all. Why do you refuse it?"

Diego eyed him. "We already have wine on the table, señor, and we need no more."

"You refuse to drink with me?" the trader roared.

CAPTAIN SALCIDO had been watching, and now he hurried across the room. The captain had no wish to offend the trader, but he knew the prestige of the Vega family and didn't want to offend a member of it, and perhaps in doing so offend the rest of the gentry as well. He reached the table before Tavera could speak again, and touched the trader on the shoulder.

"One moment, senor," he said. "This gentleman is Diego Vega. Don't let the wine you've drunk cause you to make a mistake. Come back to my table with me."

Pedro Tavern blinked rapidly, and bent forward to inspect Diego's fine clothing. He peered at the jewels at Diego's throat and on his fingers. A hush came over the crowded room. Near the front door, the frightened landlord was muttering and wringing his hands.

"Ha!" Tavera said. "A caballero, no less!" In the silent room, the trader's voice seemed like a roar. "A pretty boy in satin and lace! A highborn! I wonder, señor, if I could make you dance with my ox goad."

"Try it, and you'll he dancing on the hot coals of hell," Diego said.

"You and your kind. Scum of the earth. Using peons and natives as slaves — "

"We don't use ox goads on them," Diego said.

Captain Salcido gripped the trader's thick arm. "Let's go back to our table, Señor Tavera. A new dancing girl is going to perform for us. I had the landlord send for one."

Sergeant Garcia got to his feet and stood beside Diego's chair. He, too, faced a difficult decision. He did not want to oppose his superior officer, who was treating the trader as a friend; but neither did he intend seeing Diego Vega attacked.

"I was about to escort Don Diego home, Captain," Juan Garcia said significantly.

Perhaps I can give him a swift start with my goad," Tavera said.

Diego arose and glared at the trader. "You have insulted me," he said. "Also, you have used your goad on helpless peons, men of your own caste. You should be punished severely."

A roar of rage came from Tavera's throat. Though Diego didn't realize it. He had given the trader the greatest insult possible. A man climbing from obscurity to a high position over the shoulders of weaker men does not like to be reminded of his beginnings.

Tavera raised his ox goad and lunged forward. Captain Salcido made a swift decision, and grasped the trader and held him back. Sergeant Garcia got between Tavera and Diego, ready to protect the latter.

Tavera sputtered with rage. "Out of my sight Get out, while I'm being held!"

"Come back to your table, Tavera," the captain said. "The dancing girl will be performing for us soon."

Garcia stepped close to the trader and pushed him backward. Diego remained standing against the wall, trying not to show his anger. At that instant, he would have liked to have had a sword in his hand and slash the trader to ribbons. But he was forced to act the role he had taken upon himself; Diego Vega must be a languid fop who hated violence, to protect Zorro, his other self.

"Let's leave, Don Diego," Garcia whispered to him.

Captain Salcido was urging Tavera away from the table. Diego turned to go outside the tavern, where Bernardo had been waiting.

"I'll walk to your home with you," Garcia said. "That Tavera — I'd like to tear him apart with my bare hands. It's my fond hope that the unknown Zorro gets news of what he has done with his goad, and punishes him for it."

Diego nodded, somehow preventing a smile. He was thinking how Sergeant Garcia would be shocked to learn that the man beside him was Zorro, for whose capture the Governor of Alta California had offered a huge reward.

At the house, the sergeant reluctantly refused the drink that Diego offered him, saying he had to return at once to his post. Diego told him good night and closed the door. Bernardo hurried up to him.

Diego handed over his hat and gloves. He spoke to Bernardo in a whisper.

"Zorro rides tonight. Have my horse and costume and weapons ready. A mist is drifting in from the sea, which means that the moon will be obscured. It will be a good night for my purpose."

Bernardo's eyes glittered. The mute bodyservant made a gurgling sound to reveal his pleasure, nodded that he understood, and hurried from the room.

ZORRO rode through the misty night with extreme caution. His black horse, black costume — which enveloped his entire body — and black mask made him like a part of the night itself. He circled toward the highway, toward the spot where, Fray Felipe had told him, Pedro Tavera's cart caravan was camped south of the village.

He knew the wide, open space beside the highway where such caravans usually camped, and headed toward it. His senses were keenly alert. He was Zorro now. His capture could mean a disgraceful death at the end of a rope. And even if the governor spared him, the least he could expect was death in a foul prison in Mexico, and disgrace for his aged father.

At times, streaks of light from the moon shone through the swirling mist drifting in from the sea. At such times. Zorro gave his attention to the shadows, his ears straining to catch any suspicious sound.

He had a sword at his side, two loaded pistols in the sash he wore, and a long whip coiled and fastened to the pommel of his saddle. His horse was trained to move at his touch on the reins or at the slightest pressure of his knees, and if dismounted would come at Zorro's strange call.

He neared the highway, and now he heard sounds which told him the exact location of the cart camp. Someone was singing drunkenly with all his lung power. Another man was laughing.

Zorro remembered that the trader had allowed his caravan men to go into the village for the fiesta, and that two troopers had been assigned to guard the carts. He was hoping Tavera had given them enough wine to make them drunk, so that they would be slow to think and move.

The highway ran along the brow of a low hill. The bank beside the road was about ten feet high, its crest lined with rocks and clumps of brush. Zorro rode cautiously to a spot at the end of the bank and stopped. He bent forward in the saddle and peered down the highway.

Carts were hunched together near a blazing campfire. The oxen were a short distance from the carts. Sitting on a large rock near the fire was Pedro Tavera. The trader had a wineskin across his knees, and held a mug. He waved the mug as he sang a ribald song.

Stretched out on the ground near Tavera was one of the troopers, evidently asleep. The other trooper was propped up against a wheel of one of the carts, nodding.

Zorro watched and listened. It was now about midnight. So far as he could tell, there was no one else nearby, and there were no sound's up or down the highway to indicate anyone was coming.

Zorro eased his horse along the bank until he found a break in the rocks, and then urged him down the bank and onto the highway. Once again he watched and listened, and then started the horse at a walk toward the campfire.

He stopped the horse in a spot where light from the fire did not strike him. Pedro Tavera had stopped howling his song and was busy filling his mug from the wineskin. The trooper nearest him was still stretched out on the ground, and the one by the cart had slumped down beside the wheel.

Zorro took one of his pistols from his sash, grasped the reins in his left hand, spurred his horse and jumped him into a run.

TAVERA looked up drunkenly when he heard the hoofs on the hard surface of the road. Zorro skidded the horse to a stop in a shower of gravel and dust, only a few feet front the trader. He bent forward in the saddle, pointing the pistol directly at Tavera's head.

"Who — what — ?" Tavera gasped.

Zorro's voice was stern and menacing, not at all like the soft, drawling voice of Diego Vega.

"I am Zorro," he said. "Do as I say, or I'll shoot you down! Get the muskets and pistols of the two troopers — pronto! — and toss them over by those rocks!"

Tavera lurched to his feet, dropping both the mug and the wineskin. "You — you — "

Zorro urged his horse nearer, and bent front his saddle again. He glared at the trader through the slits in the black mask and held the pistol within a foot of his head.

"Be quiet!" Zorro ordered. "Get the weapons of the trooper by the cart first, and then get those of that drunken sot on the ground."

Tavera acted as if he were befuddled. He lurched to the cart and got the musket and pistol, weaved across the road and tossed them over by the rocks. Then he reeled back to the trooper stretched on the ground, got his weapons and tossed them after the others. Then he returned to the fire.

"You — you are a robber?" he asked.

"I am Zorro, you fool! *Zorro!"*

Tavera suddenly understood. His jaw sagged, and his eyes bulged. His tongue licked feverishly at his upper lip. "You are the man they call Zorro? What do you want with me, señor? I have no quarrel with you. I am not a soldier — "

"Hand me your ox goad," Zorro ordered.

"My goad! Ha! Now I understand, senor highwayman. You would punish these troopers for getting drunk and going to sleep. It is well. They should be punished. They were going to guard my carts and me." He picked the goad off the ground and handed it up to Zorro.

Zorro swiftly transferred his pistol to his left hand and took the goad with his right. He urged the horse forward again, and Tavera backed away uncertainly until he was beside the rock upon which he had been sitting.

"Señor Tavera, you are no better than a beast," Zorro told him in a voice that rang. "A fat, greasy, arrogant, ignorant ox! Bend over that rock."

"What — what are you going to do?" Tavera muttered. "Is it money you want? I have some hidden in a cart — "

"Do as I said," Zorro told him, "or I'll shoot!"

At Zorro's kneed command, the horse went forward another step. Tavera lost his footing as he started to back away, slipped, and sprawled across the rock pleading for mercy.

Zorro bent from the saddle again. He gave two quick jabs with the goad, jabbing hard and deep. Tavera's cries of pain rang up and down the highway and echoed from the rocks. He rolled to the ground and stretched there face downward.

"Listen to me," Zorro said. "Early in the morning, start your carts northward. Never pass this way again. If you do, I'll hunt you up and kill you. And if I hear of your goading any more helpless men, anywhere along the highway, I'll do the same. Do you understand? Or do you want me to use the goad on you some more?"

Zorro swung from the saddle, holding the goad. In the sandy ground beside the rock he scratched the letter Z, then tossed the goad aside. "There's my mark," he said. "Be thankful I don't carve it on your hide."

He took the pistol in his right hand again, and backed his horse to the dying campfire. The trooper at the cart was now on his feet, groping around for his missing weapons. The trooper on the ground was sitting up, rubbing his knuckles into his eyes.

"Stay as you are, both of you!" Zorro told them. "Your muskets and pistols have been taken away. Try to draw your sabers, and I'll shoot you down!"

From the darkness nearby came a commanding voice. "Stop, Zorro! One more move, and I'll shoot you out of your saddle. This is Captain Salcido talking."

ZORRO felt the thrill of danger. He sensed a trap. The voice had scented to come from a clump of brush beside the bank of the road, about fifty feet away. He sat motionless in the saddle.

"So you are Captain Salcido?" he asked mockingly. "And what do you want with me?"

"I knew, Señor Zorro, that if you were in the neighborhood you would punish this rascal who uses a goad on other men. So I have been waiting for you. This is the end of the trail for you, my fine outlaw!"

"Is that so, Captain? We are man to man, are we not? And I am mounted. You, it seems to me, are crouching in the brush. Did you come alone to capture me so you could obtain all the reward for yourself?"

"I have two of my troopers posted down the trail, and another pair in the other direction. I intend to share the reward, but I want to take you with my own hands. Dead or alive, the official notice says. I'd rather take you alive and see you hanged."

"An interesting situation," Zorro said. "Sorry, but I can't accommodate you."

"Enough of this jesting!" Salcido roared. "Throw your pistol on the ground, and then get off your horse and hold your hands high above your head. At once!"

"That's quite a long speech, Captain. Perhaps you made it to kill time while your troopers creep up on me." He moved his right hand as if to toss the pistol upon the ground. But at the same instant he kneed his horse. The animal sprang over the dying campfire, scattering a shower of embers.

A pistol flashed and roared in the darkness. Zorro heard the zing of a slug of metal past his head. Without firing his own weapon, he bent low over his horse's neck and used his spurs. The powerful horse thundered down the highway.

Captain Salcido was shouting orders. The half-dazed troopers were searching for their weapons. Tavera was cursing and yelling for help.

A safe distance from the cart camp, Zorro pulled up his horse abruptly. He heard hoofbeats coming from both north and south as troopers raced in answer to their officer's call.

The highway was narrow where Zorro had stopped, with the high bank on one side, and on the other a deep ravine with tangled brush and heaps of rocks. He was not familiar with this ravine, and hesitated to urge the horse down into it. And he could not expect the horse to climb the steep bank at this spot. The only thing he could do was swerve the horse back off the road into a patch of black shadow.

The sound of hoofbeats became louder. The riders coming from the south seemed nearest. Zorro hoped they would ride past without noticing him, giving him a chance to find a spot where his horse could climb the bank.

The swirls of mist were suddenly wafted aside by a breeze, and bright moonlight filled the highway.

A shaft of moonlight fell upon Zorro just as the two troopers from the south bore down upon him. One was looking straight ahead, but the second glanced aside and saw the masked rider. He yelled, jerked at his reins, and fumbled for his pistol. The other rider looked back, and began pulling up his horse. And the two troopers from the north were coming swiftly.

Zorro fired one of his pistols over the head of the man nearest him, then swung his horse around and raced away. The shot had caused the troopers to rein away from one another. Then they began to fire, and took up the pursuit.

Zorro glanced back and saw the riders from the north come into view and join in the chase behind the others. He rode furiously around a curve in the highway, just as a swirl of mist drifted before the moon again.

He was at the spot where he had come down the bank beside the road. He checked his horse and put him at the bank. The horse scrambled up it, sending a cascade of gravel and loose dirt down onto the highway.

Yelling at one another, the troopers came charging along the road. Zorro knew their own hoofbeats would prevent them from realizing that no horse ahead of them was pounding the ground as he raced away. He stopped his own horse at the top of the bank behind a tangle of brush, reached forward and patted the glossy neck.

"Let them chase shadows, amigo," he said. "You've done well tonight, as usual. Now we'll go home, and Bernardo will rub you down, water you, and feed you well."

He rode back through the darkness toward the village, to the place where Bernardo was waiting. The mute's guttural sound was a question Zorro answered immediately.

"All has gone well, Bernardo," he said. "Care for the horse and hide him as usual. Stow away my costume as soon as I have removed it, and also my weapons. Then take a jar of horse salve and carry it to the chapel. Old Fray Felipe no doubt is meditating there, even at this hour. Simply hand him the jar, and he will understand. Maybe he will even smile — though he will not get a chance to salve certain wounds of which I know."

He dismounted, stripped off his costume, and stood in his usual clothing, which the costume had hidden, He gave the weapons to Bernardo to hide.

"*Buenos noches!*" he said.

Zorro was gone, for the time being, and only the languid Don Diego Vega remained. He strode toward the house, and entered it secretly so that none of the servants would know. In his own room, he undressed and stretched out on his couch to sleep.

"To goad an ox can sometimes be a pleasant pastime," he muttered.

The Mask of Zorro

This is Zorro! Hero or outlaw? Decide for yourself. They say he killed Esteban Cassara and Cassara was the beloved magistrado of Reina de Los Angeles

IN THE LATE AFTERNOON, Don Alejandro de la Vega was traveling overland from his extensive rancho holdings near Mission San Gabriel to his somewhat elaborate house in the pueblo of Reina de Los Angeles. Having been informed that stocks of new wares had come to the big warehouse in the pueblo, he'd decided to purchase what he needed for both his rancho house and his town establishment, where his housekeepers were pleading for more fashionable drapes for curtains and window hangings and garments both simple and elaborate.

Whenever shipments came to the warehouse, either from ships landing at San Diego de Alcalá or the new port called San Pedro, or from Monterey along the winding trail called El Camino Real, which connected the Franciscan missions dotting the coast of Alta California, Don Alejandro was notified immediately. This was not at all surprising, for he was by far the wealthiest *hidalgo* in the district, and the most powerful. He was also a close friend of the Viceroy, who ruled in Spain's behalf in the City of Mexico, and it was no secret that he was a liberal spender and lived on a magnificent scale.

Don Alejandro himself drove the spanking team, a thing he liked to do. Beside him in the seat was Don Diego, his son and heir and only offspring, who was infinitely adroit at reciting poetry to his frustrated father when he was not discussing the liveliest ballads and the philosophers of Spain. Behind the carriage, on a fat riding mule, rode Bernardo, young Don Diego's personal servant.

Bernardo was a born mute, but he was not deaf and had a sharp ear for what was said around him.

Where the dusty curving road ascended the side of a small hill, Don Alejandro eased the horses to a walk, and turned to face his son.

"For the moment, let me have less of music and poetry," he begged. "Such things are charming to many persons, no doubt. Pleasing to me at times, but at times only. Too much is more than enough. There are other things in the world."

"I know, Father," Don Diego replied.

"You are a *caballero*, and the last of our line. You have the sacred duty to be worthy of your heritage. You, a Vega, have no fire within you."

"I know, Father. You would have me cultivate arrogance, dominating other men, asserting my superiority with the sword, and, when necessary, the lash."

"Why do you persist in distorting what I really mean?" Don Alejandro demanded. "If strong men did not point the way to system and order, our world would be in chaos. Take pride in your superior station. Remember your responsibilities—one of which is to wed a señorita of good blood and bring forth a family to carry on the Vega line. Be a Vega, a *caballero* quick to resent a slight or an insult. Stand up to other men. Other *caballeros* ride their horses wildly, fight a little when it is necessary to dispel all doubt as to their honor, wink at a comely wench occasionally, even pinch her arm. Stir the blood in your veins! Do not make me ashamed of your mother's son."

The top of the slope fell behind, and the team bent with a clattering of hooves to the real business of getting along the trail. The carriage came to the plaza of the pueblo, passed the buildings, and finally stopped at the Vega town house, where the stable servants took charge.

A little later Don Alejandro, the trail dust cleansed from his attire, strolled toward the warehouse. He was saluted by the friends he met, and chose to ignore the sullen frowns of natives and barefooted peons.

In Don Diego's suite of rooms Bernardo was busily engaged in helping the scion of the Vegas prepare for a perfumed bath and a change of clothing. The young man was humming a few bars of classical music …

Shortly after dawn came the tumult.

Both Don Diego and his father were up at dawn, eating breakfast and preparing for the busy day ahead. They heard a wild shout, answering voices, cries of surprise and alarm. Emerging from the patio, where they had been eating, Diego and his father hurried to the front of the house. Just as they reached it another wild cry brought them up short. "Murder! Get the *commandante* at the *presidio!* Make haste! To the chapel as well. Tell Fray Felipe to come and give the last office. This man is still alive! There is a dagger in his back!"

By the time Don Alejandro and Diego reached the scene, a small crowd had gathered despite the earliness of the hour. Peons and stable servants were crossing themselves. Others stood aside, their eyes bulging.

"It is Señor Esteban Cassara, our *magistrado!"* someone in the crowd exclaimed.

Don Alejandro thrust his way through the throng with Diego at his heels. "Back!" he cried, his voice ringing out in peremptory command. "Stand back and touch nothing."

Fray Felipe hurried to the spot from the chapel, his robe flapping around his heels. He knelt beside the body, bent over and spoke to the dying man, In reply he heard two whispered words: "Zorro … punish." There came a gasp, and the *magistrado* of Reina de Los Angeles was dead.

Señor Cassara was sprawled on his side. A long dagger pierced his back. A few inches from his contorted right hand, scratched in the earth, was a large jagged letter Z.

Fray Felipe bowed his head, and remained in a kneeling position beside the body. Shouting for everyone to make room for him, Capitán Juan Ruelas, the present *commandante* stationed at Reina de Los Angeles, thrust his way through the crowd. Three of his soldiers were behind him, tossing aside peons, natives and other unimportant men. Sergeant Castro, the burly second-in-command at the post, came after them, scowling at everyone as he tugged at the ends of his enormous mustache.

CAPITÁN RUELAS stopped his rush beside the dead man as Fray Felipe arose to his feet.

"So the victim is our *magistrado*, Señor Cassara," Ruelas said. "A dagger in his back, and that all too familiar letter Z scrawled in the dirt with boastful insolence. Señor Cassara had a fine reputation for integrity in the pursuit of his office. Who would want to murder a just *magistrado?"*

Sergeant Castro grumbled the answer. "It is plain to me, *Señor el Capitán*. This rascal and thief has finally taken a human life. I'll have the troopers saddle and run down the black-hearted scoundrel! It will be a pleasure to see him at the end of a rope — and also there is a reward for his capture."

Don Alejandro tightened his lips. "He has been pursued without success through every part of the country. He has been seen repeatedly, but never caught. What we need in this pueblo is a *commandante* of merit who does more than pour wine down his throat and leer at women. And proper troopers under his command. I shall dispatch a mounted messenger immediately to the *presidio* at San Diego de Alcalá, and have the *commandante* at that post come with his soldiers as swiftly as they can ride. It should not take them long."

The eyes of Capitán Ruelas blazed and his face turned almost purple with rage. "I resent that, Don Alejandro," he declared. "I am in command here."

"Until such a time as volt are dismissed from the service," Don Alejandro snapped at him. "I have the open ear of the Governor in Monterey, and beyond him the ear of the Viceroy in the City of Mexico. It is time we have action here. Go your way, Señor Ruelas, and let me and some of the gentlemen here take care of the remains of Señor Cassara, who was the most just *magistrado* I have ever known."

The *commandante* swore an ugly oath, but took care to slur the words. He gestured to Sergeant Castro and the troopers, and turned away.

Fray Felipe touched Don Diego on his arm. "Come to the chapel with me, my son," he whispered.

"One moment, padre. My father seems to have something else to say."

Don Alejandro was saying it, and all the others were listening. "My friends we have here an infamous example of the misuse of power. The man we know as Zorro began his mysterious work by punishing self-willed men who abused natives and peons. He seemed at first to be fighting for justice and mercy. He made fools of the soldiery, appeared like a ghost in the night, did his work, and escaped while his mocking laughter was still ringing in the ears of those who tried clumsily and without success to capture him."

The group around Don Alejandro nodded in agreement.

The elder Vega continued with rising vehemence. "Power went to his head. He forgot the work he had started out to do. There were hints that he stole from the rich, but failed to give any portion of his thefts to the poor. His whip stung the backs of men who were innocent of wrong. He was accused of blackmail, and of attacking men of courage who would not pay. And now he has descended to murder.

"Why did he slay an honest *magistrado?* Perhaps because Señor Esteban Cassara was too honest an officer of the law. Perhaps he refused to make certain unjust decisions which Zorro demanded. Such a scoundrel deserves nothing but the loathing commonly reserved for vultures and snakes. He must he captured and hanged by the neck until he is dead, and buried in a grave with a black stone to mark his infamy."

Don Alejandro's face was that of an enraged zealot. Don Diego turned quickly away from his father, and took Fray Felipe by the arm. "Let us go to the chapel," he whispered.

In the sanctuary of the chapel, Fray Felipe spoke to Diego softly: "You must not feel too badly my son. Your father does not realize that your avoidance of the headstrong virtues — they are not all deserving of censure in a young man of spirit — is only a pretense covering a great and just purpose. Only two men in the entire world — I, your confessor, and Bernardo, your body-servant — know, that you are Zorro. Your father will be proud of you when he learns the truth."

"If ever there was work for Zorro to do, now is the time for him to act," Don Diego declared.

"That is true, my son. But Zorro's activities in this affair must not be conducted with weapons in his hands. You must work as your other self, as Don Diego, the lazy one, lover of poetry and music. You must pretend to be inactive, and wage your battle for justice with thoughts that are quick and skillful as rapier thrusts — not with violence."

"How can that be done, padre?"

"You have brains, my son. Use them as your weapons to seek out the truth, and point the way to the murderer. There is much that I could tell you, about injustices which have been performed by black-hearted men with cold and calculated brutality. I have had speech with some of the victims — not at confessional, naturally, but as a fatherly adviser. So let me advise you in this, my son."

"What would you have me do, Padre? How am I to begin?"

"As you know, Señor Cassara, our *magistrado* who was foully slain, has been a widower for some years, and has left one child, his daughter, Manuela. She is lovely in many ways, and quite untouched by worldliness. She likes you very much because you do not carouse with other young caballeros. It would he proper for you to go to the Cassara house to console her. Get her to open her lips while you open your ears. She may say things she has heard her father mention —"

"I understand, padre. I'll go to her house immediately. But no doubt there will he neighbor women around her."

"It should not be difficult to get the señorita aside on sonic pretext, and question her where the others will not hear. Always remember we know Zorro did not kill the *magistrado*, but others do not. They saw him dying, saw the jagged letter Z scratched in the dust beside his body. They heard his dying words 'Zorro—punish'——"

Don Diego's suddenly uplifted hand caused Fray Felipe to fall silent, and look at him with puzzled eyes.

"I believe I have an idea about those two words," Diego said. "Suppose Señor Cassara did not mean that Zorro had attacked him and he waited Zorro punished for it. Suppose he meant that he wanted Zorro to search for the murderer and bring him to justice."

Fray Felipe nodded, his eyes shining, "I said you had brains, my son. And it was not said in flattery. I believe you have the correct answer to this enigma. So now go to Señorita Manuela Cassara, and begin your work."

SENORITA MANUELA had been stunned by the sudden and cruel death of her father. Don Diego managed to get her away from the bevy of weeping women who surrounded her, and the two sat on a bench in the patio, with Manuela's aunt, her only remaining relative established just out of earshot as her *dueñña*.

"Don Diego, it was most kind for you to come in this sad hour," she told him. "I scarcely can understand what has happened. Why should my father be slain?"

The Cassara house was a neat one, though somewhat small, in a street a short distance from the plaza. Diego took the girl's hand and pressed it gently and reassuringly. "How did your father happen to be up and out so early in the day? It must have happened right after dawn."

"When he was worrying about the day's work in the court, he sometimes went out and paced back and forth, deep in thought."

"Do you know of any enemies he had, Manuela?"

He had none, as far as I know, Diego. If he had any, he perhaps did not realize it."

"Obviously he had one," Diego told her.

"You mean that terrible man they call Zorro? But why should he kill my father, who was a kind man and always tried to be just in his official dealings?"

"Manuela, I do not believe that Zorro killed your father. Perhaps it was someone who pretended to be Zorro, to direct suspicion away from himself. Did your father say anything recently about his cases in court?"

"A little, *si.* At times he discussed his affairs with me. Recently he spoke of how some of the peons were being swindled by tricksters. Hides were being stolen from the poor and were being carted away to Monterey or San de Diego Alcalá."

"And what did your father do about that in his work as *magistrado*?"

"I believe, from what he told me, that he would order the hides returned to their owners, or their values paid in full. He did say once that he had been warned to cease his judgments or harm would come to him. But he made light of the warning."

"Tell nobody else what you have revealed to me," Diego said, in an earnest tone. "I'll do everything I can to help bring the guilty man to justice. My own father thinks Zorro did the slaying. But why should Zorro kill your father? He has always helped the oppressed. And he has always appeared on a horse, and did his work either in the saddle or after dismounting. I have already ascertained that the sound of a horse's gallop was not heard by those who happened to be awake at this early hour."

"That seems strange, Diego."

"It *is* strange. There are other things, too, which must be considered. Zorro has never been known to use a dagger, and such a weapon was found in your father's back. A sword, or perhaps a pistol in the case of emergency, *si.* But never a dagger."

"That seems strange, also," she replied. "Unless Zorro has changed recently."

"I do not believe he has changed. I believe that a great many lies have been told about him by his enemies. Now I must leave you, Manuela. Please give my kind regards to your aunt. But do not tell her of our conversation. Simply tell her that I came here to try to console you a little in your hour of grief."

"I understand, Diego. I shall do as you say."

Diego smiled slightly as he looked down at her upturned face. He took her hand again and bowed over it. *"Senorita, á Dios."*

" 'Dios!"

Don Diego left the house and went to the plaza, where he lost no time in crossing to the tavern. It was the favorite gathering place for men in all walks of life, from peon to wealthy landowner. It had been operated for years by one Pedro Gonzales, who had grown prosperous and unusually fat behind his clattering tankards. Gonzales greeted each customer according to his social importance, reserving a frown, however, only for the completely unwelcome.

When Don Diego entered the tavern he found the place well crowded. He strolled to one of the benches against the wall, and sighed as he seated himself. Gonzales, who had witnessed his entrance, nodded to Rosita, not the least attractive of his girls, and strode forward. He tried to bow from the waist, but his huge paunch restrained him and the best he could do was to welcome Diego with rolling eyes, and a grotesque smile. Rosita followed him to the bench.

"My house is honored, Don Diego," Gonzales said.

Diego sighed again. "I have just come from the Cassara house, and I feel depressed. Have Rosita bring me a goblet of your best wine."

Gonzales turned to the girl. "Our very best wine," he said, giving her buttocks a slight pinch.

"I see friends in the tavern who will be approaching me," Diego said. "Watch closely, and when I am alone come to me for a talk in private."

Gonzales' eyes became small and sharp. "I will be watching carefully, Don Diego."

Gonzales left, the bench. Rosita came hurrying to it with the wine Diego had ordered. She put it upon the table, smiled and made a courtesy.

Diego smiled at her in return, and glanced around the room. A short distance from him half a dozen young *caballeros* were drinking and talking, and he knew they would join him when he indicated he wanted company. At another table, loud in talk at one moment and bending over and whispering the next, he saw Capitán Juan Ruelas in conversation with Señor Carlos Santana, a wealthy trader who was reputed to be unscrupulous in his dealings.

The others in the tavern were small businessmen and workers at the warehouse, who indulged in loud talk and tankards of the cheapest wine.

Diego spoke to Rosita, "The death of Señor Cassara is a terrible thing. He was an honest man."

She pretended to be wiping some wine off the table as she replied. Diego had always treated her kindly, never descending to the advances made by other men. "Perhaps, Don Diego, he was killed because he was honest."

"I have thought of that, Rosita. But why should *Zorro* slay him?"

"Perhaps he did not. Perhaps another stabbed him and tried to make it look as if Zorro was the guilty one."

"My own father has denounced Zorro."

"I know he did, Don Diego. I heard how he denounced Capitán Ruelas, too, and that he has sent to San Diego de Alcacá for more soldiers to bring Zorro to justice."

"If Zorro did not do this thing, can you suggest someone else who might have hated him enough to kill him or who would have profited by his death?"

"I fear I cannot. But I shall keep my eyes open, and my ears as well and report to you anything that I think suspicious or in the slightest way strange."

"Bueno. Go now, Rosita, before our speech attracts attention. I want to talk to Señor Gonzales. Please tell him so."

Rosita turned away abruptly to attend to the wishes of another customer. Capitán Ruelas was the one who had beckoned to her. "Don Diego de la Vega is not the only man in the room, little pigeon," the *capitán* called out, so loudly that the entire tavern could hear. "Is it possible that the mouse-timid poet receives from you favors denied to others?"

The others around Ruelas laughed, and Rosita slapped him. The *capitán* caught her arm and pulled her upon his lap. She bent her head quickly, and bit his wrist to make the blood come. Then, angrily, she jerked away.

"You little wildcat!" he shouted at her. "I'll have you over to my room in the barracks yet—to spend a night with me!"

Gonzales had approached Diego by this time. "Do not worry about Rosita," he whispered. "She can care for herself. The *capitán* is a swaggering braggart. He is always tormenting the girls, but a man with a sword makes him turn pale."

"I am surprised to see him so friendly with Señor Santana," Diego said.

"They are far apart in importance and wealth, yet in some things I believe they are birds of a feather, Don Diego."

"How is that?"

"If a man in my position keeps his ears open, he learns many things," Gonzales replied. "Wine, too much wine at a sitting, causes men to raise their voices and to be careless in their talk. They may have many secret conversations at the *capitán's* private room in the barracks. But when they meet here, pretending it to be an accidental meeting, and drink too heavily, they seem to forget how loud they are talking and the subject of their talk."

"And that is—?" Diego questioned.

"It appears they have been swindling the natives. They buy green hides at a small price. Then they claim the hides were not up to quality, and cut the price to almost nothing. If the swindled ones protest, the *capitán* puts them in the *quartel* and farms them out in peonage to labor a long time for no pay. The *capitán* takes pay from the men to whom he hires them, and pockets it. If the peon's family starves meanwhile, he cares nothing."

"Where is Señor Santana involved?"

"He puts up the money to buy the hides in the first place," Gonzales explained. "And he certainly gets it back twofold."

"So that explains their devilish deal. It is monstrous, inhumanly cruel! Can nothing be done to stop them?"

Gonzales lowered his voice. "I think something has been done about it, Don Diego. Our *magistrado* had guessed the situation, and several times had ordered the men released from *quartel.* So, in my humble estimation, I think the two paid Zorro to murder the *magistrado*."

Diego drew in his breath sharply. Unlike Gonzales, he had no doubts about the innocence of Zorro. Who, then? Mere suspicion was not enough.

"You have been very helpful, Gonzales," he told the tavern keeper. "I can see that some of my friends would like to talk to me now."

Gonzales bowed and turned away. Immediately six or seven young caballeros hurried to Diego, bringing their wine cups and stools and gathering around his table. "You were in the pueblo, Diego, immediately after the slaying," one said. "What do you think about it? Shall we band tip and help the soldiers catch Zorro?"

Diego brushed a scented handkerchief across his forehead. "Ride and help the soldiers? What a fatiguing thought!" he murmured. "Why must there always he trouble and tumult? If more men would read the poets, it would be a better world." They laughed immoderately at that, and shouted for Rosita to conic and bring more wine.

Capitán Ruelas was now deep in his cups. Señor Santana was unable to silence him. Several men seated near them began to lessen their own voices, and listen.

"Who is this Don Alejandro de la Vega that he should try to order me around?" Ruelas was almost shouting. "What right has he to send to San Diego de Alcalá for more troopers? If they come, I'll oppose them with my own soldiers! Has the ear of the Governor and Viceroy, has he? Any more from him, and I may cut off *his* ears. Noble blood, has he—and a lot of gold? A fine man! Look at his puny son over there. All he cares about is poetry and music. What a poor excuse for a man!"

Don Diego managed to repress outwardly the rage that seethed within him. His hands suddenly turned to fists, and his fingernails bit into his palms with force enough to lacerate the skin and draw blood. He got slowly to his feet, his voice not departing from the languid tone he habitually used.

"You are insulting my father, and I resent that, *señores,"* he said.

Ruelas roared his drunken laughter. "So you resent it, little boy who reads poetry? And just how are you going to resent it? Would you strike me down with a single blow? Would you slay me reading from a book or singing a ballad?"

Diego stood silent, Sergeant Castro, Ruelas' second-in-command, was at his superior's elbow now, attempting to quiet him, but Ruelas brushed him aside.

"If you were a man, I would invite you to step out into the -plaza with me, and let you resent what I said after the manner of a man. But you are a weakling—"

He ceased shouting as the young *caballeros* sprang to their feet in front of Diego.

"You have insulted us all," one shouted to Ruelas. "Each of us is the son of a *hidalgo*. And men like you are as common dirt for your betters to tread upon. If you desire, *señor*, one of us will step out into the plaza with you and settle this matter, though we would lower ourselves to do it. You are a *capitán*, and wear a blade at your side."

The *caballeros* surged toward Ruelas as Diego made a futile effort to prevent them. Capitán Ruelas retreated a few steps. "I regret that the Governor has issued a stern order against private duels," he said. "We can use blades only in the line of duty."

"The stern order of His Excellency the Governor, who sits in comfort in his house in Monterey, occurs to you at a very convenient time," another *caballero* shouted at him.

"I regret that duty calls me at the moment," Ruelas said. "I must lead my men and run down the outlaw Zorro before the soldiers from San Diego de Alcalá arrive here, and prove to the proud Don Alejandro that they are not needed."

Don Diego stepped out boldly in front of the others. His voice rang. "Zorro did not murder the *magistrado*. The murderer of Señor Cassara is right here in this room!"

SLIGHTLY before dawn the following day, Don Diego slipped quietly from his father's house. There had been a scene of considerable heat between them the evening before.

"What do you mean by making such a silly statement in public?" his father had demanded. "You know very well that the bandit Zorro murdered the *magistrado.* You heard me make such a declaration. The man who set out to help the poor and oppressed has become a black-hearted murderer. He probably slew Señor Cassara because he could not blackmail him to deal with the innocent unjustly, to suit some vicious scheme we can only guess at."

"But I cannot feel that Zorro did it," Diego had replied.

"You read so much poetry that you are going insane. Never in my life have I raised a hand to you. But I am tempted to now. Do not put too great a burden upon my patience."

And now, before dawn, Don Diego was slipping through the darkness, making scarcely any noise, watching the shadows with extreme caution. He reached a broad board attached to two posts at the side of the plaza, where official notices were often fastened. Diego fastened a notice which he had himself devised, and crept back to the patio of his father's house; to come out of his own room yawning an hour later to partake of the morning meal.

The notice he had fastened to the board was read at an early hour, and within a short time many others were reading it:

AVISO

WHERE WERE Capitán RUELAS AND SENOR SANTANA WHEN SENOR CASSARA WAS MURDERED?

News of the notice on the board spread rapidly. Señor Carlos Santana was the first to ridicule it in public, and Capitán Ruelas was soon beside him.

"What nonsense is this?" the *capitán* bellowed. "If I locate the clown who committed this outrage, I'll have his hide! I'll teach him what the inside of the *quartel* looks like, if he isn't, some rascal who has been in it already!"

Señor Santana held up a hand for silence. "I presume, though it is not necessary, that both the *capitán* and I should prove our innocence," he said. "At that time the *magistrado* was murdered, I was returning from San Diego de Alcalá after a business trip there, and I was riding with three men of good repute, as I can prove readily."

Capitán Ruelas laughed a little. "As for me, I was with a small detachment of my men out near San Gabriel, trying to gather a clue as to the whereabouts of that confounded Zorro. I can prove it, not only by my men, but also by two prominent and trusted acquaintances who hold high positions on a certain rancho."

Don Diego felt as if the ground beneath him had been shaken by an unforeseen earthquake. His father scoffed at him.

"Whatever made you say in public that the murderer of the *magistrado* was in the tavern?" he demanded. "You have made a complete fool of yourself. Why do you stubbornly refuse to believe that Zorro was the murderer? Have I not said so?"

For the next three days, when the funeral service was held in the chapel and the burial of Señor Cassara followed, Diego kept close at home like a man hiding in shame. More young caballeros came for the service with their fathers, and speculated regarding the murderer, most of them deciding that Zorro was the guilty man.

During the service, Manuela Cassara kept close to Diego clutching his arm at times as she sobbed, while her aunt wept beside her. Diego took her to her home afterwards, and remained for all we, because his presence seemed to comfort her.

AT THE first opportunity, he talked with Fray Felipe. "I am as puzzled as you are, my son," the padre declared. "We certainly know that Zorro did not commit this terrible crime, And the two rascals we held on suspicion have proved their innocence."

"I still think they had a hand in it somehow," Diego replied. "They could have hired some other man to do the actual killing. Many men would have done it for a few gold pieces."

"Or it could have been someone completely in their power," Fray Felipe suggested. "Perhaps sonic man Capitán Ruelas could have put into the *quartel* and charged with a serious crime. With Señor Cassara dead, Ruelas could have rushed through a conviction without too much difficulty."

"It is something to think about," Diego conceded.

He was still turning the problem over in his mind the following evening as he left the Cassara house after visiting Manuela and her aunt again. They had asked him to consult with his father regarding sonic financial details of immediate importance.

It was dark as Diego came past the house of Carlos Santana. He was walking slowly, for there was no moon, only the light of the stars to guide his steps on his homeward way. He heard the harsh voice of Capitán Ruelas, and the modulated voice of Santana coining through an open window. He heard also the voice of a third man who seemed to be frightened.

Without hesitation Diego moved closer to the window. It was the burly second-in-command, Sergeant Carlos, who seemed frightened.

"I do not like the situation," Carlos was whining. "You promised to make me a lieutenant if I did what you wanted done. Someone seems to know too much. I want to get away from here—far away. Why not do this, capitán? Give me a special message of some sort to carry to the Viceroy in the City of Mexico. It would be an opportunity for you to say that things are not just right here. You could even intimate that Don Alejandro de la Vega is taking over too much power and that the other *hidalgos* are worried about it. You might even get a promotion and a better post."

"The idea has its good points," Ruelas said. "It would get you out of the way. You might get nervous around here and let something slip. I'll think it over for a day."

Diego's breath caught in his throat. So Sergeant Castro was the murderer! But how was he to prove such a thing? If he was to succeed, he would have to act quickly. And before he slept that night, Diego had found a way.

The next morning, he went across the plaza to the tavern where some of the young caballeros were living—dashing, adventurous, wild young *caballeros* always ready for a venture which would attract attention to them, especially from certain flirtatious *señoritas*. Diego got some of them aside for a private talk.

"You know the situation," he said. "I have been listening to my father and his ideas. As you know, he has sent to San Diego de Alcalá for more soldiers to run down this rascal of a Zorro. But Capitán Ruelas and his men here will try to make a mess of things."

"And what is your ideas?" one of the young men asked.

"It would be something to get you talked about," Diego continued. "Go to the barracks. Seize Capitán Ruelas and his second-in-command, Sergeant Castro. The rest of the troop would be helpless without them. Put the *capitán* and his sergeant into the *quartel*, and keep them under guard until the other soldiers come, so they can do no mischief. Seize Carlos Santana, too, and put him in with them. He is known as a close friend of Capitán Ruelas, an active sympathizer, and if he remains outside he may be powerful enough to get the others released."

Diego saw their faces brighten. Here was a bold plan they liked and could carry out with dash and fervor. They consulted with others and made their plans. And both Capitán Ruelas and Sergeant Castro were seized as they strolled toward the tavern that afternoon, and rushed to the *quartel* where they had put so many others. There they were guarded well, while the other soldiers went around without orders, wondering what the caballeros were doing, and not caring to ask questions from the daredevil young men of noble blood who were always ready for a fight and knew how to give a good account of themselves. Certainly it would have been the height of folly even to frown at them.

Señor Santana was seized at his own house and taken to the quarrel also, muttering in violent protest and threatening dire consequences. The three prisoners were given poor food, such as quarrel prisoners generally received; and the soldiers who served it seemed to relish the job they were forced to do.

When Diego's father heard what had happened, the son was quick to pacify him with an explanation as convincing as it was eloquent.

"The caballeros discovered somehow that Capitán Ruelas and his sergeant intended to take action before the other soldiers arrived from San Diego de Alcalá," Diego explained. "They realized instantly that Ruelas would ruin everything trying to capture Zorro. They put Señor Santana into the *quartel* also, because he threatened to use his power to get the others released."

"I always did dislike that fellow," Diego's father admitted. "I agree with the action of the *caballeros*. It was clever of them, and dashing. Ah, Diego, if you could only be like them, just once, just once—that is all I ask. How proud I would be of you then, my son!"

But there was still work to be done, Diego knew. There had to be proof. He strolled up to the *quartel*, where the other *caballeros* were standing guard, and stared into the cells. He stared longest at Sergeant Castro.

With one of the caballeros at his side, Diego began talking so the sergeant could hear.

"It will soon be ended," he said to the caballero beside him. "All the evidence is at hand. So Zorro did not kill the *magistrado*, after all. These three in here—they'll be hanged immediately, possibly as soon as the soldiers from San Diego de Alcalá get here, which may be tomorrow morning."

Sergeant Castro's nerves snapped as the caballeros began gathering and staring at him through the bars of the cell.

"They made me do it!" he screeched. "The *capitán* and Señor Santana made me! Capitán Ruelas promised to promote me to the rank of lieutenant. They planned all of it! I won't hang alone!"

He beat his fists against the bars of the cell. He screeched until there was little voice left to him. Men came from the houses and the plaza to listen. The soldiers under Ruelas' command kept their distance, fearing they might become involved.

And down the trail, with a cloud of dust sent like smoke toward the sky, came the troopers from San Diego de Alcalá, to see that justice was done.

"So Zorro was not the guilty man, after all," Diego's father told him. "I made a sad mistake, my son, and am honest enough to confess it. Ah, well, we all make mistakes at times."

"I am glad all this tumult is over," Diego told him, sighing a bit. "It has about wrecked my nerves. Father, let us do our business at the warehouse now, and go back to the rancho. It is so quiet and peaceful there."

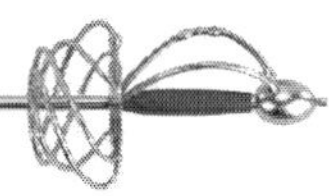

JOHNSTON McCULLEY'S AUTHORIAL AMNESIA

by Rich Harvey

ZORRO made his world debut in *The All-Story Weekly*, a revered pulp magazine which also boasted the first publication of *Tarzan of the Apes*. To the world at large, Zorro was a dashing figure of justice, protecting the down-trodden of Spanish California, punishing criminals and serenading lovely señoritas. To his fans, he was the provider of thrills and laughter, both on the printed page and on film.

But it would appear the author, Johnston McCulley, initially considered Zorro one character among many. Cast aside and forgotten after publication. That belief changed when readers wrote letters praising the serialized novel, *The Curse of Capistrano*. The world famous actor Douglas Fairbanks gave his compliment in the form of a movie deal. Fairbanks starred in *The Mark of Zorro* the following year, and Zorro was well on his way to becoming a cultural icon recognized throughout the world.

From 1919 to 1941, Zorro appeared sporadically in *The All-Story Weekly*, later merged with *Argosy* magazine. Despite this unexpected success, the fiction factory known as Johnston McCulley must have thought Zorro was a flash in the pan. The author tended to hit a figurative reset button with each story.

Zorro was unmasked at the climax of *The Curse of Capistrano* (later retitled *The Mark of Zorro*), whereupon the citizens of Reina de Los Angeles collectively gasped Don Diego Vega's name. In *The Further Adventures of Zorro* (*Argosy All-Story Weekly*, 1922) Diego was to ride again as a secret adventurer — McCulley's authorial amnesia wiped the slate clean, and the supporting characters' memories, whenever necessary.

As new stories poured fourth, continuity lapses resulted from McCulley's relentless output — novels and short stories appeared in dozens of magazines in a variety of genres. But the final verdict stands: Attempting to place the stories in a chronological sequence is a futile effort.

Beginning in 1944, McCulley began writing a *series* of Zorro adventures for *West* magazine (published by Better Publications). The masked hidalgo appeared in 52 *West* issues between 1944 and 1951, and the steady stream resulted in greater attention to continuity. By this time, it must have gradually dawned on McCulley that Zorro was his meal ticket!

TO MEET the demands of his busy writing schedule, McCulley established a basic formula for the continuing series. Typically, the languid Don Diego Vega, a wealthy scion, learns of some atrocity plaguing the peons and natives of Reina de Los Angeles. Often, the presiding commandante is the culprit, carrying out the oppressive wishes of the California governor.

In his masked guise of Zorro, the hero confounds and punishes the antagonist. Leaving the evildoer with his lethal brand — a "Z" carved deeply into the flesh — the masked highwayman takes flight, often with an army of soldiers in hot pursuit. The rotund Sergeant Manuel Juan Garcia usually leads the charge, lusting after the Governor's reward for Zorro's capture.

Upon escaping pursuit, Diego doffs the Zorro disguise and returns to his estate. Tossing back a goblet of wine, he recaps the evenings events with the only people privy to his dual identity: Don Alejandro Vega, his father, the wealthy owner of the largest rancho in Los Angeles; Bernardo, the mute servant (deaf in print, but not in the Disney television series of the 1950s); and Fray Felipe, the padre who brings misdeeds to Zorro's attention.

After relating his harrowing experience, Diego often ends the story with a reference to his Milquetoast public persona.

"My father, let us go out to the rancho for a time," Diego begged. "It is so calm and peaceful there. Here in the pueblo there is always trouble and turmoil. How can man commune with the poets?" ("Zorro Curbs a Riot," *West*, September 1950).

Fans of the Walt Disney produced *Zorro* television series (ABC network, 1957-1959) may find the *West* magazine stories most appealing, as they most closely resemble the TV episodes. The screenwriters liberally adapted elements from McCulley's stories.

McCULLEY adhered to this format for the 52 stories in *West* ... but continuity of Zorro's adventures before and after the *West* magazine varies wildly. People conveniently forget that Zorro has unmasked and revealed himself as Diego Vega — including Don Alejandro in some instances! In *The Sign of Zorro* (*Argosy,* 1941), Bernardo miraculously improves his hearing and speech. McCulley may have found it more engaging for Diego's loyal servant to trade banter. This development is abandoned with "Zorro Draws His Blade" (*West*, July 1944), and Bernardo is once again mute.

On the editorial side, Spanish words appeared in italic, *sometimes* — and sometimes *not* — which for Bold Venture Press became a challenge. The typesetters probably bear the blame in this department. For the most part, we adhered to what we saw on the pulp pages, which wasn't easy. *Zorro's Fight for Life* (*West*, July 1951) reads like the manuscript was divided among four different typesetters. We chose to retain the *italics* and accént marks throughout the story, but deferred to the original magazines for the remaining stories in this volume.

WHY did McCulley, a professional author in every sense of the word (and he wrote *millions* of them!) seem indifferent to the continuity between stories? He most likely considered Zorro a one-time effort, and no one was probably more surprised than he by the character's enduring popularity. McCulley seemed to approach every Zorro adventure as though it were the *last* story, until the editors of West commissioned the series.

McCulley may have subscribed to the common belief that pulp magazines were read once, passed around among friends, neighbors and co-workers, and discarded altogether. He most likely never imagined a time when the pulps would be preserved and cherished by dedicated collectors. I suspect he would have greeted the concept of a six-volume series, collecting the complete adventures of his hero, with mild skepticism.

Richard A. Lupoff, a noted author of mystery and science fiction, addresses some of these continuity glitches (while glossing over others) in his new series of Zorro novels, premiering in December 2017 from Bold Venture Press.

One thing remained consistent — Johnston McCulley, and Zorro, provided readers with plenty of thrills and suspense!

RICH HARVEY *is the publisher of Bold Venture Press, and the chief editor and graphic designer of* Zorro: The Complete Pulp Adventures. *He also freelances as a fiction writer and graphic designer.*

Johnston McCulley

Author, creator of Zorro

The creator of Zorro, Johnston McCulley (1883-1958) was born in Ottowa, Illinois, and raised in the neighboring town of Chilicothe. He began his writing career as a police reporter and became a prolific fiction author, filling thousands of pages of popular pulp magazines.

Southern California became a frequent backdrop for his fiction. His most notable use of the locale was in his adventures of Zorro, the masked highwayman who defended a pueblo's citizens from an oppressive government.

He contributed to popular magazines of the day like *Argosy*, *Western Story Magazine*, *Detective Story Magazine*, *Blue Book* and *Rodeo Romances*. Many of his novels were published in hardcover and paperback. Eventually he branched out into film and television screenplays.

His stable of series characters included The Crimson Clown, Thubway Tham, The Green Ghost, and The Thunderbolt. Zorro proved to be his most popular and enduring character, becoming the subject of numerous television programs, motion pictures, comic books, and cartoon programs.

After assigning all Zorro rights to agent Mitchell Gertz, Johnston McCulley retired to Los Angeles and died in 1958.

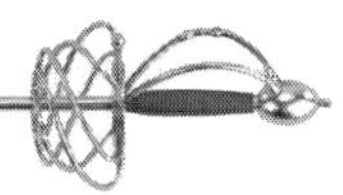

Joseph A. Farren

Illustrator

Joseph Farren (1884-1964) was born in Boston, the youngest of five sons. After high school, he drew comic strips and sports cartoons for various Boston newspapers. He was an avid golfer, and he competed in Massachusetts statewide tournaments. In 1926, he began drawing political cartoons for *The New York Times*. From his home art studio in Queens, he freelanced illustrations to pulp magazines such as *Clues Detective Stories*, *Detective Fiction Weekly*, *Popular Sports*, and *West*.

Farren balanced his art career and golf by a weekly routine of visiting midtown Manhattan to pick up and deliver illustrations, then heading to the golf course in nearby Flushing.

Publication history of Zorro by Johnston McCulley

All-Story Weekly

- The Curse of Capistrano (n) (5 issues) Aug 9 - Sep 6, 1919

Argosy All-Story Weekly

- The Further Adventures of Zorro (n) (6 issues) May 6 - June 10, 1922, etc.

Argosy

- Zorro Rides Again (n) (4 issues) Oct 3 - 24, 1931
- Zorro Saves a Friend (nv) Nov 12 1932
- Zorro Hunts a Jackal (ss) Apr 22 1933; *also known as "Zorro Hunts by Night"*
- Zorro Deals with Treason (nv) Aug 18, 1934
- Mysterious Don Miguel (nv) (2 issues) Sep 21 & Sep 28, 1935
- The Sign of Zorro (nv), (5 issues) Jan 25 - Feb 22, 1941

West magazine *(all short stories unless noted)*

- Zorro Draws His Blade, Jul 1944
- Zorro Upsets a Plot, Sep 1944
- Zorro Strikes Again, Nov 1944
- Zorro Saves a Herd, Jan 1945
- Zorro Runs the Gauntlet, Mar 1945
- Zorro Fights a Duel, May 1945
- Zorro Opens a Cage, Jul 1945
- Zorro Prevents a War, Sep 1945
- Zorro Fights a Friend, Oct 1945
- Zorro's Hour of Peril, Nov 1945
- Zorro Lays a Ghost, Dec 1945
- Zorro Frees Some Slaves, Jan 1946
- Zorro's Double Danger (nv) Feb 1946
- Zorro's Masquerade, Mar 1946
- Zorro Stops a Panic, Apr 1946
- Zorro's Twin Perils, May 1946
- Zorro Plucks a Pigeon, Jun 1946
- Zorro Rides at Dawn, Jul 1946
- Zorro Takes the Bait, Aug 1946
- Zorro Raids a Caravan, Oct 1946
- Zorro's Moment of Fear, Jan 1947
- Zorro Saves His Honor, Feb 1947
- Zorro and the Pirate, Mar 1947
- Zorro Beats a Drum, Apr 1947
- Zorro's Strange Duel, May 1947
- A Task for Zorro (na) Jun 1947
- Zorro's Masked Menace, Jul 1947
- Zorro Aids an Invalid, Aug 1947
- Zorro Saves an American, Sep 1947
- Zorro Meets a Rogue, Oct 1947
- Zorro Races with Death, Nov 1947
- Zorro Fights for Peace, Dec 1947
- Zorro Serenades a Siren, Feb 1948
- Zorro Meets a Wizard, Mar 1948
- Zorro Fights with Fire, Apr 1948
- Gold for a Tyrant, May 1948
- The Hide Hunter, Jul 1948
- Zorro Shears Some Wolves, Sep 1948
- The Face Behind the Mask, Nov 1948
- Zorro Starts the New Year, Jan 1949
- Hangnoose Reward, Mar 1949
- Zorro's Hostile Friends, May 1949
- Zorro's Hot Tortillas, Jul 1949
- An Ambush for Zorro, Sep 1949
- Zorro Gives Evidence, Nov 1949
- Rancho Marauders, Jan 1950
- Zorro's Stolen Steed, Mar 1950
- Zorro Curbs a Riot, Sep 1950
- Three Strange Peons, Nov 1950
- Zorro Nabs a Cutthroat, Jan 1951
- Zorro Gathers Taxes, Mar 1951
- Zorro's Fight for Life (na) July 1951

Max Brand's Western Magazine

- Zorro Rides the Trail! (ss) May 1954

Short Stories for Men

- The Mask of Zorro, (ss) Apr 1959

n = novel; na = novella; nv = novelette; ss = short story

Compiled from "The FictionMags Index" website edited by William G. Contento and Phil Stephensen-Payne

Watch for the Curse of Capistrano's wildest adventure!

ZORRO®

and the LITTLE DEVIL

A thrilling new novel by New York Times best-selling author

Peter David